SHADOW KISS

For my nephews, Jordan and Austin

Shadow Kiss

RAZORBILL

Published by the Penguin Group
Penguin Young Readers Group
345 Hudson Street, New York, New York 10014, U.S.A.
Penguin Group (USA) Inc., 375 Hudson Street, New York, New York 10014, U.S.A.
Penguin Group (Canada), 90 Eglinton Avenue East, Suite 700, Toronto, Ontario, Canada M4P 2Y3 (a division of
Pearson Penguin Canada Inc.)
Penguin Books Ltd, 80 Strand, London WC2R 0RL, England
Penguin Ireland, 25 St Stephen's Green, Dublin 2, Ireland
(a division of Penguin Books Ltd)
Penguin Group (Australia), 250 Camberwell Road, Camberwell,
Victoria 3124, Australia (a division of Pearson Australia Group Pty Ltd)
Penguin Books India Pvt Ltd, 11 Community Centre, Panchsheel Park,
New Delhi – 110 017, India
Penguin Group (NZ), 67 Apollo Drive, Rosedale, North Shore 0632, New Zealand
(a division of Pearson New Zealand Ltd.)
Penguin Books (South Africa) (Pty) Ltd, 24 Sturdee Avenue,
Rosebank, Johannesburg 2196, South Africa

Penguin Books Ltd, Registered Offices: 80 Strand, London WC2R 0RL, England

20 19 18 17 16 15 14 13 12

Library of Congress Cataloging-in-Publication Data is available

Printed in the United States of America

SHADOW KISS

RICHELLE MEAD

razOr
bill

ONE

His FINGERTIPS SLID ALONG my back, applying hardly any pressure, yet sending shock waves over my flesh. Slowly, slowly, his hands moved across my skin, down the sides of my stomach to finally rest in the curves of my hips. Just below my ear, I felt his lips press against my neck, followed by another kiss just below it, then another, then another. . . .

His lips moved from my neck toward my cheek and then finally found my mouth. We kissed, wrapping ourselves closer together. My blood burned within me, and I felt more alive in that moment than I ever had. I loved him, loved Christian so much that—

Christian?

Oh no.

Some coherent part of me immediately realized what was happening—and boy, was it pissed off. The rest of me, however, was still actually living in this encounter, experiencing it as though I was the one being touched and kissed. That part of me couldn't break away. I'd merged too much with Lissa, and for all intents and purposes, this *was* happening to me.

No, I told myself sternly. *It's not real—not for you. Get out of there.*

But how could I listen to logic when every nerve of my body was being set on fire?

You aren't her. This isn't your head. Get out.

His lips. There was nothing in the world right now except his lips.

It's not him. Get out.

The kisses were the same, exactly as I remembered with *him. . . .*

No, it's not Dimitri. Get out!

Dimitri's name was like cold water hitting me in the face. I got out.

I sat upright in my bed, suddenly feeling smothered. I tried kicking off the covers but mostly ended up entangling my legs even more. My heart beat hard in my chest, and I tried to take deep breaths to steady myself and return to my own reality.

Times sure had changed. A long time ago, Lissa's nightmares used to wake me from sleep. Now her sex life did. To say the two were a little different would be an understatement. I'd actually gotten the hang of blocking out her romantic interludes—at least when I was awake. This time, Lissa and Christian had (unintentionally) outsmarted me. In sleep, my defenses were down, allowing strong emotions to pass through the psychic link that connected me to my best friend. This wouldn't have been a problem if the two of them had been in bed like normal people—and by "being in bed," I mean "asleep."

"God," I muttered, sitting up and swinging my legs over the side of the bed. My voice was muffled in a yawn. Couldn't Lissa and Christian have seriously kept their hands off each other until waking hours?

Worse than being woken up, though, was the way I still felt. Sure, none of that making out had actually happened to me. It hadn't been *my* skin being touched or *my* lips being kissed. Yet my body seemed to feel the loss of it nonetheless. It had been a very long time since I'd been in that kind of situation. I ached and felt warm all over. It was idiotic, but suddenly, desperately, I wanted someone to touch me—even just to hold me. But definitely not Christian. The memory of those lips on mine flashed back through my mind, how they'd felt, and how my sleepy self had been so certain it was Dimitri kissing me.

I stood up on shaky legs, feeling restless and . . . well, sad. Sad and empty. Needing to walk off my weird mood, I put on a robe and slippers and left my room for the bathroom down the hall. I splashed cool water on my face and stared in the mirror. The reflection looking back at me had tangled hair and bloodshot eyes. I looked sleep-deprived, but I didn't want to go back to bed. I didn't want to risk falling asleep quite yet. I needed something to wake me up and shake away what I'd seen.

I left the bathroom and turned toward the stairwell, my feet light on the steps as I went downstairs. The first floor of my dorm was still and quiet. It was almost noon—the middle of the night for vampires, since they ran on a nocturnal schedule. Lurking near the edge of a doorway, I scanned the lobby. It was empty, save for the yawning Moroi man sitting at the front desk. He leafed halfheartedly through a magazine, held to consciousness only by the finest of threads. He came to the magazine's end and yawned again. Turning in his revolving chair, he tossed the magazine on a table behind him and reached for what must have been something else to read.

While his back was turned, I darted past him toward the set of double doors that opened outside. Praying the doors wouldn't squeak, I carefully opened one a crack, just enough to slip through. Once outside, I eased the door shut as gently as possible. No noise. At most, the guy would feel a draft. Feeling like a ninja, I stepped out into the light of day.

Cold wind blasted me in the face, but it was exactly what I needed. Leafless tree branches swayed in that wind, clawing at the sides of the stone dorm like fingernails. The sun peeped at me from between lead-colored clouds, further reminding me that I should be in bed and asleep. Squinting at the light, I tugged my robe tighter and walked around the side of the building, toward a spot between it and the gym that wasn't quite so exposed to the elements. The slush on the sidewalk soaked into the cloth of my slippers, but I didn't care.

Yeah, it was a typically miserable winter day in Montana, but that was the point. The crisp air did a lot to wake me up and chase off the remnants of the virtual love scene. Plus, it kept me firmly in my own head. Focusing on the cold in my body was better than remembering what it had felt like to have Christian's hands on me. Standing there, staring off at a cluster of trees without really seeing them, I was surprised to feel a spark of anger at Lissa and Christian. It must be nice, I thought bitterly, to do whatever the hell you wanted. Lissa had often commented that she wished she could feel my mind and experiences the way I could feel hers. The truth was, she had no idea how lucky she was. She had no idea what it was like to have someone else's thoughts intruding on yours, some-one else's experiences muddling yours. She didn't know what it was like to live with someone else's perfect love life when your own was nonexistent. She didn't understand what it was like to be filled with a love so strong that it made your chest ache—a love you could only feel and not express. Keeping love buried was a lot like keeping anger pent up, I'd learned. It just ate you up inside until you wanted to scream or kick something.

No, Lissa didn't understand any of that. She didn't have to. She could carry on with her own romantic affairs, with no regard for what she was doing to me.

I noticed then that I was breathing heavily again, this time with rage. The icky feeling I'd felt over Lissa and Christian's late-night hookup was gone. It had been replaced by anger and jealousy, feelings born of what I couldn't have and what came so easily to her. I tried my best to swallow those emotions back; I didn't want to feel that way toward my best friend.

"Are you sleepwalking?" a voice asked behind me.

I spun around, startled. Dimitri stood there watching me, looking both amused and curious. It would figure that while I was raging over the problems in my unfair love life, the source of those problems would be the one to find me. I hadn't heard him approach at all. So much for my ninja skills. And honestly, would it have killed me to pick up a brush before I went outside? Hastily, I ran a hand through my long hair, knowing it was a little too late. It probably looked like an animal had died on top of my head.

"I was testing dorm security," I said. "It sucks."

A hint of a smile played over his lips. The cold was really starting to seep into me now, and I couldn't help but notice how warm his long leather coat looked. I wouldn't have minded wrapping up in it.

As though reading my mind, he said, "You must be freezing. Do you want my coat?"

I shook my head, deciding not to mention that I couldn't feel my feet. "I'm fine. What are you doing out here? Are you testing security too?"

"I *am* security. This is my watch." Shifts of school guardians always patrolled the grounds while everyone else slept. Strigoi, the undead vampires who stalked living Moroi vampires like Lissa, didn't come out in sunlight, but students breaking rules—say, like, sneaking out of their dorms—were a problem night and day.

"Well, good work," I said. "I'm glad I was able to help test your awesome skills. I should be going now."

"Rose—" Dimitri's hand caught my arm, and despite all the wind and chill and slush, a flash of heat shot through me. He released me with a start, as though he too had been burned. "What are you really doing out here?"

He was using the *stop fooling around* voice, so I gave him as truthful an answer as I could. "I had a bad dream. I wanted some air."

"And so you just rushed out. Breaking the rules didn't even cross your mind—and neither did putting on a coat."

"Yeah," I said. "That pretty much sums it up."

"Rose, Rose." This time it was his exasperated voice. "You never change. Always jumping in without thinking."

"That's not true," I protested. "I've changed a lot."

The amusement on his face suddenly faded, his expression growing troubled. He studied me for several moments. Sometimes I felt as though those eyes could see right into my soul. "You're right. You have changed."

He didn't seem very happy about the admission. He was probably thinking about what had happened almost three weeks ago, when some friends and I had gotten ourselves captured by Strigoi. It was only through sheer luck that we'd managed to escape—and not all of us had gotten out. Mason, a good friend and a guy who'd been crazy about me, had been killed, and part of me would never forgive myself for it, even though I'd killed his murderers.

It had given me a darker outlook on life. Well, it had given *everyone* here at St. Vladimir's Academy a darker outlook, but me especially. Others had begun to notice the difference in me. I didn't like to see Dimitri concerned, though, so I played off his observation with a joke.

"Well, don't worry. My birthday's coming up. As soon as I'm eighteen, I'll be an adult, right? I'm sure I'll wake up that morning and be all mature and stuff."

As I'd hoped, his frown softened into a small smile. "Yes, I'm sure. What is it, about a month?"

"Thirty-one days," I announced primly.

"Not that you're counting."

I shrugged, and he laughed.

"I suppose you've made a birthday list too. Ten pages? Single-spaced? Ranked by order of priority?" The smile was still on his face. It was one of the relaxed, genuinely amused ones that were so rare to him.

I started to make another joke, but the image of Lissa and Christian flared into my mind again. That sad and empty feeling in my stomach returned. Anything I might have wanted— new clothes, an iPod, whatever—suddenly seemed trivial. What did material things like that mean compared to the one thing I wanted most of all? God, I really had changed.

"No," I said in a small voice. "No list."

He tilted his head to better look at me, making some of his shoulder-length hair blow into his face. His hair was brown, like mine, but not nearly as dark. Mine looked black at times. He brushed the unruly strands aside, only to have them immediately blow back into his face. "I can't believe you don't want anything. It's going to be a boring birthday."

Freedom, I thought. That was the only gift I longed for. Freedom to make my own choices. Freedom to love who I wanted.

"It doesn't matter," I said instead.

"What do you—" He stopped. He understood. He always did. It was part of why we connected like we did, in spite of the seven-year gap in our ages. We'd fallen for each other last fall when he'd been my combat instructor. As things heated up between us, we'd found we had more things to worry about than just age. We were both going to be protecting Lissa when she graduated, and we couldn't let our feelings for each other distract us when she was our priority.

Of course, that was easier said than done because I didn't think our feelings for each other were ever really going to go away. We'd both had moments of weakness, moments that led to stolen kisses or saying things we really shouldn't have. After I'd escaped the Strigoi, Dimitri had told me he loved me and had pretty much admitted he could never be with anyone else because of that. Yet, it had also become clear that we still couldn't be together either, and we had both slipped back into our old roles of keeping away from each other and pretending that our relationship was strictly professional.

In a not-so-obvious attempt to change the subject, he said, "You can deny it all you want, but I know you're freezing. Let's go inside. I'll take you in through the back."

I couldn't help feeling a little surprised. Dimitri was rarely one to avoid uncomfortable subjects. In fact, he was notorious for pushing me into conversations about topics I didn't want to deal with. But talking about our dysfunctional, star-crossed relationship? That was a place he apparently didn't want to go today. Yeah. Things were definitely changing.

"I think you're the one who's cold," I teased, as we walked around the side of the dorm where novice guardians lived. "Shouldn't you be all tough and stuff, since you're from Siberia?"

"I don't think Siberia's exactly what you imagine."

"I imagine it as an arctic wasteland," I said truthfully.

"Then it's definitely not what you imagine."

"Do you miss it?" I asked, glancing back to where he walked behind me. It was something I'd never considered before. In my mind, *everyone* would want to live in the U.S. Or, well, they at least wouldn't want to live in Siberia.

"All the time," he said, his voice a little wistful. "Sometimes I wish—"

"Belikov!"

A voice was carried on the wind from behind us. Dimitri muttered something, and then shoved me further around the corner I'd just rounded. "Stay out of sight."

I ducked down behind a bank of holly trees that flanked the building. They didn't have any berries, but the thick clusters of sharp, pointed leaves scratched where my skin was exposed. Considering the freezing temperature and possible discovery of my late-night walk, a few scratches were the least of my problems right now.

"You're not on watch," I heard Dimitri say several moments later.

"No, but I needed to talk to you." I recognized the voice. It belonged to Alberta, captain of the Academy's guardians. "It'll just take a minute. We need to shuffle some of the watches while you're at the trial."

"I figured," he said. There was a funny, almost uncomfortable note in his voice. "It's going to put a strain on everyone else—bad timing."

"Yes, well, the queen runs on her own schedule." Alberta sounded frustrated, and I tried to figure out what was going on. "Celeste will take your watches, and she and Emil will divide up your training times."

Training times? Dimitri wouldn't be conducting any trainings next week because— Ah. That was it, I realized. The field experience. Tomorrow kicked off six weeks of hands-on practice for us novices. We'd have no classes and would get to protect Moroi night and day while the adults tested us. The "training times" must be when Dimitri would be out participating in that. But what was this trial she'd mentioned? Did they mean like the final trials we had to undergo at the end of the school year?

"They say they don't mind the extra work," continued Alberta, "but I was wondering if you could even things out and take some of their shifts before you leave?"

"Absolutely," he said, words still short and stiff.

"Thanks. I think that'll help." She sighed. "I wish I knew how long this trial was going to be. I don't want to be away that long. You'd think it'd be a done deal with Dashkov, but now I hear the queen's getting cold feet about imprisoning a major royal."

I stiffened. The chill running through me now had nothing to do with the winter day. *Dashkov?*

"I'm sure they'll do the right thing," said Dimitri. I realized at that moment why he wasn't saying much. This wasn't something I was supposed to hear.

"I hope so. And I hope it'll only take a few days, like they claim. Look, it's miserable out here. Would you mind coming into the office for a second to look at the schedule?"

"Sure," he said. "Let me check on something first."

"All right. See you soon."

Silence fell, and I had to assume Alberta was walking away. Sure enough, Dimitri rounded the corner and stood in front of the holly. I shot up from my hiding spot. The look on his face told me he already knew what was coming.

"Rose—"

"Dashkov?" I exclaimed, trying to keep my voice low so Alberta wouldn't hear. "As in Victor Dashkov?"

He didn't bother denying it. "Yes. Victor Dashkov."

"And you guys were talking about . . . Do you mean . . ." I was so startled, so dumbstruck, that I could barely get my thoughts together. This was unbelievable. "I thought he was locked up! Are you saying he hasn't been on trial yet?"

Yes. This was definitely unbelievable. Victor Dashkov. The guy who'd stalked Lissa and tortured her mind and body in order to control her powers. Every Moroi could use magic in one of the four elements: earth, air, water, or fire. Lissa, however, worked an almost unheard of fifth element called spirit. She could heal anything—including the dead. It was the reason I was now psychically linked to her—"shadow-kissed," some called it. She'd brought me back from the car accident that had killed her parents and brother, binding us together in a way that allowed me to feel her thoughts and experiences.

Victor had learned long before any of us that she could heal, and he'd wanted to lock her away and use her as his own personal Fountain of Youth. He also hadn't hesitated to kill anyone who got in his way—or, in the case of Dimitri and me, use more creative ways to stop his opponents. I'd made a lot of enemies in seventeen years, but I was pretty sure there was no one I hated as much as Victor Dashkov—at least among the living.

Dimitri had a look on his face I knew well. It was the one he got when he thought I might punch someone. "He's been locked up—but no, no trial yet. Legal proceedings sometimes take a long time."

"But there's going to be a trial now? And you're going?" I spoke through clenched teeth, trying to be calm. I suspected I still had the *I'm going to punch someone* look on my face.

"Next week. They need me and some of the other guardians to testify about what happened to you and Lissa that night." His expression changed at the mention of what had occurred four months ago, and again, I recognized the look. It was the fierce, protective one he got when those he cared about were in danger.

"Call me crazy for asking this, but, um, are Lissa and I going with you?" I had already guessed the answer, and I didn't like it.

"No."

"No?"

"No."

I put my hands on my hips. "Look, doesn't it seem reasonable that if you're going to talk about what happened to *us*, then you should have *us* there?"

Dimitri, fully in strict-instructor mode now, shook his head. "The queen and some of the other guardians thought it'd be best if you didn't go. There's enough evidence between the rest of us, and besides, criminal or not, he is—or was—one of the most powerful royals in the world. Those who know about this trial want to keep it quiet."

"So, what, you thought if you brought us, we'd tell everyone?" I exclaimed. "Come on, comrade. You really think we'd do that? The only thing we want is to see Victor locked up. Forever. Maybe longer. And if there's a chance he might walk free, you have to let us go."

After Victor had been caught, he'd been taken to prison, and I'd thought that was where the story had ended. I'd figured they'd locked him up to rot. It had never occurred to me—though it should have—that he'd need a trial first. At the time, his crimes had seemed so obvious. But, although the Moroi government was secret and separate from the human one, it operated in a lot of the same ways. Due process and all that.

"It's not my decision to make," Dimitri said.

"But you have influence. You could speak up for us, especially if . . ." Some of my anger dimmed just a little, replaced by a sudden and startling fear. I almost couldn't say the next words. "Especially if there really is a chance he might get off. Is there? Is there really a chance the queen could let him go?"

"I don't know. There's no telling what she or some of the other high-up royals will do sometimes." He suddenly looked tired. He reached into his pocket and tossed over a set of keys. "Look, I know you're upset, but we can't talk about it now. I have to go meet Alberta, and you need to get inside. The square key will let you in the far side door. You know the one."

I did. "Yeah. Thanks."

I was sulking and hated to be that way—especially since he was saving me from getting in trouble—but I couldn't help it. Victor Dashkov was a criminal—a villain, even. He was power-hungry and greedy and didn't care who he stepped on to get his way. If he were loose again . . . well, there was no telling what might happen to Lissa or any other Moroi. It enraged me to think that I could do something to help put him away but that no one would let me do it.

I'd taken a few steps forward when Dimitri called out from behind me. "Rose?" I glanced back. "I'm sorry," he said. He paused, and his expression of regret turned wary. "And you'd better bring the keys back tomorrow."

I turned away and kept going. It was probably unfair, but some childish part of me believed Dimitri could do anything. If he'd really wanted to get Lissa and me to the trial, I was certain he could have.

When I was almost to the side door, I caught movement in my peripheral vision. My mood plummeted. Great. Dimitri had given me keys to sneak back in, and now someone else had busted me. That was typical of my luck. Half-expecting a teacher to demand to know what I was doing, I turned and prepared an excuse.

But it wasn't a teacher.

"No," I said softly. This had to be a trick. "No."

For half an instant, I wondered if I'd ever really woken up. Maybe I was actually still in bed, asleep and dreaming.

Because surely, *surely* that was the only explanation for what I was now seeing in front of me on the Academy's lawn, lurking in the shadow of an ancient, gnarled oak.

It was Mason.

TWO

OR, WELL, IT LOOKED LIKE MASON.

He—or it or whatever—was hard to see. I had to keep squinting and blinking to get him in focus. His form was insubstantial—almost translucent—and kept fading in and out of my field of vision.

But yes, from what I could see, he definitely looked like Mason. His features were washed out, making his fair skin look whiter than I recalled. His reddish hair now appeared as a faint, watery orange. I could barely even see his freckles. He was wearing exactly what I'd last seen him in: jeans and a yellow fleece jacket. The edge of a green sweater peeped out from underneath the coat's hem. Those colors, too, were all softened. He looked like a photograph that someone had left out in the sun, causing it to fade. A very, very faint glow seemed to outline his features.

The part that struck me the most—aside from the fact that he was supposed to be dead—was the look on his face. It was sad—so, so sad. Looking into his eyes, I felt my heart break. All the memories of what had taken place just a few weeks ago came rushing back to me. I saw it all again: his body falling, the cruel look on the Strigoi faces. . . . A lump formed in my throat. I stood there frozen, stunned and unable to move.

He studied me too, his expression never changing. Sad. Grim. Serious. He opened his mouth, like he might speak, and then closed it. Several more heavy moments hung between us, and then he lifted his hand and extended it toward me. Something in that motion snapped me out of my daze. No, this could *not* be happening. I wasn't seeing this. Mason was dead. I'd seen him die. I'd held his body.

His fingers moved slightly, like he was beckoning, and I panicked. Backing up a few steps, I put distance between us and waited to see what would happen. He didn't follow. He simply stood there, hand still in the air. My heart lurched, and I turned and ran. When I'd almost reached the door, I stopped and glanced back, letting my ragged breathing calm down. The clearing he'd stood in was completely empty.

I made it up to my room and slammed the door behind me, hands shaking. I sank onto my bed and replayed what had just happened.

What the hell? That had *not* been real. No way. Impossible. Mason was dead, and everyone knows the dead don't come back. Well, yeah, I had come back . . . but that was a different situation.

Clearly, I'd imagined this. That was it. It *had* to be. I was overtired and still reeling from Lissa and Christian, not to mention that Victor Dashkov news. Probably the cold had frozen part of my brain too. Yes, the more I thought about it, the more I decided there had to be a hundred explanations for what had just happened.

Yet, no matter how often I told myself that, I couldn't fall back asleep. I lay in my bed, covers pulled to my chin as I tried to banish that haunting image from my mind. I couldn't. All I could see were those sad, sad eyes, those eyes that seemed to say, *Rose, why did you let this happen to me?*

I squeezed my eyes shut, trying not to think about him. Since Mason's funeral, I'd been working so hard to go on and act like I was strong. But the truth was, I was nowhere near being over his death. I tortured myself day after day with *what if?* questions. What if I'd been faster and stronger during the Strigoi fight? What if I hadn't told him where the Strigoi were in the first place? And what if I'd simply been able to return his love? Any of those could have kept him alive, but none of them had happened. And it was all my fault.

"I imagined it," I whispered out loud into the darkness of my room. I had to have imagined it. Mason already haunted my dreams. I didn't need to see him when I was awake too. "It wasn't him."

It couldn't have been him, because the only way it could have been was . . . Well, that was something I didn't want to think about. Because while I believed in vampires and magic and psychic powers, I most certainly did *not* believe in ghosts.

I apparently didn't believe in sleep, either, because I didn't get much of it that night. I tossed and turned, unable to quiet my racing mind. I eventually did drift off, but it seemed like my alarm went off so soon after that I could have hardly slept for more than a few minutes.

Among humans, the light of day tends to chase off night-mares and fear. I had no such daylight; I awoke to increas-ing darkness. But just being out with real and living people had nearly the same effect, and as I went to breakfast and my morning practice, I found that what I'd seen last night—or what I *thought* I'd seen last night—was growing fainter and fainter in my memory.

The weirdness of that encounter was also being replaced by something else: excitement. This was it. The big day. The start of our field experience.

For the next six weeks, I wouldn't have any classes. I'd get to spend my days hanging out with Lissa, and the most I'd have to do was write a daily field report that was only about a half-page long. Easy. And, yeah, of course I'd be on guard duty, but I wasn't concerned. That was second nature to me. She and I had lived among humans for two years, and I'd pro-tected her the whole time. Before that, when I'd been a fresh-man, I'd seen the kinds of tests the adult guardians planned for novices during this phase. The ordeals were tricky, abso-lutely. A novice had to be on watch and not slack—*and* be ready to defend and attack if necessary. None of that wor-ried me, though. Lissa and I had been away from the school our sophomore and junior years, and I'd fallen behind then. Thanks to my extra practices with Dimitri, I'd quickly caught up and was now one of the best in my class.

"Hey, Rose."

Eddie Castile caught up to me as I walked into the gym where our field experience orientation would kick off. For a brief moment, looking at Eddie, my heart sank. Suddenly, it was like I was out in the quad again with Mason, staring at his sorrowful face.

Eddie—along with Lissa's boyfriend, Christian, and a Moroi named Mia—had been with our group when we'd been captured by Strigoi. Eddie hadn't died, obviously, but he'd come very close to it. The Strigoi who'd held us had used him as food, feeding from him throughout our capture in an effort to tease the Moroi and scare the dhampirs. It had worked; I'd been terrified. Poor Eddie had been unconscious for most of the ordeal, thanks to blood loss and the endorphins that came from a vampire's bite. He'd been Mason's best friend and nearly as funny and lighthearted.

But since we'd escaped, Eddie had changed, just like I had. He was still quick to smile and laugh, but there was a grimness to him now, a dark and serious look in his eyes that was always on guard for the worst to happen. That was understandable, of course. He pretty much *had* seen the worst happen. Just like with Mason's death, I held myself responsible for this transformation in Eddie and for what he'd suffered at the hands of the Strigoi. That may not have been fair to me, but I couldn't help it. I felt like I owed him now, like I needed to protect him or make things up to him somehow.

And that was kind of funny, because I think Eddie was trying to protect me. He wasn't stalking me or anything, but

I'd noticed him keeping an eye on me. I think after what had happened, he felt he owed it to Mason to watch over his girlfriend. I never bothered to tell Eddie that I hadn't been Mason's girlfriend, not in the real sense of the word, just as I never rebuked Eddie for his big brother behavior. I could certainly take care of myself. But whenever I heard him warning other guys away from me, pointing out that I wasn't ready to date anyone yet, I saw no point in interfering. It was all true. I wasn't ready to date.

Eddie gave me a lopsided smile that added a little boy type of cuteness to his long face. "Are you excited?"

"Hell, yeah," I said. Our classmates were filling in bleachers on one side of the gym, and we found a clear spot near the middle. "It's going to be like a vacation. Me and Lissa, together for six weeks." As frustrating as our bond was sometimes, it nonetheless made me her ideal guardian. I always knew where she was and what was happening to her. Once we graduated and were out in the world, I'd be assigned to her officially.

He turned thoughtful. "Yeah, I guess you don't have to worry as much. You know your assignment when you graduate. The rest of us aren't so lucky."

"You got your sights set on someone royal?" I teased.

"Well, it doesn't matter. Most guardians are assigned to royals lately anyway."

That was true. Dhampirs—half-vampires like me—were in short supply, and royals usually got first pick of guardians.

There was a time in the past when more Moroi, royal and non-royal alike, would have gotten guardians, and novices like us would have competed fiercely to get assigned to someone important. Now it was almost a given that every guardian would work for a royal family. There weren't enough of us to go around, and less influential families were on their own.

"Still," I said, "I guess it's a question of which royal you get, right? I mean, some are total snobs, but lots of them are cool. Get someone really rich and powerful, and you could be living at the Royal Court or traveling to exotic places." That last part appealed to me a lot, and I often had fantasies of Lissa and me traveling the world.

"Yup," agreed Eddie. He nodded toward a few guys in the front row. "You wouldn't believe the way those three have been sucking up to some of the Ivashkovs and Szelskys. It won't affect their assignments here, of course, but you can tell they're already trying to set things up after graduation."

"Well, the field experience can affect that. How we're rated on this will go into our records."

Eddie nodded again and started to say something when a loud, clear feminine voice cut through the murmur of our conversation. We both looked up. While we'd been talking, our instructors had gathered in front of the bleachers and now stood facing us in an impressive line. Dimitri was among them, dark and imposing and irresistible. Alberta was trying to call us to attention. The crowd fell silent.

"All right," she began. Alberta was in her fifties, wiry and

tough. Seeing her reminded me of the conversation she and
Dimitri had had last night, but I filed that away for later. Victor Dashkov was not going to ruin this moment. "You all know
why you're here." We'd become so quiet, so tense and excited,
that her voice now rang through the gym. "This is the most
important day of your education before you take your final trials. Today you will find out which Moroi you've been placed
with. Last week, you were given a booklet with the full details
of how the next six weeks will play out. I trust you've all read
it by now." I had, actually. I'd probably never read anything so
thoroughly in my life. "Just to recap, Guardian Alto will high-
light the main rules of this exercise."

She handed a clipboard to Guardian Stan Alto. He was
one of my least favorite instructors, but after Mason's death,
some of the tension between us had lightened. We understood
each other better now.

"Here we go," said Stan gruffly. "You'll be on duty six
days a week. This is actually a treat for you guys. In the real
world, you're usually working every day. You will accompany
your Moroi everywhere—to class, to their dorms, to their
feedings. Everything. It's up to you to figure out how you fit
into their lives. Some Moroi interact with their guardians just
like friends; some Moroi prefer you to be more of an invisible
ghost who doesn't talk to them." Did he have to use the word
ghost? "Every situation is different, and you two will have to
find a way to work it out to best ensure their safety.

"Attacks may come at any time, anywhere, and we'll be

dressed in all black when it happens. You should always be on your guard. Remember, even though you'll obviously know it's *us* doing the attacking and not real Strigoi, you should respond as though your lives are in terrible, immediate danger. Don't be afraid of hurting us. Some of you, I'm sure, won't have any qualms about getting us back for past grievances." Students in the crowd giggled at this. "But some of you may feel like you have to hold back, for fear of getting in trouble. Don't. You'll get in more trouble if you do hold back. Don't worry. We can take it."

He flipped to the next page of his clipboard. "You will be on duty twenty-four hours a day for your six-day cycles, but you may sleep during daylight when your Moroi does. Just be aware that although Strigoi attacks are rare in daylight, they aren't impossible indoors, and you will not necessarily be 'safe' during these times."

Stan read over a few more technicalities, and I found myself tuning them out. I knew this stuff. We all did. Glancing around, I could see I wasn't alone in my impatience. Excitement and apprehension crackled in the crowd. Hands were clenched. Eyes were wide. We all wanted our assignments. We all wanted this to begin.

When Stan finished, he handed the clipboard to Alberta. "Okay," she said. "I'm going to call out your names one by one and announce who you're paired with. At that time, come down here to the floor, and Guardian Chase will give you a packet containing information about your Moroi's schedule, past, etcetera."

We all straightened up as she leafed through her papers. Students whispered. Beside me, Eddie exhaled heavily. "Oh man. I hope I get someone good," he muttered. "I don't want to be miserable for the next six weeks."

I squeezed his arm reassuringly. "You will," I whispered back. "Er, get someone good, I mean. Not be miserable."

"Ryan Aylesworth," Alberta announced clearly. Eddie flinched, and I instantly knew why. Before, Mason Ashford had always been the first one called on any class lists. That would never happen again. "You are assigned to Camille Conta."

"Damn," muttered someone behind us, who'd apparently been hoping to get Camille.

Ryan was one of the suck-ups in the front row, and he grinned broadly as he walked over to take his packet. The Contas were an up-and-coming royal family. It was rumored that one of their members was a candidate for when the Moroi queen eventually named her heir. Plus, Camille was pretty cute. Following her around wouldn't be too hard for any guy. Ryan, walking with a swagger, seemed very pleased with himself.

"Dean Barnes," she said next. "You have Jesse Zeklos."

"Ugh," Eddie and I both said together. If I'd been assigned to Jesse, he would have needed an extra person to protect him. From me.

Alberta kept reading names, and I noticed Eddie was

sweating. "Please, please let me get someone good," he muttered.

"You will," I said. "You will."

"Edison Castile," Alberta announced. He gulped. "Vasilisa Dragomir."

Eddie and I both froze for the space of a heartbeat, and then duty made him stand up and head toward the floor. As he stepped down the bleachers, he shot me a quick, panicked look over his shoulder. His expression seemed to say, *I don't know! I don't know!*

That made two of us. The world around me slowed to a blur. Alberta kept calling names, but I didn't hear any of them. What was going on? Clearly, someone had made a mistake. Lissa was *my* assignment. She had to be. I was going to be her guardian when we graduated. This made no sense. Heart racing, I watched Eddie walk over to Guardian Chase and get his packet and practice stake. He glanced down at the papers immediately, and I suspected he was double-checking the name, certain there was a mix-up. The expression on his face when he looked up told me that it was Lissa's name he'd found.

I took a deep breath. Okay. No need to panic just yet. Someone had made a clerical error here, one that could be fixed. In fact, they'd have to fix it soon. When they got to me and read Lissa's name *again*, they were going to realize they'd double-booked one of the Moroi. They'd straighten it out and give Eddie someone else. After all, there were plenty of Moroi to go around. They outnumbered dhampirs at the school.

"Rosemarie Hathaway." I tensed. "Christian Ozera."

I simply stared at Alberta, unable to move or respond. No. She had *not* just said what I thought. A few people, noticing my lack of movement, glanced back at me. But I was dumb-struck. This wasn't happening. My Mason delusion from last night seemed more real than this. A few moments later, Alberta also realized I wasn't moving. She looked up from her clipboard with annoyance, scanning the crowd.

"Rose Hathaway?"

Someone elbowed me, like maybe I didn't recognize my own name. Swallowing, I stood and walked down the bleach-ers, robotlike. There was a mistake. There *had* to be a mistake. I headed toward Guardian Chase, feeling like a puppet that someone else was controlling. He handed me my packet and a practice stake meant to "kill" the adult guardians with, and I stepped out of the way for the next person.

Disbelieving, I read the words on the packet's cover three times. *Christian Ozera.* Flipping it open, I saw his life spread out before me. A current picture. His class schedule. His fam-ily tree. His bio. It even went into detail about his parents' tragic history, how they'd chosen to become Strigoi and had murdered several people before finally being hunted down and killed.

Our directions at this point had been to read through our dossiers, pack a bag, and then meet up with our Moroi at lunch. As more names were called, many of my classmates lingered around the gym, talking to their friends and showing off their packets. I hovered near one group, discreetly waiting for a chance to talk to Alberta and Dimitri. It was a sign of my newly developing patience that I didn't walk right up to them then and there and demand answers. Believe me, I wanted to. Instead, I let them go through their list, but it felt like forever. Honestly, how long did it take to read a bunch of names?

When the last novice had been assigned his Moroi, Stan shouted above the din for us to move on to the next stage of the assignment and tried to herd out my classmates. I cut through the crowd and stalked up to Dimitri and Alberta, who blessedly were standing with each other. They were chatting about something administrative and didn't notice me right away.

When they did glance at me, I held up my packet and pointed. "What's this?"

Alberta's face looked blank and confused. Something in Dimitri's told me he'd been expecting this. "It's your assignment, Miss Hathaway," Alberta said.

"No," I said through gritted teeth. "It's not. This is somebody else's assignment."

"The assignments in your field experience aren't optional," she told me sternly. "Just as your assignments in the real world won't be. You can't pick who you protect based on whim and mood, not here and certainly not after graduation."

"But after graduation, I'm going to be Lissa's guardian!" I exclaimed. "Everyone knows that. I'm supposed to have her for this thing."

"I know it's an accepted idea that you'll be together after graduation, but I do not recall any mandatory rulings that say you're 'supposed' to have her or anyone *here* at school. You take who you're assigned."

"Christian?" I threw my packet on the floor. "You're out of your mind if you think I'm guarding him."

"Rose!" snapped Dimitri, joining the conversation at last. His voice was so hard and so sharp that I flinched and forgot what I was saying for half a second. "You're out of line. You do *not* speak to your instructors like that."

I hated being chastised by anyone. I especially hated being chastised by him. And I *especially* hated being chastised by him when he was right. But I couldn't help it. I was too angry, and the lack of sleep was taking its toll. My nerves felt raw and strained, and suddenly, little things seemed difficult to bear. And big things like this? Impossible to bear.

"Sorry," I said with great reluctance. "But this is stupid. Nearly as stupid as not bringing us to Victor Dashkov's trial."

Alberta blinked in surprise. "How did you know—Never mind. We'll deal with that later. For now, this is your assignment, and you need to do it."

Eddie suddenly spoke up beside me, his voice filled with apprehension. I'd lost track of him earlier. "Look . . . I don't mind. . . . We can switch. . . ."

Alberta turned her stony gaze from me to him. "No, you certainly cannot. Vasilisa Dragomir is *your* assignment." She looked back at me. "And Christian Ozera is yours. End of discussion."

"This is stupid!" I repeated. "Why should I waste my time with Christian? Lissa's the one I'm going to be with when I graduate. Seems like if you want me to be able to do a good job, you should have me practice with her."

"You will do a good job with her," said Dimitri. "Because you know her. And you have your bond. But somewhere, someday, you could end up with a different Moroi. You need to learn how to guard someone with whom you have absolutely no experience."

"I have experience with Christian," I grumbled. "That's the problem. I hate him." Okay, that was a huge exaggeration. Christian annoyed me, true, but I didn't really hate him. As I'd said, working together against the Strigoi had changed a lot of things. Again, I felt like my lack of sleep and general irritability were cranking up the magnitude of everything.

"So much the better," said Alberta. "Not everyone you protect will be your friend. Not everyone you protect will be someone you like. You need to learn this."

"I need to learn how to fight Strigoi," I said. "I've learned that in class." I fixed them with a sharp look, ready to play my trump card. "*And* I've done it in person."

"There's more to this job than the technicalities, Miss Hathaway. There's a whole personal aspect—a bedside manner, if you will—that we don't touch on much in class. We teach you how to deal with the Strigoi. You need to learn how to deal with the Moroi yourselves. And *you* in particular need to deal with someone who has not been your best friend for years."

"You also need to learn what it's like to work with someone when you can't instantly sense that they're in danger," added Dimitri.

"Right," agreed Alberta. "That's a handicap. If you want to be a good guardian—if you want to be an excellent guardian—then you need to do as we say."

I opened my mouth to fight this, to argue that having someone I was so close to would train me up faster and make me a better guardian for any other Moroi. Dimitri cut me off.

"Working with another Moroi will also help keep Lissa alive," he said.

That shut me down. It was pretty much the only thing that could have, and damn him, he knew it.

"What do you mean?" I asked.

"Lissa's got a handicap too—you. If she never has a chance to learn what it's like to be guarded by someone without a psychic connection, she could be at greater risk if attacked. Guarding someone is really a two-person relationship. This assignment for your field experience is as much for her as for you."

I stayed silent as I processed his words. They almost made sense.

"And," added Alberta, "it's the only assignment you're going to get. If you don't take it, then you opt out of the field experience."

Opt out? Was she crazy? It wasn't like a class I could sit

out from for one day. If I didn't do my field experience, I didn't graduate. I wanted to explode about unfairness, but Dimitri stopped me without saying a word. The constant, calm look in his dark eyes held me back, encouraging me to accept this gracefully—or as close as I could manage.

Reluctantly, I picked up the packet. "Fine," I said icily. "I'll do this. But I want it noted that I'm doing this against my will."

"I think we already figured that out, Miss Hathaway," remarked Alberta dryly.

"Whatever. I still think it's a horrible idea, and you eventually will too."

I turned and stormed off across the gym before any of them could respond. In doing so, I fully realized what a bitchy little brat I sounded like. But if they'd just endured their best friend's sex life, seen a ghost, and hardly gotten any sleep, they'd have been bitchy too. Plus, I was about to spend six weeks with Christian Ozera. He was sarcastic, difficult, and made jokes about everything.

Actually, he was a lot like me.

It was going to be a long six weeks.

THREE

"WHY SO GLUM, LITTLE DHAMPIR?"

I was heading across the quad, toward the commons, when I detected the scent of clove cigarettes. I sighed.

"Adrian, you are the last person I want to see right now."

Adrian Ivashkov hurried up beside me, blowing a cloud of smoke into the air that of course drifted right toward me. I waved it off and made a great show of exaggerated coughing. Adrian was a royal Moroi we'd "acquired" on our recent ski trip. He was a few years older than me and had come back to St. Vladimir's to work on learning spirit with Lissa. So far, he was the only other spirit user we knew of. He was arrogant and spoiled and spent a lot of his time indulging in cigarettes, alcohol, and women. He also had a crush on me—or at least wanted to get me into bed.

"Apparently," he said. "I've hardly seen you at all since we got back. If I didn't know better, I'd say you were avoiding me."

"I *am* avoiding you."

He exhaled loudly and raked a hand through the sable brown hair he always kept stylishly messy. "Look, Rose. You don't have to keep up with the hard-to-get thing. You've already got me."

Adrian knew perfectly well I wasn't playing hard-to-get, but he always took a particular delight in teasing me. "I'm really not in the mood for your so-called charm today."

"What happened, then? You're stomping through every puddle you can find and look like you're going to punch the first person you see."

"Why are you hanging around, then? Aren't you worried about getting hit?"

"Aw, you'd never hurt me. My face is too pretty."

"Not pretty enough to make up for the gross, carcinogenic smoke blowing in my face. How can you do that? Smoking's not allowed on campus. Abby Badica got two weeks' detention when she got caught."

"I'm above the rules, Rose. I'm neither student nor staff, merely a free spirit wandering your fair school as I will."

"Maybe you should go do some wandering now."

"You want to get rid of me, you tell me what's going on."

There was no avoiding it. Besides, he'd know soon enough. Everyone would know. "I got assigned to Christian for my field experience."

There was a pause, and then Adrian burst out laughing. "Wow. Now I understand. In light of that, you actually seem remarkably calm."

"I was supposed to have Lissa," I growled. "I can't believe they did this to me."

"Why *did* they do it? Is there some chance you might not be with her when you graduate?"

"No. They just all seem to think this is going to help me train better now. Dimitri and I will still be her real guardians later."

Adrian gave me a sidelong glance. "Oh, I'm sure that'll be quite the hardship for you."

It had to be one of the weirdest things in the universe that Lissa had never come close to suspecting my feelings for Dimitri but that Adrian had figured it out.

"Like I said, your commentary isn't appreciated today."

He apparently didn't agree. I had a suspicious feeling he'd been drinking already, and it was barely even lunchtime. "What's the problem? Christian'll be with Lissa all the time anyway."

Adrian had a point. Not that I'd have admitted it. Then, in that short-attention-span way of his, he switched subjects just as we neared the building.

"Have I mentioned your aura to you?" he asked suddenly. There was a strange note to his voice. Hesitant. Curious. It was *very* uncharacteristic. Everything he usually said was mocking.

"I don't know. Yeah, once. You said it was dark or something. Why?" Auras were fields of light that surrounded every person. Their colors and brightness were allegedly linked to a person's personality and energy. Only spirit users could see them. Adrian had been doing it for as long as he could remember, but Lissa was still learning.

"Hard to explain. Maybe it's nothing." He came to a stop

near the door and inhaled deeply on his cigarette. He went out of his way to blow a cloud of smoke away from me, but the wind carried it back. "Auras are strange. They ebb and flow and change colors and brightness. Some are vivid, some are pale. Every once in a while, someone's will settle and burn with such a pure color that you can . . ." He tipped his head back, staring into the sky. I recognized the signs of that weird "unhinged" state he sometimes fell into. "You can instantly grasp what it means. It's like seeing into their soul."

I smiled. "But you haven't figured mine out, huh? Or what any of these colors mean?"

He shrugged. "I'm figuring it out. You talk to enough people, get a feel for what they're like and then start to see the same kinds of people with the same kinds of colors. . . . After a while, the colors start to mean something."

"What's mine look like right now?"

He glanced over at me. "Eh, I can't quite get a fix on it today."

"I knew it. You've been drinking." Substances, like alcohol or certain medications, numbed spirit's effects.

"Just enough to chase the chill away. I can guess what your aura's like, though. It's usually like the others, sort of those swirling colors—it's just kind of edged in darkness. Like you've always got a shadow following you."

Something in his voice made me shiver. Although I'd heard him and Lissa talk about auras a lot, I'd never really thought of them as anything I needed to worry about. They were more like some kind of stage trick—a cool thing with little substance.

"That's so cheerful," I said. "You ever think about motivational speaking?"

His scattered look faded, and his normal mirth returned. "Don't worry, little dhampir. You might be surrounded by clouds, but you'll always be like sunshine to me." I rolled my eyes. He dropped his cigarette onto the sidewalk and put it out with his foot. "Gotta go. See you later." He swept me a gallant bow and started walking away toward guest housing.

"You just littered!" I yelled.

"Above the rules, Rose," he called back. "Above the rules."

Shaking my head, I picked up the now-cold cigarette butt and took it to a garbage can that was outside the building. When I entered, the warmth inside was a welcome change as I shook off the slush on my boots. Down in the cafeteria, I found lunch wrapping up for the afternoon. Here, dhampirs sat side by side with Moroi, providing a study in contrasts. Dhampirs, with our half-human blood, were bigger—though not taller—and more solidly built. The girl novices were curvier than the ultra-slim Moroi girls, the boy novices far more muscular than their vampire counterparts. The Moroi complexions were pale and delicate, like porcelain, while ours were tanned from being outside in the sun so much.

Lissa sat at a table by herself, looking serene and angelic in a white sweater. Her pale blond hair cascaded over her shoulders. She glanced up at my approach, and welcoming feelings flowed to me through our bond.

She grinned. "Oh, look at your face. It's true, isn't it? You really are assigned to Christian."

I glared.

"Would it kill you to be a *little* less miserable?" She gave me a censuring yet amused look as she licked the last of her strawberry yogurt off her spoon. "I mean, he's my boyfriend, after all. I hang out with him all the time. It's not that bad."

"You have the patience of a saint," I grumbled, slouching into a chair. "And besides, you don't hang out with him 24/7."

"Neither will you. It's only 24/6."

"Same difference. It might as well be 24/10."

She frowned. "That doesn't make any sense."

I waved off my idiotic remark and stared blankly around the lunchroom. The room was buzzing with news of the impending field exercise, which would kick off as soon as lunch ended. Camille's best friend had gotten assigned to Ryan's best friend, and the four of them huddled gleefully together, looking as though they were about to embark on a six-week double date. At least someone would enjoy all this. I sighed. Christian, my soon-to-be charge, was off with the feeders—humans who willingly donated blood to Moroi.

Through our bond, I sensed Lissa wanting to tell me something. She was holding off because she was worried about my bad mood and wanted to make sure I got enough support. I smiled. "Stop worrying about me. What's up?"

She smiled back, her pink-glossed lips hiding her fangs. "I got permission."

"Permission for—?" The answer flitted from her mind faster than she could have voiced it. "What?" I exclaimed. "You're going to stop your meds?"

Spirit was an amazing power, one whose cool abilities we were just starting to figure out. It had a very nasty side effect, however: It could lead to depression and insanity. Part of the reason Adrian indulged in drinking so much (aside from his party nature) was to numb himself against these side effects. Lissa had a much healthier way of doing it. She took antidepressants, which completely cut her off from the magic altogether. She hated not being able to work with spirit anymore, but that was an acceptable trade-off for not going crazy. Well, I thought it was. She apparently disagreed if she was considering this insane experiment. I knew she'd been wanting to try the magic again, but I hadn't really thought she'd go through with it—or that anyone would let her.

"I have to check in with Ms. Carmack every day *and* regularly talk to a counselor." Lissa made a face at this last part, but her overall feelings were still quite upbeat. "I can't wait to see what I can do with Adrian."

"Adrian's a bad influence."

"He didn't make me do this, Rose. I chose it." When I didn't answer, she lightly touched my arm. "Hey, listen. Don't worry. I've been so much better, and lots of people are going to have my back."

"Everyone except me," I told her wistfully. Across the room, Christian entered through a set of double doors and approached us. The clock read five minutes until the end of lunch. "Oh man. The zero hour is almost here."

Christian pulled up a chair at our table and flipped it backwards, letting his chin rest on its slatted back. He brushed his black hair away from his blue eyes and gave us a smug smile. I felt Lissa's heart lighten at his presence.

"I can't wait until this show gets on the road," he said. "You and me are going to have so much fun, Rose. Picking out curtains, doing each other's hair, telling ghost stories. . . ."

The reference to "ghost stories" hit a little closer to home than I was comfortable with. Not that choosing curtains or brushing Christian's hair was much more appealing.

I shook my head in exasperation and stood up. "I'll leave you two alone for your last few private moments." They laughed.

I walked over to the lunch line, hoping to find some leftover doughnuts from breakfast. So far, I could see croissants, quiche, and poached pears. It must have been highbrow day at the cafeteria. Was deep-fried dough really too much to ask for? Eddie stood in front of me. His face turned apologetic as soon as he saw me.

"Rose, I'm really sorry—"

I put up a hand to stop him. "Don't worry. It's not your fault. Just promise me you'll do a good job protecting her."

It was a silly sentiment since she was in no real danger, but I could never really stop worrying about her—particularly in light of this new development with her medication.

Eddie stayed serious, apparently not thinking my request was silly at all. He was one of the few who knew about Lissa's abilities—and their downsides, which was probably why he'd been selected to guard her. "I won't let anything happen to her. I mean it."

I couldn't help a smile, in spite of my glum mood. His experiences with the Strigoi made him take all of this more seriously than almost any other novice. Aside from me, he was probably the best choice to guard her.

"Rose, is it true you punched Guardian Petrov?"

I turned and looked into the faces of two Moroi, Jesse Zeklos and Ralf Sarcozy. They'd just stepped in line behind Eddie and me and looked more self-satisfied and annoying than usual. Jesse was all bronzed good looks and quick thinking. Ralf was his slightly less attractive and slightly less intelligent sidekick. They were quite possibly the two people I hated most at this school, mainly due to some nasty rumors they'd spread about me doing some very explicit things with them. It was Mason's strong-arming that had forced them to tell the truth to the school, and I don't think they'd ever forgiven me for that.

"Punch Alberta? Hardly." I started to turn around, but Ralf kept talking.

"We heard you threw a big hissy fit in the gym when you

found out who you were with."

"'Hissy fit'? What are you, sixty? All I did was—" I paused and carefully chose my words. "—register my opinion."

"Well," said Jesse. "I suppose if anyone's going to keep an eye on that Strigoi wannabe, it might as well be you. You're the biggest badass around here."

The grudging tone in his voice made it sound like he was complimenting me. I didn't see it that way at all. Before he could utter another word, I was standing right in front of him, with barely any space between us. In what I considered a true sign of discipline, I didn't put my hand around his throat. His eyes widened in surprise.

"Christian has nothing to do with any Strigoi," I said in a low voice.

"His parents—"

"Are his parents. And he's Christian. Don't confuse them." Jesse had been on the wrong side of my anger before. He was clearly remembering that, and his fear warred with his desire to trash-talk Christian in front of me. Surprisingly, the latter won out.

"Earlier you acted like being with him was the end of the world, and now you're defending him? You know how he is—he breaks rules all the time. Are you saying you seriously don't believe there's any chance at all he might turn Strigoi like his parents?"

"None," I said. "Absolutely none. Christian's more willing to take a stand against Strigoi than probably any other Moroi here." Jesse's eyes flicked curiously toward Ralf before return-ing to me. "He even helped me fight against those ones in Spokane. There is no chance of him ever, *ever* turning Strigoi." I racked my brain, trying to recall who had been assigned to Jesse for the field experience. "And if I hear you spreading that crap around, Dean isn't going to be able to save you from me."

"Or me," added Eddie, who had come to stand right beside me.

Jesse swallowed and took a step back. "You're such a liar. You can't lay a hand on me. If you get suspended now, you'll never graduate."

He was right, of course, but I smiled anyway. "Might be worth it. We'll have to see, huh?"

It was at that point that Jesse and Ralf decided they didn't want anything from the lunch line after all. They stalked off, and I heard something that sounded suspiciously like "crazy bitch."

"Jerks," I muttered. Then I brightened. "Oh, hey. Dough-nuts."

I got a chocolate-glazed, and then Eddie and I hurried off to find our Moroi and get to class. He grinned at me. "If I didn't know any better, I'd say you just defended Christian's honor. Isn't he a pain in the ass?"

"Yes," I said, licking icing off my fingers. "He is. But for the next six weeks, he's *my* pain in the ass."

FOUR

IT BEGAN.

At first, things weren't too different from any other day. Dhampirs and Moroi attended separate classes in the first half of the school day, then joined up after lunch. Christian had most of the same afternoon classes I'd had last semester, so it was almost like following my own schedule again. The difference was that I was no longer a student in these classes. I didn't sit at a desk or have to do any of the work. I was also a lot more uncomfortable since I had to stand at the back of the room the entire time, along with other novices who were guarding Moroi. Outside the school, this was what it was usually like. Moroi came first. Guardians were shadows.

There was a strong temptation to talk to our fellow novices, particularly during times when the Moroi were working on their own and talking amongst themselves. None of us cracked, though. The pressure and adrenaline of the first day had us all on good behavior.

After biology, Eddie and I started using a bodyguard technique called pair guarding. I was near guard and walked with Lissa and Christian for immediate defense. Eddie, being far guard, walked farther away and scanned the larger area for any potential threats.

We followed this pattern for the rest of the day, up until the last class came around. Lissa gave Christian a quick kiss on the cheek, and I realized they were parting.

"You guys don't have the same schedule this time?" I asked with dismay, stepping over to the side of the hall to stay out of student traffic. Eddie had already deduced that we were parting and had stopped far guard duties to come talk to us. I hadn't known how Lissa and Christian's schedules lined up for this new semester.

Lissa took in my disappointed look and gave me a sympathetic smile. "Sorry. We're going to study together after school, but right now, I've got to go to creative writing."

"And I," declared Christian loftily, "have to go to culinary science."

"Culinary science?" I cried. "You elected *culinary science*? That's like the most brainless class ever."

"It is not," he countered. "And even if it was . . . well, hey, it's my last semester, right?" I groaned.

"Come on, Rose," laughed Lissa. "It's just one class period. It won't be that—"

She was cut off when a commotion broke out farther down the hall. We and everyone near us stopped and stared. One of my guardian instructors, Emil, had practically appeared out of nowhere and—playing Strigoi—reached for a Moroi girl. He swung her away, pressing her to his chest and exposing her neck as though he would bite her. I couldn't see who she was, just a tangle of brown hair, but her assigned protector was Shane Reyes. The attack had caught him by surprise—it was the first one of the day—but he fumbled only a little as he kicked Emil in the side and wrested the girl away. The two guys squared off, and everyone watched eagerly. A few even whistled and shouted, cheering Shane on.

One of the catcallers was Ryan Aylesworth. He was so fixated on watching the fight—which Shane, wielding his practice stake, had just about won—that he didn't notice two other adult guardians sneaking up on him and Camille. Eddie and I realized it at the same time and stiffened, instinct readying both of us to spring forward.

"Stay with them," Eddie told me. He headed toward Ryan and Camille, who had just discovered they were being set upon. Ryan didn't react as well as Shane had, particularly since he faced two attackers. One of the guardians distracted Ryan while the other—Dimitri, I now saw—grabbed Camille. She screamed, not faking her fear. She apparently didn't find being in Dimitri's arms as thrilling as I did.

Eddie headed toward them, approaching from behind, and landed a blow on the side of Dimitri's head. It hardly fazed Dimitri, but I was still amazed. I'd barely ever been able to land a hit on him in all our trainings. Eddie's attack forced Dimitri to release Camille and face this new threat. He spun around, graceful as a dancer, and advanced on Eddie.

Meanwhile, Shane had "staked" his Strigoi and jumped in to help Eddie, moving around to Dimitri's other side. I watched, fists clenched in excitement, intrigued with the fighting in general and with watching Dimitri in particular. It amazed me that someone so deadly could be so beautiful. I wished I was part of the fray but knew I had to watch the area around me in case any "Strigoi" attacked here.

But they didn't. Shane and Eddie successfully "finished off" Dimitri. Part of me was a little sad at this. I wanted Dimitri to be good at everything. However, Ryan had tried to help and failed. Dimitri had technically "killed" him, so I felt a twisted comfort in thinking that Dimitri had still been a badass Strigoi. He and Emil praised Shane for being fast on his feet and Eddie for realizing we had to treat this as a group endeavor rather than one-on-one trials. I got a nod for watching Eddie's back, and Ryan was chastised for not paying attention to his Moroi.

Eddie and I grinned at each other, happy over getting high marks on this first test. I wouldn't have minded a slightly bigger role, but this wasn't a bad start to the field experience. We high-fived, and I saw Dimitri shake his head at us as he left.

With the drama over, our foursome split up. Lissa gave me one last smile over her shoulder and spoke to me through the bond, *Have fun in culinary science!* I rolled my eyes, but she and Eddie had already rounded a corner.

"Culinary science" sounded pretty impressive, but really, it was just a fancy term for what was essentially a cooking class. Despite my teasing Christian about it being brainless, I had some respect for it. I could barely boil water, after all. Still, it was a lot different from an elective like creative writing or debate, and I had no doubts Christian was taking it as a blow-off class and not because he wanted to be a chef someday. At least I might get some satisfaction out of watching him mix a cake or something. Maybe he'd even wear an apron.

There were three other novices in the class who were guarding Moroi. Since the culinary science room was large and open, with lots of windows, the four of us worked together to come up with a plan to pool our efforts and secure the whole room. When I'd watched novices do their field experiences in past years, I'd only ever paid attention to the fights. I'd never noticed the teamwork and strategizing that must have been going on. Theoretically, the four of us were here to only protect our assigned Moroi, but we'd slipped into a role where we were protecting the whole class.

My post was by a fire door that led outside of the school. Coincidentally, it was right by the station Christian was working at. The class normally cooked in pairs, but there was an odd number of students. Rather than work in a group of three, Christian had volunteered to be by himself. No one had seemed to mind. Many still regarded him and his family with the same prejudice that Jesse did. To my disappointment, Christian wasn't making a cake.

"What is that?" I asked, watching him take out a bowl of some kind of raw, ground-up meat from the refrigerator.

"Meat," he said, dumping it onto a cutting board.

"I know that, you idiot. What kind?"

"Ground beef." He pulled another container out and then

another. "And this is veal. And this is pork."

"Do you have, like, a T. rex that you're going to feed?"

"Only if you want some. This is for meatloaf."

I stared. "With three kinds of meat?"

"Why eat something called meatloaf if you aren't actually going to get some meat out of it?"

I shook my head. "I can't believe this is only the first day with you."

He glanced down, focusing on kneading his tri-meat creation together. "You sure are making a big deal out of this. Do you really hate me that much? I heard you were screaming at the top of your lungs back in the gym."

"No, I wasn't. And . . . I don't hate you at all," I admitted.

"You're just taking it out on me because you didn't get paired with Lissa."

I didn't answer. He wasn't that far off.

"You know," he continued, "it might actually be a good idea for you to practice with someone different."

"I know. That's what Dimitri says too."

Christian put the meat into a bowl and started adding some other ingredients. "Then why question it? Belikov knows what he's doing. I'd trust anything he says. It sucks that they're going to lose him after we graduate, but I'd rather see him with Lissa."

"Me too."

He paused and looked up, meeting my eyes. We both smiled, amused at how shocked we were to have agreed with each other. A moment later, he returned to his work.

"You're good too," he said, not *too* grudgingly. "The way you handled yourself . . ."

He didn't finish the thought, but I knew what he was talking about. Spokane. Christian hadn't been around when I killed the Strigoi, but he'd been instrumental in helping with the escape. He and I had teamed up, using his fire magic as a means of letting me subdue our captors. We'd worked well together, all of our animosity put aside.

"I guess you and I have better things to do than fight all the time," I mused. Like worry about Victor Dashkov's trial, I realized. For a moment, I considered telling Christian what I'd learned. He'd been around the night it had all gone down with Victor last fall, but I decided not to mention the news just yet. Lissa needed to hear it first.

"Yup," Christian said, unaware of my thoughts. "Brace yourself, but we aren't that different. I mean, I'm smarter and a lot funnier, but at the end of the day, we both want to keep her safe." He hesitated. "You know . . . I'm not going to take her away from you. I can't. No one can, not as long as you guys have that bond."

I was surprised he'd brought this up. I honestly suspected that there were two reasons he and I argued a lot. One was that we both had personalities that liked to argue. The other reason—the big one—was that we were each envious of the other's relationship with Lissa. But, as he'd said, we really had the same motives. We cared about her.

"And don't think the bond will keep you guys apart," I said. I knew the link bothered him. How could you ever get romantically close to someone when they had that kind of connection with another person, even if that other person was just a friend? "She cares about you. . . ." I couldn't bring myself to say "loves." "She has a whole separate place for you in her heart."

Christian put his dish in the oven. "You did *not* just say that. I have a feeling we're on the verge of hugging and coming up with cute nicknames for each other." He was trying to look disgusted at my sentiment, but I could tell he liked being told that Lissa cared about him.

"I already have a nickname for you, but I'll get in trouble if I say it in class."

"Ah," he said happily. "*That's* the Rose I know."

He went off to talk to another friend while his meatloaf cooked, which was probably just as well. My door was a vulnerable position, and I shouldn't have been chatting away, even if the rest of the class was. Across the room, I saw Jesse and Ralf working together. Like Christian, they'd chosen a blow-off class too.

No attacks occurred, but a guardian named Dustin did come in to make notes on us novices as we held our positions. He was standing near me right when Jesse chose to stroll by. At first, I thought it was a coincidence—until Jesse spoke.

"I take back what I said earlier, Rose. I figured it out. You aren't upset because of Lissa or Christian. You're upset because the rules say you have to be with a student, and Adrian Ivash-kov's too old. The way I hear it, you guys have already had a lot of practice watching each other's bodies."

That joke could have been *so* much funnier, but I'd learned not to expect too much from Jesse. I knew for a fact that he didn't care about Adrian and me. I also suspected he didn't even believe we had anything going on. But Jesse was still bitter about me threatening him earlier, and here was his chance to get back at me. Dustin, standing within earshot, had no interest in Jesse's idiotic teasing. Dustin would probably have an interest, however, if I slammed Jesse's face into the wall.

That didn't mean I had to be silent, though. Guardians talked to Moroi all the time; they just tended to be respectful and still keep an eye on their surroundings. So I gave Jesse a small smile and simply said, "Your wit is always such a delight, Mr. Zeklos. I can barely contain myself around it." I then turned away and surveyed the rest of the room.

When Jesse realized I wasn't going to do anything else, he laughed and walked away, apparently thinking he'd won some great victory. Dustin left shortly thereafter.

"Asshole," muttered Christian, returning to his station. Class had about five minutes left.

My eyes followed Jesse across the room. "You know something, Christian? I'm pretty happy to be guarding you."

"If you're comparing me to Zeklos, I don't really take that as much of a compliment. But here, try this. Then you'll really be glad you're with me."

His masterpiece was finished, and he gave me a piece. I hadn't realized it, but just before the meatloaf had gone in, he'd wrapped it in bacon.

"Good God," I said. "This is the most stereotypical vampire food ever."

"Only if it was raw. What do you think?"

"It's good," I said reluctantly. Who knew that bacon would make all the difference? "Really good. I think you have a promising future as a housewife while Lissa works and makes millions of dollars."

"Funny, that's exactly my dream."

We left the class in lighter moods. Things had grown more friendly between us, and I decided that I could handle the next six weeks protecting him.

He and Lissa were going to meet in the library to study— or pretend to study—but he had to stop by his dorm first. So I followed him across the quad, back into the winter air that had grown chillier since sunset seven hours ago. The snow on the paths, which had turned slushy in the sun, had now frozen up and made walking treacherous. Along the way, we were joined by Brandon Lazar, a Moroi who lived in Christian's hall. Brandon could barely contain himself, recapping a fight he'd witnessed in his math class. We listened to his rendition, all of us laughing at the thought of Alberta sneaking in through the window.

"Hey, she might be old, but she could take on almost any of us," I told them. I gave Brandon a puzzled look. He had bruises and red splotches on his face. He also had a few weird welts near his ear. "What happened to you? Have you been fighting guardians too?"

His smile promptly disappeared, and he looked away from me. "Nah, just fell."

"Come on," I said. Moroi might not train to fight like dhampirs did, but they got in brawls with each other just as often as anyone else. I tried to think of any Moroi he might have a conflict with. For the most part, Brandon was pretty likeable. "That's the lamest, most unoriginal excuse in the world."

"It's true," he said, still avoiding my eyes.

"If someone's screwing with you, I can give you a few pointers."

He turned back to me, locking eyes. "Just let it go." He wasn't hostile or anything, but there was a firm note in his voice. It was almost like he believed saying the words alone would make me obey him.

I chuckled. "What are you trying to do? Compel me—"

Suddenly, I saw movement on my left. A slight shadow blending in with the dark shapes of a cluster of snowy pine trees—but moving just enough to catch my attention. Stan's face emerged from the darkness as he sprang toward us.

Finally, my first test.

Adrenaline shot through me just as strongly as if a real Strigoi were approaching. I reacted instantly, reaching out to grab both Brandon and Christian. That was always the first move, to throw my own life before theirs. I jerked the two guys to a halt and turned toward my attacker, reaching for my stake in order to defend the Moroi—

And that's when he appeared.

Mason.

He stood several feet in front of me, off to Stan's right, looking just as he had last night. Translucent. Shimmering. Sad.

The hair on the back of my neck stood up. I froze, unable to move or finish going for my stake. I forgot about what I'd been doing and completely lost track of the people and commotion around me. The world slowed down, everything fading around me. There was only Mason—that ghostly, shimmering Mason who glowed in the dark and seemed like he so badly wanted to tell me something. The same feeling of helplessness I'd experienced in Spokane returned to me. I hadn't been able to help him then. I couldn't help him now. My stomach turned cold and hollow. I could do nothing except stand there, wondering what he was trying to say.

He lifted one translucent hand and pointed off toward the other side of campus, but I didn't know what it meant. There was so much over there, and it wasn't clear what he was pointing at. I shook my head, not understanding but desperately wishing I could. The sorrow on his face seemed to grow.

Suddenly, something slammed into my shoulder, and I stumbled forward. The world suddenly started up again, snapping me out of the dreamy state I'd just been in. I only barely managed to throw out my hands in time to stop myself from hitting the ground. I looked up and saw Stan standing over me.

"Hathaway!" he barked. "What are you doing?"

I blinked, still trying to shake off the weirdness of seeing Mason again. I felt sluggish and dazed. I looked into Stan's angry face and then glanced over at where Mason had been. He was gone. I turned my attention back to Stan and realized what had happened. In my distraction, I'd completely spaced while he'd staged his attack. He now had one arm around Christian's neck and one around Brandon's. He wasn't hurting them, but his point was made.

"If I had been a Strigoi," he growled, "these two would be dead."

FIVE

MOST DISCIPLINARY ISSUES AT the Academy went to Headmistress Kirova. She oversaw Moroi and dhampirs alike and was known for her creative and oft-used repertoire of punishments. She wasn't cruel, exactly, but she wasn't soft, either. She simply took student behavior seriously and dealt with it as she saw fit.

There were some issues, however, that were beyond her jurisdiction.

The school's guardians calling together a disciplinary committee wasn't unheard of, but it was very, very rare. You had to do something pretty serious to piss them off to get that sort of response. Like, say, willfully endangering a Moroi. Or *hypothetically* willfully endangering a Moroi.

"For the last time," I growled, "I didn't do it on purpose."

I sat in one of the guardians' meeting rooms, facing my committee: Alberta, Emil, and one of the other rare female guardians on campus, Celeste. They sat at a long table, looking imposing, while I sat in a single chair and felt very vulnerable. Several other guardians were sitting in and watching, but thankfully, none of my classmates were there to see this humiliation. Dimitri was among the watchers. He was not on the committee, and I wondered if they'd kept him off because of his potentially biased role as my mentor.

"Miss Hathaway," said Alberta, fully in her strict-captain mode, "you must know why we have a hard time believing that."

Celeste nodded. "Guardian Alto saw you. You refused to protect two Moroi—including the one whose protection you were specifically assigned to."

"I didn't refuse!" I exclaimed. "I . . . fumbled."

"That wasn't a fumble," said Stan from the watchers. He glanced at Alberta for permission to speak. "May I?" She nodded, and he turned back to me. "If you'd blocked or attacked me and then messed up, that would be a fumble. But you didn't block. You didn't attack. You didn't even try. You just stood there like a statue and did nothing."

Understandably, I was outraged. The thought that I would purposely leave Christian and Brandon to be "killed" by a Strigoi was ridiculous. But what could I do? I either confessed to screwing up majorly or to having seen a ghost. Neither option was appealing, but I had to cut my losses. One made me look incompetent. The other made me look insane. I didn't want to be associated with either of those. I much preferred my usual description of "reckless" and "disruptive."

"Why am I getting in trouble for messing up?" I asked tightly. "I mean, I saw Ryan mess up earlier. He didn't get in trouble. Isn't that the point of this whole exercise? *Practice*? If we were perfect, you'd already have unleashed us upon the world!"

"Weren't you listening?" said Stan. I swore I could see a vein throbbing in his forehead. I think he was the only one there as upset as I was. At the very least, he was the only one (aside from me) showing his emotions. The others wore poker faces, but then, none of them had witnessed what had happened. If I'd been in Stan's place, I might have thought the worst of me too. "You didn't mess up, because 'messing up' implies that you have to actually *do* something."

"Okay, then. I froze." I looked at him defiantly. "Does that count as messing up? I cracked under the pressure and blanked out. It turns out I wasn't prepared. The moment came, and I panicked. It happens to novices all the time."

"To a novice who has already killed Strigoi?" asked Emil. He was from Romania, his accent a bit thicker than Dimitri's Russian one. It wasn't nearly as nice, though. "It seems unlikely."

I dealt out glares to him and everyone else in the room. "Oh, I see. After one incident, I'm now expected to be an expert Strigoi killer? I can't panic or be afraid or anything? Makes sense. Thanks, guys. Fair. Real fair." I slumped back in my seat, arms crossed over my chest. There was no need to fake bitchy defiance. I had plenty of it to dish out.

Alberta sighed and leaned forward. "We're arguing semantics. Technicalities aren't the point here. What's important is that this morning, you made it very clear you did not want to guard Christian Ozera. In fact . . . I think you even said you wanted us to be sure we knew that you were doing it against your will *and* that we'd soon see what a horrible idea it was." Ugh. I *had* said that. Honestly, what had I been thinking? "And then, when your first test comes around, we find you completely and utterly unresponsive."

I nearly flew out of my chair. "That's what this is about? You think I didn't protect him because of some kind of weird revenge thing?"

All three of them stared at me expectantly.

"You aren't exactly known for calmly and gracefully accepting things you don't like," she replied wryly.

This time, I did stand up, pointing my finger at her accusingly. "*Not* true. I have followed every rule Kirova laid down for me since coming back here. I've gone to every practice and obeyed every curfew." Well, I'd fudged some of the curfews but not willfully. It had always been for the greater good. "There's no reason I'd do this as some kind of revenge! What good would it do? Sta— Guardian Alto wasn't going to really hurt Christian, so it's not like I'd get to see him punched or anything. The only thing I would accomplish is getting dragged into the middle of something like *this* and possibly facing removal from the field experience."

"You *are* facing removal from the field experience," replied Celeste flatly.

"Oh." I sat down, suddenly not feeling as bold. Silence hung in the room for several moments, and then I heard Dimitri's voice speak from behind me.

"She has a point," he said. My heart thumped loudly in

my chest. Dimitri knew I wouldn't take revenge like that. He didn't think I was petty. "If she were going to protest or take revenge, she'd do it in a different way." Well, not *too* petty, at least.

Celeste frowned. "Yes, but after the scene she made this morning . . ."

Dimitri took a few steps forward and stood beside my chair. Having his solid presence nearby comforted me. I had a flash of déjà vu, back to when Lissa and I had returned to the Academy last autumn. Headmistress Kirova had nearly expelled me, and Dimitri had stood up for me then too.

"This is all circumstantial," he said. "Regardless of how suspicious you think it looks, there's no proof. Removing her from the experience—and essentially ruining her gradua-tion—is a bit extreme without any certainties."

The committee looked thoughtful, and I focused my atten-tion on Alberta. She had the most power here. I'd always liked her, and in our time together, she'd been strict but always scrupulously fair. I hoped that would still hold true. She beck-oned Celeste and Emil toward her, and the other two guard-ians leaned closer. They had a whispered conference. Alberta gave a resigned nod, and the others leaned back.

"Miss Hathaway, do you have anything you'd like to say before we tell you our conclusions?"

That I'd *like* to say? Hell, yeah. There were tons of things. I wanted to say that I wasn't incompetent. I wanted to tell them that I was one of the best novices here. I wanted to tell them

that I had seen Stan coming *and* had been on the verge of react-
ing. I especially wanted to tell them that I *didn't* want to have
this mark on my record. Even if I stayed in the field experience, I'd essentially have an F for this first test. It would affect
my overall grade, which could subsequently affect my future.

But again, what choice did I have? Tell them that I'd seen
a ghost? The ghost of a guy who'd had a major crush on me
and who had quite likely died because of that crush? I still
didn't know what was going on with these sightings. One
time I could write off to exhaustion . . . but I'd seen him—or
it—twice now. Was he real? My higher reasoning said no, but
honestly, it didn't matter at the moment. If he was real and I
told them, they'd think I was crazy. If he wasn't real and I told
them, they'd think I was crazy—and they'd be right. I couldn't
win here.

"No, Guardian Petrov," I said, hoping I sounded meek.
"Nothing more to add."

"All right," she said wearily. "Here's what we've decided.
You're lucky you have Guardian Belikov to advocate for you,
or this decision might have been different. We're giving you
the benefit of the doubt. You'll go on with the field experience
and continue to guard Mr. Ozera. You'll just be on a probation
of sorts."

"That's okay," I said. I'd been on probation for most of my
academic life. "Thank you."

"And," she added. *Uh-oh.* "Because the suspicion isn't
entirely removed, you'll be spending your day off this week

doing community service."

I jumped out of my chair again. "What?"

Dimitri's hand wrapped around my wrist, his fingers warm and controlling. "Sit down," he murmured in my ear, tugging me toward the chair. "Take what you can get."

"If that's a problem, we can make it next week too," warned Celeste. "And the next five after that."

I sat down and shook my head. "I'm sorry. Thank you."

The hearing dispersed, and I was left feeling weary and beaten. Had only one day gone by? Surely the happy excitement I'd felt before the field experience had been weeks ago and not this morning. Alberta told me to go find Christian, but Dimitri asked if he could have some time alone with me. She agreed, no doubt hoping he'd set me on the straight and narrow.

The room emptied, and I thought he'd sit and talk to me then and there, but instead he walked over to a small table that held a water dispenser, coffee, and other beverages.

"You want some hot chocolate?" he asked.

I hadn't expected that. "Sure."

He dumped four packets of instant hot chocolate into two Styrofoam cups and then added in hot water.

"Doubling it is the secret," he said when the cups were full.

He handed me mine, along with a wooden stirrer, and then walked toward a side door. Presuming I was supposed to follow him, I scurried to catch up without spilling my hot chocolate.

"Where are we—oh."

I stepped through the doorway and found myself in a little glass-enclosed porch filled with small patio tables. I'd had no idea this porch was adjacent to the meeting room, but then, this was the building the guardians conducted all campus business out of. Novices were rarely allowed. I also hadn't realized the building was built around a small courtyard, which was what this porch looked out to. In the summer, I imagined one could open the windows and be surrounded in greenery and warm air. Now, encased in glass and frost, I felt like I was in some kind of an ice palace.

Dimitri swept his hand over a chair, brushing off dust. I did the same and sat down opposite him. Apparently this room didn't see a lot of use in the winter. Because it was enclosed, the room was warmer than outdoors, but it wasn't heated otherwise. The air felt chilly, and I warmed my hands on my cup. Silence fell between Dimitri and me. The only noise came from me blowing on my hot chocolate. He drank his right away. He'd been killing Strigoi for years. What was a little scalding water here and there?

As we sat, and the quiet grew, I studied him over the edge of my cup. He wasn't looking at me, but I knew he knew I was watching. Like every other time I looked at him, I was always struck by his looks first. The soft dark hair that he often tucked behind his ears without realizing it, hair that never *quite* wanted to stay in its tie at the back of his neck. His eyes were brown too, somehow gentle and fierce at the same time. His lips had that same contradictory quality, I realized. When he was fighting or dealing with something grim, those lips would flatten and turn hard. But in lighter times . . . when he laughed or kissed . . . well, then they'd become soft and wonderful.

Today, more than his exterior hit me. I felt warm and safe just being with him. He brought comfort after my terrible day. So often with other people, I felt a need to be the center of attention, to be funny and always have something clever to say. It was a habit I needed to shake to be a guardian, seeing as that job required so much silence. But with Dimitri, I never felt like I had to be anything more than what I already was. I didn't have to entertain him or think up jokes or even flirt. It was enough to just be together, to be so completely comfortable in each other's presence—smoldering sexual tension aside—that we lost all sense of self-consciousness. I exhaled and drank my cocoa.

"What happened out there?" he asked at last, meeting my gaze. "You didn't crack under the pressure."

His voice was curious, not accusatory. He wasn't treating me as a student right now, I realized. He was regarding me as an equal. He simply wanted to know what was going on with me. There was no discipline or lecturing here.

And that just made it all the worse when I had to lie to him.

"Of course it was," I told him, looking down into my cup.

"Unless you believe I really did let Stan 'attack' Christian."

"No," he said. "I don't believe that. I never did. I knew you'd be unhappy when you found out about the assignments, but I never once doubted that you'd do what you'd have to for this. I knew you wouldn't let your personal feelings get in the way of your duty."

I looked up again and met his eyes, so full of faith and absolute confidence in me. "I didn't. I was mad. . . . Still am a little. But once I said I'd do it, I meant it. And after spending some time with him . . . well, I don't hate him. I actually think he's good for Lissa, and he cares about her, so I can't get upset about that. He and I just clash sometimes, that's all . . . but we did really well together against the Strigoi. I remembered that while I was with him today, and arguing against this assignment just seemed stupid. So I decided to do the best job I could."

I hadn't meant to talk so much, but it felt good to let out what was inside of me, and the look on Dimitri's face would have gotten me to say anything. Almost anything.

"What happened then?" he asked. "With Stan?"

I averted my eyes and played with my cup again. I hated keeping things from him, but I couldn't tell him about this. In the human world, vampires and dhampirs were creatures of myth and legend—bedtime stories to scare children. Humans didn't know we were real and walking the earth. But just because we were real didn't mean that every other story-time paranormal creature was. We knew that and had our own myths and bedtime stories about things we didn't believe in. Werewolves. Bogeymen. Ghosts.

Ghosts played no real role in our culture, short of being fodder for pranks and campfire tales. Ghosts inevitably came up on Halloween, and some legends endured over the years. But in real life? No ghosts. If you came back after death, it was because you were a Strigoi.

At least, that's what I'd always been taught. I honestly didn't know enough now to say what was going on. Me imagining Mason seemed more likely than him being a true ghost, but man, that meant I might seriously be heading into crazy territory. All this time I'd worried about Lissa losing it. Who had known it might be me?

Dimitri was still watching me, waiting for an answer.

"I don't know what happened out there. My intentions were good . . . I just . . . I just messed up."

"Rose. You're a terrible liar."

I glanced up. "No, I'm not. I've told a lot of good lies in my life. People have believed them."

He smiled slightly. "I'm sure. But it doesn't work with me. For one thing, you won't look me in the eye. As for the other . . . I don't know. I can just tell."

Damn. He *could* tell. He just knew me that well. I stood up and moved to the door, keeping my back to him. Normally, I treasured every minute with him, but I couldn't stick around today. I hated lying, but I didn't want to tell the truth either. I had to leave.

"Look, I appreciate you being worried about me . . . but really, it's okay. I just messed up. I'm embarrassed about it—and sorry I put your awesome training to shame—but I'll rebound. Next time, Stan's ass is mine."

I hadn't even heard him get up, but suddenly, Dimitri was right behind me. He placed a hand on my shoulder, and I froze in front of the door leading out. He didn't touch me anywhere else. He didn't try to pull me closer. But, oh, that one hand on my shoulder held all the power in the world.

"Rose," he said, and I knew he was no longer smiling. "I don't know why you're lying, but I know you wouldn't do it without a good reason. And if there's something wrong—something you're afraid to tell the others—"

I spun around rapidly, somehow managing to pivot in place in such a way that his hand never moved yet ended up on my other shoulder.

"I'm not afraid," I cried. "I do have my reasons, and believe me, what happened with Stan was nothing. Really. All of this is just something stupid that got blown out of proportion. Don't feel sorry for me or feel like you have to do anything. What happened sucks, but I'll just roll with it and take the black mark. I'll take care of everything. I'll take care of me." It took all of my strength just then not to shake. How had this day gotten so bizarre and out of control?

Dimitri didn't say anything. He just looked down at me, and the expression on his face was one I'd never seen before. I couldn't interpret it. Was he mad? Disapproving? I just couldn't tell. The fingers on my shoulder tightened slightly and then relaxed.

"You don't have to do this alone," he said at last. He sounded almost wistful, which made no sense. He was the one who'd been telling me for so long that I needed to be strong. I wanted to throw myself into his arms just then, but I knew I couldn't.

I couldn't help a smile. "You say that . . . but tell me the truth. Do *you* go running to others when you have problems?"

"That's the not the same—"

"Answer the question, comrade."

"Don't call me that."

"And don't avoid the question either."

"No," he said. "I try to deal with my problems on my own."

I slipped away from his hand. "See?"

"But you have a lot of people in your life you can trust, people who care about you. That changes things."

I looked at him in surprise. "You don't have people who care about you?"

He frowned, obviously rethinking his words. "Well, I've always had good people in my life . . . and there have been people who cared about me. But that doesn't necessarily mean I could trust them or tell them everything."

I was often so distracted by the weirdness of our relationship that I rarely thought about Dimitri as someone with a life away from me. He was respected by everyone on campus. Teachers and students alike knew him as one of the deadliest guardians here. Whenever we ran into guardians from outside the school, they always seemed to know and respect him too. But I couldn't recall ever having seen him in any sort of social setting. He didn't appear to have any close friends among the other guardians—just coworkers he liked. The friendliest I'd ever seen him get with someone had been when Christian's aunt, Tasha Ozera, visited. They'd known each other for a long time, but even that hadn't been enough for Dimitri to pursue once her visit was over.

Dimitri was alone an awful lot, I realized, content to hole up with his cowboy novels when not working. I *felt* alone a lot, but in truth, I was almost always surrounded by people. With him being my teacher, I tended to view things as one-sided: He was the one always giving me something, be it advice or instruction. But I gave him something too, something harder to define—a connection with another person.

"Do you trust me?" I asked him.

The hesitation was brief. "Yes."

"Then trust me now, and don't worry about me just this once."

I stepped away, out of the reach of his arm, and he didn't say anything more or try to stop me. Cutting through the room that I'd had the hearing in, I headed for the building's main exit, tossing the remnants of my hot chocolate in a garbage can as I walked past.

SIX

THERE HAD ONLY BEEN THREE other witnesses to what had happened out on the quad. Yet, unsurprisingly, everyone seemed to know about it when I returned to the commons later on. Classes were done, but plenty of students moved about in the corridors, off to study or retake tests or whatever. They tried to hide their glances and whispers, but they didn't do a very good job. Those who made eye contact with me either gave me tight-lipped smiles or immediately looked away. Wonderful.

With no psychic link to Christian, I had no clue where to find him. I could sense that Lissa was in the library and figured that would be a good place to start looking. On my way there, I heard a guy's voice call out behind me.

"Took things a bit far, didn't you?"

I turned around and saw Ryan and Camille walking several steps back. If I'd been a guy, the appropriate response would have been, "You mean with your mom?" Because I was not a guy, though, and because I had manners, I just said, "Don't know what you're talking about."

Ryan hurried to catch up with me. "You know exactly what I mean. With Christian. I heard that when Stan attacked, you were just like, 'Here, take him,' and walked away."

"Oh good God," I groaned. It was bad enough when everyone was talking about you, but why did the stories always end up changing? "That is *not* what happened."

"Oh yeah?" he asked. "Then why did you get called in to see Alberta?"

"Look," I said, not feeling so well mannered anymore, "I just messed up the attack . . . you know, kind of like you did earlier when you weren't paying attention in the hall?"

"Hey," he said, flushing slightly. "I ended up getting in on that—I did my part."

"Is that what they're calling getting killed nowadays?"

"At least I wasn't a whiny bitch who refused to fight."

I had just about calmed down after speaking with Dimitri, but now my temper was rising already. It was like a thermometer ready to burst. "You know, maybe instead of criticizing others, you should pay more attention to your own guardian duties." I nodded toward Camille. She had thus far been quiet, but her face showed me she was eating all of this up.

Ryan shrugged. "I can do both. Shane's farther behind us, and the area ahead is clear. No doors. Easy." He patted Camille's shoulder. "She's safe."

"It's an easy place to secure. You wouldn't do so well in the real world with real Strigoi."

His smile faded. Anger glinted in his eyes. "Right. The way I hear it, you didn't do such a great job out there either, at least not as far as Mason was concerned."

Taunting over what had happened with Stan and Christian

was one thing. But implying that I was at fault for Mason's death? Unacceptable. *I* was the one who'd kept Lissa safe for two years in the human world. *I* was the one who had killed two Strigoi in Spokane. *I* was the only novice at this school with *molnija* marks, the little tattoos given to guardians to mark Strigoi kills. I'd known there had been some whispers about what had happened to Mason, but no one had ever actually said anything to me. The thought of Ryan or anyone else thinking I was to blame for Mason dying was too much. I blamed myself plenty enough already without their help.

The thermometer broke.

In one smooth motion, I reached past him, grabbed Camille, and swung her up against the wall. I hadn't thrown her hard enough to hurt her, but she was clearly startled. Her eyes widened in shock, and I used my forearm to pin her, pressing it against her throat.

"What are you doing?" exclaimed Ryan, peering back and forth between our faces. I shifted my stance slightly, still keeping the pressure on Camille.

"Furthering your education," I said pleasantly. "Sometimes places aren't as easy to secure as you think."

"You're crazy! You can't hurt a Moroi. If the guardians find out—"

"I'm not," I argued. I glanced toward her. "Am I hurting you? Are you in extreme pain?"

There was a hesitation; then she gave as much of a shake of her head as she could manage.

"Are you uncomfortable?"

A small nod.

"See?" I told Ryan. "Discomfort isn't the same thing as pain."

"You're insane. Let her go."

"I'm not done, Ry. Pay attention because here's the point: Danger can come from anywhere. Not just Strigoi—or guardians dressed up like Strigoi. Keep acting like an arrogant asshole who thinks he knows everything"—I pressed my arm in a little harder, still not enough to affect her breathing or cause real pain—"and you miss things. And those things can kill your Moroi."

"Okay, okay. Whatever. Please, stop it," he said. His voice wavered. There was no more attitude. "You're scaring her."

"I'd be scared too, if my life was in your hands."

The scent of cloves alerted me to Adrian's presence. I also knew that Shane and a few others had come to watch. The other novices looked uncertain, like they wanted to pry me off but were afraid of getting Camille hurt. I knew I should let her go, but Ryan had just made me so angry. I needed to prove a point to him. I needed to get him back. And really, I didn't even feel sorry for Camille either since I was sure she'd done her fair share of gossiping about me too.

"This is fascinating," said Adrian, his voice as lazy as usual. "But I think you've made your point."

"I don't know," I said. The tone of my voice managed to be both sweet and menacing at the same time. "I still don't think Ryan gets it."

"For God's sake, Rose! I get it," cried Ryan. "Just let her go."

Adrian moved around me, going over to stand beside Camille. She and I were pressed close together, but he managed to squeeze in so that his face was in my line of sight, almost beside hers. He wore that goofy smirk he normally had, but there was something serious in his dark green eyes.

"Yes, little dhampir. Let her go. You're done here."

I wanted to tell Adrian to get away from me, that *I* would be the one to say when this was finished. Somehow, I couldn't get the words out. A part of me was enraged at his interference. The other part of me thought he sounded . . . reasonable.

"Let her go," he repeated.

My eyes were all over Adrian now, not Camille. Suddenly, all of me decided he sounded reasonable. Completely reasonable. I needed to let her go. I moved my arm and stepped away. With a gulp, Camille darted behind Ryan, using him like a shield. I saw now that she was on the verge of tears. Ryan simply looked stunned.

Adrian straightened up and made a dismissive gesture toward Ryan. "I'd get out of here—before you *really* annoy Rose."

Ryan, Camille, and the others slowly backed off from us. Adrian put his arm around me and hurried me away toward the library. I felt weird, kind of like I was waking up, but then, with each step, things grew clearer and clearer. I pushed his arm off me and jerked away.

"You just used compulsion on me!" I exclaimed. "You made me let her go."

"Someone needed to. You looked like you were seconds away from strangling her."

"I wasn't. And I wouldn't have." I pushed open the library door. "You had no right to do that to me. No right at all." Compulsion—making people do what you wanted—was a skill all vampires had to a very small degree. Using it was considered immoral, and most couldn't control it well enough to do any real damage. Spirit strengthened the ability, however, making both Adrian and Lissa very dangerous.

"And *you* had no right to tackle some poor girl in the hall just to soothe your own hurt pride."

"Ryan had no right to say those things."

"I don't even know what 'those things' are, but unless I've misjudged your age, you're too old to be throwing a tantrum over idle gossip."

"Throwing a—"

My words fell short as we reached Lissa working at a table. Her face and feelings told me trouble was coming. Eddie stood a couple feet away from her, leaning against a wall and watching the room. His eyes widened when he saw me, but he didn't say anything at my approach.

I slid into the chair opposite Lissa.

"Hey."

She looked up and sighed, then returned her attention to the textbook open in front of her. "I wondered when you'd turn up," she said. "Did you get suspended?"

Her words were calm and polite, but I could read her underlying feelings. Annoyed. Even a little angry.

"Not this time," I said. "Just got stuck with community service."

She said nothing, but the irate mood I sensed through the bond remained unchanged.

Now I sighed. "Okay, talk to me, Liss. I know you're mad."

Adrian looked at me, then her, and then me again. "I feel like I'm missing something here."

"Oh, great," I said. "You went and busted up my fight and didn't even know what it was about."

"Fight?" asked Lissa, confusion joining her anger.

"What happened?" repeated Adrian.

I nodded to Lissa. "Go ahead, tell him."

"Rose got tested earlier and refused to protect Christian." She shook her head, exasperated, and fixed me with an accusatory glare. "I can't believe you're seriously still mad enough to do something like that to him. It's childish."

Lissa had jumped to the same conclusions as the guardians. I sighed. "I didn't do it on purpose! I just sat through a whole hearing on this crap and told them the same thing."

"Then what happened?" she demanded. "Why *did* you do it?"

I hesitated, unsure what to say. My reluctance to talk didn't even have anything to do with Adrian and Eddie overhearing—though I certainly didn't want them to. The problem was more complex.

Dimitri had been right—there were people I could trust, and two of them I trusted unconditionally: him and Lissa. I'd already held back from telling him the truth. Would I—could I—do the same with her? Although she was mad, I knew without a doubt that Lissa would always support me and be there for me. But just like with Dimitri, I balked at the idea of telling my ghost story. Also just like with Dimitri, it left me in the same bind: crazy or incompetent?

Through our bond, I felt her mind, pure and clear. There was no taint, no darkness, or sign of madness—and yet, something tingled in the background. A slight stirring. Antidepressants took awhile to fully get into and out of one's system, but her magic was already waking up after one day. I thought back to my ghostly encounters, dredging up the memory of that sad, translucent Mason. How could I even begin to explain that to her? How could I bring up something as weird and fantastic as that when she'd been trying so hard to get a little normality in her life and now faced the challenge of getting her magic under control?

No, I realized. I couldn't tell her. Not yet—especially when it suddenly occurred to me that there was still something else big I needed to let her know about.

"I froze," I said finally. "It's stupid. I'd been so cocky about being able to take out anyone, and then Stan . . ." I shrugged. "I don't know. I just couldn't react. It . . . it's really embarrassing. And him of all people."

Lissa studied me intently, looking for any sign of dishonesty. It hurt to think that she'd mistrust me, except . . . well, I *was* actually lying. As I'd told Dimitri, though, I could be a good liar when I wanted to be. Lissa couldn't tell.

"I wish I could read your mind," she mused.

"Come on," I said. "You know me. Do you really think I'd do this? Abandon Christian and make myself look stupid on purpose just to get back at my teachers?"

"No," she said finally. "You'd probably do it in a way where you wouldn't get caught."

"Dimitri said the same thing," I grumbled. "I'm glad everyone has so much faith in me."

"We do," she countered. "That's why all of this is so weird."

"Even I make mistakes." I put on my brash, overconfident face. "I know it's hard to believe—kind of surprises me myself—but I guess it has to happen. It's probably some kind of karmic way to balance out the universe. Otherwise, it wouldn't be fair to have one person so full of awesomeness."

Adrian, blessedly silent for a change, was watching the two of us talk, much as one would look back and forth at a tennis match. His eyes were narrowed slightly, and I suspected he was studying our auras.

Lissa rolled her eyes, but fortunately, the anger I'd felt earlier lightened. She believed me. Her gaze then lifted from my face to someone beyond me. I felt the happy, golden emotions that signaled Christian's presence.

"My loyal bodyguard returns," he declared, pulling up a chair. He glanced at Lissa. "Are you done yet?"

"Done with what?" she asked.

He inclined his head toward me. "Giving her a hard time about how she threw me into the deadly clutches of Alto."

Lissa blushed. She was already feeling a little bad about jumping on me, now that I'd defended myself sufficiently. Christian's flippant, knowing observation just made her feel more foolish.

"We were just talking about it, that's all."

Adrian yawned and slouched back in his chair. "Actually, I think I've figured it all out. This was a scam, wasn't it? A scam to scare me off since I'm always talking about you being my guardian. You thought if you pretended to be a bad guardian, I wouldn't want you. Well, it's not going to work, so there's no point in risking anyone else's life."

I was grateful he didn't mention the incident in the hall. Ryan had absolutely been out of line, but as more time passed, it became harder and harder for me to believe I'd snapped like that. It was like something that had happened to someone else, something that I'd simply been watching. Of course, I seemed to be snapping over everything lately. I'd been mad about getting Christian, mad about the guardians' accusation, mad about—

Oh, right. It was probably time for me to drop the bomb.

"So, um . . . there's something you guys should know."

Four sets of eyes—even Eddie's—turned to me.

"What's wrong?" asked Lissa.

There was really no easy way to tell them, so I just pushed forward. "Well, it turns out that Victor Dashkov was never found guilty of what he did to us. He's just been locked up. But they're finally going to have an official trial—in another week or so."

Lissa's reaction to hearing his name was similar to mine. Shock shot through the bond, followed immediately by fear. A slide show of images flashed through her mind. The way Victor's sick game had made her question her sanity. The torture his henchman had subjected her to. The bloody state she'd found Christian in after he'd been attacked by Victor's hounds. She clenched her fists on the table, knuckles going white. Christian couldn't sense her reaction the way I could, but he didn't need to. He moved his hand over hers. She barely noticed.

"But . . . but . . ." She took a deep, steadying breath, fighting to stay calm. "How could he not be guilty already? Everyone knows. . . . They all saw. . . ."

"It's the law. They supposedly have to give him a fighting chance."

There was confusion all over her, and slowly, she came to the same realization that I had last night with Dimitri. "So . . . wait . . . are you saying there's a chance they might not find him guilty?"

I looked into her wide, frightened eyes and couldn't bring myself to tell her. Apparently, my face said it all.

Christian slammed his fist against the table. "This is bullshit." Several people at other tables glanced over at his outburst.

"This is politics," said Adrian. "People in power never have to play by the same rules."

"But he nearly killed Rose and Christian!" cried Lissa. "And he kidnapped me! How can there be any question?"

Lissa's emotions were all over the place. Fear. Sorrow. Anger. Outrage. Confusion. Helplessness. I didn't want her delving into those dark feelings and hoped desperately that she'd grow calm again. Slowly, steadily, she did—but then I started getting angry again. It was like Ryan all over.

"It's a formality, I'm sure," said Adrian. "When all the evidence is in, there probably isn't going to be much of a debate."

"That's the thing," I said bitterly. "They're not going to have all the evidence. We aren't allowed to go."

"What?" exclaimed Christian. "Then who's testifying?"

"The other guardians who were there. We apparently can't be trusted to keep the whole thing quiet. The queen doesn't want the world to know that one of her precious royals might have done something wrong."

Lissa didn't seem to take offense at me trashing royals. "But we're the reason he's on trial."

Christian stood up, glancing around as though Victor

might be in the library. "I'm going to go take care of this right now."

"Sure," said Adrian. "I bet going in there and kicking down the door will change their minds. Take Rose with you, and you guys'll make a really good impression."

"Yeah?" asked Christian, clenching the back of his chair and fixing Adrian with a stormy glare. "You have a better idea?"

Lissa's calmness began to waver again. "If Victor was free, would he come after us again?"

"If he gets loose again, he won't stay that way for long," I said. "I'll make sure of it."

"Careful there," said Adrian. He seemed to find all of this funny. "Even you couldn't get away with a royal assassination."

I started to tell him that I'd practice on him first, but then Eddie's sharp voice interrupted my thoughts.

"Rose."

Instinct born from years of training instantly kicked into place. I looked up and immediately saw what he'd noticed. Emil had just entered the library and was scanning for novices, taking notes. I shot up out of my chair, taking a position not far from Eddie that gave me a view of Christian and most of the library. Damn it. I had to get a grip, or I'd end up proving Ryan right. Between my brawl in the hall and now this Victor thing, I was completely neglecting my guardian duties. I might not even need Mason to fail this.

Emil hadn't seen me sitting and socializing. He strolled by, glanced at us, and made a few notes before heading off to scout the rest of the library. Relieved at escaping my close call, I tried to gain control of myself. It was hard. That black mood had seized me again, and listening to Lissa and Christian rage over Victor's trial wasn't really helping me relax. I wanted to go over there and weigh in. I wanted to yell and rant and share my own frustration. But that wasn't a luxury I had as a guardian. My first duty was to protect Moroi and not give into my own impulses. Over and over, I repeated the guardian mantra: *They come first.*

Those words were really starting to annoy me.

SEVEN

When the first warning for curfew came around, the Moroi packed their things up. Adrian took off right away, but Lissa and Christian took their time walking back to the dorm. They held hands and kept their heads close together, whispering about something that I could have "spied" on if I'd gone inside Lissa's head. They were still outraged over the Victor news.

I gave them their privacy and kept my distance, scouting while Eddie walked off to their side. Since there were more Moroi than dhampirs on campus, the Moroi actually had two side-by-side dorms. Lissa and Christian lived in different ones. The two of them stopped when they came to the spot outside the buildings where the path through the quad split. They kissed goodbye, and I did my best to do the guardian seeing-without-actually-seeing thing. Lissa called goodbye to me and then headed off to her dorm with Eddie. I followed Christian to his.

If I'd been guarding Adrian or someone like him, I would probably have had to put up with sexual jokes about us sleeping near each other for the next six weeks. But Christian treated me in the casual, brusque way one might a sister. He cleared a spot on the floor for me, and by the time he returned from brushing his teeth, I'd made myself a cozy bed out of blankets. He flipped off the lights and climbed into his own bed.

After several quiet moments, I asked, "Christian?"

"This is the time when we sleep, Rose."

I yawned. "Believe me, I want that too. But I have a question."

"Is it about Victor? Because I need to sleep, and that's just going to piss me off again."

"No, it's about something else."

"Okay, shoot."

"Why didn't you make fun of me over what happened with Stan? Everyone else is trying to figure out if I messed up or did it on purpose. Lissa gave me a hard time. Adrian did a little. And the guardians . . . well, never mind about them. But you didn't say anything. I figured you'd be the first one with a snappy comment."

More silence fell, and I hoped he was thinking about his answer and not falling asleep.

"There was no point in giving you a hard time," he said at last. "I know you didn't do it on purpose."

"Why not? I mean, not that I'm contradicting you— because I *didn't* do it on purpose—but why are you so sure?"

"Because of our conversation in culinary science. And because of the way you are. I saw you in Spokane. Anyone who did what you did to save us . . . well, you wouldn't do something childish like this."

"Wow. Thanks. I . . . well, that means a lot." Christian

believed me when no one else did. "You're like the first person who actually believes I just messed up without any ulterior motives."

"Well," he said, "I don't believe that either."

"Believe what? That I messed up? Why not?"

"Weren't you just listening? I saw you in Spokane. Someone like you doesn't mess up or freeze." I started to give him the same line I'd given the guardians, that killing Strigoi didn't make me invincible, but he cut me off: "Plus, I saw your face out there."

"Out . . . on the quad?"

"Yeah." Several more quiet moments passed. "I don't know what happened, but the way you looked . . . that wasn't the look of someone trying to get back at a person. It wasn't the look of someone blanking out at Alto's attack either. It was something different. . . . I don't know. But you were completely consumed by something else—and honestly? Your expression? Kind of scary."

"Yet . . . you aren't giving me a hard time over that either."

"Not my business. If it was big enough to take you over like that, then it must be serious. But if push comes to shove, I feel safe with you, Rose. I know you'd protect me if there was really a Strigoi there." He yawned. "Okay. Now that I've bared my soul, can we please go to bed? Maybe you don't need beauty sleep, but some of us aren't that lucky."

I let him sleep and soon gave into exhaustion myself. I'd

had a long day and was still short on rest from the previous night. Once heavily asleep, I began to dream. As I did, I felt the telltale signs of one of Adrian's contrived dreams.

"Oh no," I groaned.

I stood in a garden in the middle of summer. The air was heavy and humid, and sunshine beat down on me in golden waves. Flowers of every color bloomed around me, and the air was heavy with the scent of lilacs and roses. Bees and butterflies danced from blossom to blossom. I wore jeans and a linen tank top. My *nazar*, a small blue eye made of glass that allegedly warded off evil, hung around my neck. I also wore a beaded bracelet with a cross, called a *chotki*, on my wrist. It was a Dragomir heirloom Lissa had given me. I rarely wore jewelry in my daily duties, but it always showed up in these dreams.

"Where are you?" I called. "I know you're here."

Adrian stepped around from behind an apple tree that was thick with pink and white flowers. He wore jeans—something I'd never seen him in before. They looked good and were undoubtedly a designer brand. A dark green cotton T-shirt—also very simple—covered his upper body, and the sunlight brought out highlights of gold and chestnut in his brown hair.

"I told you to stay out of my dreams," I said, putting my hands on my hips.

He gave me his lazy smile. "But how else are we supposed to talk? You didn't seem very friendly earlier."

"Maybe if you didn't use compulsion on people, you'd

have more friends."

"I had to save you from yourself. Your aura was like a storm cloud."

"Okay, for once, can we please not talk about auras and my impending doom?"

The look in his eyes told me he was actually really interested in that, but he let it go. "Okay. We can talk about other things."

"But I don't want to talk at all! I want to sleep."

"You are sleeping." Adrian smiled and walked over to study a flowering vine that was winding up a post. It had orange and yellow flowers shaped like trumpets. He gently ran his fingers over one of the flowers' edges. "This was my grandmother's garden."

"Great," I said, making myself comfortable against the apple tree. It looked like we could be here for a while. "Now I get to hear your family history."

"Hey, she was a cool lady."

"I'm sure she was. Can I go yet?"

His eyes were still on the vine's blossoms. "You shouldn't knock Moroi family trees. You don't know anything about your father. For all you know, we could be related."

"Would that mean you'd leave me alone?"

Strolling back over to me, he switched subjects as though there'd been no interruption. "Nah, don't worry. I think we come from different trees. Isn't your dad some Turkish guy anyway?"

"Yeah, according to my— Hey, are you staring at my chest?"

He was studying me closely, but his eyes were no longer on my face. I crossed my arms over my chest and glared.

"I'm staring at your shirt," he said. "The color is all wrong."

Reaching out, he touched the strap. Like ink spreading across paper, the ivory fabric turned the same shade of rich indigo as the vine's blossoms. He narrowed his eyes like an expert artist studying his work.

"How'd you do that?" I exclaimed.

"It's my dream. Hmm. You're not a blue person. Well, at least not in the color sense. Let's try this." The blue lit up into a brilliant crimson. "Yes, that's it. Red's your color. Red like a rose, like a sweet, sweet Rose."

"Oh man," I said. "I didn't know you could kick into crazy mode even in dreams." He never got as dark and depressed as Lissa had last year, but spirit definitely made him weird sometimes.

He stepped back and threw his arms out. "I'm always crazy around you, Rose. Here, I'm going to write an impromptu poem for you." He tipped his head back and shouted to the sky:

"Rose is in red
But never in blue
Sharp as a thorn
Fights like one too."

Adrian dropped his arms and looked at me expectantly.

"How can a thorn fight?" I asked.

He shook his head. "Art doesn't have to make sense, little dhampir. Besides, I'm supposed to be crazy, right?"

"Not the craziest I've ever seen."

"Well," he said, pacing over to study some hydrangeas, "I'll work on that."

I started to ask again about when I could go "back" to sleep, but our exchange brought something to my mind.

"Adrian . . . how do you know if you're crazy or not?"

He turned from the flowers, a smile on his face. I could tell he was about to make a joke, but then he looked at me more closely. The smile faded, and he turned unusually serious.

"Do you think you're crazy?" he asked.

"I don't know," I said, looking down at the ground. I was barefoot, and sharp blades of grass tickled my feet. "I've been . . . seeing things."

"People who are crazy rarely question whether they're crazy," he said wisely.

I sighed and looked back up at him. "That doesn't really help me."

He walked back over to me and rested a hand on my shoulder. "I don't think you're crazy, Rose. I think you've been through a lot, though."

I frowned. "What's that mean?"

"It means I don't think you're crazy."

"Thanks. That clears things up. You know, these dreams are *really* starting to bug me."

"Lissa doesn't mind them," he said.

"You visit hers too? Do you seriously have no boundaries?"

"Nah, hers are instructional. She wants to learn how to do this."

"Great. So I'm just the lucky one who gets to put up with your sexual harassment."

He actually looked hurt. "I really wish you wouldn't act like I'm evil incarnate."

"Sorry. I just haven't had much reason to believe you can do anything useful."

"Right. As opposed to your cradle-robbing mentor. I don't really see you making much progress with him."

I took a step back and narrowed my eyes. "Leave Dimitri out of this."

"I will when you stop acting like he's perfect. Correct me if I'm wrong, but he's one of the people who hid the trial from you, right?"

I looked away. "That's not important right now. Besides, he had his reasons."

"Yeah, which apparently didn't involve being open with you *or* fighting to get you there. Whereas me . . ." He shrugged. "I could get you into the trial."

"You?" I asked with a harsh laugh. "How are you going to pull that off? Have a smoke break with the judge? Use compulsion on the queen and half the royals at court?"

"You shouldn't be so quick to slam people who can help you. Just wait." He placed a light kiss on my forehead that I tried to wiggle away from. "But for now, go get some rest."

The garden faded, and I fell back into the normal blackness of sleep.

EIGHT

FOR THE NEXT FEW DAYS, I followed Christian around without incident. And as I did, I found myself growing more and more impatient.

For one thing, I was discovering that a lot of being a guardian was waiting around. I'd always known that, but the reality was harder than I'd realized. Guardians were absolutely essential for when Strigoi decided to attack. But those Strigoi attacks? They were generally rare. Time could pass—*years* could pass—without a guardian ever having to engage in any sort of conflict. While my instructors certainly wouldn't make us wait that long during this exercise, they nonetheless wanted to teach us patience and how important it was *not* to slack just because there'd been no danger in a while.

We were also being held to the strictest conditions a guardian could be in: always standing and always being formal. More often than not, guardians who lived with Moroi families behaved casually in their homes and did ordinary things like reading or watching TV—while still staying perfectly aware of any threats. We couldn't always expect that, though, so we had to practice the hard way while in school.

My patience level didn't do so well with all this waiting, but my frustration was more than just restlessness. I was desperate to prove myself, to make amends for not having reacted when Stan attacked. I'd had no further Mason sightings and had decided that what I'd seen really had been fatigue- and stress-induced. That made me happy, because those were much better reasons than being crazy or inept.

But certain things were not making me happy. When Christian and I met up with Lissa after class one day, I could feel worry and fear and anger radiating off of her. It was only the bond that clued me in, though. To all outside appearances, she looked fine. Eddie and Christian, who were talking about something with each other, didn't notice a thing.

I moved close and put an arm around her as we walked. "It's okay. Everything's going to be okay." I knew what was bothering her. Victor.

We'd decided that Christian—despite his willingness to "take care of things"—probably wasn't the best choice to go see about us getting into Victor's trial. So Lissa had played diplomat the other day and very politely spoken to Alberta about the possibility of us testifying. Alberta had told her, equally politely, that it was out of the question.

"I figured if we just explained things—why it was so important—they'd let us go," she murmured to me. "Rose, I can't sleep. . . . I just keep thinking about it. What if he gets loose? What if they really set him free?"

Her voice trembled, and there was an old vulnerability there that I hadn't seen in a long time. That sort of thing usually set off my warning bells, but this time, it triggered a weird rush of memories, of times past when Lissa had depended on me so much. I was happy to see how strong she'd become and wanted to make sure she stayed that way. I tightened my arm, hard to do while still walking.

"He won't get loose," I said fiercely. "We'll get to court. I'll make sure of it. You know I'd never let anything happen to you."

She leaned her head against my shoulder, a small smile on her face. "That's what I love about you. You have no idea how you'll get us to court, but you still push forward anyway to make me feel better."

"Is it working?"

"Yes."

The worry still lurked in her, but her amusement dampened its effects a little. Plus, despite her teasing me about my bold promise, my words really had reassured her.

Unfortunately, we soon found out that Lissa had other reasons to be frustrated. She was waiting for the medication to fade from her system and allow her full access to her magic. It was there—we could both sense it—but she was having trouble touching it. Three days had passed, and nothing had changed for her. I felt for her, but my biggest concern was her mental state—which thus far had stayed clear.

"I don't know what's going on," she complained. We had almost reached the commons. Lissa and Christian had plans to watch a movie. I half-wondered how difficult it would be for me to watch the movie and be on alert. "It seems like I should be able to do *something*, but I still can't. I'm stuck."

"That might not be a bad thing," I pointed out, moving away from Lissa so I could scan the path ahead.

She shot me a rueful look. "You're such a worrier. I thought that was my job."

"Hey, it's my job to look out for you."

"Actually, it's my job," said Eddie, in a rare show of joking.

"Neither of you should be worrying," she argued. "Not about this."

Christian slipped his arm around her waist. "You're more impatient than Rose here. All you need to do is—"

It was déjà vu.

Stan leapt out from a copse of trees and reached for Lissa, wrapping his arm around her torso and jerking her toward him. My body responded instantly, no hesitation whatsoever as I moved to "save" her. The only problem was that Eddie had responded instantly too, and he was closer, which put him there ahead of me. I circled, trying to get in on the action, but the way the two were squaring off blocked me from being effective.

Eddie came at Stan from the side, fierce and swift, pulling Stan's arm away from Lissa with a strength nearly powerful enough to rip it out of the socket. Eddie's wiry frame often hid how muscular he really was. Stan's hand caught the side of Eddie's face, nails digging in, but it was enough so that Lissa could wriggle free and run to join Christian behind me. With her out of the way, I moved off to the side, hoping to assist Eddie—but there was no need. Without missing a beat, he grabbed Stan and threw him down to the ground. Half a breath later, Eddie's practice stake was poised right above Stan's heart.

Stan laughed, genuinely pleased. "Nice job, Castile."

Eddie withdrew the stake and helped his instructor up. With the action gone, I could now see how bruised and blotched Stan's face was. Attacks for us novices might be few and far between, but our guardians were picking fights daily during this exercise. All of them were taking a lot of abuse, but they handled it with grace and good humor.

"Thank you, sir," said Eddie. He looked pleased but not conceited.

"I'd be faster and stronger if I were Strigoi, of course, but I swear, you could have rivaled one with your speed there." Stan glanced at Lissa. "You okay?"

"Fine," she said, face aglow. I could sense that she'd actually enjoyed the excitement. Her adrenaline was running high.

Stan's smiling face disappeared as he turned his attention on me. "And you—what were you doing?"

I stared, aghast at his harsh tone. It was what he'd said last time too.

"What do you mean?" I exclaimed. "I didn't freeze or anything this time! I was ready to back him up, looking for a chance to join in."

"Yes," he agreed. "That's exactly the problem. You were

so eager to get a punch in that you forgot that you had two Moroi behind you. They might as well have not existed as far as you were concerned. You're out in the open, and you had your back to them."

I strode forward and glared at him, unconcerned about propriety. "That is *not* fair. If we were in the real world and a Strigoi attacked, you cannot tell me that another guardian wouldn't jump in and do everything they could to take that Strigoi down as quickly possible."

"You're probably right," Stan said. "But you weren't thinking about eliminating the threat efficiently. You weren't thinking about your exposed Moroi. You were thinking about how quickly you could do something exciting and redeem yourself."

"Wh-what? Aren't you making a few leaps there? You're grading me on what you *think* was my motivation. How can you be sure what I'm thinking?" I didn't even know half the time.

"Instinct," he replied mysteriously. He took out a small pad of paper and made some notes on it. I narrowed my eyes, wishing I could see through the notepad and discern what he was writing about me. When he finished, he slipped the pad back in his coat and nodded at all of us. "See you later."

We watched him walk across the snowy grounds toward the gym where dhampirs trained. My mouth was hanging open, and I couldn't even get any words out at first. When did it end with these people? I was getting burned again and again on stupid technicalities that had nothing to do with how I'd actually perform in the real world.

"That was not even fair. How can he judge me on what he thinks I was thinking?"

Eddie shrugged as we continued our journey toward the dorm. "He can think whatever he wants. He's our instructor."

"Yeah, but he's going to give me another bad mark! Field experience is pointless if it can't really show how we'd do against Strigoi. I can't believe this. I'm good—I'm really good. How on earth can I be failing this?"

Nobody had an actual answer for that, but Lissa noted uncomfortably, "Well . . . whether he was fair or unfair, he had one thing right: You were great, Eddie."

I glanced over at Eddie and felt bad that I was letting my own drama take away from his success. I was pissed off—*really* pissed off—but Stan's wrongness was my problem to deal with. Eddie had performed brilliantly, and everyone praised him so much on the walk back that I could see a blush creeping over his cheeks. Or maybe that was just the cold. Regardless, I was happy for him.

We settled into the lounge, pleased to find no one else had claimed it—and that it was warm and toasty. Each of the dorms had a few of these lounges, and all were stocked with movies and games and lots of comfy chairs and couches. They were only available for student use at certain times. On weekends, they were pretty much open the whole time, but on weekdays, they had limited hours—presumably to encourage us to do our homework.

Eddie and I assessed the room and made a plan, then took up our positions. Standing against the wall, I eyed the couch Lissa and Christian were sprawled out upon with considerable envy.

I'd thought the movie would distract me from being on alert, but actually, it was my own churning feelings that kept my mind spinning. I couldn't believe Stan had said what he'd said. He'd even admitted that in the heat of battle, any guardian would be trying to get into the fight. His argument about me having ulterior, glory-seeking motives was absurd. I wondered if I was in serious danger of failing this field experience. Surely, so long as I passed, they wouldn't take me from Lissa after graduation? Alberta and Dimitri had spoken like this was all just an experiment to give Lissa and me new training, but suddenly, an anxious, paranoid part of me began to wonder. Eddie was doing a great job of protecting her. Maybe they wanted to see how well she could work with other guardians. Maybe they were worried that I was only good at protecting her and not other Moroi—I'd let Mason die, after all, right? Maybe the real test here was to see if I needed to be replaced. After all, who was I, really? An expendable novice. She was the Dragomir princess. She would always have protection— and it didn't have to be me. The bond was pointless if I ultimately proved incompetent.

Adrian's entrance put my frantic paranoia on hold. He slipped into the darkened room, winking as he flounced into an armchair near me. I had figured it was only a matter of time before he would surface. I think we were his only entertainment on campus. Or maybe not, judging from the strong smell of alcohol around him.

"Are you sober?" I asked him when the movie ended.

"Sober enough. What have you guys been up to?"

Adrian hadn't visited my dreams since the one in the garden. He'd also laid off on some of his outrageous flirting. Most of his appearances with us were to work with Lissa or to ease his boredom.

We recapped our encounter with Stan for him, playing up Eddie's bravery and not mentioning my dressing-down.

"Nice work," said Adrian. "Looks like you got a battle scar too." He pointed to the side of Eddie's face where three red marks glared back at us. I remembered Stan's nails hitting Eddie during the struggle to free Lissa.

Eddie lightly touched his cheek. "I can barely feel it."

Lissa leaned forward and studied him. "You got that protecting me."

"I got that trying to pass my field experience," he teased. "Don't worry about it."

And that's when it happened. I saw it seize her, that compassion and undeniable urge to help others that so often filled her. She couldn't stand to see pain, couldn't stand to sit by if she could do something. I felt the power build up in her, a glorious and swirling feeling that made my toes tingle. I was experiencing how it affected her. It was fire and bliss. Intoxicating. She reached out and touched Eddie's face. . . .

And the marks vanished.

She dropped her hand, and the euphoria of spirit faded from both of us.

"Son of a bitch," breathed Adrian. "You weren't kidding about that." He peered at Eddie's cheek. "Not a goddamned trace of it."

Lissa had stood up and now sank back to the couch. She leaned her head back against it and closed her eyes. "I did it. I can still do it."

"Of course you can," said Adrian dismissively. "Now you have to show *me* how to do it."

She opened her eyes. "It's not that easy."

"Oh, I see," he said in an exaggerated tone. "You grill me like crazy about how to see auras and walk in dreams, but now you won't reveal your trade secrets."

"It's not a 'won't,'" she argued. "It's a 'can't.'"

"Well, cousin, *try*." Then suddenly he raked his nails across *his* hand and drew blood.

"Jesus Christ!" I yelped. "Are you insane?" Who was I kidding? Of course he was.

Lissa reached out and held his hand, and just like before, she healed the skin. Elation filled her, but my mood suddenly dropped without any real cause.

The two of them launched into a discussion I couldn't follow, using standard magical terms as well as some terms I was pretty sure they'd invented on the spot. Judging from Christian's face, it looked like he didn't understand either, and it soon became clear that Adrian and Lissa had forgotten us in their zeal over the mystery of spirit.

Christian finally stood up, looking bored. "Come on, Rose. If I wanted to listen to this, I'd be back in class. I'm hungry."

Lissa glanced up. "Dinner's not for another hour and a half."

"Feeder," he said. "I haven't had mine today."

He planted a kiss on Lissa's cheek and then left. I followed alongside him. It had started snowing again, and I glared at the flakes accusingly as they drifted down around us. When it had first started snowing in early December, I'd been excited. Now this white stuff was getting pretty damned old. As it had a few nights ago, though, being out in such harsh weather defused my mood a little, the cold air kind of snapping me out of it. With each step closer to the feeders, I felt myself calming down.

A "feeder" was what we called humans who volunteered to be regular sources of blood for Moroi. Unlike Strigoi, who killed the victims they drank from, Moroi took only small quantities each day and didn't have to kill the donor. These humans lived for the high they got from vampire bites and seemed perfectly happy to spend their lives that way and separate from normal human society. It was weird but necessary for Moroi. The school usually had a feeder or two in the Moroi dorms for overnight hours, but for most of the day, students had to go to the commons to get their daily fix.

As I continued walking, taking in the sights of white trees, white fences, and white boulders, something else white in the landscape caught my attention. Well, it wasn't white exactly. There was color—pale, washed-out color.

I came to an abrupt halt and felt my eyes go wide. Mason stood on the other side of the quad, nearly blending in with a tree and a post. *No*, I thought. I'd convinced myself that this was over, but there he was, looking at me with that sorrowful, phantom face. He pointed, off toward the back of campus. I glanced that way but again had no clue what to look for. Turning back to him, I could only stare, fear twisting within me.

An icy-cold hand touched the side of my neck, and I spun around. It was Christian.

"What's up?" he asked.

I looked back to where I'd seen Mason. He was gone, of course. I squeezed my eyes shut a moment and sighed. Then, turning back to Christian, I kept walking and said, "Nothing."

Christian usually always had some witty stream of comments whenever we were together, but he was silent as we made the rest of our journey. I was consumed with my own thoughts and worries about Mason, so I had little to say either. This sighting had only lasted a few seconds. Considering how hard it was to see out there, it seemed more than likely that he'd been a trick of the eye, right? I tried to convince myself of this for the rest of the walk. When we entered the commons and escaped the cold, it finally hit me that something was amiss with Christian.

"What's wrong?" I asked, trying not to think about Mason. "Are you okay?"

"Fine," he said.

"The way you just said that proves you aren't fine."

He ignored me as we went to the feeders' room. It was busier than I'd expected, and all of the little cubicles that feeders sat in were filled with Moroi. Brandon Lazar was one of them. As he fed, I caught a glimpse of a faded green bruise on his cheek and recalled that I never had found out who had beaten him up. Christian checked in with the Moroi at the door and then stood in the waiting area until he was called. I racked my brain, trying to figure out what could have caused Christian's bad mood.

"What's the matter? Didn't you like the movie?"

No answer.

"Grossed out by Adrian's self-mutilation?" Giving Christian a hard time was a guilty pleasure. I could do this all night.

No answer.

"Are you— Oh."

It hit me then. I was surprised I hadn't thought of this before.

"Are you upset that Lissa wanted to talk magic with Adrian?"

He shrugged, which told me all I needed to know.

"Come on, she doesn't like magic more than she likes you. It's just this thing with her, you know? She spent all these years thinking she couldn't do real magic, and then found out she could—except it was this wacky, completely unpredictable kind. She's just trying to understand it."

"I know," he said tightly, staring across the expansive room without actually focusing on any of the people. "That's not the problem."

"Then why . . ." I let my words fade as another revelation hit me. "You're jealous of Adrian."

Christian fixed his ice-blue eyes on me, and I could tell I'd hit the mark. "I'm not jealous. I'm just—"

"—feeling insecure over the fact that your girlfriend is spending a lot of time with a rich and reasonably cute guy whom she might like. Or, as we like to call it, jealous."

He turned away from me, clearly annoyed. "The honeymoon might be over between us, Rose. Damn it. Why are these people taking so long?"

"Look," I said, shifting my stance. My feet hurt after so much standing. "Didn't you listen to my romantic speech the other day about being in Lissa's heart? She's crazy about you. You're the only one she wants, and believe me, I can say that with 100 percent certainty. If there was anyone else, I'd know."

The hint of a smile crossed his lips. "You're her best friend. You could be covering for her."

I scoffed. "Not if she were with Adrian. I assure you, she has no interest in him, thank God—at least not romantically."

"He can be persuasive, though. He knows how to work his compulsion. . . ."

"He's not using it on her, though. I don't even know if he can—I think they cancel each other out. Besides, haven't you been paying attention? *I'm* the unfortunate object of Adrian's attention."

"Really?" asked Christian, clearly surprised. Guys were so oblivious to this sort of stuff. "I know he flirts—"

"And shows up in my dreams uninvited. Seeing as I can't get away, it gives him the perfect chance to torture me with his so-called charm and attempt to be romantic."

He turned suspicious. "He shows up in Lissa's dreams too."

Shoot. Shouldn't have mentioned the dreams. What had Adrian said? "Those are instructional. I don't think you need to worry."

"People wouldn't stare if she showed up at some party with Adrian."

"Ah," I said. "So this is what it's really about. You think you're going to drag her down?"

"I'm not that good . . . at those kinds of social things," he admitted in a rare show of vulnerability. "And I think Adrian's got a better reputation than me."

"Are you joking?"

"Come on, Rose. Drinking and smoking aren't even in the

same league as people thinking you're going to turn Strigoi. I saw the way everyone acted when she took me to dinners and stuff at the ski lodge. I'm a liability. She's the only representative from her family. She's going to spend the rest of her life tied up with politics, trying to get in good with people. Adrian could do a lot more for her than I could."

I resisted the urge to literally shake some sense into him. "I can see where you're coming from, but there's one flaw in your airtight logic. *There's nothing going on with her and Adrian.*"

He looked away and didn't say anything else. I suspected his feelings went beyond her simply being with another guy. As he'd even admitted, he had a whole tangle of insecurity about Lissa. Being with her had done wonders for his attitude and sociability, but at the end of the day, he still had trouble dealing with coming from a "tainted" family. He still worried he wasn't good enough for her.

"Rose is right," an unwelcome voice said behind us. Preparing my best glare, I turned around to face Jesse. Naturally, Ralf lurked nearby. Jesse's assigned novice, Dean, stood watch at the doorway. They apparently had a more formal bodyguard relationship. Jesse and Ralf hadn't been in line when we arrived, but they'd apparently wandered up and heard enough to piece together some of our conversation. "You're still royal. You have every right to be with her."

"Wow, talk about a turnaround," I said. "Weren't you guys just telling me the other day how Christian was about to turn Strigoi at any moment? I'd watch your necks, if I were you. He looks dangerous."

Jesse shrugged. "Hey, you said he was clean, and if anyone knows Strigoi, it's you. Besides, we're actually starting to think that rebellious Ozera nature is a good thing."

I eyed him suspiciously, assuming there must be some trick here. Yet he looked sincere, like he really was convinced Christian was safe.

"Thanks," said Christian, a slight sneer curling his lips. "Now that you've endorsed me and my family, I can finally get on with my life. It's the only thing that's been holding me back."

"I'm serious," said Jesse. "The Ozeras have been kind of quiet lately, but they used to be one of the strongest families out there. They could be again—especially you. You're not afraid to do things that you aren't supposed to. We like that. If you'd get over your antisocial bullshit, you could make the right friends and go far. Might make you stop worrying so much about Lissa."

Christian and I exchanged glances. "What are you getting at?" he asked.

Jesse smiled and cast a covert glance around us. "Some of us have been getting together. We've formed a group—sort of a way for those of us from the *better* families to unite, you know? Things are kind of crazy, what with those Strigoi attacks last month and people not knowing what to do. There's also talk about making us fight and finding new ways to hand out the guardians." He said it with a sneer, and I bristled at hearing guardians described like objects. "Too many non-royals are trying to take charge."

"Why is that a problem if their ideas are good?" I demanded.

"Their ideas *aren't* good. They don't know their place. Some of us have started thinking of ways to protect ourselves from that and look out for each other. I think you'd like what we've learned to do. After all, *we're* the ones who need to keep making decisions, not dhampirs and nobody Moroi. We're the elite. The best. Join us, and there are things we could do to help you with Lissa."

I couldn't help it. I laughed. Christian simply looked disgusted.

"I take back what I said earlier," he told them. "*This* is what I've been waiting for my whole life. An invitation to join your tree house club."

Ralf, big and lumbering, took a step forward. "Don't screw with us. This is serious."

Christian sighed. "Then don't screw with *me*. If you really think I want to hang out with you guys and try to make things even better for Moroi who are already spoiled and selfish, then you're even stupider than I thought you were. And *that* was pretty stupid."

Anger and embarrassment filled both Jesse and Ralf's faces, but mercifully, Christian's name was called just then. He seemed considerably cheered as we walked across the room. Nothing like a confrontation with two assholes to make you feel better about your love life.

Christian's assigned feeder tonight was a woman named Alice, who was the oldest feeder on campus. Most Moroi preferred young donors, but Christian, being the twisted person he was, liked her because she was kind of senile. She wasn't *that* old—sixties—but too many vampire endorphins over her life had permanently affected her.

"Rose," she said, turning her dazed blue eyes on me. "You aren't usually with Christian. Have you and Vasilisa had a fight?"

"Nope," I said. "Just getting a change of scenery."

"Scenery," she murmured, glancing at a nearby window. Moroi kept windows tinted to block out light, and I doubted a human could see anything. "The scenery is always changing. Have you noticed that?"

"Not our scenery," said Christian, sitting beside her. "That snow's not going anywhere. Not for a few months."

She sighed and gave him an exasperated look. "I wasn't talking about the scenery."

Christian gave me an amused smile, then leaned over and sank his teeth into her neck. Her expression grew slack, all talk of scenery or whatever she'd meant forgotten as he drank from her. I lived around vampires so much that I didn't even think about their fangs half the time. Most Moroi were actually pretty good at hiding them. It was only in moments like these that I remembered the power a vampire had.

Usually, when I watched a vampire feed, I was reminded of when Lissa and I had run away from the Academy, and I'd let her feed off of me. I'd never reached the crazy addiction levels of a feeder, but I had enjoyed the brief high. I used to want it in a way I could never admit to anybody. In our world, only humans gave blood. Dhampirs who did it were cheap and humiliated.

Now, when I watched a vampire drink, I no longer thought about how good the high felt. Instead, I flashed back to that room in Spokane where Isaiah, our Strigoi captor, had fed off of Eddie. The feelings that stirred up in me were anything but good. Eddie had suffered horribly, and I hadn't been able to do anything except sit there and watch. Grimacing, I turned away from Christian and Alice.

When we left the feeders' room, Christian looked more vibrant and upbeat. "The weekend's here, Rose. No classes—and you get your day off."

"No," I said, having almost forgotten. Damn it. Why did he have to remind me? I was almost starting to feel better after the Stan incident. I sighed. "I have community service."

NINE

WITH SO MANY MOROI tracing their roots back to Eastern Europe, Orthodox Christianity was the dominant religion on campus. Other religions were represented too, and I'd say all in all, only about half of the student body attended any sort of services regularly. Lissa was one such student. She went to church every Sunday because she believed. Christian also attended. He did it because she went and because it made him look good and seem less likely to become Strigoi. Since Strigoi couldn't enter holy ground, regular church service provided a small front of respectability for him.

When I wasn't sleeping in, I showed up at church for the social aspect. Lissa and my friends usually hung out and did something fun afterward, so church made for a good meeting spot. If God minded me using his chapel as a way to further my social life, He hadn't let me know. Either that, or He was biding his time before punishing me.

When the service ended that Sunday, however, I had to stick around the chapel, because that was where my community service was going to happen. When the place had cleared out, I was surprised to see one other person had lingered with me: Dimitri.

"What are you doing here?" I asked.

"Thought you might need some help. I hear the priest wants to do a lot of housecleaning."

"Yeah, but you're not the one being punished here. And this is your day off too. We—well, everyone else—spent the whole week battling it out, but you guys were the ones picking the fights the whole time." In fact, I noticed now that Dimitri had a couple bruises too—though not nearly as many as Stan had. It had been a long week for everyone, and it was only the first of six.

"What else would I do today?"

"I could think of a hundred other things," I noted dryly. "There's probably a John Wayne movie on somewhere that you haven't seen."

He shook his head. "No, there isn't. I've seen them all. Look—the priest is waiting for us."

I turned around. Sure enough. Father Andrew stood at the front, watching us expectantly. He'd taken off the rich robes he'd worn during service and now stood in simple slacks and a button down shirt. He looked like he was ready to work too, and I wondered whatever happened to Sunday being a day of rest.

As Dimitri and I approached to get our assignments, I pondered what could have actually made Dimitri stay here in the first place. Surely he hadn't *really* wanted to work on his day off. I wasn't used to puzzles with him. His intentions were usually straightforward, and I had to assume there was a simple explanation now. It just wasn't clear yet.

"Thank you both for volunteering to help me." Father Andrew smiled at us. I tried not to scoff at the "volunteering" reference. He was a Moroi in his late forties, with thinning gray hair. Even without much faith in religion, I still liked and respected him. "We aren't doing anything particularly complex today," he continued. "It's a bit boring, really. We'll have to do the regular cleaning, of course, and then I'd like to sort the boxes of old supplies I have sitting up in the attic."

"We're happy to do whatever you need," Dimitri said solemnly. I repressed a sigh and tried not to think of all the other things I could be doing.

We set to it.

I was put on mop duty, and Dimitri took over dusting and polishing the wooden pews. He appeared thoughtful and intent as he cleaned, looking like he actually took pride in his work. I was still trying to figure out why he was here at all. Don't get me wrong; I was happy to have him. His presence made me feel better, and of course I always loved watching him.

I thought maybe he was there to get more information out of me about what had happened that day with Stan, Christian, and Brandon. Or maybe he wanted to chastise me about the *other* day with Stan, where I'd been accused of jumping into battle for selfish reasons. These seemed like likely explanations, yet he never said a word. Even when the priest stepped out of the sanctuary to go to his office, Dimitri continued working quietly. I would have figured if he'd had anything to say, he would have done it then.

When we finished the cleaning, Father Andrew had us haul box after box of stuff down from the attic and into a storeroom at the back of the chapel. Lissa and Christian frequently used that attic as a secret getaway, and I wondered if having it cleaner would be a pro or a con for their romantic interludes. Maybe they would abandon it, and I could start getting some sleep.

With all of the stuff downstairs, the three of us settled on the floor and began sorting it all out. Father Andrew gave us instructions on what to save and what to throw out, and it was a relief to be off my feet for a change this week. He made small talk as we worked, asking me about classes and other things. It wasn't so bad.

And as we worked, a thought came to me. I'd done a good job convincing myself that Mason had been a delusion brought on by lack of sleep, but getting assurance from an authority figure that ghosts weren't real would go a long way toward making me feel better.

"Hey," I said to Father Andrew. "Do you believe in ghosts? I mean, is there any mention of them in—" I gestured around us. "—in this stuff?"

The question clearly surprised him, but he didn't appear to take offense at me calling his vocation and life's work "this stuff." Or at the fact that I was obviously ignorant about it all, despite seventeen years of sitting through services. A bemused expression crossed his face, and he paused in his work.

"Well . . . it depends on how you define 'ghost,' I suppose."

I tapped a theology book with my finger. "The whole point of this is that when you die, you go to heaven or hell. That makes ghosts just stories, right? They're not in the Bible or anything."

"Again," he said, "it depends on your definition. Our faith has always held that after death, the spirit separates from the body and may indeed linger in this world."

"What?" A dusty bowl I was holding dropped out of my hand. Fortunately, it was wood and didn't break. I quickly retrieved it. That was *not* the answer I'd been expecting. "For how long? Forever?"

"No, no, of course not. That flies in the face of the resurrection and salvation, which form the cornerstone of our beliefs. But it's believed the soul can stay on earth for three to forty days after death. It eventually receives a 'temporary' judgment that sends it on from this world to heaven or hell—although no one will truly experience either until the actual Judgment Day, when the soul and body are reunited to live out eternity as one."

The salvation stuff was lost on me. The "three to forty days" was what caught my attention. I completely forgot about my sorting. "Yeah, but is it true or not? Are spirits really walking the earth for forty days after death?"

"Ah, Rose. Those who have to ask if faith is true are opening up a discussion they may not be ready for."

I had a feeling he was right. I sighed and turned back to the box in front of me.

"But," he said kindly, "if it helps you, some of these ideas parallel folk beliefs from Eastern Europe about ghosts that existed before the spread of Christianity. Those traditions have long upheld the idea of spirits staying around for a short time after death—particularly if the person in question died young or violently."

I froze. Whatever progress I'd made in convincing myself Mason had been brought on by stress instantly vanished. *Young or violently.*

"Why?" I asked in a small voice. "Why would they stay? Is it . . . is it for revenge?"

"I'm sure there are some who believe that, just as some believe it's because the soul has trouble finding peace after something so unsettling."

"What do you believe?" I asked.

He smiled. "I believe the soul separates from the body, just as our fathers teach us, but I doubt the soul's time on earth is anything the living can perceive. It's not like in the movies, with ghosts haunting buildings or coming to visit those they knew. I envision these spirits as more of an energy existing around us, something beyond our perception as they wait to move on and find peace. Ultimately, what matters is what happens beyond this earth when we attain the eternal life our savior bought for us with his great sacrifice. That's what's important."

I wondered if Father Andrew would be so quick to say that if he'd seen what I'd seen. *Young or violently*. Both had applied to Mason, and he had died less than forty days ago. That sad, sad face came back to me, and I wondered what it had meant. Revenge? Or could he truly not find peace?

And how did Father Andrew's theology about heaven and hell fit with someone like me, who had died and come back to life? Victor Dashkov had said I'd gone to the world of the dead and returned when Lissa had healed me. What world of the dead? Was that heaven or hell? Or was it another way of referring to this in-between state on earth that Father Andrew was talking about?

I didn't say anything after that, because the idea of a revenge-seeking Mason was so startling. Father Andrew sensed the change in me, but he obviously didn't know what had brought it about. He tried to coax me out.

"I just got some new books in from a friend in another parish. Interesting stories about St. Vladimir." He tilted his head. "Are you still interested in him? And Anna?"

Theoretically, I was. Until we'd met Adrian, we'd only known of two other spirit users. One was our former teacher, Ms. Karp, who'd gone completely nuts from spirit and become a Strigoi to stop the madness. The other person was St. Vladimir, the school's namesake. He'd lived centuries ago and had brought his guardian, Anna, back from the dead, just as Lissa had me. It had made Anna shadow-kissed and created a bond between them too.

Normally, Lissa and I tried to get our hands on everything we could about Anna and Vlad, in order to learn more about ourselves. But, as incredible as it was for me to admit, I had bigger problems right now than the ever-present and ever-puzzling psychic link between Lissa and me. It had just been trumped by a ghost who could possibly be pissed off over my role in his untimely death.

"Yeah," I said evasively, not making eye contact. "I'm interested . . . but I don't think I can get to it anytime soon. I'm kind of busy with all this . . . you know, field experience stuff."

I fell silent again. He took the hint and let me work on without further interruption. Dimitri never said a word throughout any of this. When we finally finished sorting, Father Andrew told us we had one more task before our work was done. He pointed to some boxes that we'd organized and repacked.

"I need you to carry these over to the elementary campus," he said. "Leave them off at the Moroi dorm there. Ms. Davis has been teaching Sunday school for some of the kindergartners and might be able to use those."

It would take at least two trips between Dimitri and me, and the elementary campus was a fair distance away. Still, that put me one step closer to freedom.

"Why are you interested in ghosts?" Dimitri asked me on our first trip.

"Just making conversation," I said.

"I can't see your face right now, but I have a feeling you're lying again."

"Jeez, everyone thinks the worst of me lately. Stan accused me of glory-seeking."

"I heard about that," said Dimitri, as we rounded a corner. The buildings of the elementary campus loomed up in front of us. "That might have been a little unfair of him."

"A little, huh?" Hearing him admit that thrilled me, but it didn't change my anger against Stan. That dark, grouchy feeling that had plagued me lately sprang to life. "Well, thanks, but I'm starting to lose faith in this field experience. Sometimes in the whole Academy."

"You don't mean that."

"I don't know. The school just seems so caught up in rules and policies that don't have anything to do with real life. I saw what was out there, comrade. I went right to the monster's lair. In some ways . . . I don't know if this really prepares us."

I expected him to argue, but to my surprise he said, "Sometimes I agree."

I nearly stumbled as we stepped inside one of the two Moroi dorms on the elementary campus. The lobby looked a lot like the ones on the secondary campus. "Really?" I asked.

"Really," he said, a small smile on his face. "I mean, I don't agree that novices should be put out in the world when they're ten or anything, but sometimes I've thought the field experience should actually be in the field. I probably learned more in my first year as a guardian than I did in all my years of training. Well . . . maybe not all. But it's a different situation, absolutely."

We exchanged looks, pleased over our agreement. Something warm fluttered up in me, putting the lid on my earlier
anger. Dimitri understood my frustration with the system, but
then, Dimitri understood *me*. He glanced around, but there
was no one at the desk. A few students in their early teens
were working or talking in the lobby.

"Oh," I said, shifting the weight of the box I held. "We're
in the middle school dorm. The younger kids are next door."

"Yes, but Ms. Davis lives in this building. Let me try to
find her and see where she wants these." He set his box down
carefully. "I'll be right back."

I watched him go and set my own box down. Leaning
against a wall, I glanced around and nearly jumped when I
saw a Moroi girl only a couple feet away. She'd been standing
so perfectly still, I hadn't noticed her. She looked like she could
be mid-teens—thirteen or fourteen—but she was tall, much
taller than me. The slimness of her Moroi build made her look
even taller. Her hair was a cloud of brown curls, and she had
freckles—rare among the normally pale Moroi—across her
face. Her eyes widened when she saw me looking at her.

"Oh. My. God. You're Rose Hathaway, aren't you?"

"Yeah," I said with surprise. "Do you know me?"

"Everyone knows you. I mean, everyone heard about
you. You're the one who ran away. And then you came back
and killed those Strigoi. That is *so* cool. Did you get *molnija*
marks?" Her words came out in one long string. She hardly
took a breath.

"Yeah. I have two." Thinking about the tiny tattoos on the back of my neck made my skin itch.

Her pale green eyes—if possible—grew wider. "Oh my God. Wow."

I usually grew irate when people made a big deal about the *molnija* marks. After all, the circumstances had *not* been cool. But this girl was young, and there was something appealing about her.

"What's your name?" I asked.

"Jillian—Jill. I mean, just Jill. Not both. Jillian's my full name. Jill's what everyone calls me."

"Right," I said, hiding a smile. "I figured it out."

"I heard Moroi used magic on that trip to fight. Is that true? I would *love* to do that. I wish someone would teach me. I use air. Do you think I could fight Strigoi with that? Everyone says I'm crazy." For centuries, Moroi using magic to fight had been viewed as a sin. Everyone believed it should be used peacefully. Recently, some had started to question that, particularly after Christian had proved useful in the Spokane escape.

"I don't know," I said. "You should talk to Christian Ozera."

She gaped. "Would he talk to *me*?"

"If you bring up fighting the establishment, yeah, he'll talk to you."

"Okay, cool. Was that Guardian Belikov?" she asked, switching subjects abruptly.

"Yeah."

I swore I thought she might faint then and there. "Really? He's even cuter than I heard. He's your teacher, right? Like, your own personal teacher?"

"Yeah." I wondered where he was. Talking to Jill was exhausting.

"Wow. You know, you guys don't even act like teacher and student. You seem like friends. Do you hang out when you're not training?"

"Er, well, kind of. Sometimes." I remembered my earlier thoughts, about how I was one of the few people Dimitri was social with outside of his guardian duties.

"I knew it! I can't even imagine that—I'd be freaking out all the time around him. I'd never get anything done, but you're so cool about it all, kind of like, 'Yeah, I'm with this totally hot guy, but whatever, it doesn't matter.'"

I laughed in spite of myself. "I think you're giving me more credit than I deserve."

"No way. And I don't believe any of those stories, you know."

"Um, stories?"

"Yeah, about you beating up Christian Ozera."

"Thanks," I said. Now rumors of my humiliation were trickling down to the lower campus. If I walked over to the elementary dorms, some six-year-old would probably tell me she'd heard that I killed Christian.

Jill's expression turned momentarily uncertain. "But I didn't know about the other story."

"What other story?"

"About how you and Adrian Ivashkov are—"

"No," I interrupted, not wanting to hear the rest. "Whatever you heard, it's not true."

"But it was really romantic."

"Then it's definitely not true."

Her face fell, and then she perked back up a few seconds later. "Hey, can you teach me to punch someone?"

"Wai— What? Why would you want to know that?"

"Well, I figure if I'm going to fight with magic someday, I should learn to fight the regular way too."

"I'm probably not the right person to ask," I told her. "Maybe you should, um, ask your P.E. teacher."

"I did!" Her face looked distraught. "And he said no."

I couldn't help but laugh. "I was joking about asking him."

"Come on, it could help me fight a Strigoi someday."

My laughter dried up. "No, it really wouldn't."

She bit her lip, still desperate to convince me. "Well, it would at least help against that psycho."

"What? What psycho?"

"People keep getting beat up around here. Last week it was Dane Zeklos, and just the other day it was Brett."

"Dane . . ." I ran through my knowledge of Moroi genealogy. There were a gazillion Zeklos students around. "That's Jesse's younger brother, yeah?"

Jill nodded. "Yup. One of our teachers was *so* mad, too,

but Dane wouldn't say a word. Neither would Brett."

"Brett who?"

"Ozera."

I did a double take. "Ozera?"

I had the impression she was really excited to tell me things I didn't know. "He's my friend Aimee's boyfriend. He was all bruised up yesterday—had some weird things that looked like welts, too. Maybe burns? But he wasn't as bad as Dane. And when Mrs. Callahan asked him about it, Brett convinced her it was nothing, and she let it go, which was weird. He was also in a really good mood—which was also weird, since you'd kind of think getting beat up would bring you down."

Somewhere in the back of my mind, her words tickled a memory. There was some connection I should be making, but I couldn't quite grasp it. Between Victor, ghosts, and the field experiences, it was honestly a wonder I could string words together anymore.

"So can you teach me so that I won't get beat up?" Jill asked, clearly hoping she'd convinced me. She balled her fist up. "I just do this, right? Thumb across the fingers and swing?"

"Uh, well, it's a little more complicated than that. You need to stand a certain way, or you'll hurt yourself more than the other person. There are a lot of things you need to do with your elbows and hips."

"Show me, please?" she begged. "I bet you're really good."

I *was* really good, but corrupting minors was one offense I didn't yet have on my record, and I preferred to keep it that way. Fortunately, Dimitri came back just then with Ms. Davis.

"Hey," I told him. "I have someone who wants to meet you. Dimitri, this is Jill. Jill, Dimitri."

He looked surprised, but he smiled and shook her hand. She turned bright red and became speechless for a change. As soon as he released her hand, she stammered out a goodbye and ran off. We finished up with Ms. Davis and headed back toward the chapel for our second load.

"Jill knew who I was," I told Dimitri as we walked. "She had kind of a hero-worship thing going on."

"Does that surprise you?" he asked. "That younger students would look up to you?"

"I don't know. I just never thought about it. I don't think I'm that good of a role model."

"I disagree. You're outgoing, dedicated, and excel at everything you do. You've earned more respect than you think."

I gave him a sidelong glance. "And yet not enough to go to Victor's trial, apparently."

"Not this again."

"Yes, this again! Why don't you get how major this is? Victor's a huge threat."

"I know he is."

"And if he gets loose, he'll just start in on his crazy plans again."

"It's really unlikely he will get loose, you know. Most of

those rumors about the queen letting him off are just that—rumors. You of all people should know not to believe everything you hear."

I stared stonily ahead, refusing to acknowledge his point. "You should still let us go. Or"—I took a deep breath—"you should at least let Lissa go."

It was harder for me to say those words than it should have been, but it was something I'd been thinking about. I didn't think I was a glory seeker like Stan had said, but there was a part of me that always wanted to be the one in the middle of a fight. I wanted to rush forward, doing what was right and helping others. Likewise, I wanted to be there at Victor's trial. I wanted to look him in the eye and make sure he was punished.

But as time went on, it seemed less likely that that would happen. They really weren't going to let us go. Maybe, though, maybe they'd let *one* of us go, and if it should be anyone, it should be Lissa. She'd been the target of Victor's plan, and though her going alone stirred up that nervous idea about how maybe she didn't need me to guard her, I'd still rather take the chance and see him put away.

Dimitri, understanding my need to rush in and take action, seemed surprised by my unusual behavior. "You're right—she should be there, but again, it's nothing I can do anything about. You keep thinking I can control this, but I can't."

"But did you do *everything* you could?" I thought back to Adrian's words in the dream, about how Dimitri could have done more. "You have a lot of influence. There must be something. Anything."

"Not as much influence as you think. I've got a high position here at the Academy, but in the rest of the guardian world, I'm still pretty young. And yes, I did actually speak up for you."

"Maybe you should have spoken up louder."

I could sense him shutting down. He'd discuss most things reasonably but wouldn't encourage me when I was just being a bitch. So, I tried to be more reasonable.

"Victor knows about us," I said. "He could say something."

"Victor has bigger things to worry about with this trial than us."

"Yeah, but you know him. He doesn't exactly act like a normal person would. If he feels like he's lost all hope of getting off, he might decide to bust us just for the sake of revenge."

I'd never been able to confess my relationship with Dimitri to Lissa, yet our worst enemy knew about it. It was weirder even than Adrian knowing. Victor had figured it out by watching us and gathering data. I guess when you're a scheming villain, you get good at that stuff. He'd never made the knowledge public, though. Instead, he'd used it against us with the lust charm he'd made from earth magic. A charm like that wouldn't work if there wasn't already attraction in place. The charm just cranked things up. Dimitri and I had been all over each other and had been only a heartbeat away from having sex. It had been a pretty smart way for Victor to distract us without using violence. If anyone had tried to attack us, we could have put up a good fight. But turn us loose on each other? We had trouble fighting that.

Dimitri was silent for several moments. I knew he knew I had a point. "Then we'll have to deal with that as best we can," he said at last. "But if Victor's going to tell, he's going to do it whether or not you testify."

I refused to say anything else until we got to the church. When we did, Father Andrew told us that after going over some more things, he'd decided he really only needed one more box brought over to Ms. Davis.

"I'll do it," I told Dimitri crisply, once the priest was out of earshot. "You don't have to come."

"Rose, please don't make a big deal about this."

"It is a big deal!" I hissed. "And you don't seem to get it."

"I *do* get it. Do you really think I want to see Victor loose? Do you think I want us all at risk again?" It was the first time in a long time I'd seen his control on the verge of snapping. "But I told you, I've done all I can do. I'm not like you—I can't keep making a scene when things don't go my way."

"I do not."

"You're doing it right now."

He was right. Some part of me knew I'd crossed a line . . . but just like with everything else recently, I couldn't stop talking.

"Why did you even help me today?" I demanded. "Why

are you here?"

"Is that so strange?" he asked. He *almost* looked hurt.

"Yes. I mean, are you are you trying to spy on me? Figure out why I messed up? Make sure I don't get into any trouble?"

He studied me, brushing hair out of his eyes. "Why does there have to be some ulterior motive?"

I wanted to blurt out a hundred different things. Like, if there wasn't a motive, then that meant he just wanted to spend time with me. And that made no sense, because we both knew we were only supposed to have a teacher-student relationship. *He* of all people should know that. He was the one who'd told me.

"Because everyone has motives."

"Yes. But not always the motives you think." He pushed open the door. "I'll see you later."

I watched him go, my feelings a tangle of confusion and anger. If the situation hadn't been so strange, I would have almost said it was like we'd just gone on a date.

TEN

T HE NEXT DAY, MY guardian duties with Christian resumed. Once again, I found my own life put on hold for someone else's.

"How was your penance?" he asked as we walked across campus from his dorm.

I stifled a yawn. I hadn't been able to sleep well last night, both because of my feelings for Dimitri and because of what Father Andrew had told me. Nonetheless, I kept a sharp eye out. This was the location where Stan had attacked us twice before, and besides, the guardians were sick and twisted enough to come after me on a day when I was so exhausted.

"It was okay. The priest let us go early."

"Us?"

"Dimitri came and helped me. I think he felt bad about me being stuck with that work."

"Either that or he has nothing else to do now that he's not doing your extra sessions."

"Maybe, but I doubt it. All in all, I guess it wasn't that bad a day." Unless you considered learning about spiteful ghosts bad.

"I had a great day," said Christian, the smallest amount of smugness in his voice.

I repressed the urge to roll my eyes. "Yeah, I know."

He and Lissa had taken advantage of their guardianless day to take advantage of each other. I supposed I should be glad they'd held off until Eddie and I weren't around, but in a lot of ways, it didn't matter. True, when I was awake, I could block out all of the details, but I still knew what was going on. A bit of the jealousy and anger I'd felt from the last time they'd been together returned. It was the same problem all over again: Lissa doing all the things I couldn't do.

I was dying to go eat breakfast. I could smell French toast and hot maple syrup. Carbs wrapped in more carbs. Yum. But Christian wanted blood before we ate solid food, and his needs trumped mine. *They come first.* He'd apparently skipped his daily blood dose yesterday—probably to maximize his romantic time.

The feeder room wasn't crowded, but we still had to wait.

"Hey," I said. "Do you know Brett Ozera? You're related, right?" After my encounter with Jill, I'd finally put some pieces together. Brett Ozera and Dane Zeklos had reminded me of how Brandon had looked the day of Stan's first attack. The disaster of that attack had made me completely forget about Brandon, but the coincidences here suddenly stirred my curiosity. All three had been beaten up. All three had been in denial.

Christian nodded. "Yeah, in the way we're all kind of related. I don't know him that well—he's like a third or fourth cousin or something. His branch of the family hasn't had much to do with mine since . . . well, you know."

"I heard something weird about him." I then related what Jill had told me about Dane and Brett.

"That's weird," agreed Christian. "But people get in fights."

"Yeah, but there are some weird connections here. And royals aren't usually on the losing ends of fights—all three of these guys were."

"Well, maybe that's it. You know how it's been. A lot of royals are getting pissed off that non-royals want to change how guardians are assigned and learn to start fighting. That's the whole point of Jesse and Ralf's stupid little club. They want to make sure royals stay on top. Non-royals are probably getting just as pissed off and fighting back."

"So, what, some kind of vigilante is out making royals pay?"

"Wouldn't be the weirdest thing that's happened around here," he pointed out.

"That's for damn sure," I muttered.

Christian's name was called, and he peered ahead. "Look at that," he said happily. "Alice again."

"I don't get your fascination with her," I observed as we approached the old feeder. "Lissa's always kind of excited to see her too. But Alice is nuts."

"I know," he said. "That's what's so great."

Alice greeted us as Christian sat down beside her. I leaned against the wall, arms crossed over my chest. Feeling uppity, I said, "Alice, the scenery hasn't changed. It's exactly the same as last time."

She turned her dazed eyes on me. "Patience, Rose. You must be patient. And prepared. Are you prepared?"

The switch in subject threw me a little. It was like talking to Jill, except less sane. "Um, prepared how? For the scenery?"

In what had to be a prime moment of irony, she looked at me as though I were the one who was crazy. "Armed. Are you armed? You're going to protect us, aren't you?"

I reached inside my coat and pulled out the practice stake I'd been given for the field experience. "Got you covered," I said.

She looked immensely relieved and apparently couldn't tell the difference between a real stake and a fake one. "Good," she said. "Now we'll be safe."

"That's right," said Christian. "With Rose armed, we have nothing to worry about. The Moroi world can rest easy."

Alice was oblivious to his sarcasm. "Yes. Well, nowhere is ever safe."

I concealed the stake again. "We're safe. We've got the best guardians in the world protecting us, not to mention the wards. Strigoi aren't getting in here."

I didn't add what I'd recently learned: that Strigoi could get *humans* to break the wards. Wards were invisible lines of power that were composed of all four elements. They were created when four Moroi, each one strong in a different element, walked around an area and laid the magic in a circle upon the ground, creating a protective border. Moroi magic was imbued with life, and a strong field of it kept out Strigoi, since they were devoid of life. So wards were frequently laid around Moroi dwellings. Tons of them were laid around this school. Since stakes were also imbued with all four elements, driving a stake through a ward line in the ground pierced the ward and canceled out the protective effect. This had never been much of a concern because Strigoi couldn't touch stakes. However, in some recent attacks, humans—who could touch stakes—had served Strigoi and broken some wards. We believed the Strigoi I'd killed had been the ringleaders in that group, but we still didn't know for sure.

Alice studied me closely with her cloudy eyes, almost as though she knew what I was thinking. "Nowhere is safe. Wards fade. Guardians die."

I glanced over at Christian, who shrugged in a sort of *what did you expect from her?* kind of way.

"If you guys are done with your girl talk, can I eat now?" he asked.

Alice was more than happy to comply; he was her first hit of the day. She soon forgot about wards or anything else and simply lost herself to the ecstasy of his bite. I forgot about wards too. I had a one-track mind, really: I still wanted to know if Mason had been real or not. The priest's frightening explanation aside, I had to admit Mason's visits hadn't been threatening, just scary. If he was out to get me, he was kind of doing a half-assed job of it. Once again, I started putting more stock in the stress-and-fatigue theory.

"Now it's time for *me* to eat," I said when Christian finished. I was pretty sure I could smell bacon now. That'd probably make Christian happy. He could wrap it around his
French toast.

We'd barely stepped out of the room when Lissa came running up to us, Eddie trailing behind. Excitement lit her face,
though the feelings in the bond weren't exactly happy.

"Did you hear?" she asked, a little breathless.

"Hear what?" I asked.

"You have to hurry—go pack your things. We're going to
Victor's trial. Right now."

There'd been no warning at all about when Victor's trial
would even occur, let alone that someone had apparently
decided we could go. Christian and I exchanged brief, startled
looks and then hurried off to his room to gather our things.

Packing was a breeze. My bag was ready to go already,
and Christian only took a minute to throw his together. In less
than a half hour, we were out on the Academy's landing strip.
Two private jets sat in attendance, one of which was fired up
and waiting to go. A couple of Moroi hurried about, doing
last-minute things with the plane and the runway.

No one seemed to know what was going on. Lissa had
simply been told that she, Christian, and I were going to testify and that Eddie could come along to continue his field
experience. There'd been no explanation as to why things

had changed, and a weird mix of eagerness and apprehension crackled around us. We all wanted to see Victor locked away for good, but now that we were actually faced with the reality of the trial and of seeing him—well, it was kind of scary.

A few guardians lingered near the steps going up to the plane. I recognized them as the ones who had helped capture Victor. They were probably going to do double duty and serve as witnesses and as our protection. Dimitri hovered near the outskirts, and I hurried over to him.

"I'm sorry," I gulped out. "I'm so sorry."

He turned toward me, his face schooled to that perfect picture of neutrality that he was so good at. "Sorry for what?"

"For all the horrible things I said yesterday. You did it— you really did it. You got them to let us go."

Despite my nervousness about seeing Victor, I was filled with elation. Dimitri had come through. I'd known all along that he really cared about me—this just proved it. If there hadn't been so many people around, I would have hugged him.

Dimitri's face didn't change. "It wasn't me, Rose. I had nothing to do with it."

Alberta signaled that we could board, and he turned away to join the others. I stood frozen for a moment, watching him and trying to figure out what had happened. If he hadn't intervened, then why were we going? Lissa's diplomatic efforts had been shot down a while ago. Why the change of heart?

My friends were already on board, so I hurried to catch

up. As soon as I stepped into the cabin, a voice called to me. "Little dhampir! About time you got here."

I looked and saw Adrian waving, a drink in his hand. Great. We'd had to beg and plead to go along, yet Adrian had somehow just glided on in. Lissa and Christian were sitting together, so I joined Eddie in the hopes of staying away from Adrian. Eddie gave me the window seat. Adrian moved to the seat in front of us, though, and might as well have been sitting in our row, as often as he turned around to talk to me. His chatter and outrageous flirting indicated he'd been sipping cocktails long before the rest of us had come aboard. I kind of wished I'd had a few myself once we were airborne. A wicked headache set in almost immediately after liftoff, and I entertained a fantasy of vodka numbing the pain.

"We're going to Court," Adrian said. "Aren't you excited about it?"

I closed my eyes and rubbed my temples. "About which one? The royal one or the legal one?"

"The royal one. Did you bring a dress?"

"Nobody told me to."

"So . . . that's a 'no.'"

"Yes."

"Yes? I thought you meant no."

I opened one eye and glared. "I did mean no, and you know it. No, I did not bring a dress."

"We'll get you one," he said loftily.

"You're going to take me shopping? I'm going to go out

on a limb and guess they won't consider you a reliable chap-
erone."

"Shopping? As if. There are tailors that live there. We'll get
you something custom-made."

"We're not staying that long. And do I really need a dress
for what we're doing there?"

"No, I'd just kind of like to see you in one."

I sighed and leaned my head against the window. The
pain in my skull was still throbbing. It was like the air was
pressing in on me. Something flashed in my peripheral vision,
and I turned in surprise, but there was nothing but stars outside the window.

"Something black," he continued. "Satin, I think . . . maybe
with lace trim. Do you like lace? Some women think it itches."

"Adrian." It was like a hammer, a hammer inside and outside my head.

"You could get a nice velvet trim too, though. That
wouldn't itch."

"Adrian." Even my eye sockets seemed to hurt.

"And then a slit up the side to show off what great legs
you have. It could go nearly to the hip and have this cute little
bow—"

"*Adrian!*" Something inside of me burst. "Will you shut
the hell up for five seconds?" I yelled so loud that the pilot had
probably heard me. Adrian had that rare look of astonishment
on his face.

Alberta, sitting across the aisle from Adrian, shot up in her seat. "Rose," she exclaimed. "What's going on?"

I gritted my teeth and rubbed my forehead. "I have the *worst* fucking headache in the world, and he won't shut up." I didn't even realize I'd sworn in front of an instructor until several seconds later. From the other side of my field of vision, I thought I saw something else—another shadow darting through the plane, reminding me of black wings. Like a bat or a raven. I covered my eyes. There was nothing flying through the plane. "God, why won't it go away?"

I expected Alberta to chastise me for the outburst, but instead, Christian spoke: "She hasn't eaten today. She was really hungry earlier."

I uncovered my eyes. Alberta's face was filled with concern, and Dimitri now hovered behind her. More shadowy shapes flitted across my vision. Most were indistinct, but I could have sworn I saw something that looked like a skull mixed in with the darkness. I blinked rapidly, and it all disappeared. Alberta turned to one of the flight attendants.

"Can you get her something to eat? And find a painkiller?"

"Where's it at?" Dimitri asked me. "The pain?"

With all of this attention, my explosion suddenly seemed excessive. "It's a headache. . . . I'm sure it'll go away. . . ." Seeing his stern look, I pointed to the center of my forehead. "It's like something pushing on my skull. And there's pain kind of behind my eyes. I keep feeling like . . . well, it's like I've got something in my eye. I think I'm seeing a shadow or something. Then I blink and it's gone."

"Ah," said Alberta. "That's a migraine symptom—having vision problems. It's called an aura. People sometimes get it before the headache sets in."

"An aura?" I asked, startled. I glanced up at Adrian. He was looking at me over the top of his seat, his long arms hanging over the back of it.

"Not that kind," he said, a small smile turning up his lips. "Same name. Like Court and court. Migraine auras are images and light you see when a migraine's coming on. They have nothing to do with the auras around people I see. But I tell you . . . the aura I can see . . . the one around you . . . wow."

"Black?"

"And then some. It's obvious even after all the drinks I've had. Never seen anything like it."

I didn't exactly know what to make of that, but then the flight attendant returned with a banana, a granola bar, and some ibuprofen. It was a far cry from French toast, but it sounded good on my empty stomach. I consumed it all and then propped a pillow up against the window. Closing my eyes, I rested my head and hoped I could sleep the headache off before we landed. Mercifully, everyone else stayed quiet.

I had drifted off a little when I felt a slight touch on my arm. "Rose?"

Opening my eyes, I peered at Lissa as she sat in Eddie's seat. Those bat-winged shapes flitted behind her, and my head still hurt. In those swirling shadows, I again saw what looked like a face, this time with a wide gaping mouth and eyes like fire. I flinched.

"You're still in pain?" Lissa asked, peering at me. I blinked, and the face was gone.

"Yeah, I—oh no." I realized what she was going to do. "Don't do it. Don't waste it on me."

"It's easy," she said. "It hardly fazes me."

"Yeah, but the more you use it . . . the more it hurts you in the long run. Even if it's easy now."

"I'll worry about that later. Here."

She clasped my hand between hers and closed her eyes. Through our bond, I felt the magic welling up in her as she drew upon spirit's healing power. To her, magic felt warm and golden. I'd been healed before, and it always came through to me as varying temperatures: hot, then cold, then hot, etc. But this time, when she released the magic and sent it into me, I didn't feel anything except a very faint tingle. Her eyelids fluttered open.

"Wh—what happened?" she asked.

"Nothing," I said. "The headache's still going strong."

"But I . . ." The confusion and shock on her face mirrored what I sensed in her. "I had it. I felt the magic. It worked."

"I don't know, Liss. It's okay, really. You haven't been off the meds that long, you know."

"Yeah, but I healed Eddie the other day without any problems. *And* Adrian," she added dryly. He was hanging over the seat again, watching us intently.

"Those were scrapes," I said. "This is a five-alarm migraine we're talking about. Maybe you've got to build back up."

Lissa bit her lower lip. "You don't think the pills permanently hurt my magic, do you?"

"Nah," said Adrian, head tilted to the side. "You lit up like a supernova when you were summoning it. You had magic. I just don't think it had any effect on her."

"Why not?" she demanded.

"Maybe she's got something you can't heal."

"A headache?" I asked in disbelief.

He shrugged. "What do I look like, a doctor? I don't know. Just telling you what I saw."

I sighed and placed a hand on my forehead. "Well, I appreciate the help, Liss, and I appreciate your annoying commentary, Adrian. But I think sleep might be the best thing for now. Maybe it's stress or something." Sure, why not? Stress was the answer to everything lately. Ghosts. Incurable headaches. Weird faces floating in the air. "Probably can't heal that."

"Maybe," she said, sounding as though she took personal offense at me having something she couldn't fix. Inside her mind, though, her accusations were turned toward herself, not me. She worried she wasn't good enough.

"It's okay," I said soothingly. "You're just getting your stride back. Once you're up to full power, I'll go crack a rib or something so we can test it."

She groaned. "The horrible part is that I don't think you're joking." After a quick squeeze of my hand, she stood up. "Sleep well."

She left, and I soon realized Eddie wasn't coming back. He'd taken a new seat so that I'd have more room. Appreciative, I fluffed and repositioned the pillow while stretching my legs out as best I could across the seats. A few more phantom clouds danced across my vision, and then I closed my eyes to sleep.

I woke up later when the plane touched down, the sounds of its engines kicking into reverse startling me out of a deep sleep. To my relief, the headache was gone. So were the weird shapes floating around me.

"Better?" Lissa asked when I stood up and yawned.

I nodded. "Much. Better still if I can get some real food."

"Well," she laughed, "somehow I doubt there's any shortage of food around here."

She was right. Glancing out the windows, I tried to get my first look at our surroundings. We'd made it. We were at the Moroi Royal Court.

ELEVEN

W E STEPPED OFF THE plane and were immediately hit with wet, blustery weather. Sleet cracked into us, far worse than the flaky white stuff falling back in Montana. We were on the East Coast now, or well, close to it. The queen's court was in Pennsylvania, near the Pocono Mountains, a range I had only a vague idea about. I knew we weren't too close to any major cities, like Philadelphia or Pittsburgh, which were the only ones I knew in the state.

The runway we'd landed on was part of the Court's property, so we were already behind wards. It was just like the Academy's small landing strip. In fact, in many ways, the Royal Court was laid out exactly like the school. It was what they told humans the compound was, actually. The Court was a collection of buildings, beautiful and ornate, spreading across well-tended grounds adorned with trees and flowers. At least, the land would be adorned with them when spring came. Just like in Montana, the vegetation was bleak and leafless.

We were met by a group of five guardians, all dressed in black pants and matching coats, with white shirts underneath. They weren't uniforms exactly, but custom usually dictated that for formal occasions, guardians wear some sort of nice ensemble. By comparison, in our jeans and T-shirts, our group looked like somebody's poor relations. Yet I couldn't help but think we'd be a lot more comfortable if it came to a fight with Strigoi.

The guardians knew Alberta and Dimitri—honestly, those two knew *everybody*—and after some formalities, everyone relaxed and became friendly. We were all eager to get in out of the cold, and our escorts led us toward the buildings. I knew enough about the Court to know that the largest and most elaborate of the buildings was where all official Moroi business was conducted. It resembled some sort of gothic palace on the outside, but inside, I suspected it probably looked like any set of modern government offices you'd find among humans.

We weren't taken there, however. We were led to an adjacent building, just as exquisite on the outside, but half the size. One of the guardians explained that this was where all guests and dignitaries traveling in and out of the Court stayed. To my surprise, we each got our own room.

Eddie started to protest this, adamantly saying he needed to stay with Lissa. Dimitri smiled and told him it wasn't necessary. In a place like this, guardians didn't need to stay as close to their Moroi. In fact, they often separated to do their own things. The Court was as heavily warded as the Academy. And really, Moroi visitors at the Academy were rarely trailed so closely by their guardians either. It was only for the sake of the field experience that it was being done with us.

Eddie agreed with some reluctance, and again, I was amazed at his dedication.

Alberta spoke briefly and then turned to the rest of us. "Decompress for a bit and be ready for dinner in four hours. Lissa, the queen wants to see you in an hour."

A jolt of surprise ran through Lissa, and she and I exchanged brief, puzzled looks. The last time Lissa had seen the queen, Tatiana had snubbed her and embarrassed her in front of the school for having running away with me. Both of us wondered what she'd want to see Lissa about now.

"Sure," said Lissa. "Rose and I'll be ready."

Alberta shook her head. "Rose isn't going. The queen specifically asked for you alone."

Of course she had. What interest would the queen have in Vasilisa Dragomir's shadow? A nasty voice whispered in my head, *Expendable, expendable. . . .*

The dark sentiment startled me, and I shoved it aside. I went to my room, relieved to see it had a TV. The thought of vegging for the next four hours sounded fantastic. The rest of the room was pretty fancy, very modern looking, with sleek black tables and white leather furniture. I was kind of afraid to sit on it. Ironically, despite how nice it all was, the place wasn't as decked out as the ski resort that we'd stay in over the holidays. I guessed when you came to the Royal Court, you came for business, not a vacation.

I had just sprawled on the leather couch and turned on the TV when I felt Lissa in my mind. *Come talk*, she said. I sat up, surprised by the message itself and the content. Usually our bond was all about feelings and impressions. Specific requests like this were rare.

I got up and left the room, going to the one next door. Lissa opened the door.

"What, you couldn't have come to me?" I asked.

"Sorry," she said, looking like she genuinely meant it. It was hard to be grouchy around someone so nice. "I just didn't have the time. I'm trying to decide what to wear."

Her suitcase was already open on the bed, with things hung up in the closet. Unlike me, she'd come prepared for every occasion, formal and casual alike. I lay down on the couch. Hers was plush velvet, not leather.

"Wear the print blouse with the black slacks," I told her. "Not a dress."

"Why not a dress?"

"Because you don't want to look like you're groveling."

"This is the queen, Rose. Dressing up is showing respect, not groveling."

"If you say so."

But Lissa wore the outfit I suggested anyway. She talked to me as she finished getting ready, and I watched with envy as she applied makeup. I hadn't realized how much I'd missed cosmetics myself. When she and I had lived with humans, I'd been pretty diligent about primping every day. Now, there never seemed to be enough time—or any reason. I was always in some kind of scuffle that made makeup pointless and ruined it anyway. The most I could do was to slather my face with moisturizer. It seemed excessive in the mornings—like I was putting on a mask—yet by the time I faced the cold weather and other harsh conditions, I was always surprised to see my skin had sucked all the moisture up.

The smallest pang of regret shot through me that I'd rarely have any opportunities to do this for the rest of my life. Lissa would spend most of her days dressed up, out at royal functions. No one would notice me. It was weird, considering that until this last year, I'd always been the one who was always noticed.

"Why do you think she wants to see me?" Lissa asked.

"Maybe to explain why we're here."

"Maybe."

Unease filled Lissa, despite her calm exterior. She still hadn't entirely recovered from the queen's brutal humiliation last fall. My own petty jealousy and moping suddenly seemed stupid when compared with what she had to go through. I mentally slapped myself, reminding myself that I wasn't just her unseen guardian. I was also her best friend, and we hadn't talked very much lately.

"You have nothing to be afraid of, Liss. You haven't done anything wrong. And really, you've been doing everything right. Your grades are perfect. Your behavior's perfect. Remember all those people you impressed on the ski trip? That bitch has nothing to get on you about."

"You shouldn't say that," said Lissa automatically. She

applied mascara to her eyelashes, studied them, and then added another coat.

"Just call 'em like I see 'em. If she gives you any grief, then it's just going to be because she's afraid of you."

Lissa laughed. "Why would she be afraid of me?"

"Because people are drawn to you, and people like her don't like it when others steal all the attention." I was a bit astonished at how wise I sounded. "Plus, you're the last Dragomir. You're always going to be in the spotlight. Who's she? Just another Ivashkov. There are a ton of them. Probably because all the guys are like Adrian and have all sorts of illegitimate children."

"Adrian doesn't have any children."

"That we know of," I said mysteriously.

She snickered and stepped back from the mirror, pleased with her face. "Why are you always so mean to Adrian?"

I gave her a look of mock astonishment. "You're standing up for Adrian now? Whatever happened to you warning me to stay away from him? You practically bit my head off the first time I hung out with him—and that wasn't even by my choice."

She took a thin golden chain out of her suitcase and tried to fasten it around her neck. "Well, yeah . . . I didn't really know him then. He's not so bad. And it's true. . . . I mean, he's not a great role model or anything, but I also think some of those stories about him and other girls are exaggerated."

"I don't," I said, jumping up. She still hadn't managed to

fasten the chain, so I took it and put the clasp together for her.

"Thanks," she said, running her hands over the necklace. "I think Adrian really likes you. Like, in a wanting-to-be-serious way."

I shook my head and stepped back. "Nope. He likes me in a wanting-to-get-the-clothes-off-the-cute-dhampir way."

"I don't believe that."

"That's because you believe the best about everyone."

She looked skeptical as she began brushing her hair smooth over her shoulders. "I don't know about that either. But I do think he's not as bad as you think. I know it hasn't been that long since Mason, but you should think about going out with someone else. . . ."

"Wear your hair up." I handed her a barrette from her suitcase. "Mason and I were never really going out. You know that."

"Yeah. Well, I guess that's more reason to start thinking about dating someone. High school's not over yet. Seems like you should be doing something fun."

Fun. It was ironic. Months ago, I'd argued with Dimitri about how it wasn't fair that, as a guardian-in-training, I had to watch my reputation and not act too crazy. He'd agreed it wasn't fair that I couldn't do the kinds of things other girls my age could, but that that was the price I paid for my future. I'd been upset, but after Victor's meddling, I started to see Dimitri's point—to such an extent that he'd actually hinted I shouldn't try to limit myself *that* much. Now, after Spokane, I felt like a completely different girl from the one who'd talked to Dimitri last fall about having fun. I was only a couple months from graduation. High school things . . . dances . . . boyfriends . . . what did they matter in the grand scheme of things? Everything at the Academy seemed so trivial—unless it was making me a better guardian.

"I don't really think I need a boyfriend to complete my high school experience," I told her.

"I don't think you do either," she agreed, tugging her ponytail straight. "But you used to flirt and go out sometimes. I feel like it'd just be nice for you to do a little of that. It's not like you'd have to have anything serious with Adrian."

"Well, you won't get any arguments from him on that. I think the last thing he wants is anything serious, that's the problem."

"Well, according to some of the stories, he's very serious. I heard the other day that you were engaged. Someone else said that he'd been disowned because he told his dad he'd never love anyone else."

"Ahhhh." There was really no other adequate response to all these silly rumors. "The creepy thing is that the same stories are all over the place at the elementary campus too." I stared at the ceiling. "Why does this stuff keep happening to me?"

She walked over to the couch and looked down at me. "Because you're awesome, and everyone loves you."

"Nah. You're the one everyone loves."

"Well, then, I guess we're both awesome and loveble. And one of these days"—a mischievous sparkle danced in her eyes—"we'll find a guy you love back."

"Don't hold your breath. None of that matters. Not right now. You're the one I've got to worry about. We're going to graduate, and you'll go off to college, and it'll be great. No more rules, just us on our own."

"It's a little scary," she mused. "Thinking about being on my own. But you'll be with me. And Dimitri too." She sighed. "I can't imagine not having you around. I can't even really remember when you weren't around."

I sat up and gave her a light punch in her arm. "Hey, be careful. You're going to make Christian jealous. Oh crap. I suppose he's going to be around too, huh? No matter where we end up going?"

"Probably. You, me, him, Dimitri, and any guardians Christian gets. One big happy family."

I scoffed, but inside of me, there was a warm fuzzy feeling building. Things were crazy in our world right now, but I had all these great people in my life. As long as we were all together, everything would be okay.

She looked at the clock, and her fear returned. "I've gotta go. Will you . . . will you go with me?"

"You know I can't."

"I know . . . not in body . . . but like, will you do that thing? Where you're watching in my head? It'll make me feel like I'm not alone."

It was the first time Lissa had ever asked me to purposely do that. Normally, she hated the thought of me seeing through her eyes. It was a sign of how nervous she really was.

"Sure," I said. "It's probably better than anything on TV anyway."

I returned to my own room, taking up an identical position on the couch. Clearing my thoughts, I opened myself up to Lissa's mind, going beyond simply knowing her feelings. It was something the shadow-kissed bond allowed me to do and was the most intense part of our connection. It wasn't just feeling her thoughts—it was actually being inside of her, looking through her eyes and sharing her experiences. I'd learned to control it only recently. I used to slip in without wanting to, much as I sometimes couldn't keep her feelings out. I could control my out-of-body experiences now and even summon up the phenomenon at will—just like I was about to do.

Lissa had just reached the parlor the queen was waiting in. Moroi might use terms like "royal" and even kneel sometimes, but there were no thrones or anything like that here. Tatiana sat in an ordinary armchair, dressed in a navy blue skirt and blazer, looking more like a corporate businesswoman than any sort of monarch. She wasn't alone, either. A tall, stately Moroi whose blond hair was laced with silver sat near her. I recognized her: Priscilla Voda, the queen's friend and adviser. We'd met her on the ski trip, and she'd been impressed with Lissa. I took her presence as a good sign. Silent guardians, dressed in black and white, stood along the wall. To my astonishment,

Adrian was there too. He reclined on a small love seat, seeming completely oblivious to the fact that he was hanging out with the Moroi's ultimate leader. The guardian with Lissa announced her.

"Princess Vasilisa Dragomir."

Tatiana nodded in acknowledgment. "Welcome, Vasilisa. Please sit down."

Lissa sat down near Adrian, her apprehension growing by leaps and bounds. A Moroi servant came by and offered tea or coffee, but Lissa declined. Tatiana meanwhile sipped from a teacup and scrutinized Lissa from head to toe. Priscilla Voda broke the awkward silence.

"Remember what I said about her?" Priscilla asked cheerfully. "She was very impressive at our state dinner in Idaho. Settled a huge spat over Moroi fighting with guardians. She even managed to calm Adrian's father down."

A frosty smile crossed Tatiana's cold features. "That is impressive. Half the time, I still feel like Nathan is twelve years old."

"Me too," said Adrian, drinking from a wine glass.

Tatiana ignored him and again focused on Lissa. "*Everyone* seems impressed with you, really. I hear nothing but good things about you, in spite of your past transgressions . . . which I'm given to understand weren't entirely without their reasons." Lissa's look of surprise actually made the queen laugh. There wasn't much warmth or humor in the laugh, though. "Yes, yes . . . I know all about your powers, and of course I know what happened with Victor. Adrian's been filling me in about spirit as well. It's so strange. Tell me . . . can you . . ." She glanced to a nearby table. A flowerpot sat on it, dark green shoots sticking through the soil. It was some kind of bulb-based plant that someone was growing indoors. Like its outside counterparts, it was waiting for spring.

Lissa hesitated. Using her powers in front of others was a strange thing for her. But, Tatiana was watching expectantly. After only a few moments more, Lissa leaned over and touched the shoots. The stems shot up through the dirt, growing taller—almost a foot high. Huge pods formed along the sides as it grew, bursting open to reveal fragrant white flowers. Easter lilies. Lissa withdrew her hand.

Wonder showed on Tatiana's face, and she muttered something in a language I didn't understand. She hadn't been born in the United States but had chosen to hold her Court here. She spoke with no accent, but, as they did for Dimitri, moments of surprise apparently brought out her native tongue. Within seconds, she put her stately mask back on.

"Hmm. Interesting," she said. Talk about an understatement.

"It could be very useful," said Priscilla. "Vasilisa and Adrian can't be the only two out there with it. If we could find others, so much could be learned. The healing itself is a gift, let alone anything else they can conjure. Just think what we could do with it."

Lissa turned optimistic. For a while, she'd been going out

of her way to find others like her. Adrian had been the only one she'd discovered, and that had been through sheer luck. If the queen and Moroi council put their resources into it, there was no telling what they might find. Yet something about Priscilla's words troubled Lissa.

"Begging your pardon, Princess Voda . . . I'm not sure we should be so eager to use my—or others'—healing powers as much as you might want to."

"Why not?" asked Tatiana. "From what I understand, you can heal almost anything."

"I can . . ." said Lissa slowly. "And I want to. I wish I could help everybody, but I can't. I mean, don't get me wrong, I'll definitely help some people. But I know we'd run into other people like Victor, who want to abuse it. And after a while . . . I mean, how do you choose? Who gets to live? Part of life is that . . . well, some people have to die. My powers aren't a prescription you can get filled as needed, and honestly, I'm afraid they would only be used for, uh, certain kinds of people. Just like the guardians are."

A slight tension built in the room. What Lissa had insinuated was rarely ever mentioned in public.

"What are you talking about?" asked Tatiana with narrowed eyes. I could tell she already knew.

Lissa was scared to say her next words, but she did it anyway. "Everyone knows that there's a certain, um, method to how guardians are distributed. Only the elite get them. Royals. Rich people. People in power."

A chill fell over the room. Tatiana's mouth settled into a straight line. She didn't speak for several moments, and I had a feeling everyone else was holding their breath. I certainly was. "You don't think our royals deserve special protection?" she asked finally. "You don't think *you* do—the last of the Dragomirs?"

"I think keeping our leaders safe is important, yeah. But I also think we need to stop sometimes and look at what we're doing. It could be time to reconsider the way we've always done things."

Lissa sounded so wise and so self-assured. I was proud of her. Watching Priscilla Voda, I could see that she was proud too. She'd liked Lissa from the beginning. But I could also tell that Priscilla was nervous. She answered to the queen and knew that Lissa was swimming in dangerous waters.

Tatiana sipped her tea. I think it was an excuse to gather her thoughts. "I understand," she said, "that you're also in favor of Moroi fighting with the guardians and attacking Strigoi?"

Another dangerous topic, one Lissa pushed forward into. "I think if there are Moroi who want to, they shouldn't be denied the chance." Jill suddenly popped into my head.

"Moroi lives are precious," said the queen. "They shouldn't be risked."

"Dhampir lives are precious too," Lissa countered. "If they fight with Moroi, it could save everybody. And again, if Moroi are willing, why deny them? They deserve to know how to defend themselves. And people like Tasha Ozera have developed ways of fighting with magic."

The mention of Christian's aunt brought a frown to the queen's face. Tasha had been attacked by Strigoi when younger and had spent the rest of her life learning to fight back. "Tasha Ozera . . . she's a troublemaker. She's starting to gather a lot of other troublemakers."

"She's trying to introduce new ideas." I noticed then that Lissa wasn't afraid any longer. She was confident in her beliefs and wanted them expressed. "Throughout history, people with new ideas—who think differently and try to change things—have always been called troublemakers. But seriously? Do you want the truth?"

A wry look crossed Tatiana's face, almost a smile. "Always."

"We need change. I mean, our traditions are important. We shouldn't give up on those. But sometimes, I think we're misguided."

"Misguided?"

"As time's gone on, we've gone along with other changes. We've evolved. Computers. Electricity. Technology in general. We all agree those make our lives better. Why can't we be the same in the way we act? Why are we still clinging to the past when there are better ways to do things?"

Lissa was breathless, worked up and excited. Her cheeks felt warm, and her heart raced. All of us were watching Tatiana, searching for any clue in that stony face.

"You're very interesting to talk to," she finally said. She made *interesting* sound like a dirty word. "But I have things I must do now." She stood up, and everyone hastily followed suit, even Adrian. "I won't be joining you for dinner, but you and your companions will have everything you need. I'll see you tomorrow at the trial. No matter how radical and naively idealistic your ideas are, I'm glad you'll be there to complete his sentencing. His imprisonment, at least, is something we can all agree on."

Tatiana swept out, two guardians immediately following. Priscilla followed too, leaving Lissa and Adrian alone.

"Well done, cousin. Aren't many people who can throw the old lady off-balance like that."

"She didn't seem very off-balance."

"Oh, she was. Believe me. Most of the people she deals with every day wouldn't talk to her like that, let alone someone your age." He stood up and extended a hand to Lissa. "Come on. I'll show you around this place. Take your mind off things."

"I've been here before," she said. "When I was younger."

"Yeah, well, the things we get to see when we're young are different than the things we get to see when we're older. Did you know there's a twenty-four-hour bar in here? We'll get you a drink."

"I don't want a drink."

"You will before this trip's over."

I left Lissa's head and returned to my room. The meeting

with the queen was over, and Lissa didn't need my unseen support. Besides, I really didn't want to hang out with Adrian right now. Sitting up, I discovered I felt surprisingly alert. Being in her head had kind of been like taking a nap.

I decided to do a little exploring of my own. I'd never been to the Royal Court. It really was supposed to be like a mini-town, and I wondered what other things there were to see, aside from the bar that Adrian probably lived in while visiting.

I headed downstairs, figuring I'd have to go outside. As far as I knew, this building only held guestrooms. It was kind of like the palace's hotel. When I got to the entryway, however, I saw Christian and Eddie standing and talking with someone I couldn't see. Eddie, ever vigilant, saw me and grinned.

"Hey, Rose. Look who we found."

As I approached, Christian stepped aside, revealing the mystery person. I came to a halt, and she grinned at me.

"Hi, Rose."

A moment later, I felt a smile slowly creep over my face. "Hello, Mia."

TWELVE

IF YOU'D ASKED ME six months ago, I would have said there was no way I'd be happy to run into Mia Rinaldi at the Royal Court. She was a year younger than me and had held a grudge against Lissa since freshman year—a grudge so big that Mia had gone to great extremes to make life miserable for us. She'd done a good job. Jesse and Ralf's rumors about me had been a result of her efforts.

But then Mia had gone with us to Spokane and been captured by the Strigoi. And, just like for Christian and Eddie, that had changed everything. She'd seen the same horrors the rest of us had. In fact, she was the only one of my friends who had witnessed Mason's death and me killing Strigoi. She had even saved my life then by using her water magic to temporarily drown one of the Strigoi. In the great Moroi argument about whether or not they should learn to fight with the guardians, she was firmly on the fighting side.

I hadn't seen Mia in almost a month, ever since Mason's funeral. In studying her, I felt like it'd been a year. I had always thought Mia looked like a doll. She was short compared to most Moroi and had young, round-cheeked features. The fact that she'd always curled her hair in perfect ringlets had sort of reinforced that image. But today, she hadn't gone to nearly that much trouble. Her golden blond hair was pulled into a ponytail, its only curl coming from a slight, natural waviness. She wore no makeup, and her face showed signs of having been outdoors a lot. Her skin looked chapped from the wind, and she had a very, very faint tan—almost unheard of for Moroi, with their aversion to sunlight. For the first time ever, she actually looked her age.

She laughed at my shock. "Come on, it hasn't been that long. You look like you don't even recognize me."

"I almost don't." We hugged, and again, it was hard to believe that she'd once plotted ways to ruin my life. Or that I'd broken her nose. "What are you doing here?"

She beckoned us out the door. "We were just about to leave. I'll explain everything."

We went to a neighboring building. It wasn't like a mall or anything, but it did have a few businesses that the Moroi who worked and visited here needed—a handful of restaurants, some small stores, and offices that offered all sorts of services. There was also a coffee shop, and that was where Mia led us.

A coffee shop seems like an ordinary thing, but I rarely got to go to them. Sitting in a public place (or semi-public) with friends, not worrying about school . . . it was great. It reminded me of when Lissa and I had been on our own, when our entire lives hadn't been contained within a school and its rules.

"My dad works here now," she told us. "And so now I live here."

Moroi children rarely lived with their parents. They were

sent off to places like St. Vladimir's, where they could grow up safely. "What about school?" I asked.

"There aren't many kids here, but there are some. Most of them are rich and have personal tutors. My dad pulled some strings and set it up so that I can go to them for different subjects. So I'm still studying the same things, just in a different way. It's actually pretty cool. Less teacher time—but more homework."

"You've been doing more than that," said Eddie. "Unless your classes are outside." He'd noticed the same things I had, and in looking at her hands as they held her latte, I could now see calluses.

She wiggled her fingers. "I made friends with some of the guardians here. They've been showing me a few things."

"That's risky," said Christian, though he sounded like he approved. "Since there's still a debate about Moroi fighting."

"You mean about Moroi fighting with magic," she corrected. "That's what's controversial. No one's really talking about Moroi fighting hand-to-hand."

"Well, they are," I said. "It's just been overshadowed by the magic controversy."

"It's not illegal," she said primly. "And until it is, I'm going to keep doing it. You think with all the events and meetings that go on around here that anyone even notices what someone like me does?" Mia's family, in addition to being non-royal, was also pretty lower class—not that there was anything wrong with that, but she had to feel the effects of that around here.

Still, I found her whole situation cheering. Mia seemed happier and more open than she had during the entire time I'd known her. She seemed . . . free. Christian spoke my thoughts before I could.

"You've changed," he said.

"We've all changed," she corrected. "Especially you, Rose. I can't quite explain it."

"I don't think there's any way the five of us couldn't have changed," Christian pointed out. A moment later he corrected himself. "Four of us."

We all fell silent, thoughts of Mason weighing us down. Being with Christian, Eddie, and Mia stirred up that grief I always tried to hide, and I could see from their faces that they continually fought the same battle.

Conversation eventually turned toward all of us catching up on what had happened here and at the Academy. Yet I kept thinking about how Mia had said that I had changed more than the others. All I could think about was how out of control I'd felt lately, how half the time my actions and feelings didn't seem like my own. Sitting there, it almost seemed like Mia was controlled by all of her positive traits now—and I was controlled by my negative ones. Conversations with Adrian replayed through my head, reminding me about how I supposedly had such a dark, dark aura.

Maybe thinking about him summoned him, but he and Lissa eventually joined us. Their bar was probably in the same building, I realized. I'd been blocking her out and not paying much attention. Adrian hadn't completely gotten her drunk, thankfully, but she'd agreed to two drinks. I could feel a slight buzz through the bond and had to carefully shield it out.

She was as surprised as we'd been to see Mia but gave her a warm welcome and wanted to catch up. I'd heard most of this already, so I just listened and drank my chai. No coffee for me. Most guardians drank it the way Moroi drank blood, but I wouldn't touch the stuff.

"How'd your thing with the queen go?" Christian asked Lissa at one point.

"Not so bad," she said. "I mean, not great either. But she didn't yell at me or humiliate me, so that's a start."

"Stop being modest," said Adrian, putting his arm around her. "Princess Dragomir totally stood her ground. You should have seen it." Lissa laughed.

"I don't suppose she mentioned why she decided to let us come to the trial?" Christian asked stiffly. He didn't look very happy about the bonding that was taking place here—or about Adrian's arm.

Lissa's laughter faded, but she was still smiling. "Adrian did it."

"What?" Christian and I asked together.

Adrian, looking very pleased with himself, stayed quiet for a change and let Lissa do the talking. "He convinced her that we needed to be here. He apparently harassed her until she gave in."

"It's called 'persuasion,' not 'harassment,'" Adrian said. Lissa laughed again.

My own words about the queen came back to haunt me. *Who's she? Just another Ivashkov. There are a ton of them.* There were indeed. I eyed Adrian.

"How closely are you guys related?" The answer popped into my head from Lissa's. "She's your aunt."

"Great-aunt. And I'm her favorite great nephew. Well, I'm her only great nephew, but that's not important. I'd still be her favorite," he said.

"Unbelievable," said Christian.

"I'll second that," I said.

"None of you appreciate me. Why is it so hard to believe that I could make a real contribution in these dark times?" Adrian stood up. He was trying to sound outraged, but the smirk on his face indicated that he still found all of this pretty funny. "My cigarettes and I are going outside. At least they show me respect."

As soon as he left, Christian asked Lissa, "Were you getting drunk with him?"

"I'm not drunk. I only had two drinks," she said. "Since when did you get all conservative?"

"Since Adrian became a bad influence."

"Come on! He helped us get here. No one else was able to do it. He didn't have to, but he did. And you and Rose are sitting there, still acting like he's the most evil person on the planet." That wasn't exactly true. I was mostly sitting there like I had been hit in the head, still too dumbstruck to react.

"Yeah, and I'm sure he did it out of the kindness of his heart," muttered Christian.

"Why else would he do it?"

"Oh, gee, I wonder."

Lissa's eyes widened. "You think he did it for me? You think there's something going on with us?"

"You guys drink together, practice magic together, and go to elitist events together. What would you think?"

Mia and Eddie looked like they wanted to be somewhere else. I was starting to share the feeling.

Anger burned through Lissa, hitting me like a wave of heat. She was utterly outraged. Her fury didn't even have that much to do with Adrian, really. She was more upset at the thought of Christian not trusting her. And as for him, I needed no psychic powers to understand how he was feeling. He wasn't jealous simply because she was hanging out with Adrian. Christian was still jealous that Adrian had the kind of influence to pull this off for her. It was just like what Jesse and Ralf had described, about how the right connections could open the right doors—connections that Christian didn't have.

I kneed Christian's leg, hoping he'd get the hint that he really should stop talking before things got worse. Lissa's anger was intensifying, muddled with embarrassment as she began to doubt herself and wonder if she *had* been getting too close to Adrian. The whole thing was ridiculous.

"Christian, for the love of God. If Adrian did this for anyone, it was because of me and his crazy obsession. He bragged awhile ago that he could do it, and I didn't believe it." I turned to Lissa. I needed to get her calm and diffuse those dark feelings that could cause so much trouble for her when they ran out of control. "Liss, you might not be wasted exactly, but you need to chill out for an hour before having this conversation. You're going to say something as stupid as Christian, and I'll be the one who has to deal with the mess—like always."

I'd gotten worked up and expected someone to tell me how bitchy I sounded. Instead, Lissa relaxed and offered Christian a smile. "Yeah, we should definitely talk about this later. A lot's kind of happened today."

He hesitated, then nodded. "Yeah. Sorry I jumped all over you." He returned her smile, fight patched up.

"So," Lissa asked Mia, "who have you met here?"

I stared at them in amazement, but no one seemed to notice. I'd fixed their fight, and there'd been no acknowledgment. No *Thank you, Rose, for pointing out how idiotic we're being.* It was bad enough I had to endure their romance day after day, with no consideration for how I felt. Now I was salvaging their relationship, and they didn't even realize it.

"I'll be right back," I said, interrupting Mia's description of some of the other teenagers here. I was afraid if I sat there, I was going to say something I'd regret or maybe break a chair. Where had this rage come from?

I went outside, hoping a gulp of cold air would calm me down. Instead, I got a face full of clove smoke.

"Don't start in about the smoking," warned Adrian. He was leaning against the building's brick wall. "You didn't have to come outside. You knew I was here."

"That's actually why I'm here. Well, that, and I felt like I was going to go crazy if I stayed inside another minute."

He tilted his head to look at my face. His eyebrows shot up. "You aren't kidding, are you? What happened? You were fine a few minutes ago."

I paced across the ground in front of him. "I don't know. I *was* fine. Then Christian and Lissa started having this stupid argument over you. It was weird. They were the ones who were mad—and then I ended up madder than both of them."

"Wait. They were arguing over me?"

"Yes. I just said that. Weren't you paying attention?"

"Hey, don't snap at me. I haven't done anything to you."

I crossed my arms over my chest. "Christian's jealous because you hang around Lissa so much."

"We're studying spirit," said Adrian. "He's welcome to join in."

"Yeah, well, no one ever said love was reasonable. Seeing you come back together kind of set him off. And then he got upset because you pulled rank with the queen for Lissa."

"I didn't do it for her. I did it for all of you—but, well, you especially."

I came to a halt in front of him. "I didn't believe you. That you could do it."

He grinned. "Guess you should have listened to my family history in that dream after all."

"I guess. I just thought . . ."

I couldn't finish. I'd thought Dimitri would be the one who came through for me, the one who—despite what he said— could make almost anything happen. But he hadn't.

"Thought what?" Adrian prompted.

"Nothing." With much effort, I managed to utter the next words. "Thank you for helping us."

"Oh my God," he said. "A kind word from Rose Hathaway. I can die a happy man."

"What are you saying? That I'm normally an ungrateful bitch?"

He just looked at me.

"Hey! Not cool."

"Maybe you could redeem yourself with a hug."

I glared.

"A small one?" he begged.

With a sigh, I walked over and put one arm around Adrian, leaning my head lightly against his arm. "Thanks, Adrian."

We stood like that for a heartbeat. I felt none of the crazy electricity or connection I did with Dimitri, but I had to admit that Lissa had been right about something. Adrian was annoying and arrogant at times, but he really wasn't the bastard I often made him out to be.

The doors opened, and Lissa and the others stepped outside. They understandably looked surprised, but I didn't care just then. Besides, they probably all thought I was pregnant with Adrian's love child, so what did it matter? I backed away.

"Heading out?" I asked.

"Yeah, Mia's got more important things to do than hang out with us," joked Christian.

"Hey, I just told my dad I'd meet him. I'll see you guys before I leave." She started to walk away, then abruptly turned around. "God, I'm so out of it." She reached into her coat pocket and handed me a folded piece of paper. "This is half the reason I found you guys. One of the court clerks wanted me to give this to you."

"Thanks," I said, puzzled. She headed off to see her dad while the rest of us strolled back to our accommodations.

I slowed my pace as I opened the note, wondering who in the world here would want to contact me.

Rose,

I was so happy to hear about your arrival. I'm sure it'll make tomorrow's proceedings that much more entertaining. I've been curious for quite some time about how Vasilisa is doing, and your romantic escapades are always an amusing diversion. I can't wait to share them in the courtroom tomorrow.

Best,
V. D.

"Who's it from?" asked Eddie, coming up beside me.

I hastily folded it up and shoved it into my pocket. "No one," I replied.

No one indeed.

V. D.

Victor Dashkov.

THIRTEEN

WHEN WE GOT BACK to our rooms, I made up an excuse to Lissa about how I needed to go take care of some guardian stuff. She was eager to patch up the earlier conflict with Christian—probably in the form of clothing removal—and didn't ask any questions. There was a phone in my room, and after calling an operator, I was able to find out which room was Dimitri's.

He was surprised to see me at his door—and a little wary. The last time this had happened, I'd been under the influence of Victor's lust charm and had behaved . . . aggressively.

"I have to talk to you," I said.

He let me come in, and I immediately handed over the note.

"V. D.—"

"Yeah, I know," said Dimitri. He handed the note back. "Victor Dashkov."

"What are we going to do? I mean, we talked about this, but now he really is saying he's going to sell us out."

Dimitri didn't answer, and I could tell he was assessing every angle of this, just like he would a fight. Finally, he pulled out his cell phone, which was a lot cooler than having to rely on the room's phone. "Give me a moment."

I started to sit on his bed, decided that was dangerous, and instead sat on the couch. I didn't know who he was calling, but the conversation took place in Russian.

"What's going on?" I asked when he finished.

"I'll let you know soon. For now, we have to wait."

"Great. My favorite thing to do."

He dragged an armchair up and sat opposite me. It seemed too small for someone as tall as him, but, as always, he managed to make it work and appear graceful in the process.

Beside me was one of the Western novels he always carried around. I picked it up, again thinking about how alone he was. Even now, at the Court, he'd chosen to stay in his room. "Why do you read these?"

"Some people read books for fun," he observed.

"Hey, watch the dig. And I do read books. I read them to solve mysteries that threaten my best friend's life and sanity. I don't think reading this cowboy stuff is really saving the world like I do."

He took it from me and flipped it over, face thoughtful and not as intense as usual. "Like any book, it's an escape. And there's something . . . mmm. I don't know. Something appealing about the Old West. No rules. Everyone just lives by their own code. You don't have to be tied down by others' ideas of right and wrong in order to bring justice."

"Wait," I laughed. "I thought I was the one who wanted to break rules."

"I didn't say I wanted to. Just that I can see the appeal."

"You can't fool me, comrade. You want to put on a cowboy hat and keep lawless bank robbers in line."

"No time. I have enough trouble keeping you in line."

I grinned, and suddenly, it was a lot like when we cleaned the church—before the fight, at least. Easy. Comfortable. In fact, it was a lot like the old days when we'd first begun training together, way back before everything had gotten so complicated. Well, okay . . . things had always been complicated, but for a while, they'd been less complicated. It made me sad. I wished we could relive those early days. There'd been no Victor Dashkov, no blood on my hands.

"I'm sorry," Dimitri said all of a sudden.

"For what? Reading cheesy novels?"

"For not being able to get you here. I feel like I let you down." I glimpsed a shadow of worry on his face, like he was concerned he might have caused some irreparable damage.

The apology totally caught me off guard. For a moment, I wondered if he was jealous of Adrian's influence in the same way Christian had been. Then I realized it was completely different. I'd been giving Dimitri a hard time because I'd been convinced he could do anything. Somewhere—deep inside—he felt the same, at least where I was concerned. He didn't want to deny me anything. My earlier bad mood had long since vanished, and I suddenly just felt drained. And stupid.

"You didn't," I told him. "I acted like a total brat. You've never let me down before. You didn't let me down with this."

The grateful look he gave me made me feel as if I had

wings. If another moment had passed, I suspected he would have said something so sweet that I would have flown away. Instead, his phone rang.

Another conversation in Russian took place, and then he stood up. "All right, let's go."

"Where?"

"To see Victor Dashkov."

It turned out that Dimitri had a friend who had a friend, and somehow, despite the best security in the Moroi world, we managed to get into the Court's prison facilities.

"Why are we doing this?" I whispered as we walked down the hall toward Victor's cell. I'd really, really hoped for stone walls and torches, but the place looked very modern and efficient, with marble floors and stark white walls. At least there were no windows. "You think we can talk him out of it?"

Dimitri shook his head. "If Victor wanted to take revenge on us, he'd just do it without any warning. He doesn't do things without a reason. The fact that he told you first means he wants something, and now we're going to find out what it is."

We reached Victor's cell. He was the only prisoner currently being held. Like the rest of the facility, his room reminded me of something you'd find at a hospital. Everything was clean, bright, and sterile—and very bare. It was a place without any sort of stimulus or distraction whatsoever, which would have driven me crazy in one hour. The cell had silvery bars that looked very hard to break, which was the most important part.

Victor sat in a chair, idly examining his nails. It had been three months since our last meeting, and seeing him again made my skin crawl. Feelings I hadn't known were buried in me suddenly burst to the surface.

One of the hardest things of all was seeing him look so healthy and young. He'd bought that health by torturing Lissa, and I hated him for it. If his disease had run its normal course, he might be dead by now.

He had receding black hair, with only the slightest touch of silver. He was in his forties and had a regal, almost handsome cut to his face. He glanced up at our approach. Eyes the same pale jade as Lissa's met mine. The Dragomir and Dashkov families had a lot of intertwined history, and it was creepy seeing that eye color in someone else. A smile lit his face.

"Oh my. This is a treat. Lovely Rosemarie, practically an adult now." His eyes flicked toward Dimitri. "Of course, some have been treating you that way for quite a while."

I pressed my face to the bars. "Stop screwing with us, you son of a bitch. What do you want?"

Dimitri put a gentle hand on my shoulder and pulled me back. "Easy, Rose."

I took a deep breath and then slowly stepped backward. Victor straightened up in his chair and laughed.

"After all this time, your cub still hasn't learned any control. But then, maybe you never really wanted her to."

"We aren't here to banter," said Dimitri calmly. "You wanted to lure Rose over, and now we need to know why."

"Does there have to be some sinister reason? I just wanted to know how she was doing, and something tells me we aren't going to have a chance for any friendly chats tomorrow." That annoying smirk stayed on his face, and I decided then that he was lucky to be behind bars and out of my reach.

"We're not going to have a friendly chat now," I growled.

"You think I'm joking, but I'm not. I really do want to know how you're doing. You've always been a fascinating subject to me, Rosemarie. The only shadow-kissed person we know of. I told you before, that isn't the kind of thing you walk away from unscathed. There's no way you can quietly sink into the regimented routine of academic life. People like you aren't meant to blend in."

"I'm not some kind of science experiment."

He acted like I hadn't said anything. "What's it been like? What have you noticed?"

"There's no time for this. If you don't get to the point," warned Dimitri, "we're going to leave."

I didn't understand how Dimitri could sound so calm. I leaned forward and gave Victor my coldest smile. "There's no way they'll let you off tomorrow. I hope you enjoy prison. I bet it'll be great once you get sick again—and you will, you know."

Victor regarded me levelly, still with that amused look that made me want to choke him. "All things die, Rose. Well, except for you, I suppose. Or maybe you are dead. I don't know. Those who visit the world of the dead can probably never fully shake their connection to it."

There was a snarky retort on my lips, but something held me back. *Those who visit the world of the dead.* What if my Mason sightings weren't because I was crazy or because he was seeking revenge? What if there was something about me—something that had happened when I'd died and come back—that was now connecting me to Mason? It was Victor who had first explained what it meant to be shadow-kissed. I wondered now if he had any of the answers I'd been looking for.

My face must have given away something, because Victor gave me a speculative look. "Yes? There's something you'd like to say?"

I hated to ask him for anything. It made my stomach turn. Swallowing my pride, I asked, "What is the world of the dead? Is it heaven or hell?"

"Neither," he said.

"What lives there?" I exclaimed. "Ghosts? Will I go back? Do things come out of it?"

Victor was taking great pleasure in me having to come to him for information, just as I'd feared he would. I saw that smirk intensify.

"Well, clearly some things come out of it, because here you stand before us."

"He's baiting you," said Dimitri. "Let it go."

Victor gave Dimitri a brief glare. "I'm *helping* her." He

turned back to me. "Honestly? I don't know that much about it. You're the one who has been there, Rose. Not me. Not yet. Someday, you'll probably be the one educating me. I'm sure the more you deal death out, the closer you'll become to it."

"Enough," said Dimitri, voice harsh. "We're going."

"Wait, wait," said Victor, voice congenial. "You haven't told me about Vasilisa yet."

I moved forward again. "Stay away from her. She doesn't have anything to do with this."

Victor gave me a dry look. "Seeing as I'm locked away here, I have no choice but to stay away from her, my dear. And you're wrong—Vasilisa has everything to do with every-thing."

"That's it," I said, suddenly getting it. "That's why you sent the note. You wanted me here because you wanted to know about her, and you knew there was no way she'd come talk to you herself. You had nothing to blackmail her with."

"*Blackmail*'s an ugly word."

"There's no way you're going to see her—at least outside of the courtroom. She's never going to heal you. I told you: You're going to get sick again, and you're going to die. You're going to be the one sending me postcards from the other side."

"You think that's what this is about? You think my needs are that petty?" The mockery was gone, replaced by a feverish and almost fanatical look in his green eyes. The tight set of his mouth stretched the skin of his face a little, and I noticed he'd lost weight since our last encounter. Maybe prison had been harder on him than I'd thought. "You've forgotten everything, why I did what I did. You've been so caught up in your own shortsightedness that you missed the big picture I was looking at."

I racked my brain, thinking back to that time last fall. He was right. My focus had been on the wrongs he'd committed against Lissa and me personally. I'd forgotten other conversations, his insane explanations of his grand scheme.

"You wanted to stage a revolution—still want to. That's crazy. It's not going to happen," I said.

"It's already happening. Do you think I don't know what's going on out in the world? I still have contacts. People can be bought off—how do you think I was able to send you that message? I know about the unrest—I know about Natasha Ozera's movement to get Moroi to fight with guardians. You stand by her and vilify me, Rosemarie, but I pushed for the very same thing last fall. Yet, somehow, you don't seem to regard her in the same way."

"Tasha Ozera is working on her cause a bit differently than you did," noted Dimitri.

"And that's why she's getting nowhere," Victor retorted. "Tatiana and her council are being held back by centuries of archaic traditions. So long as that sort of power rules us, nothing will change. We will never learn to fight. Non-royal Moroi will never have a voice. Dhampirs like you will continually be sent out to battle."

"It's what we dedicate our lives to," said Dimitri. I could sense the tension building in him. He might show better self-control than me, but I knew he was getting just as frustrated here.

"And it's what you lose your lives for. You're all but enslaved and don't even realize it. And for what? Why do you protect us?"

"Because . . . we need you," I faltered. "For our race to survive."

"You don't need to throw yourselves into battle for that. Making children isn't really that difficult."

I ignored his quip. "And because the Moroi . . . the Moroi and their magic are important. They can do amazing things."

Victor threw his hands up in exasperation. "We *used* to do amazing things. Humans used to revere us as gods, but over time, we grew lazy. The advent of technology made our magic more and more obsolete. Now, all we do is parlor tricks."

"If you have so many ideas," said Dimitri, with a dangerous glint in his dark eyes, "then do something useful in prison and write a manifesto."

"And what's this have to do with Lissa anyway?" I asked.

"Because Vasilisa is a vehicle for change."

I stared incredulously. "You think she's going to lead your revolution?"

"Well, I'd prefer that I lead it—someday. But, regardless, I think that she's going to be part of it. I've heard about her too. She's a rising star—still young, certainly, but people are taking notice. All royals aren't created equal, you know. The Dragomir symbol is a dragon, the king of the beasts. Likewise, the Dragomir blood has always been powerful—that's why the Strigoi have targeted them so consistently. A Dragomir returning to power is no small thing—particularly one such as her. My impression from the reports is that she must have mastered her magic. If that's so—with her gifts—there's no telling what she could do. People are drawn to her with almost no effort on her part. And when she actually tries to influence them . . . well, they'll do anything she wants." His eyes were wide as he spoke, wonder and happiness on his face as he imagined Lissa living out his dreams.

"Unbelievable," I said. "First you wanted to hide her away to keep you alive. Now you actually want her out in the world to use her compulsion for your own psycho plans."

"I told you, she's a force for change. And like you being shadow-kissed, she's the only one of her kind that we know about. That makes her dangerous—and very valuable."

Well, that was something. Victor wasn't all-knowing after all. He didn't know about Adrian's spirit use.

"Lissa will never do it," I said. "She's not going to abuse her powers."

"And Victor's not going to say anything about us," said Dimitri, tugging my arm. "He's achieved his goal. He brought you here because he wanted to know about Lissa."

"He didn't find out much," I said.

"You'd be surprised," said Victor. He grinned at Dimitri.

"And what makes you so certain I won't enlighten the world about your romantic indiscretions?"

"Because it won't save you from prison. And if you ruin Rose, you'll destroy whatever weak chance you had of Lissa helping you with your warped fantasy." Victor flinched just a little; Dimitri was right. Dimitri stepped forward, pressing close to the bars as I had earlier. I'd thought I had a scary voice, but when he spoke his next words, I realized I wasn't even close. "And it'll all be pointless anyway, because you won't stay alive long enough in prison to stage your grand plans. You aren't the only one with connections."

My breath caught a little. Dimitri brought so many things to my life: love, comfort, and instruction. I got so used to him sometimes that I forgot just how dangerous he could be. As he stood there, tall and threatening while he glared down at Victor, I felt a chill run down my spine. I remembered how when I had first come to the Academy, people had said Dimitri was a god. In this moment, he looked it.

If Victor was frightened by Dimitri's threat, he didn't show it. His jade green eyes glanced between the two of us. "You two are a match made in heaven. Or somewhere."

"See you in court," I said.

Dimitri and I left. On our way out, he said a few words in Russian to the guardian on duty. From their manners, my guess was Dimitri was offering thanks.

We ventured outdoors, walking across a wide, beautiful parklike space to get back to our rooms. The sleet had stopped, and it had left everything—buildings and trees alike—coated in ice. It was like the world was made of glass. Glancing at Dimitri, I saw him staring straight ahead. It was hard to tell while walking, but I could have sworn he was shaking.

"Are you okay?" I asked.

"Yes."

"You sure?"

"As okay as I can be."

"Do you think he'll tell everyone about us?"

"No."

We walked in silence for a bit. I finally asked the question I'd been dying to know.

"Did you mean it . . . that if Victor did tell . . . that you'd . . ." I couldn't finish. I couldn't bring myself to say the words *have him killed*.

"I don't have much influence in the upper levels of Moroi royalty, but I have plenty among the guardians who handle the dirty work in our world."

"You didn't answer the question. If you'd really do it."

"I'd do a lot of things to protect you, Roza."

My heart pounded. He only used "Roza" when he was feeling particularly affectionate toward me.

"It wouldn't exactly be protecting me. It'd be after the fact—cold-blooded. You don't do that kind of thing," I told him. "Revenge is more my thing. I'll have to kill him."

I meant it as a joke, but he didn't think it was funny. "Don't talk like that. And anyway, it doesn't matter. Victor's not going to say anything."

He left me to go to his own room when we got inside. As I was opening the door to mine, Lissa rounded the hall corner.

"There you are. What happened? You missed dinner."

I'd completely forgotten. "Sorry . . . got carried away with some guardian stuff. It's a long story."

She'd changed for dinner. Her hair was still pulled up, and she now wore a form-fitting dress made out of silver raw silk. She looked beautiful. She looked royal. I thought about Victor's words and wondered if she really could be the power for change he swore she was. Looking like she did now, so glamorous and self-composed, I could imagine people following her anywhere. I certainly would, but then, I was biased.

"Why are you looking at me like that?" she asked with a small smile.

I couldn't tell her that I'd just seen the man who frightened her the most. I couldn't tell her that while she'd been out living it up, I'd been off watching her back in the shadows, like I would always do.

Instead, I returned her smile. "I like the dress."

FOURTEEN

ABOUT A HALF HOUR before my alarm was scheduled to go off the next morning, I heard a knock at my door. I expected it to be Lissa, but a sleepy check of our bond showed that she was still fast asleep. Puzzled, I staggered out of the bed and opened the door. A Moroi girl I didn't recognize handed me some folded clothes with a note attached. I wondered if I should tip her or something, but she left too quickly for me to react.

I sat back on my bed and unfolded the clothing. Black slacks, white blouse, and a black jacket. It was the same ensemble that the other guardians wore around here, and it was in my size. Wow. I was about to become part of the team. A slow grin spread over my face, and I opened the note. It was in Dimitri's writing: *Wear your hair up.*

The grin stayed on my face. A lot of female guardians cut their hair to show off their *molnija* marks. I'd reluctantly considered it once, and Dimitri had told me not to. He loved my hair and had told me to wear it up. The way he'd said it back then had given me chills, just like now.

An hour later, I was on my way to the trial with Lissa, Christian, and Eddie. Someone had rustled up a black-and-white outfit for Eddie too, and I think we both kind of felt like kids playing dress-up with their parents' clothing. My cropped jacket and stretchy blouse were actually pretty cute, and I wondered if I'd be able to bring these back with me.

The courtroom was over in the large, ornate building we'd passed upon arrival. Walking through its halls, I saw a mix of the old and the new. Outside, it was all arched windows and stone spires. Inside, it was a hub of modern activity. People worked in offices with flat-screen monitors. Elevators led to upper floors. Yet, despite that, a few antique touches could still be found. Sculptures on pedestals. Chandeliers in the halls.

The courtroom itself had beautiful murals that stretched from floor to ceiling, and in the front of the room, seals from all the royal families hung on the walls. Lissa stopped as we walked in, her eyes falling on the Dragomir dragon. *King of the beasts.* A sea of conflicting emotions swirled within her as she stared at the seal and felt the full weight of being the only one left to carry on her name. Pride to be part of that family. Fear that she wouldn't be good enough to live up to the name. Giving her a gentle nudge, I urged her on toward our seats.

The seating was split by an aisle down the middle of the room. We sat at the front of the right-hand section. There were still several minutes to go before proceedings began, but the room wasn't very full yet. I suspected that wouldn't change, due to the secrecy surrounding what had happened with Victor. A judge sat at the front, but there was no jury. An elevated seat on one side of the room marked where the queen would sit when she arrived. She would be the one who made the ultimate decision. That was how it worked with royal criminal cases.

I pointed it out to Lissa. "Let's hope that she's against him. Looks like she'll be the only one making the decision."

Lissa frowned. "Not having a jury feels kind of weird."

"That's because we spent so much time around humans."

She smiled. "Maybe. I don't know. Just seems like there's a lot of room for corruption."

"Well, yeah. But this is Victor we're talking about."

Moments later, Prince Victor Dashkov himself entered the courtroom. Or, rather, just Victor Dashkov did. He'd been stripped of his title when he'd been imprisoned. It had gone to the next oldest person in the Dashkov family.

Fear shot through Lissa, and the little color that was in her cheeks completely disappeared. Mingled with that fear was an emotion I hadn't expected: regret. Before he'd kidnapped her, Victor had been like an uncle to her—that was even how she'd referred to him. She'd loved him, and he'd betrayed her. I put my hand over hers. "Easy," I murmured. "It's going to be okay."

His eyes, narrowed and cunning, looked around the courtroom as though it were a party. He had that same unconcerned look he'd had while talking to Dimitri and me. I felt my lips curl into a sneer. A red haze tinged my vision, and I worked hard to be as serene as the other guardians in the room. He finally focused on Lissa, and she flinched at seeing the same eye color she and others of her family had. When he nodded a sort of greeting to her, I felt my control snap. Before I could actually do anything, I felt new words in my mind—Lissa's. *Breathe, Rose. Just breathe.* It looked like we were going to have to rely on each other to get through this. A heartbeat later, Victor was walking again, off to take his seat on the left side of the room.

"Thanks," I said to her, once he was gone. "It's like you can read my mind."

"No," she said gently. "I could just feel your hand."

I looked down at where I'd put my hand over hers. I'd done it to comfort her and had ended up clenching her fingers in my own agitation. "Yikes," I said, jerking away and hoping I hadn't broken her bones. "Sorry."

Queen Tatiana's entrance followed his, which distracted me and helped calm my dark feelings. We all stood when she appeared and then knelt. It was all kind of archaic, but it was a custom the Moroi had held onto over the years. We didn't rise until she took her seat, and then the rest of us were able to sit too.

The trial started. One by one, those who had witnessed the events with Victor gave their account of what they'd seen. Largely, this involved the guardians who had pursued Lissa when Victor had taken her away and who had subsequently been part of the raid on Victor's hideout.

Dimitri was the last of the guardians to go. On the surface, his testimony wasn't much different than theirs. They'd all been part of the rescue squad, but his part in the story had begun a little earlier.

"I was with my student, Rose Hathaway," he said. "She shares a bond with the princess and was the first to sense what had happened."

Victor's lawyer—I couldn't even imagine how they'd gotten anyone to represent him—glanced at some papers and then looked back up at Dimitri. "Based on the events, it sounds like there was a delay between when she discovered that and when you alerted the others."

Dimitri nodded, his mask of composure never slipping. "She couldn't act on it because Mr. Dashkov had inflicted a charm on her, one that caused her to attack me." He spoke the words so levelly, it amazed me. Not even the lawyer seemed to notice anything. Only I could see—or maybe it was just because I *knew* him—how much it hurt for Dimitri to lie. Oh, he wanted to protect us—wanted to protect me in particular—which was why he was doing this. But it killed a piece of him to stand up there, under oath, and lie. Dimitri was not perfect, no matter how much I thought he was some days, but he always tried to be truthful. Today he couldn't be.

"Mr. Dashkov works with earth magic, and some who use that power and are strong in compulsion can influence our base instincts," continued Dimitri. "In this case, he affected her anger and violence through an object."

Off to my left, I heard a sound—like someone choking on their own laughter. The judge, an elderly but fierce Moroi woman, glared.

"Mr. Dashkov, please respect the decorum of this court-room."

Victor, still smiling, waved his hands in apology. "I'm terribly sorry, Your Honor and Your Majesty. Something in Guardian Belikov's testimony just tickled my fancy, that's all. It won't happen again."

I held my breath, waiting for the blow to fall. It didn't. Dimitri finished his statement, and then Christian was called up. His part was short. He'd been with Lissa when she'd been taken and had been knocked out. His contribution was being able to ID some of Victor's guardians as the kidnappers. Once Christian sat down, it was my turn.

I walked up, hoping I looked calm in front of all those eyes—and in front of Victor. In fact, I went out of my way to not look at him at all. As I said my name and gave my oath to tell the truth, I suddenly felt the full force of what Dimitri must have experienced. I was standing before all these people, swearing I'd be honest, but I would lie in an instant if the lust charm came up.

My version was pretty straightforward. I had details to offer from before the night of the kidnapping, like about when Victor had laid his sick traps to test Lissa's power. Otherwise, my story lined up with Dimitri's and the other guardians'.

I'd said before that I could lie well, and I brushed over the "attack" charm part with such ease that no one paid any attention. Except Victor. Despite my refusal to look at him, I inadvertently glanced in his direction when I mentioned the charm. His eyes bored into me, and a small smirk sat on his lips. His smugness, I realized, was more than just because he knew I was lying. It was also because he actually knew the precise truth—and the look he gave me told me that he had that power over me and Dimitri, the power to ruin everything for us in front of all these people—no matter what Dimitri had threatened. All the while, I kept my face calm enough to make Dimitri proud, but inside my chest, my heart thudded loudly.

It seemed to last forever, but I knew I was only on the stand for a few minutes. I finished, sagging with relief that Victor hadn't called me out, and then it was Lissa's turn. As the victim, she offered the first new perspective thus far, and everyone there grew caught up in her story. It was compelling; no one had ever heard anything like it. I also realized that, without even trying, Lissa was using her spirit-induced charisma. I think it came from the same place compulsion did. People were enraptured and sympathetic. When Lissa described the torture Victor had put her through to force her to heal him, I saw faces go pale with shock. Even Tatiana's stern mask faltered a little, though whether she felt pity or just simple surprise, I couldn't say.

The most amazing thing, though, was how calmly Lissa managed to deliver the story. On the outside, she was steady and beautiful. But as she spoke the words, describing exactly how Victor's henchman had tortured her, she relived the pain and terror of that night. The guy had been an air user, and he'd toyed with that element, sometimes taking it away so she couldn't breathe and at other times smothering her with it. It had been horrible, and I'd experienced it right along with her. In fact, I experienced it with her again now as she spoke about the events on the stand. Each painful detail was still etched in her mind, the pain echoing back to both of us. We were both relieved when her testimony finished.

Finally, it was Victor's turn. From the look on his face, you never would have guessed he was on trial. He wasn't angry or outraged. He wasn't contrite. He didn't plead. He looked like we were all hanging out somewhere, like he had nothing in the world to worry about. Somehow, that made me that much angrier.

Even when answering, he spoke as though he made perfect sense. When the prosecuting lawyer asked why he'd done what he had, he looked at her as though she were crazy.

"Why, I had no choice," he said pleasantly. "I was dying. No one was going to condone me openly experimenting with the princess's powers. What would you have done in my place?"

The lawyer ignored that. She was having a hard time keeping the disgust off of her face. "And you found coaxing your own daughter into turning Strigoi also necessary?"

Everyone in the courtroom shifted uncomfortably. One of

the most awful things about Strigoi was that they were made, not born. A Strigoi could force a human, a dhampir, or a Moroi into becoming Strigoi if the Strigoi drank the victim's blood and then fed Strigoi blood back to the victim. It didn't matter if the victim wanted it or not, and once she became Strigoi, she lost all sense of her old, moral self. She embraced becoming a monster and killing others to survive. Strigoi converted others if they found someone they thought would strengthen their ranks. Sometimes they did it just out of cruelty.

The other way a Strigoi could be made was if a Moroi willingly chose to kill another person during feeding, destroying all the magic and life within themselves. Christian's parents had done that because they'd wanted to be immortal, no matter the cost. Victor's daughter Natalie had done it because he had talked her into it. The extra strength and speed she'd gotten from being a Strigoi had helped her free him, and he'd felt his goals were worth the sacrifice.

Again, Victor showed no remorse. His answer was simple. "Natalie made that decision."

"Can you say that about everyone you used to meet your ends? Guardian Belikov and Miss Hathaway had no say in what you made them do."

Victor chuckled. "Well, that's a matter of opinion. I honestly don't think they minded. But if you have time after this case, Your Honor, you might want to consider trying a statutory rape case."

I froze. He'd done it. He'd really done it. I expected everyone in the room to turn and point at Dimitri and me. No one even looked in our direction, though. Most people were giving Victor appalled looks. I realized that was exactly what Victor had known would happen. He just wanted to tease us; he didn't actually expect anyone to take him seriously. Lissa's feelings through the bond confirmed as much. She felt like Victor was trying to shift attention off of himself by making up stories about Dimitri and me. She was horrified that Victor would stoop so low.

The judge was too, and she chastised Victor for getting off topic. By that point, most of the questioning was done. The lawyers wrapped up, and it was time for the queen to deliver her verdict. I held my breath again, wondering what she would do. He hadn't denied any of the charges. The evidence was overwhelming, thanks to my friends' testimonies, but as even Victor had pointed out, there was a lot of corruption among royals. The queen could very well decide that she didn't want the scandal involved with imprisoning someone so well known. Even if no one knew the details, his imprisonment would start a buzz. Maybe she didn't want to deal with that. Maybe Victor had bought her off too.

But in the end, she found Victor guilty and sentenced him to life in prison—a different prison, not the one at Court. I'd heard stories about Moroi prisons, and they were terrible places. I suspected his new home would be very different from the cell we'd found him in. Victor remained calm and amused throughout it all, just as he had yesterday. I didn't like that. The conversation I'd had with him made me think he wasn't going to accept this as serenely as he pretended. I hoped they'd watch him closely.

A gesture from the queen ended formalities. The rest of us stood up and began talking while she surveyed the room with a sharp eye, probably taking notes. Victor's escort started to lead him out. He passed by us again. This time, he stopped and spoke.

"Vasilisa, I trust you've been well."

She didn't answer. She still hated and feared him, but with this verdict, she finally believed he could no longer hurt her. It was like the end of a chapter she'd been stuck in for months. She could finally move on and hopefully let those horrible memories fade.

"I'm sorry we didn't get a chance to talk, but I'm sure we will next time," he added.

"Come on," said one of the guardians with him. They led him away.

"He's crazy," muttered Lissa once he was gone. "I can't believe he said that stuff about you and Dimitri."

Dimitri was standing behind her. I looked up and met his eyes as he moved past us. His relief mirrored my own. We'd danced with danger today—and we'd won.

Christian came up to her and hugged her, holding her for a long time. I watched them fondly, surprised at my own kind feelings for them. When a hand touched my arm, I jumped. It was Adrian.

"You okay, little dhampir?" he asked softly. "Dashkov said a few . . . uh . . . suggestive things."

I stepped closer, keeping my voice low as well. "No one believed him. I think it's okay. Thanks for asking, though."

He smiled and tapped my nose. "Two thank-yous in as many days. I don't suppose I'll get to see any, uh, special gratitude?"

I scoffed. "Nope. You'll just have to imagine it."

He gave me a half-hug and released me. "Fair enough. But I have a good imagination."

We started to leave, and then Priscilla Voda hurried over to Lissa. "The queen would like to meet with you before you leave. In private."

I glanced over to the raised chair where the queen sat. Her gaze was fixed on us, and I wondered what this could be about.

"Sure," said Lissa, as confused as I was. To me, she sent through the bond: *Will you listen again?*

I gave her a quick nod before Priscilla spirited her off. I returned to my room, tuning in to Lissa while I packed my things up. It took a little while because Tatiana had to finish a few courtroom formalities, but she finally arrived in the same room as yesterday. Lissa and Priscilla bowed as she entered and waited for the queen to sit.

Tatiana made herself comfortable. "Vasilisa, you need to be in the air soon, so I'll make this brief. I would like to make an offer to you."

"What kind of an offer, Your Majesty?"

"You'll need to go to college soon." She spoke like it was a done deal. And yeah, Lissa did plan on going to college, but I didn't like the presumption. "I understand you're dissatisfied with your choices."

"Well . . . it's not that I'm dissatisfied, exactly. It's just, all the places Moroi are supposed to go are small. I mean, I understand it's for safety, but I don't know. I'd like to go somewhere bigger. Somewhere prestigious." Guardians monitored a handful of select colleges in the country so that Moroi could safely attend them. As Lissa had noted, though, they tended to be smaller schools.

Tatiana nodded impatiently, like she already knew this. "I'm going to give you an opportunity that no one else has ever been given, to my knowledge. After graduation, I would like you to come live here, at the Royal Court. You have no family, and I think you'd benefit from learning politics right in the heart of our government. Along with this, we would make arrangements for you to attend Lehigh University. It's less than an hour from here. Have you heard of it?"

Lissa nodded. I'd never heard of it, but she was enough of a nerd to have researched every college in the U.S. "It's a good school, Your Majesty. But . . . still small."

"It's bigger than the ones Moroi usually attend," she pointed out.

"True." In her mind, Lissa was trying to puzzle out what

was going on here. Why was Tatiana making this offer? Especially considering how she'd seemed to disagree with Lissa earlier. There was something weird going on here, and she decided to see how far she could push it. "The University of Pennsylvania isn't that far either, Your Majesty."

"That school is *enormous*, Vasilisa. We couldn't ensure your safety there."

Lissa shrugged. "Well, then it probably doesn't matter if I go to Lehigh or one of the others."

The queen looked shocked. So did Priscilla. They couldn't believe Lissa seemed indifferent to the offer. Truthfully, Lissa wasn't indifferent. Lehigh was a step up from what she'd expected, and she wanted to go. But she also wanted to see how badly the queen wanted her to go.

Tatiana frowned and appeared to be weighing matters. "Depending on your grades and experiences at Lehigh, we could possibly arrange for you to transfer in a couple years. Again, the safety logistics would be very difficult."

Wow. The queen did want her around. But why? Lissa decided to simply ask.

"I'm very flattered, Your Majesty. And grateful. But why are you offering me this?"

"As the last Dragomir, you're a precious commodity. I'd like to make sure your future is secure. And I do so hate to see bright minds wasted. Besides . . ." She paused, hesitant to speak her next words. "You were right to a certain extent. The

Moroi do have trouble changing. It could be useful to have a dissenting voice around here."

Lissa didn't answer right away. She was still analyzing this offer from every possible angle. She wished I was there to advise her, but I wasn't sure I'd have much of an opinion. Splitting my guardian duty between the Court and a cool university could be pretty neat. On the other hand, we'd have more freedom elsewhere. In the end, Lissa decided in favor of higher education.

"All right," she said at last. "I accept. Thank you, Your Majesty."

"Excellent," said Tatiana. "We'll see that the arrangements are made. You may go now."

The queen made no signs of moving, so Lissa bowed again and scurried to the door, still reeling with this news. Tatiana suddenly called out to her.

"Vasilisa? Will you send your friend here to talk to me? The Hathaway girl?"

"Rose?" she asked in astonishment. "Why do you—? Yes, of course. I'll get her."

Lissa hurried toward guest housing, but I met her halfway. "What's going on?" I asked.

"I have no idea," said Lissa. "Did you hear what she said?"

"Yup. Maybe she wants to tell me how I have to be extra careful with you going to that school."

"Maybe. I don't know." Lissa gave me a quick hug. "Good

luck. I'll see you soon."

I went to the same room and found Tatiana standing with her hands clasped, posture stiff and impatient. She was dressed like a corporate businesswoman again, with a sleek brown blazer and skirt set. That color wouldn't have been my first choice to go with her dark gray hair, but that was her style adviser's problem, not mine.

I bowed just as Lissa had and glanced around the room. Priscilla was gone; only a couple guardians remained. I expected Tatiana to tell me to sit, but instead, she stood up and walked right over to me. Her face did not look happy.

"Miss Hathaway," she said sharply, "I'm going to keep this brief. You are going to stop this atrocious affair you're having with my great-nephew. Immediately."

FIFTEEN

"I . . . WHAT?"

"You heard me. I don't know how far things have gone, and honestly, I really don't want to know the details. That's not the point. The point is that it's going to go no farther."

The queen was looking down on me, hands on her hips, clearly waiting for me to swear I'd do whatever she wanted. Except I kind of couldn't. I glanced around the room, certain this was some sort of joke. I looked to the two guardians across the room, half-hoping they'd explain what was going on, but they were doing that seeing-without-actually-seeing thing. No eye contact. I turned back to the queen.

"Um, Your Majesty . . . there's been some kind of mistake. There's nothing going on between Adrian and me."

"Do you think I'm an idiot?" she asked.

Wow. That was an opening.

"No, Your Majesty."

"Well, that's a start. There's no point in lying to me. People have seen you together, here and back at your school. *I* saw you myself in the courtroom." Damn it. Why had Adrian chosen that moment to be chivalrous and sneak another hug? "I've heard all the illicit details about what's going on, and it is going to stop right here, right now. Adrian Ivashkov is not going to run off with some cheap dhampir girl, so you might as well rid yourself of that delusion right now."

"I never thought he was going to—seeing as how we're not involved," I said. "I mean, we're friends, that's all. He likes me. He's a flirt. And if you want to talk illicit stuff, then . . . yeah, I'm pretty sure he's got a list of illicit things he'd like to do with me. Lots of illicit things. But we're not doing them. Your Majesty."

As soon as the words left my mouth, I felt like an idiot. From the look on her face, however, it didn't seem like things could really get any worse for me.

"I know about you," she said. "All anyone talks about are your recent awards and accolades, but I haven't forgotten that it was *you* who took Vasilisa away. I also know about the trouble you used to get into—I know about the drinking, about the men. If it was up to me, I'd pack you up and send you off to some blood whore commune. You'd probably fit in well."

Drinking and men? She made me sound like an alcoholic prostitute when, honestly, I'd probably drunk no more than other teenagers at high school parties. Telling her this seemed useless, though. Pointing out that I was still a virgin probably wouldn't have made much of a difference either.

"But," she continued, "your recent . . . achievements make sending you away impossible. Everyone believes you have some glorious future ahead of you. Maybe you do. Regardless, if I can't stop you from being a guardian, I *can* affect whose guardian you are."

I stiffened. "What are you saying? Are you threatening me?" I spoke the words tentatively, not as a challenge. She couldn't be serious. Taking me away from Lissa during the field experience was one thing, but we were talking about an entirely different matter now.

"I'm just saying I have a great interest in Vasilisa's future, that's all. And if I have to protect her from corrupting influences, I will. We can find her another guardian. We can find you another Moroi."

"You can't do that!" I exclaimed. I could tell by the look on her face that she was happy to finally get a real reaction out of me. I was both angry and afraid, and I fought hard against my normal explosive instincts. Diplomacy and honesty were what I needed now. "I'm not doing anything with Adrian. Really. You can't punish me for something I'm not doing." I quickly remembered to add: "Your Majesty."

"I don't want to punish you at all, Rose. I just want to make sure we understand each other. Moroi men don't marry dhampir girls. They play with them. Every girl thinks it's going to be different with her—even your mother did with Ibrahim, but she was wrong too."

"With who?" I asked, the name hitting me like a slap in the face. Ibrahim? I'd never even heard of that name, let alone someone called that. I wanted to ask who he was and what his connection to my mother was, but Tatiana just kept talking.

"They're always wrong. And you can try your hardest to change that, but it's a waste of time." She shook her head, like she felt sorry for these dhampir girls, but her smug air contradicted any true sympathy. "You can use your pretty face and easy body as much as you want, but in the end, you're the one who'll get used. He may say he loves you now, but in the end, he'll get tired of you. Save yourself the grief. I'm doing you a favor."

"But he isn't saying he loves—" There was no point. The ironic thing here was that I was fairly certain Adrian did just want to use me for sex. I didn't have any delusions about that. But seeing as I wasn't actually sleeping with him, there was no problem—except, well, that Tatiana seemed to see of all this as a problem. I sighed, suspecting no argument was going to make her believe that I wasn't interested in Adrian. "Look, if you're so certain we can't have a future together, then why are you telling me this? According to you, he's going to throw me away anyway. Your Majesty."

She hesitated for just a second, and I nearly laughed. Despite her trash-talking about me, my mom, and other dhampirs, some part of her really was worried that I might indeed be charming and pretty enough to seduce Adrian into a disgraceful marriage. She quickly hid her uncertainty.

"I like to take care of things before they become messy, that's all. Besides, it's going to make things easier for him and Vasilisa if they aren't dragging around baggage from you."

Whoa, whoa. My moment of brief satisfaction shattered— into confusion. I was as lost now as I'd been when she first started accusing me of being involved with Adrian.

"Him and . . . Vasilisa? Lissa? What are you talking about?" I forgot the *Your Majesty*, but I don't think she cared at this point.

"The two of them are an excellent match," she said, sounding like she was about ready to purchase some artwork. "Despite your bad influence, Vasilisa's grown into a very promising young woman. She has a very serious, very dedicated nature that will cure some of his recklessness. And being together would allow them to continue examining their . . . unusual magical situation."

Five minutes ago, me marrying Adrian had been the craziest thing I'd ever heard. It had just been trumped, however, by the thought of Lissa marrying Adrian.

"Lissa and Adrian. Together. You can't be serious. Your Majesty."

"If they're both here together, I think they'll come around to it. They already have a certain charisma around each other. Plus, both of Adrian's grandmothers came from branches of the Dragomir family. He has more than enough blood to help her carry on the Dragomir line."

"So does Christian Ozera." In one of their more disgustingly cute moments, Lissa and Christian had looked up his family tree to see if he had enough Dragomir genes to be able to pass on the name. When they found out he did, they'd then starting naming their future children. It had been horrible. I'd left after Lissa told me they'd name their third daughter after me.

"Christian Ozera?" That condescending smile of hers tightened. "There is no way Vasilisa Dragomir is going to marry him."

"Well, yeah. Not anytime soon. I mean, they're going to go to college and—"

"Not now, not ever," interrupted Tatiana. "The Dragomirs are an ancient and exalted line of royalty. Their last descendent is not going to attach herself to someone like him."

"He's royal," I said in a low voice that was on the verge of becoming my scary voice. For whatever reason, her insulting Christian made me angrier than her insulting me. "The Ozera line is every bit as important as the Dragomirs and Ivashkovs. He's royal, just like Lissa, like Adrian, and like you."

She snorted. "He is *not* like us. Yes, the Ozeras are one of the royal houses, and yes, he has several respectable distant cousins. But we aren't talking about them. We're talking about the son of someone who purposely became a Strigoi. Do you know how many times that's happened in my lifetime? Nine. Nine in fifty years. And his parents were two of them."

"Yes—his *parents*," I said. "Not him."

"It doesn't matter. The Dragomir princess cannot associate with someone like him. That position is simply too prestigious."

"But your nephew is the perfect choice," I said bitterly. "Your Majesty."

"If you're such a smart girl, then you tell me—back at St. Vladimir's, how are they treated? How do your classmates view Christian? How do they view Christian and Vasilisa together?" Her eyes gleamed knowingly.

"Fine," I said. "They have lots of friends."

"And Christian is fully accepted?"

Immediately, I thought of Jesse and Ralf grilling me about Christian. And yes, there were plenty of people who still avoided Christian like he was already Strigoi. It was why he'd had no partner in culinary science. I tried to hide my thoughts, but my hesitation had given me away.

"You see?" she exclaimed. "And that's just a microcosm of society. Imagine it on a bigger scale. Imagine how it'll be when she's active in the government and trying to get others to support her. He'll be a liability. She'll make enemies just because of him. Do you really want that to happen to her?"

It was exactly what Christian had feared, and I denied it now as much as I had to him. "It won't happen. You're wrong."

"And you're very young, Miss Hathaway. You're also delaying your flight." She moved toward the door. The guardians across the room were by her side in the blink of an eye. "I have nothing more to say and hope this will be the last time we ever have a discussion like this." *Or any discussion,* I thought.

She left, and as soon as etiquette said I could go, I sprinted off to catch my plane. My head reeled as I went. How insane was that lady? Not only was she convinced that I was on the verge of eloping with Adrian, she also believed that she could work some kind of arranged marriage with him and Lissa. It was almost impossible to figure out which part of that conversation had been the most ridiculous.

I could hardly wait to tell the others what had happened and have a good laugh over it. But, as I returned to my room to get my bag, I reconsidered. There was already so much gossip about me and Adrian going around; I didn't think I should be fueling the fire. I also didn't think Christian should hear about this. He was already insecure about his position with Lissa. How would he feel if he found out the queen was already making plans to get rid of him?

So I decided to sit on the information for a while, which was hard because Lissa was practically waiting outside my door when I got back.

"Hey," I said. "I thought you'd be on the plane?"

"Nope. They delayed it by a few hours."

"Oh." Going home suddenly sounded like the best idea ever.

"What'd the queen want?" asked Lissa.

"To congratulate me," I said glibly. "Over my Strigoi kills. I didn't expect that from her—it was kind of weird."

"Not that weird," she said. "What you did was amazing. I'm sure she just wanted to recognize you for what you did."

"Yeah, I guess. So what's going on? What are we going to do with the extra time?" There was excitement in both her eyes and her feelings, and I welcomed a change in subject.

"Well . . . I was thinking. Since we're at the Royal Court . . . don't you want to check it out? There's gotta be more to it than a bar and a coffee shop. Seems like we should know this stuff if we're going to be living here. Besides, we've got a lot to celebrate."

The full force of our situation hit me. I'd been so distracted by Victor that I hadn't even really let things sink in: We were at the Royal Court, the center of Moroi leadership. It was nearly as big as the Academy, and there had to be more to it than the all-business side we'd seen so far. Plus, she was right. We had a lot to be happy about. Victor had been put away. She'd gotten a sweet college deal. Only my alleged affair with Adrian had been a downside, but I was willing to put that aside as Lissa's contagious excitement seized me.

"Where's Christian?" I asked.

"Doing his own thing," she said. "You think we need him along?"

"Well, he usually *is* along lately."

"Yeah," she admitted, "but I'd kind of like just us to hang out." I sensed the thoughts behind her decision. Our brief conversation just before she'd gone to see the queen had made her nostalgic for the old days, back when it had just been the two of us on our own.

"No complaints here," I said. "How much can we cover in three hours?"

A mischievous grin lit her face. "The essentials." I could tell she had something special in mind, but she was trying to keep it in hidden. She couldn't block me out of the bond, but she had learned that if she didn't think too *hard* about certain things, then I wouldn't pick up on them easily. She liked being able to think that she could surprise me sometimes. Trying to hide big issues or problems from me never worked, though.

We set back out into the cold weather, with Lissa leading the way. She steered us away from the administrative buildings, off toward some others set at the farther end of the Court's grounds.

"The queen lives in that first building," Lissa explained. "It's not exactly a palace but the closest we have. Back when the Court was in Europe, Moroi royalty used to live in castles."

I made a face. "You make that sound like a good thing."

"Stone walls? Turrets? Even you have to admit that sounds pretty neat."

"Yeah, but I bet they had crap Internet access."

Lissa shook her head at me, smiling, and didn't dignify my comment with a response. We passed some other buildings that had the same ornate stonework as the others but were tall and built in a style that reminded me of apartments. She confirmed as much.

"Those are town houses, where people who live here year-round stay."

I eyed them, wondering what they were like on the inside, and a happy thought came to me. "You think that's where we'll live?"

The thought caught her off guard, but she soon grew just as excited as me. She, too, liked the idea of us having our own place, free to decorate it and come and go as we wanted. I rather liked the idea of Dimitri living with us too, but here at Court, he wouldn't be with her 24/7. For that matter, I actually wouldn't need to be with her 24/7 either. Would they let me live with her? Or would this be another chance to show I wasn't needed?

"I hope so," she said, oblivious to my worries. "Top floor with a view."

I mustered another smile. "And a pool."

"How can you think about a pool in this weather?"

"Hey, if we're fantasizing here, we might as well go the whole way. I bet Tatiana's got one. I bet she wears a bikini and has hot guys rubbing her down with suntan lotion."

I expected another eye roll, but Lissa just grinned as she led me into a building that was near the town houses. "Funny you mention that."

"What?" I exclaimed. She was about ready to burst with her secret. I was *this* close to pulling it out of her mind. I would have, too, if I hadn't been so stunned by our surroundings. It was sensory overload: delicate music, fountains, plants, people in white robes, everything gleaming and silver . . .

It was a spa, a full-fledged luxury spa hidden away in an old stone building here at Court. Who would have guessed? A long granite receptionist's desk guarded the entrance, so we only had a partial view, but what I could see was pretty sweet. Women sat along a wall getting pedicures and manicures. Moroi men and women were getting haircuts and color. What looked like a maze of halls could just be seen in the back of the salon, with a directory of arrows pointing to other sections: massage, sauna, facials, etc.

Lissa grinned at me. "What do you think?"

"I think Adrian was right about the Court having all sorts of secrets." I gave a mock sigh. "And I *hate* having to admit that he's right."

"You've been so down about the field experience and . . . other stuff." She didn't have to mention Mason's death and the Strigoi fight. I read it from her mind. "I figured you could use a treat. I checked their openings here while you were with the queen, and they were able to squeeze us in."

Lissa walked up to the receptionist and told her who we were. The woman immediately recognized our names but seemed surprised to be letting a dhampir in. I didn't care, though. I was too bedazzled by the sights and sounds around me. Compared to the harsh, practical lifestyle I usually led, this sort of luxury almost defied belief.

After checking in, Lissa turned to me, face eager and radiant. "I got us set up to get massages with these—"

"Nails," I interrupted.

"What?"

"I want my nails done. Can I get a manicure?"

It was the most exotic, completely useless thing I could imagine. Well, it wasn't useless for ordinary women. But for me? With the way I used my hands and subjected them to blisters, bruises, dirt, and wind? Yes. Useless. I hadn't painted my nails in ages. There was no reason. Half the nail polish would probably chip off after one practice session. A novice like me couldn't afford that kind of luxury. And that was why I so, so desperately wanted one. Seeing Lissa wear makeup had awakened that longing in me for some beautification of my own. I accepted that it could never be a regular part of my life, but if I was in a place like this today, then by God, I wanted my nails done.

Lissa faltered a little. She'd apparently had big plans for this massage thing. But, she had a hard time refusing me and spoke to the receptionist again. It sounded like the receptionist had to do a bit of juggling with her schedule, but she said she could make it work.

"Of course, Princess." She smiled happily, entranced by Lissa's natural charisma. Half the time, Lissa didn't even need spirit to get people to help her.

"I don't want to be an inconvenience," Lissa said.

"No, no. Definitely not!"

We soon found ourselves sitting at adjacent tables while Moroi women soaked our hands in hot water and started scrubbing them with weird combinations of sugar and seaweed.

"Why the manicure?" Lissa wanted to know. I explained my reasoning to her, about how I hardly had time for makeup anymore and how the abuse my hands went through made any sort of pampering impractical. Her face turned thoughtful. "I never thought about that before. I just figured you weren't into it lately. Or, well, that you didn't need it. Not with your looks."

"Whatever," I said. "You're the one guys worship."

"Because of my name. You're the one that guys—like a certain one we know—actually want for other reasons."

Gee, I wondered who she could be referring to. "Yeah, but those other reasons aren't very noble."

She shrugged. "The point's the same. You don't need makeup for them to drool all over you."

Then I felt the weirdest thing through the bond. I saw myself through her eyes. It was like looking in a mirror, except she only had a profile view of me. But when she looked at me, she really did think I was beautiful. With my tan and dark brown hair, I seemed exotic to her. She felt pale and washed out compared to me, skinny next to my curves. It was surreal, considering how often I felt scruffy next to her luminous beauty. Her envy wasn't malicious; that wasn't in her nature. It was more wistful, an admiration of a look she could never have.

I wanted to reassure her but had a feeling she didn't want me knowing about her insecurities. Besides, my thoughts were interrupted when the woman doing my nails asked what color I wanted. I picked a color that looked like gold glitter. Gaudy, perhaps, but I actually thought it looked kind of cool, and it wasn't like it was going to last long anyway. Lissa picked pale pink, a color as refined and elegant as she was. Hers got painted a lot faster than mine, though, because my manicurist had to spend so long softening my hands and filing the nails. Lissa finished long before I did.

When we both had glamorous hands, we proudly held them up side by side. "You look gorgeous, darling," she declared, affecting a sophisticated air.

Laughing, we went off to the massage area. Lissa had originally scheduled us for extensive massages, but the manicure had cut into a chunk of that time. So we modified the full-body massage into a foot massage, which was just as well since we couldn't have put on robes or any other changes of clothes with our nails still wet. All we had to do was remove our shoes and roll up our pants. I sat down in a chair while my feet soaked in warm, bubbling water. Someone put something into the tub that smelled like violets, but I didn't pay much attention. I was too entranced by my hands. They were perfect. The manicurist had buffed and hydrated them to silky softness, and my nails had been transformed into gleaming gold ovals.

"Rose," I heard Lissa say.

"Hmm?" The lady had also put a clear coat of nail polish over the gold. I wondered if that would give the nails a longer lease on life.

"Rose."

Sensing that Lissa wanted my undivided attention, I finally looked up from my awesome hands. She was grinning from ear to ear. I could feel that excited news burning in her again, the secret she'd had while we'd been walking over here.

"What's up?" I asked.

She nodded downward. "Rose, this is Ambrose."

I glanced absentmindedly toward the masseuse at my feet. "Hey, Ambrose, how's it—" I cut myself off before the words *holy crap* or *whoa* left my lips.

The guy massaging my feet couldn't have been much older than me. He had curly black hair and muscles everywhere. I knew this for a fact because he was shirtless and offered us both a good view of his sculpted pecs and biceps. His deep golden skin was a color achievable only by excessive time in the sun, indicating he was human. The bite marks on his neck confirmed it. A pretty boy feeder. *Very* pretty.

His attractiveness was almost unreal, though. Dimitri was gorgeous, but he had little flaws that made him that much more gorgeous. Ambrose was too perfect, like a piece of art. I didn't want to throw myself into his arms or anything, but he was certainly nice to look at.

Lissa, still worried about my love life, had apparently thought this was exactly what I needed. Her masseuse was female.

"It's very nice to meet you, Rose," said Ambrose. He had a musical voice.

"It's nice to meet you too," I said, suddenly self-conscious as he lifted my feet out of the water and toweled them off. I was especially self-conscious of the appearance of my feet.

They weren't gross or anything, since they weren't usually exposed to the elements like my hands. I just kind of wished they'd been polished up too if this male model was going to handle them so much.

Lissa, astute enough to sense me being flustered, could barely stop from laughing. I heard her thoughts in my head: *Cute, huh?* I cut her a look, refusing to voice my thoughts out loud. *He's Tatiana's personal masseuse. That practically makes you royalty.* I sighed loudly to let her know she wasn't as funny as she thought she was. *And when I say personal, I mean personal.*

I jerked in surprise, accidentally kicking one of my feet out. Ambrose's deft hands caught it before I hit him in his pretty face, thankfully. I might not have been able to communicate telepathically, but I was pretty sure there could be no question to Lissa that the look on my face said, *You can't be serious because if you are, you're in big trouble.*

Her grin widened. *I thought you'd like that. Pampered by the queen's secret lover.*

Pampered wasn't exactly the word that came to mind. Looking at Ambrose's young, beautiful features, I just couldn't picture him getting it on with that old hag. Of course, that denial might have just been my brain's way of refusing to acknowledge that someone who had touched her was now touching me. Ew.

Ambrose's hands were checking out my calves along with my feet, and he struck up a conversation about what elegant legs I had. His dazzling white smile never left his face, but most of my answers were curt. I still couldn't get over the thought of him and Tatiana together.

Silently, Lissa groaned. *He's flirting with you, Rose!* she thought to me. *What are you doing? You can do better than that. I went to all this trouble to get you the hottest guy here, and this is what I get!*

This one-sided-conversation thing was becoming a pain in the ass. I wanted to tell her that I'd never asked for her to rent out this guy for me. In fact, I suddenly had images of the queen calling me in for another meeting to yell at me for having a nonexistent affair with Ambrose too. Wouldn't that be perfect?

Ambrose continued smiling as he rubbed the soles of one foot with his thumbs. It hurt—but in a good way. I hadn't realized how sore that spot was. "They go to such trouble to make sure you wear the right black and white clothes, but no one ever thinks about your feet," he mused. "How are you supposed to stand around all day *and* still manage roundhouse kicks and cat stances in bad shoes?"

I was about to tell them that he really didn't need to keep worrying about my feet, but something odd suddenly struck me. "Roundhouse kicks" and "cat stances" weren't top-secret guardian terms. Anyone could Google "martial arts" and find out about those kinds of things. Still, it wasn't the kind of topic I'd expect a Moroi to casually throw around, let alone a feeder. I studied Ambrose closer, noting the way his dark eyes so carefully darted around and observed everything. I recalled his fast reflexes in stopping my kick.

I felt my jaw start to drop, and I shut it before I looked like an idiot.

"You're a dhampir," I breathed.

SIXTEEN

"SO ARE YOU," HE TEASED.

"Yeah, but I just thought—"

"That I was human? Because of the bite marks?"

"Yeah," I admitted. No point in lying.

"We all have to survive," he said. "And dhampirs are good at figuring out ways to."

"Yeah, but most of us become guardians," I pointed out. "Especially men." I still couldn't believe he was a dhampir—or that I hadn't spotted it right away.

Long ago, dhampirs had been born from humans and Moroi getting together. We were half-vampire, half-human. Over time, Moroi started keeping themselves separate from humans. Humans grew too plentiful and no longer needed Moroi for magic. Moroi now feared they'd become human experiments if ever discovered. So no more dhampirs were being made that way, and in a bizarre genetic twist, dhampirs getting together with dhampirs couldn't make more dhampirs.

The only way my race kept reproducing was through Moroi mixing with dhampirs. Normal logic would make you think that a dhampir and a Moroi would make children who were ¾ Moroi. Nope. We came out with perfect dhampir genes, half and half, mixing some of the best traits of both races. Most dhampirs came from dhampir women and Moroi men. For centuries, these women had sent their kids off to be raised somewhere else, so that the mothers could go back to being guardians. That's what mine had done.

Over time, though, some dhampir women had decided they wanted to raise their children themselves. They refused to be guardians and instead banded together in communities. That's what Dimitri's mother had done. Lots of ugly rumors surrounded these women because Moroi men often visited in the hopes of getting cheap sex. Dimitri had told me that a lot of these stories were exaggerated and that most dhampir women weren't that easy. The rumors came from the fact that these women were almost always single mothers who had no contact with their kids' fathers—and because some dhampirs would let Moroi drink blood during sex. It was a kinky, dirty thing in our culture and was where the nickname for these non-guardian dhampirs had come from: blood whores.

But I'd never even thought about a *male* blood whore.

My mind was reeling. "Most guys who don't want to be guardians just run off," I said. It was rare, but it happened. Guys bailed on guardian school and disappeared to hide out among humans. It was another disgraceful thing.

"I didn't want to run off," said Ambrose, seeming very cheerful about all this. "But I didn't want to fight Strigoi either. So I did this."

Beside me, Lissa was stunned. Blood whores stayed on the

fringes of our world. Having one right in front of her—a guy, no less—was incredible.

"This is better than being a guardian?" I asked in disbelief.

"Well, let's see. Guardians spend all their time watching out for others, risking their lives, and wearing bad shoes. Me? I have great shoes, am currently massaging a pretty girl, and sleep in an awesome bed."

I made a face. "Let's not talk about where you sleep, okay?"

"And giving blood isn't as bad as you think. I don't give as much as a feeder, but the high's pretty neat."

"Let's not talk about that either," I said. No way would I admit that I knew Moroi bites were indeed "pretty neat."

"Fine. But say what you want, my life's good." He gave me a lopsided smile.

"But aren't people, like . . . well, aren't they mean to you? They must say things. . . ."

"Oh yes," he agreed. "Horrible things. I get called a lot of ugly names. But you know where I get the most grief from? Other dhampirs. Moroi tend to leave me alone."

"That's because they don't understand what it's like to be a guardian, how important it is." It occurred to me, with some unease, that I sounded exactly like my mother. "It's what dhampirs are meant to do."

Ambrose rose, unkinking his legs and giving me a face full of muscled chest. "You sure? How would you like to find out what you're really meant to do? I know someone who might be able to tell you."

"Ambrose, don't do it," groaned Lissa's manicurist. "That woman's crazy."

"She's psychic, Eve."

"She's not psychic, and you *cannot* take the Dragomir princess to go see her."

"The queen herself goes to her for advice," he argued back.

"That's a mistake too," grumbled Eve.

Lissa and I exchanged looks. She'd latched onto the word *psychic*. Psychics and fortune-tellers were generally regarded with the same disbelief as ghosts—except that Lissa and I had recently learned that psychic abilities we'd previously believed to be fantasy were actually part of spirit. Hope that she might have stumbled onto another spirit user shot through Lissa.

"We'd love to see a psychic. Can we go? Please?" Lissa glanced at a nearby clock. "And soon? We have a flight to catch."

Eve clearly thought it was a waste of our time, but Ambrose could hardly wait to show us. We put our shoes back on and were led out of the massage area. The spa rooms had been in a maze of halls behind the front salon, and we soon found ourselves in another maze that was farther back still.

"There's no directory here," I said as we walked past closed doors. "What are these rooms for?"

"Everything and anything people will pay money for," he

said.

"Like what?"

"Ah, Rose. You're such an innocent."

We finally reached a door at the end of the hall. We stepped inside and found a small room that only held a desk. A closed door sat beyond it. A Moroi at the desk looked up, obviously recognizing Ambrose. He walked over to her, and the two got into a quiet argument as he tried to get her to let us in.

Lissa turned to me, keeping her voice soft. "What do you think?"

My eyes were on Ambrose. "That all that muscle's going to waste."

"Forget the blood whore thing already. I mean about this psychic. Do you think we've found another spirit user?" she asked eagerly.

"If a party boy like Adrian can be a spirit user, then a woman who tells the future probably can be too."

Ambrose returned to us, grinning. "Suzanne was happy to fit you into the schedule before your flight. It'll be just a minute while Rhonda finishes up with her current client."

Suzanne didn't look very happy about fitting us in, but I didn't have time to ponder that because the inner door opened and an older Moroi man walked out, entranced. He gave Suzanne some cash, nodded at the rest of us, and left. Ambrose stood and made a wide sweeping motion toward the door.

"Your turn."

Lissa and I walked inside the other room. Ambrose followed and closed the door behind us. It was like walking into someone's heart. Everything was red. Plush red carpet, a red velvet couch, velvet brocade wallpaper, and red satin cushions on the floor. Sitting on the cushions was a Moroi in her forties, with curly black hair and equally dark eyes. There was a very faint olive cast to her skin, but her overall look was pale, like all Moroi. Her black clothing stood out in stark contrast to the red room, and jewelry the color of my nails gleamed on her neck and hands. I expected her to speak in a spooky, mysterious voice—one with an exotic accent—but her words sounded blandly American.

"Please, sit down." She pointed to some cushions across from her. Ambrose sat on the couch. "Who've you brought?" she asked him as Lissa and I settled down.

"Princess Vasilisa Dragomir, and her guardian-to-be, Rose. They need a fast fortune."

"Why do you always want to rush these things?" Rhonda asked.

"Hey, it's not me. They have a plane to catch."

"It'd be the same if you didn't. You're always in a rush."

I shook off my awe of the room enough to pay attention to their easy banter and similar hair. "Are you guys related?"

"This is my aunt," said Ambrose fondly. "She adores me." Rhonda rolled her eyes.

That was a surprise. Dhampirs rarely had contact with their extended Moroi family, but then, Ambrose was hardly normal. Lissa was intrigued by all of this too, but her interest was different from mine. She was studying Rhonda intently, trying to find any indication that the woman might be a spirit user.

"Are you a gypsy?" I asked.

Rhonda made a face and began shuffling some cards. "I'm Roma," she said. "A lot of people call us gypsies, though the term isn't exactly accurate. And really, I'm Moroi first." She gave the cards a few more shuffles, then handed them to Lissa. "Cut, please."

Lissa was still staring, half-hoping she might see an aura. Adrian could sense other spirit users, but she didn't have that skill yet. She cut the cards and handed them back. Rhonda put the deck back together and dealt out three cards to Lissa.

I leaned forward. "Cool." They were tarot cards. I didn't know much about them, only that they supposedly had mystical powers and could tell the future. I didn't believe in that stuff much more than I'd ever believed in religion, but then, until recently, I'd never really believed in ghosts, either.

The three cards were the Moon, the Empress, and the Ace of Cups. Ambrose leaned over my shoulder to peer at the cards. "Ooh," he said. "Very interesting."

Rhonda glanced up at him. "Hush. You don't know what you're talking about." She turned back to the cards and tapped the Ace of Cups. "You're on the verge of a new beginning, a rebirth of great power and emotion. Your life will change, but it will be a change that takes you in a direction that, while difficult, will ultimately illuminate the world."

"Whoa," I said.

Rhonda then pointed to the Empress. "Power and leadership lie ahead of you, which you will handle with grace and intelligence. The seeds are already in place, though there's an edge of uncertainty—an enigmatic set of influences that hang around you like mist." Her attention was on the Moon as she said those words. "But my overall impression is that those unknown factors won't deter you from your destiny."

Lissa's eyes were wide. "You can tell that just from the cards?"

Rhonda shrugged. "It's in the cards, yes, but I also have a gift that lets me see forces beyond what ordinary people can perceive."

She shuffled the cards again and then handed them to me to cut. I did, and she flipped three more over. The Nine of Swords, the Sun, and the Ace of Swords. The Sun card was upside down.

Now, I knew nothing about this stuff, but I immediately got the feeling I was about to get a raw deal compared to Lissa. The Empress card had shown a woman in a long dress, with stars on her head. The Moon had shown a full moon with two dogs below it, and the Ace of Cups had shown a bejeweled chalice filled with flowers.

Meanwhile, my Nine of Swords showed a woman sobbing in front of a wall of swords, and the Ace of Swords was a boring hand holding a plain iron sword. The Sun at least looked cheerful. It had what looked like an angel riding a white horse, with a brilliant sun shining above.

"Shouldn't that be flipped right-side up?" I asked.

"No," she said, eyes on the cards. After several moments of heavy silence, she said, "You will destroy that which is undead."

I waited about thirty seconds for her to continue, but she didn't. "Wait, that's it?"

She nodded. "That's what the cards say to me."

I pointed at them. "Seems like they've got a little bit more to say than that. You gave Lissa a whole encyclopedia worth of information! And I already know I'm going to kill the undead. That's my job." Bad enough I'd gotten a minuscule fortune. It was also totally unoriginal.

Rhonda shrugged, as though that were some sort of explanation.

I started to say that she'd better not even think about charging me for that crap reading when there was a soft knock at the door. It opened, and to my surprise, Dimitri stuck his head inside. His eyes fell on Lissa and me. "Ah, they said you were in here." He walked in and noticed Rhonda. To my further surprise, he gave her a low nod of respect and said very politely, "I'm sorry to interrupt, but I need to bring these two to their flight."

Rhonda examined him—but not in a checking-him-out kind of way. It was more like he was mystery she wanted to figure out. "There's nothing to apologize for. But maybe you've got time for a reading of your own?"

With our similar views on religion, I expected Dimitri to tell her he had no time for her scam-artist fortune-telling. Yet the look on his face stayed serious, and he finally nodded, sitting down beside me, letting me smell the sweet scent of leather and aftershave. "Thank you." His words were still perfectly polite.

"I'll be brief." Rhonda was already shuffling up my useless cards. In record time, she had them ready for cutting and had dealt out three cards in front of Dimitri. The Knight of Rods, the Wheel of Fortune, and the Five of Cups. I couldn't get a feel for these. The Knight of Rods was what it sounded like, a man on horseback with a long wooden spear. The Wheel of Fortune was a circle with strange symbols floating in the clouds. The Five of Cups showed five knocked-over cups spilling some kind of liquid out while a man stood with his back to them.

Her eyes flicked over the cards, looked at Dimitri, then looked back at the cards. Her expression was blank. "You will lose what you value most, so treasure it while you can." She pointed to the Wheel of Fortune card. "The wheel is turning, always turning."

The reading wasn't as good as Lissa's, but he'd gotten a hell of a lot more than me. Lissa elbowed me in a silent warning to be quiet, which startled me at first. Without even realizing it, I'd opened my mouth to protest. I shut it and glowered.

Dimitri's face was dark and thoughtful as he stared at the cards. I didn't know if he knew anything about this stuff, but he was staring at the images as though they really held all the secrets of the world. At last, he gave Rhonda another respectful nod. "Thank you."

She nodded back, and then the three of us rose to catch our flight. Ambrose told us the readings were on him and that he'd settle up with Suzanne afterward. "It was worth it," he told me. "Worth it to see you think twice about your fate."

I scoffed. "No offense, but those cards didn't make me think much about anything." Like everything else, this just made him laugh.

We were about to leave Suzanne's little waiting room when Lissa suddenly dashed back to Rhonda's open doorway. I followed after her.

"Um, excuse me," Lissa said.

Rhonda looked up from more shuffling, her face troubled. "Yes?"

"This is going to sound weird, but . . . um, could you tell me what element you specialized in?"

I could feel Lissa holding her breath. She so, so wanted Rhonda to say she *hadn't* specialized, which was often the sign of having spirit. There was still so much to learn, and Lissa loved the ideas of finding others who could teach her—and she especially loved the idea of someone teaching her to foretell the future.

"Air," said Rhonda. A soft breezed rustled through our hair to prove the point. "Why?"

Lissa let go of her breath, disappointment washing over me through her link. "No reason. Thank you again."

SEVENTEEN

OUT ON THE RUNWAY, Christian stood near the entrance to the plane, along with a few of the other guardians. Lissa ran off to talk to him, leaving me and Dimitri alone. He hadn't said a word the entire way back from the spa. Strong and silent were typical behaviors for him, but something about his mood struck me as unusual this time.

"Are you still thinking about what Rhonda said? That woman's a total scam."

"Why do you say that?" he asked, stopping not far from where the others stood. A sharp wind blasted us all in the face, and I hoped we could board soon.

"Because she didn't tell us anything! You should have heard my future. It was, like, one sentence stating the obvious. Lissa had a better fortune," I admitted, "but it wasn't really anything that profound. Rhonda said she'd be a great leader. I mean, seriously, how hard is that to figure out?"

Dimitri smiled at me. "Would you be a believer if she'd given you a more interesting reading?"

"Maybe if it was good." When he just laughed, I asked, "But you're taking it seriously. Why? You really believe in that kind of stuff?"

"It's not so much that I believe . . . or that I don't believe."

He wore a black knit cap over his head today and tugged it down to better cover his ears. "I just respect people like her. They have access to knowledge other people don't."

"She's not a spirit user, though, so I'm not really sure where she's getting this knowledge. I still think she's a con artist."

"She's a *vrăjitoare*, actually."

"A..." I wasn't even going to touch that one. "A what? Is that Russian?"

"Romanian. It means ... well, there's no real translation. 'Witch' is close, but that's not right. Their idea of a witch isn't the same as an American's."

I had *never* expected to have a conversation like this with him. I just didn't think of Dimitri as the superstitious type. For half a moment, I thought that if he could believe in something like witches and fortune-tellers, maybe he could handle me seeing ghosts. I considered saying something to him but promptly decided against it. I wouldn't have had a chance to say anything anyway because Dimitri kept talking.

"My grandmother was like Rhonda," he explained. "That is, she practiced the same kind of arts. Personality-wise, they're very different."

"Your grandmother was a ... v-whatever?"

"It's called something else in Russian, but yes, same meaning. She used to read cards and give advice too. It was how she made her living."

I bit off any comments about frauds. "Was she right? In

her predictions?"

"Sometimes. Don't look at me like that."

"Like what?"

"You've got this look on your face that says you think I'm delusional, but you're too nice to say anything."

"Delusional's kind of harsh. I'm just surprised, that's all. I never expected you to buy into this stuff."

"Well, I grew up with it, so it doesn't seem that strange to me. And like I said, I'm not sure I buy into it 100 percent."

Adrian had joined the group by the plane and was protesting loudly about us not being able to board yet.

"I never thought of you as having a grandmother, either," I told Dimitri. "I mean, obviously, you'd have to. But still . . . it's just weird to think about growing up with one." Contact with my own mother was rare enough, and I'd never even met any of my other family members. "Was it weird having a witch grandma? Scary? Was she always, like, threatening to cast spells if you were bad?"

"Most of the time she just threatened to send me to my room."

"That doesn't sound so scary to me."

"That's because you haven't met her."

I noted the wording. "Is she still alive?"

He nodded. "Yeah. It'll take more than old age to kill her off. She's tough. She was actually a guardian for a while."

"Really?" Much like with Ambrose, my fixed ideas about dhampirs, guardians, and blood whores were getting muddled. "So she gave it up to become a—uh, to stay with her kids?"

"She has very strong ideas about family—ideas that probably sound kind of sexist to you. She believes all dhampirs should train and put in time as guardians, but that the women should eventually return home to raise their children together."

"But not the men?"

"No," he said wryly. "She thinks men still need to stay out there and kill Strigoi."

"Wow." I remembered Dimitri telling me a little about his family. His father had popped back every so often, but that was about it for the men in his life. All of his siblings were sisters. And honestly, the idea didn't sound so sexist. I had the same ideas about men going off to fight, which was why meeting Ambrose had been so weird. "You were the one who had to go. The women in your family kicked you out."

"Hardly," he laughed. "My mother would take me back in a second if I wanted to come home." He was smiling like it was a joke, but I saw something in his eyes that looked a lot like homesickness. It was gone in a flash, though, as Dimitri turned around when Adrian started whooping about how we could finally board.

When we were settled on the plane, Lissa could hardly wait to tell our friends about the news. She started off with how I'd been called in to see the queen. That wasn't a topic I'd wanted discussed, but she pushed forward, excited that the queen had wanted to "praise" me. Everyone seemed impressed except Adrian. The look on his face told me that he was sure that she most definitely hadn't called me in for that. However, there was enough of a puzzled look in his eyes to make me think he had no clue about the real reason. It was about time I knew something he didn't. I had a feeling he would have been as shocked by the idea of him hooking up with Lissa as I'd been.

Lissa then told them about the offer to live at Court and go to college at Lehigh. "I still can't believe it," she mused. "It sounds too good to be true."

Adrian knocked back a glass of what looked like whiskey. How had he gotten a hold of that so soon? "Coming from my great-aunt? It *is* too good to be true."

"What do you mean?" I asked. After being accused of being engaged in a fictitious romance by Tatiana and finding out she had a dhampir lover/feeder, nothing about her would surprise me anymore. "Is Lissa in trouble?"

"What, bodily? Nah. It's just, my great-aunt doesn't do things out of the kindness of her heart. Well," Adrian amended, "sometimes she does. She's not a total bitch. And I think she means it about worrying about the Dragomirs. I've heard she liked your parents. But as to why she's doing this . . . I don't know. You've got radical ideas. Maybe she does want to hear different opinions. Or maybe she wants to keep an eye on you, keep you from causing trouble." *Or maybe she wants to marry Lissa off to you*, I silently added.

Christian didn't like any of this. "He's right. They could

be trying to rein you in. You should go live with Aunt Tasha. You don't have to go to a Moroi school."

"But she'll be safer if she does," I admitted.

I was all for fighting the system—and keeping Lissa away from royal plans—but if she went to a college that wasn't one the Moroi protected, she'd be in danger, and I certainly didn't want that either. I started to add more, but just then, the plane took off. As soon as it was up in the air, my headache from yesterday returned. It was like all the air around us pressing on my skull.

"Son of a bitch," I groaned, putting my hand on my forehead.

"You're sick again?" asked Lissa, worried. I nodded.

"Have you always had trouble flying?" asked Adrian, gesturing for someone to refill his drink.

"Never," I said. "Damn it. I don't want to go through this again."

I gritted my teeth and tried to ignore the pain, as well as those black shapes again. It took some effort, but if I focused hard enough, I actually got it all to lessen a little. Weird. Still, I didn't want to talk much after that, and everyone left me alone. The college conversation dropped off.

Hours passed. It was almost time to arrive back at the Academy. One of the Moroi flight attendants walked down the aisle to our group, a frown on her face. Alberta instantly snapped to attention. "What's wrong?"

"An ice storm just blew through the area," the flight attendant said. "We can't land at St. Vladimir's because the runway isn't accessible with the ice and the winds. We need fuel, however, so we're going to land at Martinville Regional. It's a small airport a few hours away by car, but they weren't as affected as much. Our plan is to land there, refuel, and then fly into the Academy once they've cleared the runway. It's less than an hour by air."

It was annoying news, but it didn't sound too bad. Besides, what could we do? At the very least, I'd get some relief soon. If my headache behaved like before, it'd go away when we were on the ground. We settled back into our seats and put on our belts, readying for the landing. The weather looked miserable outside, but the pilot was good and landed with no difficulties.

And that's when it happened.

As soon as we touched the ground, my world exploded. The headache didn't go away; it got worse. Much worse—and I hadn't thought that was possible. It felt like my entire skull was being ripped open.

But that was just the beginning. Because suddenly, all around me, were faces. Ghostly, translucent faces and bodies—just like Mason's. And oh God, they were everywhere. I couldn't even see the seats or my friends. Just those faces—and their hands. Pale, shining hands reached out for me. Mouths opened like they would speak, and all of those faces looked as though they wanted something from me.

And the more they came at me, the more of them I started to recognize. I saw Victor's guardians, the ones who had been killed when we'd rescued Lissa. Their eyes were wide and ter-rified—over what? Were they reliving their deaths? Mixed in with them were children I didn't recognize right away. Then— I knew. They were the ones Dimitri and I had found dead after a Strigoi massacre. These children had the same washed-out look Mason had, but their necks were covered in blood, just as they'd been at the house. Its scarlet hue stood out in stark con-trast to their shadowy, luminescent bodies.

Thicker and thicker the faces grew. While none of them actually spoke, there seemed to be a buzzing in my ears that grew louder as more and more of them came. Three new fig-ures joined the crowd. They should have blended into the rest, but they stood out almost as sharply as the blood on the chil-dren's necks had.

It was Lissa's family.

Her mother, her father, and her brother Andre. They looked exactly as they had the last time I'd seen them, just before the car accident. Blond. Beautiful. Regal. Like Mason, they wore no marks of their deaths, even though I knew the crash had done horrible things to them. And like Mason, they just stared at me with sad eyes, not speaking but clearly want-ing to say something. Only, unlike with Mason, I understood the message.

There was a large patch of blackness behind Andre that was steadily growing bigger. He pointed at me, and then he pointed at it. I knew, without understanding how I knew, that it was the entrance to the world of death, the world I had come back from. Andre—who'd been my age when he died—pointed again. His parents joined him. They didn't have to speak for me to know what they were saying: *You shouldn't have lived. You need to come back with us. . . .*

I started screaming. And screaming.

I thought someone on the plane was talking to me, but I couldn't be sure, not when I couldn't see anything but those faces, hands, and the blackness behind Andre. Every so often, Mason's face materialized nearby, solemn and sad. I appealed to him for help.

"Make them go away!" I yelled. "Make them go away!"

But there was nothing he would—or could—do. Frantically, I undid my seat belt and tried to stand up. The ghosts didn't touch me, but they were all too close, still reaching and pointing with skeletal hands. I waved my arms to fend them off, screaming for someone to help me and make this all stop.

There was no help for me, though. No help for all those hands and hollow eyes or the pain that consumed me. It grew so bad that glittering black spots began to dance across my field of vision. I had a feeling I was going to pass out, and I welcomed that. It would make the pain go away and save me from the faces. The spots grew bigger and bigger, and soon I could no longer see anything. The faces disappeared, and so did the pain as sweet black waters dragged me under.

EIGHTEEN

EVERYTHING BECAME FUZZY after that. I had vague impressions of moving in and out of consciousness, of people saying my name, and of being in the air again. Eventually, I woke up in the school's infirmary and found Dr. Olendzki looking down at me.

"Hello, Rose," she said. She was a middle-aged Moroi and often joked that I was her number one patient. "How are you feeling?"

The details of what had happened came back. The faces. Mason. The other ghosts. The terrible pain in my head. All of it was gone.

"Fine," I said, half-surprised to be saying those words. For a moment, I wondered if maybe it had all been a dream. Then I looked beyond her and saw Dimitri and Alberta looming nearby. The looks on their faces told me the events on the plane had indeed been real.

Alberta cleared her throat, and Dr. Olendzki glanced back. "May we?" Alberta asked. The doctor nodded, and the other two stepped forward.

Dimitri, as always, was a balm to me. No matter what happened, I always felt a little safer in his presence. Yet even he hadn't been able to stop what had happened at the airport.

When he looked at me like he was now, with an expression of such tenderness and concern, it triggered mixed feelings. Part of me loved that he cared so much. The other part wanted to be strong for him and didn't want to make him worry.

"Rose . . ." began Alberta uncertainly. I could tell she had no clue how to go about this. What had happened was beyond her realm of experience. Dimitri took over.

"Rose, what happened back there?" Before I could utter a word, he cut me off. "And do *not* say it was nothing this time."

Well, if I couldn't fall back on that answer, then I didn't know what to say.

Dr. Olendzki pushed her glasses up the bridge of her nose. "We only want to help you."

"I don't need any help," I said. "I'm fine." I sounded just like Brandon and Brett. I was probably only one step away from saying, "I fell."

Alberta finally regained herself. "You were fine when we were in the air. When we landed, you were most definitely not fine."

"I'm fine now," I replied stonily, not meeting their eyes.

"What happened then?" she asked. "Why the screaming? What did you mean when you said we needed to make 'them' go away?"

I briefly considered my other fallback answer, the one about stress. That sounded completely stupid now. So, again, I said nothing. To my surprise, I felt tears build up in my eyes.

"Rose," murmured Dimitri, voice as soft as silk against my skin. "Please."

Something in that cracked me. It was so hard for me to stand against him. I turned my head and stared at the ceiling.

"Ghosts," I whispered. "I saw ghosts."

None of them had expected that, but honestly, how could they have? Heavy silence fell. Finally, Dr. Olendzki spoke in a faltering voice.

"W-what do you mean?"

I swallowed. "He's been following me for the last couple of weeks. Mason. On campus. I know it sounds crazy—but it's him. Or his ghost. That's what happened with Stan. I locked up because Mason was there, and I didn't know what to do. On the plane . . . I think he was there too . . . and others. But I couldn't exactly see them when we were in the air. Just glimpses . . . and the headache. But when we landed in Martinville, he was there in full form. And—and he wasn't alone. There were others with him. Other ghosts." A tear escaped from my eye, and I hastily wiped at it, hoping none of them had seen it.

I waited then, not sure what to expect. Would someone laugh? Tell me I was crazy? Accuse me of lying and demand to know what had *really* happened?

"Did you know them?" Dimitri asked finally.

I turned back and actually met his eyes. They were still serious and concerned, no mockery. "Yeah . . . I saw some of Victor's guardians and the people from the massacre. Lissa's . . . Lissa's family was there too."

Nobody said anything after that. They all just sort of exchanged glances, hoping perhaps that one of the others might shed light on all this.

Dr. Olendzki sighed. "Could I speak with the two of you privately?"

The three of them stepped out of the examining room, shutting the door behind them. Only it didn't quite catch. Scrambling off the bed, I crossed the room and stood by the door. The tiny crack was just enough for my dhampir hearing to pick up the conversation. I felt bad about eavesdropping, but they were talking about me, and I couldn't shake the feeling that my future was on the line here.

"—obvious what's going on," hissed Dr. Olendzki. It was the first time I'd ever heard her sound so irate. With patients, she was the picture of serenity. It was hard to imagine her angry, but she was clearly pissed off now. "That poor girl. She's undergoing post-traumatic stress disorder, and it's no wonder after everything that's happened."

"Are you sure?" asked Alberta. "Maybe it's something else. . . ." But as her words trailed off, I could tell she didn't really know of anything else that would explain it.

"Look at the facts: a teenage girl who witnessed one of her friends getting killed and then had to kill his killer. You don't think that's traumatic? You don't think that might have had the *tiniest* effect on her?"

"Tragedy is something all guardians have to deal with," said Alberta.

"Maybe there's not much to be done for guardians in the field, but Rose is still a student here. There are resources that can help her."

"Like what?" asked Dimitri. He sounded curious and concerned, not like he was challenging her.

"Counseling. Talking to someone about what happened can do worlds of good. You should have done that as soon as she got back. You should do it for the others who were with her while you're at it. Why doesn't anyone think of these things?"

"It's a good idea," said Dimitri. I recognized the tone in his voice—his mind was spinning. "She could do it on her day off."

"Day off? More like every day. You should pull her from this entire field experience. Fake Strigoi attacks are not the way to recover from a real one."

"No!" I had pushed open the door before I realized it. They all stared at me, and I immediately felt stupid. I'd just busted myself for spying.

"Rose," said Dr. Olendzki, returning to her caring (but slightly chastising) doctor mode. "You should go lie down."

"I'm fine. And you can't make me quit the field experience. I won't graduate if you do."

"You aren't well, Rose, and there's nothing to be ashamed of after what's happened to you. Thinking you're seeing the ghost of someone who died isn't too out there when you consider the circumstances."

I started to correct her on the *thinking you're seeing* part but then bit it off. Arguing that I'd really seen a ghost wasn't probably going to do me any favors, I decided, even if I was starting to believe that was exactly what I was seeing. Frantically, I tried to think of a convincing reason to stay in the field experience. I was usually pretty good at talking myself out of bad situations.

"Unless you're going to put me in counseling 24/7, you're just going to make it worse. I *need* something to do. Most of my classes are on hold right now. What would I do? Sit around? Think more and more about what happened? I'll go crazy— for real. I don't want to sit on the past forever. I need to get moving with my future."

This threw them into an argument about what to do with me. I listened, biting my tongue, knowing I needed to stay out of it. Finally, with some grumbling from the doctor, they all decided I would go on half-time for the field experience.

It proved to be the ideal compromise for everyone—well, except me. I just wanted life to go on exactly as it had. Still, I knew this was probably as good a deal as I'd get. They decided that I'd do three days of field experience a week, with no night duties. During the other days, I'd have to do some training and whatever bookwork they dug up for me.

I'd also have to see a counselor, which I wasn't thrilled about. It wasn't that I had anything against counselors. Lissa had been seeing one, and it had been really useful for her. Talking things out helped. It was just . . . well, this was just something I didn't want to talk about.

But if it came down to this or being kicked out of the field experience, I was more than happy to go with this. Alberta felt they could still justify passing me on half-time. She also liked the idea of having counseling going on at the same time I was dealing with fake Strigoi attacks—just in case they really were traumatizing.

After a bit more examination, Dr. Olendzki gave me a clean bill of health and told me I could go back to my dorm. Alberta left after that, but Dimitri stuck around to walk me back.

"Thanks for thinking of the half-time thing," I told him. The walkways were wet today because the weather had warmed up after the storm. It wasn't bathing suit weather or anything, but a lot of the ice and snow were melting. Water dripped steadily from trees, and we had to sidestep puddles.

Dimitri came to an abrupt stop and turned so that he stood right in front of me, blocking my path. I skidded to a halt, nearly running into him. He reached out and grabbed my arm, pulling me closer to him than I would have expected him to do in public. His fingers bit deep into me, but they didn't hurt.

"Rose," he said, the pain in his voice making my heart stop, "this shouldn't have been the first time I heard about this! Why didn't you tell me? Do you know what it was like? Do you know it was like for me to see you like that and not know what was happening? Do you know how scared I was?"

I was stunned, both from his outburst and our proximity. I

swallowed, unable to speak at first. There was so much on his face, so many emotions. I couldn't recall the last time I'd seen that much of him on display. It was wonderful and frightening at the same time. I then said the stupidest thing possible.

"You're not scared of anything."

"I'm scared of lots of things. I was scared for you." He released me, and I stepped back. There was still passion and worry written all over him. "I'm not perfect. I'm not invulnerable."

"I know, it's just . . ." I didn't know what to say. He was right. I always saw Dimitri as larger than life. All-knowing. Invincible. It was hard for me to believe that he could worry about me so much.

"And this has been going on for a long time too," he added. "It was going on with Stan, when you were talking to Father Andrew about ghosts—you were dealing with it this whole time! Why didn't you tell anyone? Why didn't you tell Lissa . . . or . . . me?"

I stared into those dark, dark eyes, those eyes I loved. "Would you have believed me?"

He frowned. "Believed what?"

"That I'm seeing ghosts."

"Well . . . they aren't ghosts, Rose. You only think they are because—"

"That's why," I interrupted. "That's why I couldn't tell you or anybody. Nobody would believe me, not without thinking I'm crazy."

"I don't think you're crazy," he said. "But I think you've been through a lot." Adrian had said almost the exact same thing when I asked him how I could tell if I was crazy or not.

"It's more than that," I said. I started walking again.

Without even taking another step, he reached out and grabbed me once more. He pulled me back to him, so that we now stood even closer than before. I glanced uneasily around again, wondering if someone might see us, but the campus was deserted. It was early, not quite sunset, so early that most people probably weren't even up for the school day yet. We wouldn't see activity around here for at least another hour. Still, I was surprised to see Dimitri was still risking it.

"Tell me then," he said. "Tell me how it's more than that."

"You won't believe me," I said. "Don't you get it? No one will. Even you . . . of all people." Something in that thought made my voice catch. Dimitri understood so much about me. I wanted—*needed*—him to understand this too.

"I'll . . . try. But I still don't think you really understand what's happening to you."

"I do," I said firmly. "That's what no one realizes. Look, you have to decide once and for all if you really do trust me. If you think I'm a child, too naive to get what's going on with her fragile mind, then you should just keep walking. But if you trust me enough to remember that I've seen things and know things that kind of surpass those of others my age . . . well, then you should also realize that I might know a little about what I'm talking about."

A lukewarm breeze, damp with the scent of melted snow, swirled around us. "I do trust you, Roza. But . . . I don't believe in ghosts."

The earnestness was there. He did want to reach out to me, to understand . . . but even as he did, it warred with beliefs he wasn't ready to change yet. It was ironic, considering tarot cards apparently spooked him.

"Will you try to?" I asked. "Or at the very least try not to write this off to some psychosis?"

"Yes. That I can do."

So I told him about my first couple of Mason sightings and how I'd been afraid to explain the Stan incident to anyone. I talked about the shapes I'd seen on the plane and described in more detail what I'd seen on the ground.

"Doesn't it seem kind of, um, specific for a random stress reaction?" I asked when I finished.

"I don't know that you can really expect 'stress reactions' to be random or specific. They're unpredictable by nature." He had that thoughtful expression I knew so well, the one that told me he was turning over all sorts of things in his head. I could also tell that he still wasn't buying this as a real ghost story but that he was trying very hard to keep an open mind. He affirmed as much a moment later: "Why are you so certain these aren't just things you're imagining?"

"Well, at first I thought I was imagining it all. But now . . . I don't know. There's something about it that feels real . . . even though I know that isn't actually evidence. But you heard what Father Andrew said—about ghosts sticking around after they die young or violently."

Dimitri actually bit his lip. He'd been about to tell me not to take the priest literally. Instead he asked, "So you think Mason's back for revenge?"

"I thought that at first, but now I'm not so sure. He's never tried to hurt me. He just seems like he wants something. And then . . . all those other ghosts seemed to want something too—even the ones I didn't know. Why?"

Dimitri gave me a sage look. "You have a theory."

"I do. I was thinking about what Victor said. He mentioned that because I'm shadow-kissed—because I died—I have a connection to the world of the dead. That I'll never entirely leave it behind me."

His expression hardened. "I wouldn't put a lot of stock in what Victor Dashkov tells you."

"But he knows things! You know he does, no matter how big an asshole he is."

"Okay, supposing that's true, that being shadow-kissed lets you see ghosts, why is it happening now? Why didn't it happen right after the car accident?"

"I thought of that," I said eagerly. "It was something else Victor said—that now that I was dealing in death, I was that much closer to the other side. What if causing someone else's death strengthened my connection and now makes this possible? I just had my first real kill. Kills, even."

"Why is it so haphazard?" asked Dimitri. "Why does it occur when it does? Why the airplane? Why not at Court?"

My enthusiasm dimmed a little. "What are you, a lawyer?" I snapped. "You question everything I'm saying. I thought you were going to have an open mind."

"I am. But you need to too. Think about it. Why this pattern of sightings?"

"I don't know," I admitted. I sagged in defeat. "You still think I'm crazy."

He reached out and cupped my chin, tipping my face up to look at his. "No. Never. Not one of these theories makes me think you're crazy. But I've always believed the simplest explanation makes sense. Dr. Olendzki's does. The ghost one has holes. But, if you can find out more . . . then we may have something to work with."

"We?" I asked.

"Of course. I'm not leaving you alone on this, no matter what. You know I'd never abandon you."

There was something very sweet and noble about his words, and I felt the need to return them, though mostly I ended up sounding idiotic. "And I won't ever abandon you, you know. I mean it . . . not that this stuff ever happens to you, of course, but if you start seeing ghosts or anything, I'll help you through it."

He gave a small, soft laugh. "Thanks."

Our hands found each other's, fingers lacing together.

We stood like that for almost a full minute, neither of us saying anything. The only place we touched was our hands. The breeze picked up again, and although the temperature was probably only in the forties, it felt like spring to me. I expected flowers to burst into bloom around us. As though sharing the same thought, we released our hands at the same time.

We reached my dorm shortly after that, and Dimitri asked if I'd be okay going in on my own. I told him I'd be fine and that he should go do his own thing. He left, but just as I was about to step through the lobby door, I realized my overnight bag was still back at the med clinic. Muttering a few things that would have gotten me a detention, I turned around and hurried back in the direction I'd just come.

Dr. Olendzski's receptionist motioned me toward the examining rooms when I told her why I was there. I retrieved the bag from my now-empty room and turned into the hall to leave. Suddenly, in the room opposite mine, I saw someone lying in bed. There was no sign of any of the clinic's staff, and my curiosity—always getting the better of me—made me peek inside.

It was Abby Badica, a senior Moroi. *Cute* and *perky* were the adjectives that usually came to mind when I described Abby, but this time, she was anything but. She was bruised and scratched up, and when she turned her face to look at me, I saw red welts.

"Let me guess," I said. "You fell."

"W-what?"

"You fell. I hear that's the standard answer: Brandon, Brett, and Dane. But I'll tell you the truth—you guys need to come up with something else. I think the doctor's getting suspicious."

Her eyes went wide. "You know?"

It was then that I realized my mistake with Brandon. I'd come at him demanding answers, which had made him reluctant to share anything. Those who'd questioned Brett and Dane had faced similar results. With Abby, I realized that I just had to act like I already knew the answers, and then she'd give up the information.

"Of course I know. They told me everything."

"What?" she squeaked. "They swore not to. It's part of the rules."

Rules? What was she talking about? The royal-bashing vigilante group I'd been picturing didn't really seem like the type to have rules. There was something else going on here.

"Well, they didn't have much of a choice. I don't know why, but I keep finding you guys afterward. I had to help cover for them. I'm telling you, I don't know how much longer this can go on without someone asking more questions." I spoke like I was a sympathizer, wanting to help if I could.

"I should have been stronger. I tried, but it wasn't enough." She looked tired—and in pain. "Just keep quiet until everything's set, okay? Please?"

"Sure," I said, dying to know what she'd "tried." "I'm not going to drag anyone else in. How'd you even end up here? You're supposed to avoid attracting attention." Or so I assumed. I was totally making this up as I went along.

She grimaced. "The dorm matron noticed and made me come in. If the rest of the Mână finds out, I'm going to get in trouble."

"Hopefully the doctor'll send you on your way before any of them find out. She's kind of busy. You've got the same marks as Brett and Brandon, and none of theirs were that serious." So I hoped. "The . . . uh, burn marks were a little tricky, but they haven't had any problems."

It was a gamble in my game here. Not only did I have no clue about the specifics of Brett's injuries, I also didn't actually know if those marks Jill had described on him were burns. If they weren't, I might have just blown my insider act. But, she didn't correct me, and her fingers absentmindedly touched one of the welts.

"Yeah, they said the damage wouldn't last. I'll just have to make up something for Olendzki." A small flicker of hope shone in her eyes. "They said they wouldn't, but maybe . . . maybe they'll let me try again."

It was at that moment that the good doctor returned. She was surprised to see me still there and told me I needed to get back home and rest. I said goodbye to both of them and trekked back out into the cold. I barely noticed the weather as I walked, though. Finally, finally, I had a clue in this puzzle. Mână.

NINETEEN

LISSA HAD BEEN MY best friend ever since elementary school, which was why keeping so many secrets from her lately had hurt so much. She was always open with me, always willing to share what was on her mind—but then, maybe that was because she had no choice. I used to be that way with her, yet at some point, I'd started locking my secrets in, unable to tell her about Dimitri or the real reason I'd messed up with Stan. I hated it being that way. It ate me up inside and made me feel guilty around her.

Today, however, there was absolutely *no* way I could wiggle out of explaining what had happened at the airport. Even if I made up something, the fact that I was on half-time with Christian would be a huge tip-off that something was going on. No excuses this time.

So, as much as it hurt, I gave her and Christian—as well as Eddie and Adrian, who were hanging around—the short version of what had happened.

"You think you saw ghosts?" Christian exclaimed. "Seriously?" The look on his face showed me that he was already building a list of snide comments to make.

"Look," I snapped, "I told you what was going on, but I don't want to elaborate on it. It's getting worked out, so just let it drop."

"Rose . . ." began Lissa uneasily. A hurricane of emotions was beating through to me from her. Fear. Concern. Shock. Her compassion made me feel that much worse.

I shook my head. "No, Liss. Please. You guys can think whatever you want about me or make up your own theories, but we're not going to talk about it. Not now. Just leave me alone about it."

I expected Lissa to badger me because of her normal persistence. I expected Adrian and Christian to because of their irritating natures. But even though my words had been simple, I realized I'd delivered them with a harshness both in voice and manner. It was Lissa's surprised mental reaction that alerted me to that, and then I needed only to look at the guys' faces to realize I must have sounded incredibly bitchy.

"Sorry," I mumbled. "I appreciate the concern, but I'm just not in the mood."

Lissa eyed me. *Later*, she said in my mind. I gave her a brief nod, secretly wondering how I could avoid that conversation.

She and Adrian had met to practice magic again. I still liked being able to be close to her, but I was only able to do so because Christian was hanging around too. And honestly, I couldn't figure out why he stayed. I guess he was still a little jealous, despite everything that had happened. Of course, if he'd known about the queen's matchmaking schemes, he might have had good reason. Nonetheless, it was clear these magic lessons were starting to bore him. We were in Ms. Meissner's classroom today, and he pulled two desks together and stretched out across them, tossing an arm over his eyes.

"Wake me when it gets interesting," he said.

Eddie and I stood in a central position that let us watch the door and windows while also staying near the Moroi.

"You really saw Mason?" Eddie whispered to me. He turned sheepish. "Sorry . . . you said you didn't want to talk about it. . . ."

I started to say yes, that was exactly what I'd said . . . but then I saw the look on Eddie's face. He wasn't asking me about this out of perverse curiosity. He asked because of Mason, because of their closeness, and because Eddie wasn't over his best friend's death any more than I was. I think he found the idea of Mason communicating from beyond the grave reassuring, but then, he hadn't been the one to actually see Mason's ghost.

"I think it was him," I murmured back. "I don't know. Everyone thinks I imagined it."

"How did he look? Was he upset?"

"He looked . . . sad. Really sad."

"If it was really him . . . I mean, I don't know." Eddie looked at the ground, momentarily forgetting to watch the room. "I've always wondered if he was upset that we didn't save him."

"There was nothing we could have done," I told him, reiterating exactly what everyone had told me. "But I wondered that too, because Father Andrew had mentioned that ghosts sometimes come back for revenge. But Mason didn't look that way. He just seemed like he wanted to tell me something."

Eddie looked back up suddenly, realizing he was still on guard duty. He didn't say anything else after that, but I knew where his thoughts were.

Meanwhile, Adrian and Lissa were making progress. Or rather, Adrian was. The two of them had dug up a bunch of scraggly plants that had died or gone dormant for the winter and put them in little pots. The pots were now lined up in a row on a long table. Lissa touched one, and I felt the euphoria of magic burn within her. A moment later, the scrappy little plant turned green and sprouted leaves.

Adrian stared hard at it, as though it held all the secrets of the universe, and then exhaled deeply. "Okay. Here goes nothing."

He lightly placed his fingers on a different plant. *Here goes nothing* might have been an accurate statement, because nothing actually happened. Then, a few moments later, the plant shuddered a little. A hint of green started to grow in it and then it stopped.

"You did it," said Lissa, impressed. I could also feel that she was a little jealous. Adrian had learned one of her tricks, but she still hadn't learned any of his.

"Hardly," he said, glaring at the plant. He was completely sober, with none of his vices to mellow him. Spirit had nothing to stop it from making him feel irritable. With our moods, we actually had something in common tonight. "Damn it."

"Are you kidding?" she asked. "It was great. You made a plant grow—*with your mind*. That's amazing."

"Not as good as you, though," he said, still sounding like he was ten years old.

I couldn't help but pipe in. "Then stop bitching and try again."

He glanced over at me, a smile twisting his lips. "Hey, no advice, Ghost Girl. Guardians should be seen and not heard." I flipped him off for the "Ghost Girl" comment, but he didn't notice because Lissa was talking to him again.

"She's right. Try it again."

"You do it one more time," he said. "I want to watch you. . . . I can kind of feel what you do to it."

She performed her trick on another plant. I again felt the magic flare up, as well as the joy that came with it—and then she faltered. A flash of fear and instability tinged the magic, smacking a little of when her mental state had deteriorated so badly. *No, no*, I begged silently. *It's happening. I knew it would if she kept using the magic. Please don't let it happen again.*

And like that, the dark spot within her magic went away. All of her thoughts and feelings returned to normal. I noticed then that she'd also made the plant grow. I'd missed it because I'd been distracted by her lapse. Adrian had missed the magic too because his eyes were on me. His expression was troubled and very, very confused.

"Okay," said Lissa happily. She didn't realize he hadn't

paid attention. "Try again."

Adrian focused his attention back on their work. Sighing, he moved to a new plant, but she gestured him back. "No, keep working on the one you started. Maybe you can only do it in small bursts."

Nodding, he turned his attention to his original plant. For a few minutes, he just did nothing but stare. Silence reigned in the room. I'd never seen him so focused on anything, and sweat was actually forming on his forehead. Finally, at long last, the plant twitched again. It grew even greener, and tiny buds appeared on it. Glancing up at him, I saw him narrow his eyes and grit his teeth, no doubt concentrating for all he was worth. The buds burst. Leaves and tiny white flowers appeared.

Lissa made what could only be called a whoop of joy. "You did it!" She hugged him, and feelings of delight washed over me from her. She was sincerely happy that he'd been able to do it. And while she was still disappointed at her lack of progress, it inspired hope in her that he'd replicated her abilities. That meant they truly could learn from each other.

"I can't wait until I'm able to do something new," she said, still a tiny bit jealous.

Adrian tapped a notebook. "Well, there are plenty of other tricks in the world of spirit. You've got to be able to learn at least one of them."

"What's that?" I asked.

"Remember that research I did on people who'd shown

weird behaviors?" she asked. "We made a list of all the different things that showed up." I did remember. In her search to find others with spirit, she'd uncovered claims about Moroi demonstrating abilities no one had ever seen. Few people believed the reports were true, but Lissa was convinced they were spirit users.

"Along with healing, auras, and dream walking, we seem to also have some super compulsion going on."

"You already knew that," I said.

"No, this is even more hard-core. It's not just telling people what to do. It's also making them see and feel things that aren't even there."

"What, like hallucinations?" I asked.

"Kind of," he said. "There are stories of people using compulsion to make others live through their worst nightmares, thinking they're being attacked or whatever."

I shivered. "That's actually kind of scary."

"And awesome," said Adrian.

Lissa agreed with me. "I don't know. Regular compulsion is one thing, but that just seems wrong."

Christian yawned. "Now that victory has been achieved, can we call it a night with the magic?"

Glancing behind me, I saw that Christian was sitting up and alert. His eyes were on Lissa and Adrian, and he did *not* look happy about the victory hug. Lissa and Christian had broken apart, though not because they'd noticed his reaction. They were both too distracted by their own excitement to notice his glare.

"Can you do it again?" asked Lissa eagerly. "Make it grow?"

Adrian shook his head. "Not right away. That took a lot out of me. I think I need a cigarette." He gestured in Christian's direction. "Go do something with your guy. He's been terribly patient through all of this."

Lissa walked over to Christian, her face alight with joy. She looked beautiful and radiant, and I could tell it was hard for him to stay too mad at her. The harsh expression on his face softened, and I saw the rare gentleness that only she could bring out in him. "Let's go back to the dorm," she said, grabbing his hand.

We set off. Eddie walked near guard with Lissa and Christian, which left me with far guard. It also left me with Adrian, who had chosen to lag behind and talk to me. He was smoking, so I got to be the one to deal with the toxic cloud that generated. Honestly, I couldn't figure out why no one in charge had busted him for this. I wrinkled my nose at the smell.

"You know, you can always be our far-far guard and stay behind with that thing," I told him.

"Mm, I've had enough." He dropped the cigarette and stamped it out, leaving it behind. I hated that almost as much as him smoking in the first place.

"What do you think, little dhampir?" he asked. "I was pretty badass with that plant, wasn't I? Of course, it would have been more badass if I'd, I dunno, helped an amputee grow a limb back. Or maybe separated Siamese twins. But that'll come with more practice."

"If you want some advice—which I'm sure you don't—you guys should lay off on the magic. Christian still thinks you're moving in on Lissa."

"What?" he asked in mock astonishment. "Doesn't he know my heart belongs to you?"

"It does not. And no, he's still worried about it, despite what I've told him."

"You know, I bet if we started making out right now, it would make him feel better."

"If you touch me," I said pleasantly, "I'll provide you with the opportunity to see if you can heal yourself. Then we'd see how badass you really are."

"I'd get Lissa to heal me," he said smugly. "It'd be easy for her. Although . . ." The sardonic smirk faded. "Something weird happened when she used her magic."

"Yeah," I said. "I know. Could you sense it too?"

"No. But I *saw* it." He frowned. "Rose . . . remember when you asked about being crazy and I said you weren't?"

"Yeah . . ."

"I think I might have been wrong. I think you are crazy."

I nearly stopped walking. "What the hell does that mean?"

"Well . . . you see, the thing is, when Lissa did the second plant . . . her aura dimmed a little."

"That would go along with what I felt," I said. "It was

kind of like she . . . I don't know, grew mentally fragile for a moment, kind of like she used to. But it went away."

He nodded. "Yeah, that's the thing . . . the darkness in her aura went away and into yours. Like, I've noticed before that you guys have a big difference in auras, but this time, I *saw* it happening. It was like that spot of darkness jumped out of hers and into yours."

Something about that made me shiver. "What does it mean?"

"Well, this is why I think you're crazy. Lissa isn't having any side effects from the magic anymore, right? And you, well . . . you've been feeling kind of short-tempered lately and you're, like, seeing ghosts." He said the words casually, like seeing ghosts was just something that happened from time to time. "I think whatever harmful thing there is in spirit that screws with the mind is leaking out of her and into you. It's making her stay stable, and you, well . . . as I said, you're seeing ghosts."

It was like being smacked in the face. A new theory. Not trauma. Not real ghosts. Me "catching" Lissa's madness. I remembered how she'd been at her worst, depressed and self-destructive. I remembered our former teacher, Ms. Karp, who'd also been a spirit user—and completely out of her mind enough to become Strigoi.

"No," I said in a strained voice. "That's not happening to me."

"What about your bond? You have that connection. Her

thoughts and feelings creep into you . . . why not the madness too?" Adrian's manner was typically light and curious. He didn't realize just how much this was starting to freak me out.

"Because it doesn't make any—"

And then, it hit me. The answer we'd been searching for this whole time.

St. Vladimir had struggled his whole life with spirit's side effects. He'd had dreams and delusions, experiences he wrote off to "demons." But he hadn't gone completely crazy or tried to kill himself. Lissa and I had felt certain that it was because he had a shadow-kissed guardian, Anna, and that sharing that bond with her had helped him. We'd assumed it was simply the act of having such a close friend around, someone who could support him and talk him through the bad times since they hadn't had antidepressants or antianxiety drugs back then.

But what if . . . what if . . .

I couldn't breathe. I couldn't go another single moment without knowing the answer. What time was it anyway? An hour or so before curfew? I had to find out. I came to an abrupt halt, nearly slipping on the slick ground.

"Christian!"

The group in front of us stopped and looked back at me and Adrian. "Yeah?" Christian asked.

"I need to take a detour—or rather, *we* do since I can't go anywhere without you. We need to go to the church."

His eyebrows rose in surprise. "What, you need to confess

something?"

"Don't ask questions. Please. It'll only take a few minutes."

Concern crossed Lissa's face. "Well, we can all go—"

"No, we'll be fast." I didn't want her there. I didn't want her to hear the answer I was certain I'd get. "Go to the dorm. We'll catch up. Please, Christian?"

He studied me, expression oscillating between wanting to mock me and wanting to help. He wasn't a complete jerk, after all. The latter emotion won out. "Okay, but if you try to get me to pray with you, I walk."

He and I split off toward the chapel. I moved so fast that he had to scurry to keep up.

"I don't suppose you want to tell me what this is about?" he asked.

"Nope. I appreciate your cooperation, though."

"Always glad to help," he said. I was certain he was rolling his eyes, but I was more focused on the path ahead.

We reached the chapel, and the door was locked, unsurprisingly. I knocked on it, staring anxiously around to see if any lights shone through the windows. It didn't look like it.

"You know, I've broken in here before," said Christian. "If you need inside—"

"No, more than that. I need to see the priest. Damn it, he's not here."

"He's probably in bed."

"Damn it," I repeated, feeling only a little bad about swearing on a church's doorstep. If the priest was in bed, he'd be off in Moroi staff housing and inaccessible. "I need to—"

The door opened, and Father Andrew peered out at us. He looked surprised but not upset. "Rose? Christian? Is something wrong?"

"I have to ask you a question," I told him. "It won't take long."

His surprise grew, but he stepped aside so we could enter. We all stopped and stood in the chapel's lobby, just outside the main sanctuary.

"I was just about to go home for the night," Father Andrew told us. "I was shutting everything down."

"You told me that St. Vladimir lived a long life and died of old age. Is that true?"

"Yes," he said slowly. "To the best of my knowledge. All the books I've read—including these latest ones—say as much."

"But what about Anna?" I demanded. I sounded like I was on the verge of hysteria. Which I kind of was.

"What about her?"

"What happened to her? How did she die?"

All this time. All this time, Lissa and I had worried about Vlad's outcome. We'd never considered Anna's.

"Ah, well." Father Andrew sighed. "Her end wasn't as good, I'm afraid. She spent her whole life protecting him, though there are hints that in her old age, she started growing a little unstable too. And then . . ."

"And then?" I asked. Christian was looking between the

priest and me, completely lost.

"And then, well, a couple months after St. Vladimir passed on, she committed suicide."

I squeezed my eyes shut for half a second and then opened them. This was what I'd been afraid of.

"I'm sorry," Father Andrew said. "I know how closely you've followed their story. I didn't even learn this about her until reading it recently. Taking one's life is a sin, of course . . . but, well, considering how close they were, it's not hard to imagine how she may have felt when he was gone."

"And you also said that she was starting to go a little crazy."

He nodded and spread his hands out. "It's hard to say what that poor woman was thinking. Many factors were probably involved. Why was this so pressing?"

I shook my head. "It's a long story. Thanks for helping me."

Christian and I were halfway to the dorm before he finally asked, "What was that all about? I remember when you guys were looking into this. Vladimir and Anna were like Lissa and you, right?"

"Yeah," I said glumly. "Look, I don't want to get between you guys, but *please* don't tell Lissa about this. Not until I find out more. Just tell her . . . I don't know. I'll tell her that I suddenly panicked because I thought I had more community service scheduled."

"Both of us lying to her, huh?"

"I hate it, believe me. But it's also best for her at the moment."

Because if Lissa knew that she might potentially make me insane . . . yeah, she'd take that hard. She'd want to stop working her magic. Of course, that was what I'd always wanted . . . and yet, I'd felt that joy in her when she used it. Could I take that away from her? Could I sacrifice myself?

There was no easy answer, and I couldn't start jumping to conclusions. Not until I knew more. Christian agreed to keep it secret, and by the time we joined the others, it was almost time for curfew anyway. We had only about a half hour together, and then we all split off for bed—including me, since the part-time field experience agreement said I couldn't do nighttime duty. The Strigoi risk was low in general anyway, and my instructors were more concerned about me getting a full night's sleep.

So when curfew came, I walked back to the dhampir dorm alone. And then, when I was almost there, he appeared again.

Mason.

I came to an abrupt halt and glanced around me, wishing someone else was there to witness this and settle the crazy-or-not thing once and for all. His pearly form stood there, hands in the pockets of his coat in an almost casual way that somehow made the experience that much weirder.

"Well," I said, feeling surprisingly calm, despite the sorrow that washed over me whenever I saw him. "Glad to see you're alone again. I didn't really like the extras on the plane."

He stared, expression blank and eyes sad. It made me feel worse, guilt twisting my stomach into knots. I broke.

"What are you?" I cried. "Are you real? Am I going crazy?"

To my surprise, he nodded.

"Which?" I squeaked. "Yes, you're real?"

He nodded.

"Yes, I'm crazy?"

He shook his head.

"Well," I said, forcing a joke through my hurricane of emotions. "That's a relief, but honestly, what else would you say if you're a hallucination?"

Mason just stared. I glanced around again, wishing someone would come by.

"Why are you here? Are you mad at us and looking for revenge?"

He shook his head, and something in me relaxed. Until that moment, I hadn't realized how worried I'd been about that. The guilt and grief had been wound up so tightly in me. Him blaming me—just as Ryan had—had seemed inevitable.

"Are you . . . are you having trouble finding peace?"

Mason nodded and seemed to grow sadder. I thought back to his final moments and swallowed back tears. I'd probably have a hard time finding peace too, taken from my life before it began.

"Is there more than that, though? Another reason you keep coming to me?"

He nodded.

"What?" I asked. There were too many questions lately. I needed answers. "What is it? What do I need to do?"

But anything other than a yes or no question was beyond us, apparently. He opened up his mouth as though he would say something. He looked like he was trying hard, like Adrian had with the plant. But no sound came out.

"I'm sorry," I whispered. "I'm sorry I don't understand . . . and . . . I'm sorry for everything else."

Mason gave me one last wistful look and then vanished.

TWENTY

"LET'S TALK ABOUT YOUR MOTHER."

I sighed. "What about her?"

It was my first day of counseling, and so far, I wasn't impressed. Last night's Mason sighting was probably something I should have brought up right away. But I didn't want school officials to have any more reason to think I was losing my mind—even if I was.

And honestly, I didn't know I was for sure. Adrian's analysis of my aura and the story of Anna certainly lent credence to me being on the road to Crazyville. Yet I didn't feel crazy. Did crazy people know if they really were? Adrian had said they didn't. *Crazy* itself was a weird term. I'd learned enough about psychology to know that it was also a very broad classification. Most forms of mental illness were actually very specific and had select symptoms—anxiety, depression, mood swings, etc. I didn't know where I fell on that scale, if I did at all.

"How do you feel about her?" continued the counselor. "About your mother?"

"That she's a great guardian and a so-so mother."

The counselor, whose name was Deirdre, wrote something in her notebook. She was blond and Moroi-slim, clad in a teal cashmere sweater dress. She actually didn't look much older than me, but certificates on her desk swore she had all sorts of degrees in psychotherapy. Her office was in the administrative building, the same place the headmistress's office was, and where all other sorts of Academy business was conducted. I'd kind of been hoping for a couch to lie on, like therapists always had on TV, but the best I had was a chair. It was a comfy chair, at least. The walls were covered in nature pictures, things like butterflies and daffodils. I guess they were supposed to be soothing.

"Do you want to elaborate on 'so-so'?" Deirdre asked.

"It's an upgrade. A month ago I would have said 'horrible.' What's this have to do with Mason?"

"Do you want to talk about Mason?"

I'd noticed she had a habit of answering my questions with questions.

"I don't know," I admitted. "I guess that's what I'm here for."

"How do you feel about him? About his death?"

"Sad. How else should I feel?"

"Angry?"

I thought about the Strigoi, their leering faces and casual attitudes toward killing. "Yeah, a little."

"Guilty?"

"Sure, of course."

"Why 'of course'?"

"Because it's my fault he was there. I'd upset him . . . and he had this thing to prove. I told him where the Strigoi were, and I wasn't supposed to. If he hadn't known about them, he wouldn't have done it. He'd still be alive."

"You don't think he was responsible for his own actions? That he was the one who chose to do that?"

"Well . . . yeah. I guess he did. I didn't make him do it."

"Any other reason you might feel guilty?"

I looked away from her and focused on a picture of a ladybug. "He liked me—like romantically. We kind of dated, but I couldn't get into it. That hurt him."

"Why couldn't you get into it?"

"I don't know," I said. The image of his body, lying on the floor, flashed into my mind and I shoved it away. No way would I cry in front of Deirdre. "That's the thing. I should have. He was nice. He was funny. We got along really well . . . but it just didn't feel right. Even kissing or anything like that . . . I eventually just couldn't do it."

"Do you feel like you have a problem with intimate contact?"

"What do you—? Oh. No! Of course not."

"Have you ever had sex with anyone?"

"No. Are you saying I should have?"

"Do you think you should have?"

Damn. I'd thought I had her. I'd thought for sure she wouldn't have a question for that one. "Mason wasn't the right person."

"Is there someone else? Someone you think might be the

right person?"

I hesitated. I'd lost track of how this related to me seeing ghosts. According to some paperwork I'd signed, everything we said in here was confidential. She couldn't tell anyone unless I was a danger to myself or doing something illegal. I wasn't entirely sure where a relationship with an older man fell there.

"Yeah . . . but I can't tell you who he is."

"How long have you known him?"

"Almost six months."

"Do you feel close?"

"Yeah, sure. But we're not . . ." How exactly did one describe this? "We're not actually really involved. He's kind of . . . unavailable." She could think what she wanted about that, like that maybe I was interested in a guy with a girlfriend.

"Is he the reason you couldn't get close to Mason?"

"Yes."

"And is he holding you back from dating someone else?"

"Well . . . he's not like purposely doing anything."

"But as long as you care about him, you're not interested in anyone else?"

"Right. But it doesn't matter. I probably shouldn't even be dating anyone at all."

"Why not?"

"Because there's no time. I'm training to be a guardian. I have to give all my attention to Lissa."

"And you don't think you can do that and be romantically

involved with someone?"

I shook my head. "No. I have to be willing to lay down my life for hers. I can't be distracted by someone else. We have this saying with the guardians: 'They come first.' You guys. Moroi."

"And so you figure you'll always have to put Lissa's needs ahead of yours?"

"Of course." I frowned. "What else would I do? I'm going to be her guardian."

"How does that make you feel? Giving up what you want for her?"

"She's my best friend. And she's the last of her family."

"That's not what I asked."

"Yeah, but—" I stopped. "Hey, you didn't ask a question."

"You think I always ask questions?"

"Never mind. Look, I love Lissa. I'm happy to spend my life protecting her. End of story. Besides, are you, a Moroi, going to tell me, a dhampir, that I shouldn't be putting Moroi first? You know how the system works."

"I do," she said. "But I'm not here to analyze it. I'm here to help you get better."

"Seems like you might not be able to do one without the other."

Deirdre's lips quirked into a smile, and then her eyes flicked to the clock. "We're out of time today. We'll have to pick this up next time."

I crossed my arms over my chest. "I thought you'd be giving me some kind of awesome advice or telling me what to do. But you just kept making me talk."

She laughed softly. "Therapy isn't so much about what I think as you do."

"Then why do it at all?"

"Because we don't always know what it is we're thinking or feeling. When you have a guide, it's easier to figure things out. You'll often discover that you already know what to do. I can help you ask questions and go places you might not have on your own."

"Well, you're good at the question part," I noted dryly.

"While I don't have any 'awesome advice,' I do have some things I want you to think about for when we talk again." She glanced down at her notepad and tapped it with her pencil while she thought. "First, I want you to think again about what I asked about Lissa—how you really feel about dedicating your life to her."

"I already told you."

"I know. Just think about it some more. If your answer's the same, that's fine. Then, I want you to consider something else. I want you to think about whether maybe the reason you're attracted to this unavailable guy is *because* he's unavailable."

"That's crazy. That doesn't make any sense."

"Is it? You just told me that you can't ever be involved

with anyone. Do you think it's possible that wanting someone you can't have is your subconscious mind's way of coping? If it's impossible for you to have him, then you never have to confront feeling conflicted about Lissa. You'll never have to choose."

"This is confusing," I grumbled.

"It's supposed to be. That's why I'm here."

"What's this have to do with Mason?"

"It has to do with you, Rose. That's what's important."

I left therapy feeling like my brain had melted. I also kind of felt like I'd been on trial. If Deirdre had been there to grill Victor, they probably would have finished up in half the time.

I *also* thought Deirdre had totally been going in the wrong direction. Of course I didn't resent Lissa. And the thought that I'd fallen for Dimitri because I couldn't have him was ridiculous. I'd never even thought of the conflict with guarding until he'd mentioned it. I'd fallen for him because . . . well, because he was Dimitri. Because he was sweet, strong, funny, fierce, and gorgeous. Because he understood me.

And yet, as I walked back to the commons, I found her question spinning around in my brain. I might not have been thinking about a relationship distracting us in our guard duties, but I'd certainly known from the start that his age and job were huge barriers. Could that have really played a part? Had some piece of me known we could never really have anything—thus allowing me to always stay dedicated to Lissa?

No, I decided firmly. That was ridiculous. Deirdre might be good at asking questions, but she was clearly asking the wrong ones.

"Rose!"

I looked to my right and saw Adrian cutting across the lawn toward me, oblivious to the slush's effects on his designer shoes.

"Did you just call me 'Rose'?" I asked. "And not 'little dhampir'? I don't think that's ever happened."

"It happens all the time," he countered, catching up to me.

We stepped inside the commons. School was in session, so the halls were empty.

"Where's your better half?" he asked.

"Christian?"

"No, Lissa. You can tell where she is, right?"

"Yeah, I can tell because it's last period, and she's in class like everyone else. You keep forgetting that for the rest of us, this is a school."

He looked disappointed. "I found more case files I wanted to talk to her about. More super-compulsion stuff."

"Whoa, you've been doing something productive? I'm impressed."

"You're one to talk," he said. "Especially considering your whole existence here revolves around beating people up. You dhampirs are uncivilized—but then, that's why we love you."

"Actually," I mused, "we aren't the only ones doing beatings lately." I'd nearly forgotten about my royal fight club mystery. There were so many things I had to worry about lately. It was like trying to hold water in my hands. It was a long shot, but I had to ask him. "Does the word *Mână* mean anything to you?"

He leaned against the wall and reached for his cigarettes. "Sure."

"You're inside the school," I warned.

"What—oh, right." With a sigh, he put the pack back in his coat. "Don't half of you study Romanian here? It means 'hand.'"

"I study English here." Hand. That didn't make any sense.

"Why the interest in translation?"

"I don't know. I think I got it wrong. I thought it had some connection to this thing that's been going on with these royals."

Recognition flashed in his eyes. "Oh Lord. Not that. Are they really doing it here too?"

"Doing what?"

"The Mână. The Hand. It's this stupid secret society that pops up at schools. We had a chapter of it back at Alder. It's mostly a bunch of royals getting together and having secret meetings to talk about how much better they are than everyone else."

"That's it then," I said. The pieces clicked together. "That's Jesse and Ralf's little group—the one they tried to get Christian to join. That's what this Mână is."

"Him?" Adrian laughed. "They must have been desper-ate—and I don't mean that as a slam against Christian. He's just not really the type to get into that kind of thing."

"Yeah, well, he turned them down pretty hard. What's the point of this secret society exactly?"

He shrugged. "The same as any other. It's a way to make people feel better about themselves. Everyone likes feeling special. Being part of an elite group is a way to do that."

"But you weren't part of it?"

"No need. I already know I'm special."

"Jesse and Ralf made it sound like royals had to stick together because of all the controversies that are going on—about fighting and guardians and all that. They made it sound like they could do something about it."

"Not at this age," said Adrian. "Mostly all they can do is talk. When they get older, Mână members sometimes cut deals for each other and still have secret meetings."

"That's it then? They're just hanging out and talking to hear themselves talk?"

He turned contemplative. "Well, yes, of course they're doing lots of that. But I mean, whenever these little chapters form, there's usually something *specific* they want to do in secret. Each group's kind of different that way, so this one's probably got some plan or scheme or whatever." A plan or scheme. I didn't like the sound of that. Especially with Jesse and Ralf.

"You know a lot for someone who wasn't in it."

"My dad was. He never talks much about it—hence the secret part—but I picked up things, and then I heard about it while I was at school."

I leaned against the wall. The clock across the hall told me classes were almost over. "Did you hear anything about them beating up people? There are at least four Moroi I know of who were attacked. And they won't talk about it."

"Who? Like non-royals?"

"No. Other royals."

"That doesn't make any sense. The whole point of it is for elite royals to band together to protect themselves from change. Unless, perhaps, they're going after royals who refuse or are supporting non-royals."

"Maybe. But one of them was Jesse's brother, and Jesse seems to be a founding member. Seems like he'd have to make the cut. *And* they didn't do anything when Christian refused."

Adrian spread his hands wide. "Even I don't know everything, and like I said, this one's probably got its own little agenda they're keeping hidden." I sighed in frustration, and he gave me a curious look. "Why do you care so much?"

"Because it isn't right. The people I saw were in bad shape. If some group's going around and ganging up on victims, they need to be stopped."

Adrian laughed and played with a strand of my hair. "You can't save everyone, though God knows you try."

"I just want to do what's right." I remembered Dimitri's

comments about Westerns and couldn't help a small smile. "I need to bring justice where it's needed."

"The crazy thing, little dhampir, is that you mean that. I can tell by your aura."

"What, are you saying it's not black anymore?"

"No . . . still dark, definitely. But it's got a little light in it, streaks of gold. Like sunlight."

"Maybe your theory about me catching it from Lissa is wrong then." I'd been trying very hard not to think about last night, when I'd learned about Anna. Mentioning it now stirred up all those fears all over again. Insanity. Suicide.

"Depends," he said. "When was the last time you saw her?"

I gave him a light punch. "You have no clue, do you? You're making this up as you go along."

He caught my wrist and pulled me closer. "Isn't that the way you normally operate?"

I grinned in spite of myself. This close to him I could appreciate just how lovely the green of his eyes was. In fact, despite continually making fun of him, I couldn't deny that the rest of him was pretty good-looking too. His fingers were warm on my wrist, and there was something kind of sexy about the way he held it. Thinking back to Deirdre's words, I tried to assess how it all made me feel. The queen's warnings aside, Adrian was a guy who was technically available. Was I attracted to him? Did I get a thrill out of this?

The answer: no. Not in the same way I did with Dimitri.

Adrian was sexy in his way, but he didn't drive me wild the way Dimitri did. Was it because Adrian was so readily available? Was Deirdre right about me purposely wanting relationships that were impossible?

"You know," he said, interrupting my thoughts, "under any other circumstances, this would be hot. Instead, you're looking at me like I'm some kind of science fair project."

That was exactly how I was treating this, actually. "Why don't you ever use compulsion on me?" I asked. "And I don't mean just to stop me from getting in fights."

"Because half the fun of you is that you're so difficult."

A new idea occurred to me. "Do it."

"Do what?"

"Use compulsion on me."

"What?" It was another of those rare shocked Adrian moments.

"Use compulsion to make me want to kiss you—except you have to promise not to actually kiss me."

"That's pretty weird—and when I say something's weird, you know it's serious."

"Please."

He sighed and then focused his eyes right on me. It was like drowning, drowning in seas of green. There was nothing in the world except for those eyes.

"I want to kiss you, Rose," he said softly. "And I want you to want me too."

Every aspect of his body—his lips, his hands, his scent—

suddenly overpowered me. I felt warm all over. I wanted him to kiss me with every ounce of my being. There was nothing in life I wanted more than that kiss. I tilted my face up toward his, and he leaned down. I could practically taste his lips.

"Do you want to?" he asked, voice still like velvet. "Do you want to kiss me?"

Did I ever. Everything around me had blurred. Only his lips were in focus.

"Yes," I said. His face moved closer, his mouth only a breath away from mine. We were so, so close, and then—

He stopped. "We're done," he said, stepping back.

I snapped out of it instantly. The dreamy haze was gone, as was the yearning in my body. But I'd discovered something. Under compulsion, I had definitely wanted him to kiss me. Yet even under compulsion, it hadn't been the electric, all-encompassing feeling I had when I was with Dimitri, that feeling that we were practically the same person and were bound by forces bigger than both of us. With Adrian, it had simply been mechanical.

Deirdre had been wrong. If my attraction to Dimitri was just some subconscious reaction, then it should have been as superficial as that forced attraction to Adrian. Yet they were completely different. With Dimitri, it was love—not just some trick my mind was playing on me.

"Hmm," I said.

"Hmm?" asked Adrian, eyeing me with amusement.

"Hmm."

The third "hmm" hadn't come from either of us. I looked across the hall and saw Christian watching us. I separated from Adrian, just as the bell rang. The sounds of students pouring out of classrooms rumbled through the hallway.

"Now I can see Lissa," said Adrian happily.

"Rose, will you come with me to the feeders?" asked Christian. He spoke in a flat tone, and his expression was unreadable.

"I'm not guarding you today."

"Yeah, well, I miss your charming company."

I told Adrian goodbye and cut through the cafeteria with Christian. "What's up?" I asked.

"You tell me," he said. "You were the one about ready to start making out with Adrian."

"It was an experiment," I said. "It was part of my therapy."

"What the hell kind of therapy are you in?"

We reached the feeders' room. Somehow, despite him getting out of class early, there were still a few people ahead of us in line.

"Why do you care?" I asked him. "You should be happy. It means he isn't moving in on Lissa."

"He could be moving in on both of you."

"What are you, my big brother now?"

"Annoyed," he said. "That's what I am."

I looked beyond him and saw Jesse and Ralf enter. "Well, keep it to yourself, or our good friends will overhear."

Jesse, however, was too busy to hear, because he was arguing with the feeding coordinator. "I don't have time to wait," he told her. "I've got to be somewhere."

She pointed to us and the others in line. "These people are ahead of you."

Jesse met her eyes and smiled. "You can make an exception this time."

"Yeah, he's in a hurry," added Ralf in a voice I'd never heard him use before. It was smooth and less grating than usual. "Just write his name down at the top of the list."

The coordinator looked like she was going to tell them off, but then a funny, distracted look came over her face. She glanced at her clipboard and wrote something. A few seconds after she looked away, her head jerked up again, eyes sharp once more. She frowned.

"What was I doing?"

"You were signing me up," said Jesse. He pointed at the board. "See?"

She looked down, startled. "Why is your name first? Didn't you just get here?"

"We were here earlier and checked in. You told us it was okay."

She looked down again, clearly puzzled. She didn't remember them coming earlier—because they hadn't—but she apparently couldn't figure out why Jesse's name was at the top now. A moment later, she shrugged and must have decided it wasn't worth overthinking. "Stand with the others, and I'll call you next."

As soon as Jesse and Ralf came near us, I turned on them. "You just used compulsion on her," I hissed.

Jesse looked panicked for a fraction of a second; then his normal swagger took over. "Whatever. I just convinced her, that's all. What, are you going to try to tell on me or something?"

"Nothing to tell," scoffed Christian. "That was the worst compulsion I've ever seen."

"Like you've seen compulsion," said Ralf.

"Plenty," said Christian. "From people prettier than you. Of course, maybe that's part of why yours isn't as good."

Ralf seemed highly offended at not being considered pretty, but Jesse just nudged him and started to turn away. "Forget him. He had his chance."

"His chance at—" I remembered how Brandon had attempted weak compulsion when trying to convince me his bruises were nothing. Jill had said that Brett Ozera actually *had* convinced a teacher that his were nothing. The teacher had dropped the matter, much to Jill's surprise. Brett must have used compulsion. Lightbulbs went off in different parts of my brain. The connections were all around me. The problem was, I couldn't untangle the wires quite yet. "That's what this is about, isn't it? Your stupid Mână and its need to beat up on people. It's got something to do with compulsion. . . ."

I didn't understand how it all fit together, but the surprised look on Jesse's face told me I was on to something, even though he said, "You don't know what you're talking about."

I pushed forward, hoping some blind hits would make him mad and say something he wasn't supposed to. "What's the point? Does it give you guys some kind of power trip to do these little tricks? That's all they are, you know. You seriously don't know the first thing about compulsion. I've seen compulsion that would make you do handstands and throw yourself out a window."

"We're learning more than you can even imagine," said Jesse. "And when I find out who told—"

He didn't get a chance to finish his threat because he was called over to the feeder just then. He and Ralf stalked away, and Christian immediately turned to me.

"What's going on? What's a Mână?"

I gave him a hasty recap of Adrian's explanation. "That's what they wanted you to join. They must secretly be practicing compulsion. Adrian said these groups are always royals who have some plan to change and control things in dangerous times. They must think compulsion is the answer—it's what they meant when they told you they had ways to help you get what you wanted. If they knew how crappy your compulsion was, they probably wouldn't have asked."

He scowled, not liking me reminding him of the one time he'd attempted—and failed—to compel someone at the ski lodge. "So where's the beating-people-up part come in?"

"That's the mystery," I said. Christian was summoned over to feed just then, and I put my theories on hold until I could get more info and take action. I noticed which feeder we were being led to. "Is that Alice *again*? How do you always get her? Do you request her?"

"No, but I think some people specifically un-request her."

Alice was happy to see us, as always. "Rose. Are you still keeping us safe?"

"I will if they'll let me," I told her.

"Don't be too hasty," she warned. "Conserve your strength. If you're too eager to fight the undead, you may find yourselves joining them. Then you'd never see us again, and we'd be very sad."

"Yes," said Christian. "I'd cry into my pillow every night."

I resisted the urge to kick him. "Well, I couldn't visit if I was Strigoi, yeah, but hopefully I'd just die a normal death. Then I could come see you as a ghost."

How sad, I thought, that I was now making jokes about the very thing that was freaking me out lately. Alice found no amusement in it whatsoever. She shook her head.

"No, you wouldn't. The wards would keep you out."

"The wards only keep Strigoi out," I reminded her gently.

A defiant look replaced her scattered one. "The wards keep anything that isn't alive out. Dead or undead."

"Now you've done it," said Christian.

"The wards don't keep ghosts out," I said. "I've seen them."

Considering Alice's own instability, I didn't mind discussing mine with her. In fact, it was kind of refreshing to talk about this stuff with someone who wouldn't judge me. Indeed, she treated this as a perfectly normal conversation.

"If you've seen ghosts, then we're not safe anymore."

"I told you last time, the security's too good."

"Maybe someone made a mistake," she argued, sounding remarkably coherent. "Maybe someone missed something. Wards are made of magic. Magic is alive. Ghosts can't cross them for the same reason as Strigoi. They aren't alive. If you saw a ghost, the wards have failed." She paused. "Or you're crazy."

Christian laughed out loud. "There you go, Rose. Straight from the source." I shot him a glare. He smiled at Alice. "In Rose's defense, though, I think she's right about the wards. The school checks them all the time. The only place guarded better than here is the Royal Court, and both places are over-flowing with guardians. Stop being so paranoid."

He fed, and I glanced away. I should have known better than to listen to Alice. She was hardly a reputable source of information, even if she'd been around for a while. And yet . . . her weird logic did make sense. If wards kept Strigoi out, why not ghosts? True, Strigoi were the dead who had come back to walk the earth, but her point was sound: *All* of them were dead. But Christian and I were right too: The wards around the school were solid. It took a lot of power to lay wards. Not every Moroi home could have them, but places like schools and the Royal Court had theirs maintained diligently.

The Royal Court . . .

I'd had no ghostly encounters whatsoever while we there, yet that had been incredibly stressful. If my sightings were stress-induced, wouldn't the Court and encounters with Victor and the queen have provided great opportunities for them to occur? The fact that I'd seen nothing seemed to negate the PTSD theory. I hadn't seen ghosts until we'd landed at the Martinville airport.

Which didn't have wards.

I nearly gasped. The Court had strong wards. I'd seen no ghosts. The airport, which was part of the human world, had no wards. I'd been bombarded with ghosts there. I'd also seen flashes of them on the plane—which was unwarded when we were in the air.

I looked over at Alice and Christian. They were just about finished. Could she be right? Did wards keep out ghosts? And if so, what was going on with the school? If the wards were intact, I should see nothing—just like at Court. If the wards were broken, I should be overrun—just like at the airport. Instead, the Academy was somewhere in the middle. I had sightings only occasionally. It didn't make sense.

The only thing I knew for sure was that if something was wrong with the school's wards, then I wasn't the only one in danger.

TWENTY-ONE

I COULD HARDLY WAIT for my day to end. I'd promised Lissa I'd hang out with her and the others after school. It should have been fun, but the minutes dragged by. I was too restless. When curfew came around, I split off from them ran back to my dorm. I asked the woman at the front desk if she could call up to Dimitri's room—off-limits to students—because I had an "urgent" question for him. She had just picked up the phone when Celeste walked past.

"He's not there," she told me. She had a large bruise on the side of her face. Some novice had gotten the better of her—some novice who wasn't me. "I think he was going to the chapel. You'll have to see him tomorrow—you can't be there and back before curfew comes."

I nodded meekly and acted like I was heading for the student wing. Instead, as soon as she was out of sight, I headed back outside again and ran to the chapel. She was right. I wasn't going to make curfew, but hopefully Dimitri could make sure I got back without getting in trouble.

The chapel's doors were unlocked when I reached them. I walked in and saw all the candles lit, making all the gold ornaments in the room sparkle. The priest must still be working. But, when I stepped inside the sanctuary, he wasn't there.

Dimitri was, however.

He sat in the last pew. He wasn't praying or kneeling or anything. He just sat there, looking quite relaxed. Although he wasn't a practicing member of the church, he'd told me he often found peace there. It gave him a chance to think about his life and the deeds he'd done.

I always thought he looked good, but just then, something about him nearly made me come to a standstill. Maybe it was because of the background, all the polished wood and colorful icons of saints. Maybe it was just the way the candlelight shone on his dark hair. Maybe it was just because he looked unguarded, almost vulnerable. He was normally so wound up, so on edge . . . but even he needed the occasional moment of rest. He seemed to glow in my eyes, kind of in the way Lissa always did. His normal tension returned when he heard me come in.

"Rose, is everything okay?" He started to stand, and I motioned him down as I slid into the spot beside him. The faint smell of incense lingered in the air.

"Yeah . . . well, kind of. No breakdowns, if that's what you're worried about. I just had a question. Or, well, a theory."

I explained the conversation with Alice and what I'd deduced from it. He listened patiently, expression thoughtful.

"I know Alice. I'm not sure she's credible," he said when I finished. It was similar to what he'd said about Victor.

"I know. I thought the same thing. But a lot of it makes sense."

"Not quite. As you pointed out, why are your visions so irregular here? That doesn't go along with the ward theory. You should feel like you did on the plane."

"What if the wards are just weak?" I asked.

He shook his head. "That's impossible. Wards take months to wear down. New ones are put in place here every two weeks."

"That often?" I asked, unable to hide my disappointment. I'd known maintenance was frequent but not *that* frequent. Alice's theory had almost provided a sound explanation, one that didn't involve me being insane.

"Maybe they're getting staked," I suggested. "By humans or something—like we saw before."

"Guardians walk the grounds a few times a day. If there was a stake in the borders of campus, we'd notice."

I sighed.

Dimitri moved his hand over mine, and I flinched. He didn't remove it, though, and as he did so frequently, guessed my thoughts. "You thought if she was right, it would explain everything."

I nodded. "I don't want to be crazy."

"You aren't crazy."

"But you don't believe I'm really seeing ghosts."

He glanced away, his eyes staring at the flickering of candles on the altar. "I don't know. I'm still trying to keep an open mind. And being stressed isn't the same as being crazy."

"I know," I admitted, still very conscious of how warm his

hand was. I shouldn't have been thinking about things like that in a church. "But . . . well . . . there's something else. . . ."

I told him then about Anna possibly "catching" Vladimir's insanity. I also explained Adrian's aura observations. He turned his gaze back on me, expression speculative.

"Have you told anyone else about this? Lissa? Your counselor?"

"No," I said in a small voice, unable to meet his eyes. "I was afraid of what they'd think."

He squeezed my hand. "You have to stop this. You aren't afraid of throwing yourself in the path of danger, but you're terrified of letting anyone in."

"I . . . I don't know," I said, looking up at him. "I guess."

"Then why'd you tell me?"

I smiled. "Because you told me I should trust people. I trust you."

"You don't trust Lissa?"

My smile faltered. "I trust her, absolutely. But I don't want to tell her things that'll make her worry. I guess it's a way of protecting her, just like keeping Strigoi away."

"She's stronger than you think," he said. "And she would go out of her way to help you."

"So what? You want me to confide in her and not you?"

"No, I want you to confide in both of us. I think it'd be good for you. Does what happened to Anna bother you?"

"No." I looked away again. "It scares me."

I think the admission stunned both of us. I certainly hadn't expected to say it. We both froze for a moment, and then Dimitri wrapped his arms around me and pulled me to his chest. A sob built up in me as I rested my cheek against the leather of his coat and heard the steady beating of his heart.

"I don't want to be like that," I told him. "I want to be like everyone else. I want my mind to be . . . normal. Normal by Rose standards, I mean. I don't want to lose control. I don't want to be like Anna and kill myself. I love being alive. I'd die to save my friends, but I hope it doesn't happen. I hope we all live long, happy lives. Like Lissa said—one big happy family. There's so much I want to do, but I'm so scared . . . scared that I'll be like her. . . . I'm afraid I won't be able to stop it. . . ."

He held me tighter. "It's not going to happen," he murmured. "You're wild and impulsive, but at the end of the day, you're one of the strongest people I know. Even if you are the same as Anna—and I don't think you are—you two won't share the same fate."

It was funny. I'd often told Lissa the same thing about her and Vladimir. She'd always had a hard time believing it, and now I understood. Giving advice was a lot harder than following it.

"You're also missing something," he continued, running a hand over my hair. "If you are in danger from Lissa's magic, then at least you understand why. She can stop using her magic, and that'll be the end of it."

I pulled away slightly so I could look at him. Hastily, I ran my hand over my eyes in case any tears had escaped.

"But can I ask her to do that?" I said. "I've felt how it makes her feel. I don't know if I can take that away from her."

He regarded me with surprise. "Even at the cost of your own life?"

"Vladimir did great things—so could she. Besides, they come first, right?"

"Not always."

I stared. I'd had *they come first* drilled into me since I was a child. It was what all guardians believed. Only the dhampirs who'd run away from their duty didn't subscribe to that. What he said was almost like treason.

"Sometimes, Rose, you have to know when to put yourself first."

I shook my head. "Not with Lissa." I might as well have been with Deirdre or Ambrose again. Why was everyone suddenly challenging something that I'd held as absolute truth my entire life?

"She's your friend. She'll understand." To make his point, he reached forward and tugged at the *chotki* peeking out underneath my sleeve, his fingertips brushing my wrist.

"It's more than that," I said. I pointed to the cross. "If anything, *this* proves it. I'm bound to her, to protect the Dragomirs, at all costs."

"I know, but . . ." He didn't finish, and honestly, what could he have said? This was becoming an old argument, one without a solution.

"I need to get back," I said abruptly. "It's past curfew."

A wry smile crossed Dimitri's face. "And you need me to get you back or you'll get in trouble."

"Well, yeah, I was kind of hoping. . . ."

We heard some rustling near the door of the sanctuary, and Father Andrew walked in, which definitely ended our session. He was getting ready to shut down the chapel. Dimitri thanked him, and then the two of us headed back to the dhampir dorm. Neither of us spoke along the way, but it was a comfortable silence. It was weird, but since his outburst outside the med clinic, I felt like something had intensified between us, as impossible as that seemed.

Dimitri got me past the woman at the front desk, and just as I was about to head off for my wing, a guardian named Yuri walked by. Dimitri called to him.

"You've been working with security, haven't you? When was the last time they laid new wards?"

Yuri considered. "A couple days ago. Why?"

Dimitri gave me a meaningful look. "Just curious."

I nodded to Dimitri to show that I understood his point, and then I went off to bed.

After that, the next week or so played out in a repetitive pattern. I followed Christian for three days a week, had my counseling sessions, and trained with Dimitri. During those times, I could see the concern on Dimitri's face. He always asked how I was but didn't push me to talk about anything I didn't want to. Mostly, it was all physical training, which I liked since it didn't require too much ruminating.

Best of all, I didn't see Mason during this time.

I also didn't witness any attacks—of either the Mânâ type or the guardian type.

We were in full throes of the field experience, and every other novice in my class was having regular fights. The tests grew intricate and more difficult, and everyone had to stay on their toes. Eddie seemed to have to defend Lissa every other day from some guardian playing Strigoi—but it never happened when I was around. In fact, no attacks at all happened to anyone when I was around. After a while, I began to get the idea. They were going soft on me. They were worried I couldn't handle it.

"They might as well have cut me from the field experience after all," I grumbled to Christian one evening. "I'm not doing anything."

"Yeah, but if you still pass, why worry about it? I mean, do you actually want to get in a fight every day?" He then rolled his eyes. "Never mind. Of *course* you do."

"You don't understand," I told him. "This job isn't about taking the easy way out. I want to prove what I can do—to them and to myself. You can never get enough practice. I mean, Lissa's life is at stake." And also possibly my future with her. I'd worried before that they might decide to replace me—and that was *before* they thought I was nuts.

It was nearly curfew time, and I was dropping him off for the night. He shook his head. "Rose, I don't know if you're crazy or not, but I'm actually starting to think you might be the best guardian—or soon-to-be guardian—out there."

"Did you just give me a serious compliment?" I asked.

He turned his back on me and headed inside his dorm. "Good night."

My life was still in chaos, but I couldn't help a small grin as I headed back toward my dorm. The walk always made me nervous since I now lived in perpetual fear of seeing Mason. There were other people scurrying back before curfew too, though, and he mostly tended to show up when I was alone, either because he preferred the privacy or because he really was a figment of my imagination.

Talking about Lissa reminded me that I'd hardly seen her today. Comfortable and content, I let my mind slip into hers while my body continued its walk.

She was in the library, hurriedly trying to finish up some notes. Eddie stood near her, glancing around. "Better hurry up," he said teasingly. "She's making another round."

"Almost done," Lissa said, scrawling a few more words.

She shut the textbook just as the librarian came by and told them they had to leave now. With a sigh of relief, Lissa stuffed her papers into her bag and followed Eddie out. He picked it up and carried it over his shoulder as they went.

"You don't have to do that," she said. "You aren't my valet."

"You can have it back as soon as you fix that." He gestured to where she was tangled up in her coat. She'd shoved it on while trying to get out of the library on time. She laughed at her own disorderliness and adjusted the inside-out sleeve.

"Thanks," she said when he handed it back.

"No problem."

Lissa liked Eddie—though not in a romantic kind of way. She just thought he was nice. He did things like that all the time, helping her out while still doing an excellent job in his duties. His motives weren't romantic, either. He was just one of those rare guys who could be both a gentleman and a badass. She had plans for him.

"Have you ever thought about asking Rose out?"

"What?" he asked.

What? I thought.

"You guys just have so much in common," she said, trying to sound casual. Inside, she was excited. She thought this was the best idea in the world. For me, it was one of those moments where being in her mind was being *too* close to her. I would rather have been standing beside her so I could shake some sense into her.

"She's just my friend," he laughed, his face taking on kind of a cute shyness. "And I don't think we'd actually be that compatible. Besides . . ." His expression fell. "I could never go out with Mason's girlfriend."

Lissa started to say what I always told her, that I hadn't actually been Mason's girlfriend. Wisely, she instead chose to let Eddie keep believing the best. "Everyone has to move on sometime."

"It hasn't been that long, not really. Just over a month. And it's not really something you get over quickly." His eyes had a sad, faraway look that hurt both Lissa and me.

"I'm sorry," she said. "I didn't mean to make it sound like something small. What you saw—I know it was horrible."

"You know what's weird? I actually don't remember much of it. And *that's* what's horrible. I was so drugged out that I had no idea what was going on. I hate that—you have no idea. Being helpless like that . . . it's the worst thing in the world."

I felt the same way. I think it was a guardian thing. Eddie and I had never talked about it, though. We'd never even talked about Spokane much.

"It wasn't your fault," Lissa told him. "Strigoi endorphins are strong. You couldn't have fought against them."

"I should have tried harder," he countered, holding the door to her dorm open. "If I'd been even a little more conscious . . . I don't know. Mason might still be alive."

Eddie and I, I realized, should both have been in therapy as soon as we got back from winter break. I finally understood why everyone said blaming myself for Mason's death was irrational. Eddie and I were both holding ourselves responsible for things that had been beyond our control. We were torturing ourselves with guilt we didn't deserve.

"Hey, Lissa. Come here."

The serious subject was put on hold as Jesse and Ralf waved at her from across the dorm's lobby. My defenses immediately went up. So did hers. She didn't like them any better than I did.

"What's this about?" asked Eddie warily.

"I don't know," she muttered, walking over. "I hope it's fast."

Jesse gave her a dazzling smile, one that I had once found really hot. Now I saw it for the fake piece of crap it was. "How's it going?" he asked.

"It's going tired," she replied. "I need to get to bed. What's up?"

Jesse looked over at Eddie. "Would you give us a little privacy?" Eddie looked at Lissa. She nodded, and Eddie backed up enough to be out of earshot but still watch her. When he was gone, Jesse said, "We have an invitation for you."

"To what, a party?"

"Kind of. It's a group . . ." Ralf wasn't so good with words, and Jesse took over again.

"More than a group. It's only for elite people." He gestured around. "You and me and Ralf . . . we're not like a lot of other Moroi. We're not even like a lot of other royals. We have concerns and issues that we need to take care of." I thought it was funny that he'd include Ralf. Ralf's royalty came from his mother, a Voda, so he didn't even carry one of the royal names, even if he technically had the blood.

"It sounds kind of . . . snobby," she said. "No offense. Thanks for the offer, though." That was Lissa. Always polite, even to creeps like these.

"You don't understand. We aren't just sitting around.

We're working to get things done. We're—" he hesitated and then spoke more softly, " —working on ways to get our voices out there, to make people see our way no matter what."

Lissa gave an uncomfortable laugh. "Sounds like compulsion."

"So?"

I couldn't see her face, but I could feel her working hard to keep it as straight as possible. "Are you out of your mind? Compulsion's forbidden. It's wrong."

"Only to some people. And apparently not you since you're pretty good at it."

She stiffened. "Why would you think that?"

"Because someone—a couple people, actually—hinted at it." People? I tried to remember what Christian and I had said in the feeder room. We'd never mentioned her by name, though both of us had bragged about having seen someone use compulsion. And apparently, Jesse had noticed other things about her. "Besides, it's actually kind of obvious. People love you. You've gotten out of so much trouble, and I finally figured out why. You've been working people over this whole time. I was watching you in class the other day when you convinced Mr. Hill to let Christian work with you on that project. He never would have let anyone else do that."

I'd been with them in class that day. Lissa actually had used compulsion on her teacher to get help for Christian. She'd been so caught up in her pleas that she'd compelled Mr. Hill without even realizing it. Compared to other things I'd seen her do, it had actually been a pretty weak show of compulsion. No one had noticed. Well, almost no one.

"Look," Lissa said uneasily, "I seriously have no idea what you're talking about. I need to go to bed."

Jesse's face grew excited. "No, it's okay. We think it's cool. We want to help you—or actually, we want you to help us. I can't believe I never noticed it before. You're really good at it, and we need you to show us. Plus, none of the other Mână chapters has a Dragomir. We'd be the first to have every royal family represented."

She sighed. "If I could use compulsion, I'd make you guys go away. I told you, I'm not interested."

"But we need you!" exclaimed Ralf. Jesse shot him a sharp look and then turned his smile back on Lissa. I had this weird feeling he might actually be trying to compel her, but it had absolutely no effect on her—or me, since I was watching through her eyes.

"It's not just about you helping us. There are groups of Mână at every school," said Jesse. He was leaning close, and suddenly, he didn't look very friendly anymore. "Its members are all over the world. Be a part of it, and you'll have the connections to do whatever you want with your life. And if we can all learn to work compulsion, we can stop the Moroi government from doing stupid things—we can make sure the queen and everyone else make the right decision. Everything about this is good for you!"

"I'm doing fine on my own, thanks," she said, stepping

back. "And I'm not really sure you know what's best for the Moroi."

"Fine? With your Strigoi boyfriend and slutty wannabe guardian?" exclaimed Ralf. He spoke loudly enough to get Eddie's attention, and Eddie did not look happy.

"Be quiet," Jesse told him angrily. He turned to Lissa. "He shouldn't have said that . . . but he's kind of right. Your family's reputation is all on you, and the way you're going, no one's taking you seriously. The queen's already trying to keep you in line and get you away from Ozera. You're going to crash and burn."

Lissa was growing angrier and angrier. "You have no idea what you're talking about. And—" She frowned. "What do you mean she's trying to get me away from Christian?"

"She wants to marr—" Ralf started to speak, but Jesse immediately cut him off.

"That's exactly what I'm talking about," said Jesse. "We know all sorts of things that could affect you and help you— you *and* Christian."

I had a feeling that Ralf had been about to mention the queen's plans to marry Lissa off to Adrian. I was puzzling out how he would know about that until I recalled again that Ralf was related to the Vodas. Priscilla Voda was the queen's adviser and best friend. She knew all of the queen's plans and had probably told Ralf. His relationship to her must have been closer than I'd realized.

"Tell me," Lissa demanded. The thought of using compulsion on him actually crossed her mind, but she dismissed it. She wouldn't lower herself to that. "What do you know about Christian?"

"No free information," said Jesse. "Come to a meeting and we'll tell you everything."

"Whatever. I'm not interested in your elitist connections, and I don't know anything about compulsion." Despite her words, she was insanely curious about what he knew.

She started to turn away, but Jesse grabbed her arm. "Damn it! You have to—"

"Lissa's going to bed now," said Eddie. He'd shot over as soon as Jesse touched her. "Remove your hand, or I'll do it for you."

Jesse glared at Eddie. Like most Moroi-dhampir matchups, Jesse had height, and Eddie had muscle. Of course, Jesse had Ralf's bulk too, but it wouldn't matter. Everyone there knew who would win if Eddie went up against them. The beauty of it was that Eddie probably wouldn't even get in trouble if he claimed he'd done it to save Lissa from harassment.

Jesse and Ralf slowly backed off. "We need you," said Jesse. "You're the only one. Think about it."

When they were gone, Eddie asked, "Are you okay?"

"Yeah . . . thanks. God, that was so weird." They moved toward the stairs.

"What was it about?"

"They're obsessed with this royal society or something and want me to join so they can have every royal family in it.

They were kind of fanatic about it." Eddie knew about spirit, but she wasn't comfortable reminding him what a badass she was with compulsion.

He opened the door for her. "Well, they can annoy you all they want, but they can't make you join something you don't want to."

"Yeah, I suppose." Part of her still wondered what they knew about Christian or if it had been a bluff. "I just hope they don't get too annoying."

"Don't worry," he told her, his voice hard. "I'll make sure they don't."

I slipped back to my body and opened the door to my own dorm. Halfway up the stairs, I discovered I was smiling. I certainly didn't want Jesse and Ralf bothering Lissa, but if it came down to Eddie having to rough them up? Yeah. I wouldn't mind seeing them get a little payback for what they'd done to others.

TWENTY-TWO

DEIRDRE THE COUNSELOR must not have had much of a life, because she scheduled our next appointment on a Sunday. I wasn't thrilled about it, seeing as it wasn't just my day off—it was also the day my friends had off. Orders were orders, however, so I grudgingly showed up.

"You're wrong," I told her as soon as I sat down. We hadn't really addressed the questions from my first session yet. We'd spent our last couple of times talking about my mother and what I thought of the field experience.

"What about?" she asked. She wore a sleeveless floral dress that seemed too cold for a day like today. It also bore an eerie resemblance to the nature photographs that hung around the office.

"About the guy. I don't just like him because I can't have him. I like him because . . . well, because he's *him*. I've proven it to myself."

"Proven it how?"

"It's a long story," I said evasively. I didn't really want to get into the details of my Adrian compulsion experiment. "You just have to trust me."

"What about the other thing we talked about?" she asked. "What about your feelings about Lissa?"

"That idea was wrong too."

"Did you prove it to yourself?"

"No, but it wasn't the kind of thing I could really test the same way."

"Then how can you be sure?" she asked.

"Because I am." That was the best answer she was going to get.

"How have things been with her recently?"

"Recently how?"

"Have you spent a lot of time together? Kept up with what she's been doing?"

"Sure, kind of. I don't see her as much. She's doing the same things as usual though. Hanging out with Christian. Acing every test. Oh, and she's practically got Lehigh's website memorized."

"Lehigh?"

I explained the queen's offer to Deirdre. "She won't even be there until fall, but Lissa's already looking at all her classes and trying to figure out what she wants to major in."

"What about you?"

"What about me?"

"What will you do while she attends classes?"

"I'll go with her. That's what usually happens if a Moroi has a guardian close to her age. They'll probably enroll me too."

"You'll take the same classes she does?"

"Yup."

"Are there classes you'd rather take instead?"

"How do I know? She hasn't even picked the ones she's going to take, so I don't know if I want to take them or not. But it doesn't matter. I have to go with her."

"And you don't have a problem with that?"

My temper was starting to prickle. This was exactly what I hadn't wanted to talk about. "No," I said tightly.

I knew Deirdre wanted me to elaborate, but I refused to. We held each other's eyes for a few moments, almost like we were challenging the other to look away. Or maybe I was reading too much into it. She glanced down at the mysterious notepad she always held and flipped through a couple of pages. I noticed that her nails were perfectly shaped and painted red. The polish on mine had started to chip.

"Would you rather not talk about Lissa today?" she asked at last.

"We can talk about whatever you think is useful."

"What do *you* think is useful?"

Damn it. She was doing the question thing again. I wondered if one of the certificates on her wall gave her some sort of special qualification to do that.

"I think it'd be useful if you stopped talking to me like I'm a Moroi. You act like I have choices—like I have the right to be upset about any of this or pick what classes I want to take. I mean, let's say I could choose them. What good would it do? What am I going to do with those classes? Go be a lawyer or a marine biologist? There's no point in me having my own schedule. Everything's already decided for me."

"And you're okay with that." It could have been a question, but she said it like a statement of fact.

I shrugged. "I'm okay with keeping her safe, and that's what you keep missing here. Every job has bad parts. Do I want to sit through her calculus classes? No. But I have to because the other part is more important. Do you want to listen to angry teenagers try to block your efforts? No. But you have to because the rest of your job is more important."

"Actually," she said unexpectedly, "that's my favorite part of the job."

I couldn't tell if she was joking or not, but I decided not to pursue it, particularly since she hadn't responded with a question. I sighed.

"I just hate everyone acting like I'm being forced to be a guardian."

"Who's 'everyone'?"

"Well, you and this guy I met at Court . . . this dhampir named Ambrose. He's . . . well, he's a blood whore. A guy blood whore." Like that wasn't obvious. I waited to see if she'd react to the term, but she didn't. "He made it sound like I was trapped in this life and all that too. But I'm not. This is what I want. I'm good at this. I know how to fight, and I know how to defend others. Have you ever seen a Strigoi?"

She shook her head.

"Well, I have. And when I say I want to spend my life protecting Moroi and killing Strigoi, I mean it. Strigoi are evil and need to be wiped out. I'm happy to do that, and if I get to be with my best friend in the process, that's even better."

"I understand that, but what happens if you want other things—things that you can't have by choosing this lifestyle?"

I crossed my arms. "Same answer as before. There are good and bad sides to everything. We just have to balance them as best we can. I mean, are you going to try to tell me that life isn't that way? That if I can't have everything perfect, then there's something wrong with me?"

"No, of course not," she said, tilting back in her chair. "I want you to have a wonderful life, but I can't expect a perfect one. No one can. But what I think is interesting here is how you respond and cope when you have to reconcile these contradictory pieces of your life—when having one thing means you can't have another."

"Everyone goes through that." I felt like I was repeating myself.

"Yes, but not everyone sees ghosts as a result of it."

It took several heavy seconds for me to finally realize what she was getting at. "So wait. You're saying that the reason I'm seeing Mason is because I secretly resent Lissa for the things I can't have in my life? What happened to all the trauma I've been through? I thought that was the reason I'm seeing Mason?"

"I think there are a lot of reasons you're seeing Mason," she said. "And that's what we're exploring."

"And yet," I said, "we never actually talk about Mason."

Deirdre smiled serenely. "Don't we?"

Our session ended.

"Does she always answer your questions with questions?" I asked Lissa later. I was walking with her through the quad, heading toward the commons for dinner. Afterward, we were going to meet up with the others for a movie. It had been a while since she and I had hung out just by ourselves, and I realized now how much I'd missed it.

"We don't see the same counselor," she laughed. "It'd be a conflict of interest."

"Well, does yours do that then?"

"Not that I've really noticed. I take it yours does?"

"Yeah . . . it's actually pretty amazing to watch."

"Who knew the day would come when we'd be comparing notes on therapy?"

We both laughed at that. Several moments passed, and then she started to say something. She wanted to tell me about what had happened with Jesse and Ralf, not realizing I already knew. Before she could say anything, though, someone joined us. Dean Barnes.

"Hey, Rose. A bunch of us are trying to figure out why you're on half-time."

Great. I'd known somebody would ask about that sooner or later. And honestly, I was kind of surprised it hadn't happened already. Everyone had been too busy with their own field experiences to give it much thought until now. I had an excuse ready.

"I've been sick. Dr. Olendzki didn't want me going full-time."

"Really?" he asked, staggering a little. "I thought they were always talking about how in the real world, you don't get sick days. Or something like that."

"Well, this isn't the real world, and Dr. Olendzki's word is final."

"I heard it was because you're a threat to Christian."

"No, believe me, that's not it." The scent of alcohol radiating off of him gave me a convenient way to change the subject. "Have you been drinking?"

"Yeah, Shane got some stuff and had a few of us up in his room. Hey."

"Hey what?" I asked.

"Don't look at me like that."

"Like what?"

"Like you disapprove."

"I'm not," I argued.

Lissa giggled. "You are, actually."

Dean put on an offended face. "Hey, it's my day off, and even if it *is* Sunday, that doesn't mean I can't—"

Something moved beside us.

I didn't even hesitate. It was too fast, too covert to be anything friendly. And it was wearing all black. I threw myself between it and Lissa and lashed out at my attacker. In the flurry of activity, I vaguely recognized a guardian who generally taught the elementary novices. Her name was Jane or

Joan or something like that. Jean, that was it. She was taller than me, but my fist made contact with her face anyway. She staggered back, and then I noticed another shape coming up beside her. Yuri. I leapt over so that she was between him and me. I kicked her in the stomach. She fell toward him, and both stumbled. In that brief moment, I had my practice stake out and aimed for her heart. I hit the mark, and she immediately stepped aside since she was now technically "dead."

Yuri and I then faced off. Beyond me, I heard a muffled sound that I suspected was Dean fighting his own attacker or attackers. I didn't have time to check yet. I needed to dispatch Yuri, which was harder since he was stronger than Jean. He and I circled, both feinting and landing blows. Finally, he made his major move, but I was faster and wiggled out of his grip. I stayed out of his reach just long enough to stake him too.

As soon as he backed away in defeat, I turned toward Dean. Lissa stood off to the side, watching as Dean sparred with his attacker. It was pathetic, to say the least. I'd given Ryan a hard time, but his mistakes were nothing compared to this. Dean's practice stake was on the ground, and his moves were jerky and unsteady. I decided then that he was more of a liability if he stayed in the fight. I threw myself forward and shoved him out of the way, off toward Lissa. I think I might have pushed hard enough to make him fall, but I didn't care. I needed him out of the way.

Facing my opponent, I saw: Dimitri.

It was unexpected. Some little voice in the back of my head said I couldn't fight Dimitri. The rest of me reminded that voice that I'd been doing it for the last six months, and besides, he wasn't Dimitri right now. He was my enemy.

I sprang toward him with the stake, hoping to catch him by surprise. But Dimitri was hard to catch by surprise. And he was fast. Oh, so fast. It was like he knew what I was going to do before I did it. He halted my attack with a glancing blow to the side of the head. I knew it would hurt later, but my adrenaline was running too strong for me to pay attention to it now.

Distantly, I realized some other people had come to watch us. Dimitri and I were celebrities in different ways around here, and our mentoring relationship added to the drama. This was prime-time entertainment.

My eyes were only on Dimitri, though. As we tested each other, attacking and blocking, I tried to remember everything he'd taught me. I also tried to remember everything I knew about him. I'd practiced with him for months. I knew him, knew his moves, just as he knew mine. I could anticipate him the same way. Once I started using that knowledge, the fight grew tricky. We were too well matched, both of us too fast. My heart thumped in my chest, and sweat coated my skin.

Then Dimitri finally got through. He moved in for an attack, coming at me with the full force of his body. I blocked the worst of it, but he was so strong that I was the one who stumbled from the impact. He didn't waste the opportunity and dragged me to the ground, trying to pin me. Being trapped like that by a Strigoi would likely result in the neck being bitten or broken. I couldn't let that happen.

So, although he held most of me to the ground, I managed to shove my elbow up and nail him in the face. He flinched, and that was all I needed. I rolled him over and held him down. He fought to push me off, and I pushed right back while also trying to maneuver my stake. He was so strong, though. I was certain I wouldn't be able to hold him. Then, just as I thought I'd lose my hold, I got a good grip on the stake. And like that, the stake came down over his heart. It was done.

Behind me, people were clapping, but all I noticed was Dimitri. Our gazes were locked. I was still straddling him, my hands pressed against his chest. Both of us were sweaty and breathing heavily. His eyes looked at me with pride— and a hell of a lot more. He was so close, and my whole body yearned for him, again thinking he was a piece of me I needed in order to be complete. The air between us seemed warm and heady, and I would have given anything in that moment to lie down with him and have his arms wrap around me. His expression showed me that he was thinking the same thing. The fight was finished, but remnants of the adrenaline and animal intensity remained.

Then a hand reached down, and Jean helped me stand up. She and Yuri were beaming, as were the spectators who had wandered up. Even Lissa looked impressed. Dean, understandably, looked miserable. I hoped word of my stunning victory would spread around campus as fast as the recent bad stuff about me had. Probably not.

"Well done," said Yuri. "You took down all three of us. That was textbook perfect."

Dimitri was on his feet now too. I looked pointedly at the other two guardians because I was pretty sure if I looked at him, my expression would give everything away. My breathing was still heavy. "I hope . . . I hope I didn't hurt any of you," I said.

This made all of them laugh. "That's our job," said Jean. "Don't worry about us. We're tough." She glanced at Dimitri. "She got you pretty good with her elbow."

Dimitri rubbed his face near his eye, and I hoped I hadn't caused too much damage. "The student surpasses the teacher," he joked. "Or stakes, rather."

Yuri was giving Dean a hard look. "Alcohol isn't allowed on campus."

"It's Sunday!" he exclaimed. "We aren't supposed to be on duty."

"There are no rules in the real world," said Jean in a very teacherlike way. "Consider this a pop quiz. You passed it, Rose. Very nice job."

"Thanks. Wish I could say the same for my clothes." I was wet and muddy. "I'm going to have to go change, Liss. I'll meet you for dinner."

"Okay." Her face was alight. She was so proud of me, she could barely contain it. I could also sense her keeping something secret, and I wondered if there would be a congratulations surprise when I saw her later. I didn't probe too deeply, lest I ruin it.

"And you," said Yuri, tugging at Dean's sleeve, "are going to take a walk with us."

I met Dimitri's eyes. I wished he could have stuck around and talked. My adrenaline was running high, and I wanted to celebrate. I'd done it. Finally. After all the embarrassment over my fumbles and alleged incompetence, I'd finally proven what I could do. I wanted to start dancing. Dimitri had to go with the others, though, and only a slight nod of his head told me he wished it were otherwise. I sighed and watched them leave, and then I walked back to my dorm alone.

Back in my room, I discovered the situation was worse than I thought. Once I'd stripped off my muddy clothes, I realized I was going to need a shower and a good scrubbing before I was presentable. By the time it was all done, nearly an hour had passed. I'd missed most of dinner.

I ran back over to the commons, wondering why Lissa hadn't sent me any nagging thoughts. She had a tendency to do that when I was running late. Probably she'd decided I'd deserved a break after my triumph. Thinking about it again, a big grin crept over my face, one that dried up when I headed down the hallway that led to the cafeteria.

A big group of people had gathered around something, and I recognized the international sign of a fight. Considering how Jesse's band liked to conduct their beatings in secret, I figured this probably had nothing to do with them. Squeezing through people, I pushed myself forward and peeked over some heads, curious as to who could have drawn such a crowd.

It was Adrian and Christian.

And Eddie. But Eddie was clearly there in a referee role. He was standing between them, trying to keep them away from each other. Manners gone, I shoved aside the last few people in front of me and hurried to Eddie's side.

"What the hell's going on?" I demanded.

He looked relieved to see me. He might be able to fend off our instructors in combat, but this situation was clearly something he was confused about.

"No idea."

I looked at the two combatants. Fortunately, no one seemed to have hit anybody . . . yet. It also looked as though Christian was the one on the offensive.

"How long did you think you could get away with it?" he exclaimed. His eyes were like blue fire. "Did you seriously think everyone would keep buying your act?"

Adrian looked laconic as usual, but I could see some anxiety under that lazy smile. He didn't want to be in this situation, and, like Eddie, he wasn't even sure how it had happened.

"Honestly," said Adrian in a weary voice, "I have no idea what you're talking about. Can we please just go sit down and discuss this reasonably?"

"Sure. Of course you'd want that. You're afraid I might do this." Christian held up his hand, and a ball of flame danced over his palm. Even under the fluorescent lights, it glowed bright orange with a deep blue core. There were gasps from the crowd. I'd long since gotten used to the idea of Moroi fighting with magic—Christian in particular—but for most, it was still a taboo thing. Christian smirked. "What have you got to fight back with? Plants?"

"If you're going to go start fights for no reason, you should at least do it the old-fashioned way and throw a punch," said Adrian. His voice was light, but he was still uneasy. My guess was that he figured he could do better with hand-to-hand than spirit-to-fire.

"No," interrupted Eddie. "No one's going to set anyone on fire. No one's going to punch anybody. There's been some huge mistake."

"What is it?" I demanded. "What happened?"

"Your friend there thinks I'm planning to marry Lissa and carry her off into the sunset," said Adrian. He spoke to me, but his eyes never left Christian.

"Don't act like it's not true," growled Christian. "I know it is. It's been part of your plan—yours and the queen's. She's been backing you the whole time. Coming back here . . . the whole studying thing . . . it was a scam to get Lissa away from me and tied to your family instead."

"Do you have any idea how paranoid you sound?" asked Adrian. "My great-aunt has to manage the entire Moroi government! Do you think she really cares about who's dating who in high school—especially with the state of affairs lately? Look, I'm sorry about all the time I've spent with her . . . we'll find her and figure this out. I really wasn't trying to get between you. There's no conspiracy going on here."

"Yes, there is," said Christian. He glanced over at me with a scowl "Isn't there? Rose knows. Rose has known for a while about this. She even talked to the queen about it."

"That's ridiculous," said Adrian, surprised enough that he too shot me a quick glance. "Right?"

"Well . . ." I began, realizing this was getting very ugly very quickly. "Yes and no."

"See?" asked Christian triumphantly.

The fire flew from his hand, but Eddie and I jumped into motion at the same time. People screamed. Eddie grabbed Christian, forcing the fire to fly high. Meanwhile, I grabbed Adrian and slammed him to the floor. It was a lucky division of labor. I didn't want to think what would have happened if Eddie and I had gone for the same person.

"Glad you care," muttered Adrian, wincing as he lifted his head from the floor.

"Compel him," I murmured as I helped him up. "We need to sort this out without someone spontaneously combusting."

Eddie was trying to restrain Christian from leaping forward. I grabbed a hold of one arm to help. Adrian didn't look thrilled about coming any closer, but he obeyed me nonetheless. Christian tried to jerk free but couldn't fight both Eddie and me. Uneasily, probably afraid of his hair catching on fire,

Adrian leaned over Christian and made eye contact.

"Christian, stop this. Let's talk."

Christian struggled a little against his restraints, but slowly, his face went slack and his eyes started to glaze over.

"Let's talk about this," repeated Adrian.

"Okay," said Christian.

There was a collective sigh of disappointment from the crowd. Adrian had used his compulsion smoothly enough that no one suspected. It had looked as though Christian had simply seen reason. As the crowd dispersed, Eddie and I released Christian enough to a lead him over to far corner where we could talk in private. As soon as Adrian broke the gaze, Christian's face filled with fury, and he tried to leap at Adrian. Eddie and I were already holding on. He didn't move.

"What did you just do?" exclaimed Christian. Several people down the hall glanced back, no doubt hoping there'd be a fight after all. I shushed loudly in his ear. He flinched. "Ow."

"Be quiet. Something's wrong here, and we need to figure it out before you do something stupid."

"What's wrong," Christian said, glaring at Adrian, "is that they're trying to break up Lissa and me, and *you* knew about it, Rose."

Adrian glanced at me. "Did you really?"

"Yeah, long story." I turned back to Christian. "Look, Adrian didn't have anything to do with this. Not intentionally. It was Tatiana's idea—and she hasn't even actually done anything yet. It's just her long-term plan—hers alone, not his."

"Then how did you know about it?" demanded Christian.

"Because she told me—she was afraid that *I* was moving in on Adrian."

"Really? Did you defend our love?" Adrian asked.

"Be quiet," I said. "What I want to know, Christian, is who told you?"

"Ralf," he said, looking uncertain for the first time.

"You should have known better than to listen to him," remarked Eddie, face darkening at the name.

"Except, for once, Ralf was actually telling the truth— aside from Adrian being in on it. Ralf's related to the queen's best friend," I explained.

"Wonderful," said Christian. He seemed calm enough, so Eddie and I released him. "We've all been played."

I looked around, suddenly taken aback by something. "Where's Lissa? Why didn't she stop all of this?"

Adrian raised an eyebrow at me. "You tell us. Where is she? She didn't come to dinner."

"I can't. . . ." I frowned. I'd gotten so good at shielding myself when I needed to that long periods of time would go by without me feeling anything from her. This time, I sensed nothing because there was nothing coming from her. "I can't feel her."

Three sets of eyes stared at me.

"Is she asleep?" asked Eddie.

"I can tell when she's asleep. . . . This is something differ-ent. . . ." Slowly, slowly, I gained a sense of where she was.

She'd been blocking me out on purpose, trying to hide from me, but I'd found her as I always did. "There she is. She was— oh God!"

My scream rang down the hall, echoing Lissa's own screams as, far away, pain shot through her.

TWENTY-THREE

OTHERS IN THE HALL stopped and stared. I felt like I had just been hit in the face. Only it hadn't been my face. It had been Lissa's. I shifted into her mind and became instantly aware of her surroundings and everything happening to her—like the next time rocks flew up from the ground and slammed into her cheeks. They were guided by a freshman I didn't know anything about, save that he was a Drozdov. The rocks hurt both of us, but I withheld my screaming this time and gritted my teeth as I shifted back to the hallway with my friends.

"Northwest side of campus, between that weird-shaped pond and the fence," I told them.

With that, I broke away from them and headed out the door, running as hard as I could toward the part of campus where they were holding Lissa. I couldn't see all of the people gathered there through her eyes, but I recognized a few. Jesse and Ralf were there. Brandon. Brett. The Drozdov guy. Some others. The rocks were still hitting her, still cutting into her face. She didn't scream or cry, though—she just kept telling them over and over to stop while two other guys held her between them.

Jesse, meanwhile, kept telling her to *make* them stop. I only half-listened to him through her mind. The reasons didn't matter, and I'd already figured it out. They were going to torture her until she agreed to join their group. They must have forced Brandon and the others in the same way.

A suffocating feeling suddenly overwhelmed me, and I stumbled, unable to breathe as water smothered my face. Fighting hard, I separated myself from Lissa. That was happening to her, not me. Someone was torturing her with water now, using it to cut off her air. Whoever it was took their time, alternately filling her face with water, then pulling it back, then repeating. She gasped and sputtered, still asking them to stop when she could.

Jesse continued watching with calculating eyes. "Don't ask them. Make them."

I tried running harder, but I could only go so much faster. They were at one of the farthest points of campus's boundaries. It was a lot of distance to cover, and with every agonizing step, I felt more of Lissa's pain and grew angrier and angrier. What kind of a guardian could I ever be to her if I couldn't even keep her safe here on campus?

An air user went next, and suddenly, it was like she was being tortured by Victor's henchman all over again. Air was alternately taken from her, leaving her gasping, and then slammed back into her, crushing her face. It was agony, and it brought back all the memories of her capture, all the terror and horror she'd been trying to forget. The air user stopped, but it was too late. Something snapped inside of her.

When Ralf stepped up next to use fire, I was so close that I actually saw it flare up in his hand. But he didn't see me.

None of them had been paying attention to their surroundings, and there'd been too much noise from their own spectacle to hear me. I slammed into Ralf before the fire could leave his hand, pulling him to the ground and punching his face in one skilled maneuver. A few of the others—including Jesse—ran to help him and tried to pry me away. At least, they tried until they realized who it was.

Those who saw my face immediately backed off. Those who didn't quickly learned the hard way when I went after them. I'd taken out three fully trained guardians earlier today. A group of spoiled royal Moroi took hardly any effort. It was ironic, too—and a sign of how unwilling some Moroi were to lift a hand in their defense—that while this group had been so eager to use magic to torture Lissa, none of them had actually thought to use it against me.

Most of them scattered before I could even lay a hand on them, and I didn't care enough to go after them. I just wanted them away from Lissa. Admittedly, I gave Ralf a few extra punches even after he'd gone down, since I held him responsible for this whole mess. I finally left him alone, lying on the ground and groaning, as I straightened up and looked for Jesse—the other culprit here. I quickly found him. He was the only one left.

I ran over to him and then skidded to a halt, confused. He was just standing there, staring into space, mouth hanging open. I looked at him, looked at where he was staring, and then looked back at him.

"Spiders," Lissa said. Her voice made me jump. She stood off to the side with wet hair, bruised and cut, but otherwise okay. In the moonlight, her pale features made her look almost as ghostly as Mason. Her eyes never left Jesse as he spoke. "He thinks he's seeing spiders. And that they're crawling on him. What do you think? Should I have gone with snakes?"

I looked back at Jesse. The expression on his face sent chills down my spine. It was like he was locked in his own private nightmare. Scarier still was what I felt through the bond. Usually when Lissa used magic, it felt golden and warm and wonderful. This time, it was different. It was black and slimy and thick.

"I think you should stop," I said. In the distance, I heard people running toward us. "It's all over."

"It was an initiation ritual," she said. "Well, kind of. They asked me to join a couple of days ago, and I refused. But they bugged me again today and kept saying they knew something important about Christian and Adrian. It started to get to me, so . . . I finally told them I'd come to one of their sessions but that I didn't know anything about compulsion. It was an act. I just wanted to know what they knew." She tilted her head barely at all, but something must have happened to Jesse. His eyes widened further as he continued to silently scream. "Even though I hadn't technically agreed yet, they put me through their initiation ritual. They wanted to know how much I could really do. It's a way to test how strong people are in compulsion. Torture them until they can't stand it, and then, in the heat of it all, people lash out and try to compel the attackers to stop. If the victim manages any sort of compulsion at all, that person's in the group." She regarded Jesse carefully. He seemed to be in his own world, and it was a very, very bad one. "I guess this makes me their president, huh?"

"Stop it," I said. The feel of this twisted magic was making me nauseous. She and Adrian had mentioned something like this before, this idea of making people see things that weren't there. They'd jokingly called it super compulsion—and it was horrible. "This isn't how spirit is supposed to be used. This isn't you. It's wrong."

She was breathing heavily, sweat breaking out along her brow. "I can't let go of it," she said.

"You can," I said. I touched her arm. "Give it to me."

She briefly turned from Jesse and looked at me, astonished, before fixing her gaze back on him.

"What? You can't use magic."

I focused hard on the bond, on her mind. I couldn't take the magic exactly, but I could take the darkness it brought on. It was what I'd been doing for a while now, I realized. Every time I'd worried and wished she'd calm down and fight dark feelings, she had—because I was taking it all from her. I was absorbing it, just as Anna had done for St. Vladimir. It was what Adrian had seen when the darkness jumped from her aura to mine. And this—this abuse of spirit, using it to maliciously harm another and *not* for self-defense, was bringing the worst side effects of all in her. It was corrupting and wrong, and I couldn't let her have it. All thoughts of my own madness or rage were completely irrelevant at this moment.

"No," I agreed. "I can't. But you can use me to let it go. Focus on me. Release it all. It's wrong. You don't want it."

She stared at me again, eyes wide and desperate. Even without direct eye contact, she was still able to torture Jesse. I both saw and felt the fight she waged. He'd hurt her so much—she wanted him to pay. He had to. And yet, at the same time, she knew I was right. But it was hard. So hard for her to let go . . .

Suddenly, the burn of that black magic vanished from the bond, along with that sickening sensation. Something hit me like a blast of wind in the face, and I staggered backward. I shuddered as a weird sensation twisted my stomach. It was like sparks, like a coil of electricity burning within me. Then it too was gone. Jesse fell to his knees, free of the nightmare.

Lissa sank with visible relief. She was still scared and hurt over what had happened, but she was no longer consumed with that terrible, destructive rage that had driven her to punish Jesse. That urge within her had disappeared.

The only problem was, it was in *me* now.

I turned on Jesse, and it was like nothing else existed in the universe except him. He had tried to ruin me in the past. He'd tortured Lissa and hurt so many others. It was unacceptable. I lunged for him. His eyes had only a moment to widen with terror before my fist connected with his face. His head jerked back, and blood spurted from his nose. I heard Lissa scream for me to stop, but I couldn't. He had to pay for what he'd done to her. I grabbed him by the shoulders and threw him hard against the ground. He was yelling now too—begging—for me to stop. He shut up when I hit him again.

I felt Lissa's hands clawing at me, trying to pull me off, but she wasn't strong enough. I kept hitting him. There was no sign of the strategic, precise fighting I'd used earlier with him and his friends, or even against Dimitri. This was unfocused and primal. This was me being controlled by the madness I'd taken from Lissa.

Then another set of hands ripped me away. These hands were stronger, dhampir hands, backed by muscles earned through years of training. It was Eddie. I struggled against his hold. We were closely matched, but he outweighed me.

"Let me go!" I yelled.

To my complete and utter horror, Lissa was now kneeling at Jesse's side, studying him with concern. It made no sense. How could she do that? After what he'd done? I saw compassion on her face, and a moment later, the burn of her healing magic lit our bond as she took away some of the worst of his injuries.

"No!" I screamed, straining against Eddie's hold. "You can't!"

That was when the other guardians showed up, Dimitri and Celeste in the lead. Christian and Adrian were nowhere in sight; they probably couldn't have kept pace with the others.

Organized chaos followed. Those from the society who remained were gathered up and herded off for questioning. Lissa likewise was taken away, led off to get her injuries treated. A part of me that was buried in all that bloodthirsty emotion wanted to go after her, but something else had caught my attention: They were also removing Jesse for medical help. Eddie was still holding onto me, his grip never faltering despite my struggles and pleas. Most of the adults were too busy with the others to notice me, but they noticed when I started shouting again.

"You can't let him go! You can't let him go!"

"Rose, calm down," said Alberta, her voice mild. How could she not get what was going on? "It's over."

"It is *not* over! Not until I get my hands around his throat and choke the life out of him!"

Alberta and some of the others seemed to realize that something serious was happening now—but they didn't appear to think it had anything to do with Jesse. They were all giving me the Rose-is-crazy look I'd come to know so well in recent days.

"Get her out of here," said Alberta. "Get her cleaned up and calmed down." She didn't give any more instructions than that, but somehow, it was understood that Dimitri would be the one to deal with me.

He came over and took me from Eddie. In the brief change of captors, I tried to break away, but Dimitri was too fast and too strong. He grabbed my arm and started pulling me away from the scene.

"We can make this easy or difficult," said Dimitri as we walked through the woods. "There's no way I'm letting you go to Jesse. Besides, he's at the med clinic, so you'd never get near him. If you can accept that, I'll release you. If you bolt, you know I'll just restrain you again."

I weighed my options. The need to make Jesse suffer was still pounding in my blood, but Dimitri was right. For now.

"Okay," I said. He hesitated a moment, perhaps wondering if I was telling the truth, and then let go of my arm. When I didn't run off, I felt him relax very, very slightly.

"Alberta told you to clean me up," I said evenly. "So we're going to the med clinic?"

Dimitri scoffed. "Nice try. I'm not letting you near him. We'll get first aid somewhere else."

He led me off at an angle from the attack location, toward an area still at the edge of campus. I quickly realized where he was going. It was a cabin. Back when there had been more guardians on campus, some had actually stayed at these little outposts, providing regular protection for the school's boundaries. They'd long since been abandoned, but this one had been cleaned up when Christian's aunt had visited. She'd preferred hanging out here than in the school's guest housing where other Moroi regarded her as a potential Strigoi.

He opened the door. It was dark inside, but I could see well enough to watch him find matches and light a kerosene lantern. It didn't provide a huge amount of light, but it was fine for our eyes. Glancing around, I saw that Tasha really had done a good job with the place. It was clean and almost cozy, the bed made up with a soft quilt and a couple of chairs pulled up to the fireplace. There was even some food—canned and packaged—in the kitchen off to the side of the room.

"Sit down," said Dimitri, gesturing to the bed. I did, and in about a minute, he had a fire going to warm the place up. Once it was in full blaze, he grabbed a first aid kit and a bottle of water from the counter and walked back over to the bed, dragging a chair so he could sit opposite me.

"You have to let me go," I begged. "Don't you see? Don't you see how Jesse has to pay? He tortured her! He did horrible things to her."

Dimitri wet some gauze and dabbed it to the side of my forehead. It stung, so I apparently had a cut there. "He'll be punished, believe me. And the others."

"With what?" I asked bitterly. "Detention? This is as bad as Victor Dashkov. Nobody does *anything* around here! People commit crimes and get away with it. He needs to *hurt*. They all need to."

Dimitri paused his cleaning, giving me a concerned look. "Rose, I know you're upset, but you know we don't punish people like that. It's . . . savage."

"Yeah? What's wrong with that? I'd bet it'd stop them from doing it again." I could barely sit there. Every part of my body trembled with fury. "They need to suffer for what they did! And *I* want to be the one to do it! I want to hurt them all. I want to kill them all." I started to get up, suddenly feeling like I'd explode. His hands were on my shoulders in a flash, shoving me back down. The first aid was long forgotten. His expression was a mixture of both worry and fierceness as he held me down. I fought against him, and his fingers bit in tighter.

"Rose! Snap out of this!" He was yelling now too. "You don't mean any of it. You've been stressed and under a lot of pressure—it's making a terrible event that much worse."

"Stop it!" I shouted back at him. "You're doing it—just like you always do. You're always so reasonable, no matter how awful things are. What happened to you wanting to kill Victor in prison, huh? Why was that okay, but not this?"

"Because that was an exaggeration. You know it was. But this . . . this is something different. There's something wrong with you right now."

"No, there's something right with me." I was sizing him up, hoping my words distracted him. If I was fast enough, maybe—just maybe—I could get past him. "I'm the only one who wants to do anything around here, and if that's wrong, I'm sorry. You keep wanting me to be some impossible, good person, but I'm not! I'm not a saint like you."

"Neither of us is a saint," he said dryly. "Believe me, I don't—"

I made my move, leaping out and shoving him away. It got him off me, but I didn't get far. I'd barely gotten two feet from the bed when he seized me again and pinned me down, this time using the full weight of his body to keep me immobilized. Somehow, I knew I should have realized it was an impossible escape plan, but I couldn't think straight.

"Let me go!" I yelled for the hundredth time tonight, trying to free my hands.

"No," he said, voice hard and almost desperate. "Not until you break out of this. This isn't you!"

There were hot tears in my eyes. "It is! Let me go!"

"It's not. It isn't you! *It isn't you.*" There was agony in his voice.

"You're wrong! It is—"

My words suddenly dropped off. *It isn't you.* It was the same thing I'd said to Lissa when I watched, terrified, as she used her magic to torture Jesse. I'd stood there, unable to believe what she was doing. She hadn't realized she'd lost control and was on the verge of becoming a monster. And now, looking into Dimtiri's eyes, seeing his panic and love, I realized it was happening to me. I was the same as she'd been, so caught up, so blinded by irrational emotions that I didn't even recognize my own actions. It was like I was being controlled by something else.

I tried to fight it off, to shake off the feelings burning through me. They were too strong. I couldn't do it. I couldn't let them go. They would take me over completely, just as they'd done to Anna and Ms. Karp.

"Rose," said Dimitri. It was only my name, but it was

so powerful, filled with so much. Dimitri had such absolute faith me, faith in my own strength and goodness. And he had strength too, a strength I could see he wasn't afraid to lend me if I needed it. Deirdre might have been onto something about me resenting Lissa, but she was completely off about Dimitri. What we had was love. We were like two halves of a whole, always ready to support the other. Neither of us was perfect, but that didn't matter. With him, I could defeat this rage that filled me. He believed I was stronger than it. And I was.

Slowly, slowly, I felt that darkness fade away. I stopped fighting him. My body trembled, but it was no longer with fury. It was fear. Dimitri immediately recognized the change and released his hold.

"Oh my God," I said, voice shaking.

His hand touched the side of my face, fingers light on my cheek. "Rose," he breathed. "Are you okay?"

I swallowed back more tears. "I . . . I think so. For now."

"It's over," he said. He was still touching me, this time brushing the hair from my face. "It's over. Everything's all right."

I shook my head. "No. It's not. You . . . you don't understand. It's true—everything I was worried about. About Anna? About me taking away spirit's craziness? It's happening, Dimitri. Lissa lost it out there with Jesse. She was out of control, but I stopped her because I sucked away her anger and put it into myself. And it's—it's horrible. It's like I'm, I don't know, a puppet. I can't control myself."

"You're strong," he said. "It won't happen again."

"No," I said. I could hear my voice cracking as I struggled to sit up. "It *will* happen again. I'm going to be like Anna. I'm going to get worse and worse. This time it was bloodlust and hate. I wanted to destroy them. I needed to destroy them. Next time? I don't know. Maybe it'll just be craziness, like Ms. Karp. Maybe I'm already crazy, and that's why I'm seeing Mason. Maybe it'll be depression like Lissa used to get. I'll keep falling and falling into that pit, and then I'll be like Anna and kill—"

"No," Dimitri interrupted gently. He moved his face toward mine, our foreheads nearly touching. "It won't happen to you. You're too strong. You'll fight it, just like you did this time."

"I only did because you were here." He wrapped his arms around me, and I buried my face in his chest. "I can't do it by myself," I whispered.

"You can," he said. There was a tremulous note in his voice. "You're strong—you're so, so strong. It's why I love you."

I squeezed my eyes shut. "You shouldn't. I'm going to become something terrible. I might already be something terrible." I thought back to past behaviors, the way I'd been snapping at everyone. The way I'd tried to scare Ryan and Camille.

Dimitri pulled away so that he could look me in the eyes. He cupped my face in his hands. "You aren't. You won't," he said. "I won't let you. No matter what, I won't let you."

Emotion filled my body again, but now it wasn't hate or rage or anything like that. It was warm and wonderful and made my heart ache—in a good way. I wrapped my arms around his neck, and our lips met. The kiss was pure love, sweet and blissful, with no despair or darkness. Steadily, though, the intensity of our kissing increased. It was still filled with love but became much more—something hungry and powerful. The electricity that had crackled between us when I'd fought and held him down earlier returned, wrapping around us now.

It reminded me of the night we'd been under Victor's lust spell, both of us driven by inner forces we couldn't control. It was like we were starving or drowning, and only the other person could save us. I clung to him, one arm around his neck while my other hand gripped his back so hard that my nails practically dug in. He laid me back down on the bed. His hands wrapped around my waist, and then one of them slid down the back of my thigh and pulled it up so that it nearly wrapped around him.

At the same time, we both pulled back briefly, still oh so close. Everything in the world rested on that moment.

"We can't . . ." he told me.

"I know," I agreed.

Then his mouth was on mine again, and this time, I knew there would be no turning back. There were no walls this time. Our bodies wrapped together as he tried to get my coat off, then his shirt, then my shirt. . . . It really was a lot like when we'd fought out on the quad earlier—that same passion and heat. I think at the end of the day, the instincts that power fighting and sex aren't so different. They all come from an animal side of us.

Yet, as more and more clothes came off, it went beyond just animal passion. It was sweet and wonderful at the same time. When I looked into his eyes, I could see without a doubt that he loved me more than anyone else in the world, that I was his salvation, the same way that he was mine. I'd never expected my first time to be in a cabin in the woods, but I realized the place didn't matter. The person did. With someone you loved, you could be anywhere, and it would be incredible. Being in the most luxurious bed in the world wouldn't matter if you were with someone you didn't love.

And oh, I loved him. I loved him so much that it hurt. All of our clothes finally ended up in a pile on the floor, but the feel of his skin on mine was more than enough to keep me warm. I couldn't tell where my body ended and his began, and I decided then that was how I always wanted it to be. I didn't want us to ever be apart.

I wish I had the words to describe sex, but nothing I can say would really capture how amazing it was. I felt nervous, excited, and about a gazillion other things. Dimitri seemed so wise and skilled and infinitely patient—just like with our combat trainings. Following his lead seemed like a natural thing, but he was also more than willing to let me take control too. We were equals at last, and every touch held power, even the slightest brushing of his fingertips.

When it was over, I lay back against him. My body hurt . . . yet at the same time, it felt amazing, blissful and content. I wished I'd been doing this a long time ago, but I also knew it wouldn't have been right until exactly this moment.

I rested my head on Dimitri's chest, taking comfort in his warmth. He kissed my forehead and ran his fingers through my hair.

"I love you, Roza." He kissed me again. "I'll always be here for you. I'm not going to let anything happen to you."

The words were wonderful and dangerous. He shouldn't have said anything like that to me. He shouldn't have been promising he'd protect *me*, not when he was supposed to dedicate his life to protecting Moroi like Lissa. I couldn't be first in his heart, just like he couldn't be first in mine. That was why I shouldn't have said what I said next—but I did anyway.

"And I won't let anything happen to you," I promised. "I love you." He kissed me again, swallowing off any other words I might have added.

We lay together for a while after that, wrapped in each other's arms, not saying much. I could have stayed that way forever, but finally, we knew we had to go. The others would eventually come looking for us to get my report, and if they found us like that, things would almost certainly get ugly.

So we got dressed, which wasn't easy since we kept stopping to kiss. Finally, reluctantly, we left the cabin. We held hands, knowing we could only do so for a few brief moments.

Once we were closer to the heart of campus, we'd have to go back to business as usual. But for now, everything in the world was golden and wonderful. Every step I took was filled with joy, and the air around us seemed to hum.

Questions still spun in my mind, of course. What had just happened? Where had our so-called control gone? For now, I couldn't care. My body was still warm and wanting him and—I suddenly stopped. Another feeling—a very unwelcome one—was steadily creeping over me. It was strange, like faint and fleeting waves of nausea mingled with a prickling against my skin. Dimitri stopped immediately and gave me a puzzled look.

A pale, slightly luminescent form materialized in front of us. Mason. He looked the same as ever—or did he? The usual sadness was there, but I could see something else, something else I couldn't quite put my finger on. Panic? Frustration? I could have almost sworn it was fear, but honestly, what would a ghost have to be afraid of?

"What's wrong?" asked Dimitri.

"Do you see him?" I whispered.

Dimitri followed my gaze. "See who?"

"Mason."

Mason's troubled expression grew darker. I might not have been able to adequately identify it, but I knew it wasn't anything good. The nauseous feeling within me intensified, but somehow, I knew it had nothing to do with him.

"Rose . . . we should go back . . ." said Dimitri carefully. He still wasn't on board with me seeing ghosts.

But I didn't move. Mason's face was saying something else to me—or trying to. There was something here, something important that I needed to know. But he couldn't communicate it.

"What?" I asked. "What is it?

A look of frustration crossed his face. He pointed off behind me, then dropped his hand.

"Tell me," I said, my frustration mirroring his. Dimitri was looking back and forth between me and Mason, though Mason was probably only an empty space to him.

I was too fixated on Mason to worry what Dimitri might think. There was something here. Something big. Mason opened his mouth, wanting to speak as in previous times but still unable to get the words out. Except, this time, after several agonizing seconds, he managed it. The words were nearly inaudible.

"They're . . . coming. . . ."

TWENTY-FOUR

T HE WHOLE WORLD WAS still. At this time of
night, there were no birds or anything, but it seemed quieter
than usual. Even the wind had fallen silent. Mason looked at
me pleadingly. The nausea and prickling increased.

Then, I knew.

"Dimitri," I said urgently, "there are Strig—"

Too late. Dimitri and I saw him at the same time, but
Dimitri was closer. Pale face. Red eyes. The Strigoi swooped
toward us, and I could almost imagine he was flying, just like
vampire legends used to say. But Dimitri was just as fast and
nearly as strong. He had his stake—a real one, not a practice
one—in his hand and met the Strigoi's attack. I think the Strigoi had hoped for the element of surprise. They grappled, and
for a moment they seemed suspended in time, neither gaining
ground on the other. Then Dimitri's hand snaked out, plung-
ing the stake into the Strigoi's heart. The red eyes widened in
surprise, and the Strigoi's body crumpled to the ground.

Dimitri turned to me to make sure I was all right, and a
thousand silent messages passed between us. He turned away
and scanned the woods, peering into the darkness. My nausea
had increased. I didn't understand why, but somehow I could
sense the Strigoi around us. That was what was making me

feel sick. Dimitri turned back to me, and there was a look I'd never seen in his eyes.

"Rose. Listen to me. Run. Run as fast and as hard as you can back to your dorm. Tell the guardians."

I nodded. There was no questioning here.

Reaching out, he gripped my upper arm, gaze locked on me to make sure I understood his next words. "Do not stop," he said. "No matter what you hear, no matter what you see, *do not stop*. Not until you've warned the others. Don't stop unless you're directly confronted. Do you understand?"

I nodded again. He released his hold.

"Tell them *buria*."

I nodded again.

"*Run*."

I ran. I didn't look back. I didn't ask what he was going to do because I already knew. He was going to stop as many Strigoi as he could so that I could get help. And a moment later, I heard grunts and hits that told me he'd found another. For only a heartbeat, I let myself worry about him. If he died, I was certain I would too. But then I let it go. I couldn't just think about one person, not when hundreds of lives were depending on me. There were Strigoi at our school. It was impossible. It couldn't happen.

My feet hit the ground hard, splashing through the slush and mud. Around me, I thought I could hear voices and shapes—not the ghosts from the airport, but the monsters I'd been dreading for so long. But nothing stopped me. When

Dimitri and I had first begun training together, he'd made me run laps every day. I'd complained, but he'd stated over and over again that it was essential. It would make me stronger, he had said. And, he'd added, a day could come when I couldn't fight and would have to flee. This was it.

The dhampir dorm appeared before me, about half its windows lit. It was near curfew; people were going to bed. I burst in through the doors, feeling like my heart was going to explode from the exertion. The first person I saw was Stan, and I nearly knocked him over. He caught my wrists to steady me.

"Rose, wh—"

"Strigoi," I gasped out. "There are Strigoi on campus."

He stared at me, and for the first time I'd ever seen, his mouth seriously dropped open. Then, he recovered himself, and I could immediately see what he was thinking. More ghost stories. "Rose, I don't know what you're—"

"I'm not crazy!" I screamed. Everyone in the dorm's lobby was staring at us. "They're out there! They're out there, and Dimitri is fighting them alone. You have to help him." What had Dimitri told me? What was that word? "*Buria*. He said to tell you *buria*."

And like that, Stan was gone.

I had never seen any drills for Strigoi attacks, yet the guardians must have conducted them. Things moved too fast for them not to have. Every guardian in the dorm, whether they'd been awake or not, was in the lobby in a matter of minutes. Calls were made. I stood in a semicircle with other novices, who watched our elders organize themselves with amazing efficiency. Glancing around, I realized something. There were no other seniors with me. Since it was Sunday night, all of them had returned to the field experience to protect their Moroi. It was oddly relieving. The Moroi dorms had an extra line of defense.

At least, the teenage Moroi did. The elementary campus did not. It had its normal guardian protection, as well as a lot of the same defenses our dorm did, like gratings on all the first-floor windows. Things like that wouldn't keep Strigoi out, but they would slow them down. No one had ever done too much more than that. There'd been no need, not with the wards.

Alberta had joined the group and was sending out parties throughout campus. Some were sent to secure buildings. Some were hunting parties, specifically seeking out Strigoi and trying to figure out how many were around. As the guardians thinned out, I stepped forward.

"What should we do?" I asked.

Alberta turned to me. Her eyes swept over me and the others standing behind me, ages ranging from fourteen to just a little younger than me. Something flashed across her face. Sadness, I thought.

"You stay here in the dorm," she said. "No one can leave— the whole campus is under lockdown. Go up to the floors you live on. There are guardians there organizing you into groups.

The Strigoi are less likely to get up there from the outside. If they get in on this floor . . ." She scanned around us, at the door and windows being monitored. She shook her head. "Well, we'll deal with that."

"I can help," I told her. "You know I can."

I could tell she was about to disagree, but then she changed her mind. To my surprise, she nodded. "Take them upstairs. Watch them."

I started to protest being a babysitter, but then she did something really astonishing. She reached inside her coat and handed me a silver stake. A real one.

"Go on," she said. "We need them out of the way here."

I started to turn away but then paused. "What does *buria* mean?"

"Storm," she said softly. "It's Russian for 'storm.'"

I led the other novices up the stairs, directing them to their floors. Most were terrified, which was perfectly understandable. A few of them—the older ones in particular—looked like I felt. They wanted to do something, anything to help. And I knew that even though they were a year from graduation, they were still deadly in their way. I pulled a couple of them aside.

"Keep them from panicking," I said in a low voice. "And stay on watch. If something happens to the older guardians, it'll be up to you."

Their faces were sober, and they nodded at my directions. They understood perfectly. There were some novices, like

Dean, who didn't always grasp the seriousness of our lives. But most did. We grew up fast.

I went to the second floor because I figured that was where I'd be most useful. If any Strigoi got past the first floor, this was the next logical target. I showed my stake to the guardians on duty and told them what Alberta had said. They respected her wishes, but I could tell they didn't want me to be too involved. They directed me down a wing with one small window. Only someone my size or smaller could probably fit through, and I knew that particular section of the building was nearly impossible to climb up, due to its outside shape.

But, I patrolled it anyway, desperate to know what was going on. How many Strigoi were there? Where were they? I realized then that I had a good way of finding out. Still keeping an eye on my window as best I could, I cleared my mind and slipped into Lissa's head.

Lissa was with a group of other Moroi on an upper floor of her dorm too. The lockdown procedures were undoubtedly the same across campus. There was a bit more tension in this group than with mine, probably due to the fact that even while inexperienced, the novices with me right now had some idea how to fight Strigoi. The Moroi had none, despite those adamant Moroi political groups wanting to instigate some sort of training sessions. The logistics of that were still being figured out.

Eddie was near Lissa. He looked so fierce and so strong— like he could single-handedly take on every Strigoi on campus. I was so glad that he among my classmates was assigned to her.

Since I was completely inside her mind now, I got the full force of her feelings. Jesse's torture session seemed meaningless now compared to a Strigoi attack. Unsurprisingly, she was terrified. But most of her fear wasn't for herself. It was for me and Christian.

"Rose is fine," a voice nearby said. Lissa glanced over at Adrian. He'd apparently been in the dorm rather than guest housing. He had on his usual lazy face, but I could see fear masked behind his green eyes. "She can take on any Strigoi. Besides, Christian told you she was with Belikov. She's probably safer than we are."

Lissa nodded, wanting desperately to believe that. "But Christian . . ."

Adrian, for all his bravado, suddenly looked away. He wouldn't meet her eyes or offer any conciliatory words. I didn't need to hear the explanation because I read it from Lissa's mind. She and Christian had wanted to meet alone and talk about what had happened to her in the woods. They'd been supposed to sneak out and meet at his "lair" in the chapel's attic. She hadn't been fast enough and had been caught by curfew just before the attack, meaning she remained in the dorm while Christian was still out there.

It was Eddie who offered the words of comfort. "If he's in the chapel, he's fine. He really is the safest of all of us." Strigoi couldn't enter holy ground.

"Unless they burn it down," said Lissa. "They used to do that."

"Four hundred years ago," said Adrian. "I think they've got easier pickings around here without needing to go all medieval."

Lissa flinched at the words *easier pickings*. She knew Eddie was right about the chapel, but she couldn't shake the thought that Christian might have been on his way back to the dorm and been caught in the middle. The worry was eating her up, and she felt helpless with no way to do or find out anything.

I returned to my own body, standing in the second floor hallway. Finally, I really and truly grasped what Dimitri had said about the importance of guarding someone who wasn't psychically linked to me. Don't get me wrong; I was still worried about Lissa. I worried more about her than any other Moroi on campus. The only way I wouldn't have been worried would have been if she were miles away, ringed in wards and guardians. But at least I knew she was as safe as she could be right now. That was something.

But Christian . . . I had no idea. I had no link to tell me his whereabouts or to even let me know if he was alive. This was what Dimitri had meant. It was an entirely different game when you didn't have a bond—and it was a scary one.

I stared at the window without seeing it. Christian was out there. He was *my* charge. And even if the field experience was hypothetical . . . well, it didn't change things. He was a Moroi. He might be in danger. I was the one who was supposed to guard him. They came first.

I took a deep breath and wrestled with the decision before me. I'd been given orders, and guardians followed orders. With the dangers around us, following orders was what kept us organized and efficient. Playing rebel could sometimes get people killed. Mason had proven that in going after the Strigoi in Spokane.

But it wasn't like I was the only one who faced danger here. Everyone was at risk. There was no safety, not until all the Strigoi were gone from campus, and I had no clue how many there were. Guarding this window was busy work, meant to keep me out of the way. True, someone could invade the second floor, and I'd be useful then. And true, a Strigoi could try to get in through this window, but that was unlikely. It was too difficult, and, as Adrian had pointed out, they had easier ways to get prey.

But I could go through the window.

I knew it was wrong, even as I opened the window up. I was exposing myself here, but I had conflicting instincts. Obey orders. Protect Moroi.

I had to go make sure Christian was okay.

Chilly night air blew in. No sounds from outside revealed what was happening. I'd climbed out of my room's window a number of times and had some experience with it. The problem here was that the stone beneath the window was perfectly smooth. There was no handhold. There was a small ledge down by the first floor, but the distance to it was longer than my height, so I couldn't simply slide down. If I could get to that ledge, however, I could walk off to the corner of the building where some scalloped edging would let me climb down easily.

I stared at the ledge below. I was going to have to drop down to it. If I fell, I'd probably break my neck. Easy pickings for Strigoi, as Adrian would say. With a quick prayer to whoever was listening, I climbed out of the window, holding onto its sill with both hands and letting my body dangle as close to the lower ledge as I could. I still had two more feet between it and me. I counted to three and released my hold, dragging my hands along the wall as I dropped. My feet hit the ledge and I started to wobble, but my dhampir reflexes kicked in. I regained my balance and stood there, holding the wall. I'd made it. From this point, I easily moved to the corner and climbed down.

I hit the ground, barely noticing I'd skinned my hands. The quad around me was silent, though I thought I heard some screams in the distance. If I were a Strigoi, I wouldn't mess with this dorm. They'd get a fight here, and while most Strigoi could probably take out a group of novices at once, there were easier ways. Moroi were less likely to put up a real fight, and anyway, Strigoi preferred their blood to ours.

Still, I moved cautiously as I set out toward the chapel. I had the cover of darkness, but Strigoi could see in it even better than I could. I used trees as covers, looking every way I could, wishing I had eyes in the back of my head. Nothing, save more screams in the distance. I realized then that I didn't have that nauseous feeling from earlier. Somehow, that feeling was an indicator of nearby Strigoi. I didn't entirely trust it enough to walk off blindly, but it was reassuring to know I had some kind of early alarm system.

Halfway to the chapel, I saw someone move out from behind a tree. I spun around, stake in hand, and nearly struck Christian in the heart.

"God, what are you doing?" I hissed.

"Trying to get back to the dorm," he said. "What's going on? I heard screaming."

"There are Strigoi on campus," I said.

"What? How?"

"I don't know. You have to go back to the chapel. It's safe there." I could see it; we could get there easily.

Christian was as reckless as me sometimes, and I almost expected a fight. He didn't give me one. "Okay. Are you going with me?"

I started to say I would, and then I felt that nauseous feeling creep over me. "Get down!" I yelled. He dropped to the ground without hesitation.

Two Strigoi were on us. They both moved in on me, knowing I'd be an easy target for their combined strength, and then they could go after Christian. One of them slammed me into a tree. My vision blurred for half a second, but I soon recovered. I shoved back and had the satisfaction of seeing her stagger a little. The other one—a man—reached for me, and I dodged him, slipping out of his grasp.

The pair of them reminded me of Isaiah and Elena from Spokane, but I refused to get caught up in memories. Both were taller than me, but the woman was closer to my height. I feinted toward him, and then struck out as fast as I could toward her. My stake bit into her heart. It surprised both of us. My first Strigoi staking.

I'd barely pulled the stake out when the other Strigoi backhanded me, snarling. I staggered but kept my balance as I sized him up. Taller. Stronger. Just like when I'd fought Dimitri. Probably faster too. We circled and then I leapt out and kicked him. He barely budged. He reached for me, and I again managed to dodge as I scanned for some opening to stake him. My narrow escape didn't slow him down, though, and he immediately attacked again. He knocked me to the ground, pinning my arms. I tried to push him off, but he didn't move. Saliva dripped from his fangs as he leaned his face down toward mine. This Strigoi wasn't like Isaiah, wasting time with stupid speeches. This one was going to go in for the kill, draining my blood and then Christian's. I felt the fangs against my neck and knew I was going to die. It was horrible. I wanted to live so, so badly . . . but this was how it would end. With my last moments, I started to yell at Christian to run, but then the Strigoi above me suddenly lit up like a torch. He jerked back, and I rolled out from underneath him.

Thick flames covered his body, completely obscuring any of his features. He was just a man-shaped bonfire. I heard a few strangled screams before he grew silent. He fell to the ground, twitching and rolling before finally going still. Steam rose from where fire hit the snow, and the flames soon burned out, revealing nothing but ashes underneath.

I stared at the charred remains. Only moments ago, I'd expected to die. Now my attacker was dead. I nearly reeled from how close I'd been to dying. Life and death were so unpredictable. So close to each other. We existed moment to moment, never knowing who would be the next to leave this world. I was still in it, barely, and as I looked up from the ashes, everything around me seemed so sweet and so beautiful. The trees. The stars. The moon. I was alive—and I was glad I was.

I turned to Christian, who was crouched on the ground.

"Wow," I said, helping him up. Obviously, he was the one who had saved me.

"No shit," he said. "Didn't know I had that much power." He peered around, body rigid and tense. "Are there more?"

"No," I said.

"You seem pretty certain."

"Well . . . this is going to sound weird, but I can kind of sense them. Don't ask how," I said, seeing his mouth open. "Just roll with it. I think it's like the ghost thing, a shadow-kissed side effect. Whatever. Let's get back to the chapel."

He didn't move. A strange, speculative look was on his face. "Rose . . . do you really want to hole up in the chapel?"

"What do you mean?"

"We just took out two Strigoi," he said, pointing to the staked and charred bodies.

I met his eyes, the full impact of what he was saying hitting me. I could sense Strigoi. He could use his fire on them. I could stake them. Provided we didn't hit a group of ten or something, we could do some serious damage. Then reality hit.

"I can't," I told him slowly. "I can't risk your life. . . ."

"Rose. You know what we could do. I can see it in your face. It's worth risking one Moroi life—and, well, yours—to take out a bunch of Strigoi."

Putting a Moroi in danger. Taking him out to fight Strigoi. It pretty much went against everything I'd been taught. All of a sudden, I remembered that brief moment of clarity I'd just had, the wonderful joy of being alive. I could save so many others. I had to save them. I would fight as hard as I could.

"Don't use your full power on them," I finally said. "You don't need to incinerate them in ten seconds like that. Just light them up enough to distract them, and then I'll finish them. You can save your power."

A grin lit his face. "We're going hunting?"

Oh man. I was going to get in so much trouble. But the idea was too appealing, too exciting. I wanted to fight back. I wanted to protect the people I loved. What I really wanted was to go to Lissa's dorm and protect her. That wasn't the most efficient idea, though. Lissa had my classmates on hand. Others weren't so lucky. I thought about those students, students like Jill.

"Let's go to the elementary campus," I said.

We set off at a light run, taking a route we hoped would keep us away from other Strigoi. I still had no idea how many we were dealing with here, and that was driving me crazy. When we were almost to the other campus, I felt the weird nausea hit me. I called a warning to Christian, just as a Strigoi grabbed him. But Christian was fast. Flames wreathed the Strigoi's head. He screamed and released Christian, trying frantically to put the flames out. The Strigoi never saw me coming with the stake. The whole thing took under a minute. Christian and I exchanged looks.

Yeah. We were badasses.

The elementary campus proved to be a center of activity. Strigoi and guardians were actively fighting around the entrances to one of the dorms. For a moment, I froze. There were almost twenty Strigoi and half as many guardians. So many Strigoi together . . . Until recently, we'd never heard of them banding together in such large numbers. We'd thought we'd disbanded a large group of them by killing Isaiah, but apparently that wasn't true. I allowed myself only a moment more of shock, and then we jumped into the fray.

Emil was near a side entrance, fending off three Strigoi. He was battered and bruised, and the body of a fourth Strigoi lay at his feet. I lunged for one of the three. She didn't see me coming, and I managed to stake her with almost no resistance. I was lucky. Christian meanwhile set flames to the others.

Emil's face reflected surprise, but that didn't stop him from staking another of the Strigoi. I got the other.

"You shouldn't have brought him here," Emil said as we moved to help another guardian. "Moroi aren't supposed to get involved with this."

"Moroi should have been involved with this a long time ago," said Christian through gritted teeth.

We spoke little after that. The rest was a blur. Christian and I moved from fight to fight, combining his magic and my stake. Not all of our kills were as fast and easy as our early ones had been. Some fights were long and drawn out. Emil stuck with us, and I honestly lost count of how many Strigoi we took down.

"I know you."

The words startled me. In all this bloodshed, none of us, friend or foe, did much talking. The speaker was a Strigoi who looked to be my own age but was probably at least ten times older. He had shoulder-length blond hair and eyes whose color I couldn't make out. They were ringed in red, which was all that mattered.

My only answer was to swing out with my stake, but he dodged that. Christian was setting a couple of other Strigoi on fire, so I was handling this one on my own.

"There's something strange about you now, but I still remember. I saw you years ago, before I was awakened." Okay, not ten times my age, not if he'd seen me when he was a Moroi. I hoped his talking would distract him. He was actually pretty fast for a young Strigoi. "You were always with that Dragomir girl, the blonde." My foot hit him, and I jerked my kick back before he could grab me. He barely budged. "Her parents wanted you to be her guardian, right? Before they were all killed?"

"I *am* her guardian," I grunted. My stake swiped dangerously close to him.

"She's still alive, then. . . . There were rumors that she'd died last year. . . ." There was a sense of wonder in his voice, which mixed weirdly with the malice. "You have no idea what kind of reward I'd get to take down the last living Drag— Ahh!"

He'd dodged my stake from hitting his chest again, but this time I managed an upward strike that dragged the stake's tip across his face. It wouldn't kill him there, but the touch of a stake—so filled with life—would feel like acid to the undead. He screamed, but it didn't slow his defenses.

"I'll come back for you after I finish her," he snarled.

"You'll never get near her," I growled back.

Something shoved into me from the side, a Strigoi that Yuri was fighting. I stumbled but managed to drive my stake through Yuri's Strigoi's heart before he could regain his balance. Yuri gasped his thanks, and then we both turned to other parts of the battle. Only the blond Strigoi was gone. I couldn't find him anywhere. Another took his place, and as I moved toward that one, flames lit up around him, making him an easy mark for my stake. Christian had returned.

"Christian, this Strigoi—"

"I heard," he panted.

"We have to go to her!"

"He was messing with you. She's across campus, surrounded by novices and guardians. She'll be okay."

"But—"

"They need us here."

I knew he was right—and I knew how hard it was for him to say that. Like me, he wanted to run off to Lissa. Despite all the good work he was doing here, I suspected he would rather have sunk all his magic into protecting her, keeping her ringed in a wall of fire no Strigoi could cross. I had no time to deeply investigate the bond, but I could sense the important things: She was alive, and she wasn't in pain.

So I stayed on, fighting with Christian and Yuri. Lissa hovered at the back of my mind, the bond telling me she was okay. Aside from that, I let battle lust consume me. I had one goal and one alone: Kill Strigoi. I couldn't let them get into this dorm, nor could I let them leave this area and possibly go to Lissa's dorm. I lost track of time. Only the Strigoi I was currently fighting at any given moment mattered. And as soon as that one was gone, it was on to the next.

Until there wasn't a next one.

I was sore and exhausted, adrenaline burning through my body. Christian stood beside me, panting. He hadn't engaged in physical combat like me, but he'd used a lot of magic tonight, and that had taken its own physical toll. I looked around.

"We gotta find another one," I said.

"There are no others," a familiar voice said.

I turned and looked into Dimitri's face. He was alive. All the fear for him I'd held back burst through me. I wanted to throw myself at him and hold him as close to me as possible. He was alive—battered and bloody, yes—but alive.

His gaze held mine for just a moment, reminding me of what had happened in the cabin. It felt like a hundred years ago, but in that brief glance, I saw love and concern—and relief. He'd been worried about me too. Then Dimitri turned and gestured to the eastern sky. I followed the motion. The horizon was pink and purple. It was nearly sunrise.

"They're either dead or have run away," he told me. He glanced between Christian and me. "What you two did—"

"Was stupid?" I suggested.

He shook his head. "One of the most amazing things I've ever seen. Half of those are yours."

I looked back at the dorm, shocked at the number of bodies lying around it. We had killed Strigoi. We had killed a lot of them. Death and killing were horrible things . . . but I had liked doing what I just did. I had defeated the monsters who had come after me and those in my care.

Then I noticed something. My stomach twisted, but it was nothing like my earlier Strigoi-sensing feeling. This was caused by something entirely different. I turned back to Dimitri.

"There are more than just Strigoi bodies there," I said in a small voice.

"I know," he said. "We've lost a lot of people, in all senses of the word."

Christian frowned. "What do you mean?"

Dimitri's face was both hard and sad. "The Strigoi killed some Moroi and dhampirs. And some . . . some they carried away."

TWENTY-FIVE

DEAD OR TAKEN AWAY.

It wasn't enough that the Strigoi had come and attacked us, that they'd killed Moroi and dhampirs alike. They'd also carried some off. It was something Strigoi were known to do. Even they had limits on how much blood they could drink at once. So they'd often take prisoners to keep as snacks for later. Or sometimes a powerful Strigoi who didn't want to do the dirty work would send his or her minions off to bring back the prey. Every once in a while, they'd even purposely take back captives to turn into more Strigoi. Whatever the reason, it meant that some of our people might still be alive.

Students, Moroi and dhampir, were gathered up once certain buildings had been declared Strigoi-free. Adult Moroi were herded inside with us, leaving the guardians to assess the damage. I wanted desperately to be with them, to help and do my part, but they made it clear my part was over. There was nothing I could do at that point except wait and worry with the others. It still seemed unreal. Strigoi attacking our school. How could it have happened? The Academy was safe. We'd always been taught that. It had to be safe. It was why our school years were so long and why Moroi families endured being separated for most of the year. It was worth it for children to have a safe place to go.

That was no longer true.

It took only a couple hours for them to get a casualty count, but waiting while those reports trickled in felt like days. And the numbers . . . the numbers were harsh. Fifteen Moroi had been killed. Twelve guardians had been killed. A group of thirteen, both Moroi and dhampirs, had been taken away. The guardians estimated that there had been close to fifty Strigoi, which was beyond mind-boggling. They'd found twenty-eight Strigoi bodies. The rest appeared to have escaped, many taking victims with them.

For that size of a Strigoi party, our casualty count was still lower than one might have expected. A few things were credited for saving us. One was the early warning. The Strigoi had barely penetrated the school's inner grounds when I'd warned Stan. The school had gone into lockdown quickly, and the fact that most everyone was already inside for curfew had helped. Most of the Moroi victims—dead or taken—were those who had been out in the open when the Strigoi came.

The Strigoi had never made it into the elementary dorms, which Dimitri said was largely thanks to me and Christian. They had managed to breach one of the Moroi dorms, however—the one that Lissa lived in. My stomach had dropped when I heard that. And even though I could feel that she was fine through the bond, all I could see was that smirking blond Strigoi, telling me he was going to finish the Dragomirs off. I didn't know what had happened to him; the attacking Strigoi group hadn't gotten far into her dorm, thankfully, but there had been casualties.

One of them was Eddie.

"*What?*" I exclaimed when Adrian told me.

We were eating in the cafeteria. I wasn't sure which meal it was since the campus had reverted to a daylight schedule that threw my sense of timing off. The cafeteria was nearly silent, all conversations in low whispers. Meals were the only reason students could leave their dorms. There was going to be a guardian meeting later on that I was actually invited to, but for now, I was confined with the rest of my friends.

"He was with you guys," I said. I focused on Lissa, almost accusingly. "I saw him with you. Through your eyes."

She looked up at me over the tray of food she had no interest in eating, her face pale and full of grief. "When the Strigoi got in downstairs, he and some other novices went down to help."

"They didn't find his body," said Adrian. There was no smirk on his face, no humor anywhere. "He was one of the ones they took."

Christian sighed and leaned back in his chair. "He's as good as dead, then."

The cafeteria disappeared. I stopped seeing any of them. All I could see in that moment was that room back in Spokane, that room where we'd been held. They'd tortured Eddie and nearly killed him. That experience had changed him forever, affecting the way he now conducted himself as a guardian.

He'd grown extremely dedicated as a result, but it had cost him some of the light and laughter he used to have.

And now it was happening again. Eddie captured. He'd worked so hard to protect Lissa and others, risking his own life in the attack. I'd been nowhere near the Moroi dorm when it had happened, but I felt responsible—like I should have watched over him. Surely I owed it to Mason. Mason. Mason who had died on my watch and whose ghost I hadn't seen since he'd warned me earlier. I hadn't been able to save him, and now I'd lost his best friend too.

I shot up from my chair and shoved my tray away. That dark fury I'd been fighting blazed through me. If Strigoi had been around, I could have burned them up with it, without any need of Christian's magic.

"What's wrong?" asked Lissa.

I stared at her in disbelief. "What's wrong? What's *wrong*? Do you seriously have to ask that?" In the silent cafeteria, my voice rang out. People stared.

"Rose, you know what she means," said Adrian, voice unusually calm. "We're all upset. Sit back down. It's going to be okay."

For a moment, I almost listened to him. Then, I shook it off. He was trying to use compulsion to chill me out. I glared at him.

"It is not going to be okay—not unless we do something about this."

"There's nothing to be done," said Christian. Beside him,

Lissa was silent, still hurt from when I'd snapped at her.

"We'll see about that," I said.

"Rose, wait," she called. She was worried about me—and scared, too. It was tiny and selfish, but she didn't want me to leave her. She was used to me being there for her. I made her feel safe. But I couldn't stay, not right now.

I stormed out of the commons and into the bright light outside. The guardians' meeting wasn't for another couple hours, but that didn't matter. I needed to talk to someone now. I sprinted to the guardians' building. Someone else was walking into it as I was, and I bumped her in my haste.

"Rose?"

My fury turned to surprise. "Mom?"

My famous guardian mother, Janine Hathaway, stood there by the door. She looked the same as she had when I'd seen her at New Year's, her curly red hair still worn short and her face weathered from the sun. Her brown eyes seemed grimmer than last time, however, which was saying something.

"What are you doing here?" I asked.

As I'd told Deirdre, my mother and I had had a troubled relationship for most of my life, largely because of the distance that inevitably came with having a parent who was a guardian. I'd resented her for years and we still weren't super close, but she'd been there for me after Mason's death, and I think we both tentatively hoped things might improve in coming years. She'd left after New Year's, and last I'd heard, she'd gone back to Europe with the Szelsky she guarded.

She opened the door, and I followed her through. Her manner was brusque and businesslike, as always. "Replenishing the numbers. They've called in extras to reinforce campus."

Replenishing the numbers. Replacing the guardians who had been killed. All the bodies had been cleared away—Strigoi, Moroi, and dhampir alike—but the hole left behind by those who were gone was apparent to all. I could still see them when I closed my eyes. But with her here, I realized I had an opportunity. I grabbed hold of her arm, which startled her.

"We have to go after them," I said. "Rescue the ones who were taken."

She regarded me carefully, a small frown the only sign of her feelings. "We don't do that kind of thing. You know that. We have to protect those who are here."

"What about those thirteen? Shouldn't we protect them? And you went on a rescue mission once."

She shook her head. "That was different. We had a trail. We wouldn't know where to find this group if we wanted to."

I knew she was right. The Strigoi wouldn't have left an easy path to follow. And yet . . . suddenly, I had an idea.

"They put the wards back up, right?" I asked.

"Yes, almost immediately. We're still not sure how they were broken. There were no stakes used to pierce them."

I started to tell her my theory about that, but she wasn't up to speed with my ghostly shenanigans. "Do you know where Dimitri is?"

She gestured toward groups of guardians hurrying all around. "I'm sure he's busy here somewhere. Everyone is. And now I need to go check in. I know you were invited to the meeting, but that's not for a while yet—you should stay out of the way."

"I will . . . but I need to see Dimitri first. It's important—it might play a role in what happens at the meeting."

"What is it?" she asked suspiciously.

"I can't explain yet. . . . It's complicated. It'd take too much time. Help me find him, and we'll tell you later."

My mother didn't seem happy about this. After all, Janine Hathaway wasn't someone people usually said no to. But she nonetheless helped me find Dimitri. After the events over winter break, I think she'd come to regard me as more than a hapless teenager. We found Dimitri with some other guardians, studying a map of campus and planning how to distribute the newly arrived guardians. There were enough people gathered around the map that he was able to slip away.

"What's going on?" he asked as he and I stood off to the side of the room. Even in the midst of this crisis, in the midst of worrying so much about others, I could tell that there was part of him that worried just about me. "Are you okay?"

"I think we should launch a rescue mission," I said.

"You know we—"

"—don't usually do that. Yeah, yeah. And I know we don't know where they are . . . except, I might."

He frowned. "How?"

I told him how it had been Mason who'd warned us last night. Dimitri and I had had no time to talk alone since then, so we'd never really debriefed on the events of the attack. We also hadn't really had a chance to talk about what had happened in the cabin. It made me feel weird because really, that was all I wanted to think about, but I couldn't. Not with so much else going on. So I kept trying to shove those memories of sex away, only to have them keep popping up and entangle my emotions further.

Hoping I seemed cool and competent, I continued explaining my ideas. "Mason's locked out now because the wards are back up, but somehow . . . I think he knows where the Strigoi are. I think he could show us where they are." Dimitri's face told me he had his doubts about this. "Come on! You have to believe me after what happened."

"I'm still having a hard time with that," he admitted. "But okay. Suppose this is true. You think he can just lead us? You can ask him and he'll do it?"

"Yeah," I said. "I think I can. I've been fighting him all this time, but I think if I actually try to work with him, he'll help. I think that's what he's always wanted. He knew the wards were weak and that the Strigoi had been lying in wait. The Strigoi can't be too far away from us . . . they had to have stopped for daylight and hidden out somewhere. We might be able to get to them before the captives die. And once we get close enough, *I* can actually find them." I then explained the nauseous feeling I'd gotten when Strigoi were around. Dimitri didn't challenge this. I think too many weird things were going on for him to even question it.

"But Mason isn't here. You said he can't get through the wards. How will you get him to help us?" he asked.

I'd been thinking about this. "Take me to the front gates."

After a quick word to Alberta about "investigating something," Dimitri led me outside, and we walked the long way to the entrance to the school. Neither of us said anything as we walked. Even in the midst of all this, I still kept thinking of the cabin, of being in his arms. In some ways, it was part of what helped me cope with all the rest of this horror. I had a feeling it was on his mind too.

The entrance to the school consisted of a long stretch of iron fence that lay right on top of the wards. A road that wound from the main highway twenty miles away came up to the gate, which was almost always kept closed. Guardians had a small booth here, and the area was monitored at all times of the day.

They were surprised by our request, but Dimitri insisted it would just be for a moment. They slid the heavy gate open, revealing a space only big enough for one person to get through at a time. Dimitri and I stepped outside. A headache almost immediately built up behind my eyes, and I started to see faces and shapes. It was just like at the airport. When I was outside of wards, I could see all sorts of spirits. But I understood it now and no longer feared it. I needed to control it.

"Go away," I said to the gray, looming forms around

me. "I don't have time for you. *Go*." I put as much force as I could into my will and my voice, and to my astonishment, the ghosts faded. A faint hum remained with me, reminding me they were still out there, and I knew if I let down my guard even a moment, it would all hit me again. Dimitri was eyeing me with concern.

"You're okay?"

I nodded and peered around. There was one ghost I wanted to see.

"Mason," I said. "I need you." Nothing. I summoned back up the command I'd used on the other ghosts just a moment ago. "*Mason. Please. Come here.*"

I saw nothing except the road in front of us winding off into the winter-dead hills. Dimitri was giving me that look from last night, the one that said he was deeply concerned for my mental health. And actually, I was worried at that moment too. Last night's warning had been the final proof for me that Mason was real. But now . . .

A minute later, his shape materialized before me, looking a little paler than before. For the first time since all this had begun, I was happy to see him. He, of course, looked sad. Same old same old.

"Finally. You were making me look bad." He simply stared, and I immediately felt bad for joking. "I'm sorry. I need your help again. We have to find them. We have to save Eddie."

He nodded.

"Can you show me where they are?"

He nodded again and turned, pointing off in a direction that was almost directly behind me.

"They came in through the back of campus?"

He nodded yet again, and like that, I knew what had happened. I knew how the Strigoi had gotten in, but there was no time to dwell on that just now. I turned to Dimitri. "We need a map," I said.

He walked back through the gate and spoke a few words to one of the guardians on duty. A moment later, he returned with a map and unfolded it. It showed the layout of campus, as well as the surrounding roads and terrain. I took it from him and held it out to Mason, trying to keep it flat in the whipping wind.

The only true road out from the school was right in front of us. The rest of the campus was surrounded by forests and steep cliffs. I pointed to a spot at the back of the school's grounds. "This is where they came in, isn't it? Where the wards first broke?"

Mason nodded. He held out his finger and without touching the map, traced a route through the woods that flanked the edge of a small mountain. Following it long enough eventually led to a small dirt road that joined an interstate many miles away. I followed where he pointed and suddenly had my doubts about using him as a guide.

"No, that's not right," I said. "It can't be. This stretch of woods by the mountain has no roads. They'd have to go on foot, and it'd take too long to walk from the school to this other road. They wouldn't have had enough time. They'd be caught in daylight."

Mason shook his head—to disagree with me, apparently—and again traced the route back and forth. In particular, he kept pointing to a spot not far beyond the Academy's grounds. At least, it wasn't far away on the map. The map wasn't particularly detailed, and I guessed the spot was probably a few miles away. He held his finger there, looked at me, and then looked back down.

"They can't be there now," I argued. "It's outside. They might have come in through the back, but they had to have left through the front—gotten in some kind of vehicle and took off."

Mason shook his head.

I looked up at Dimitri, frustrated. I felt like the clock was ticking on us, and Mason's weird assertion that the Strigoi were a few miles away, outdoors in the daytime, was stirring up my irritable nature. I sincerely doubted they'd gotten out tents and were camping.

"Is there any building or anything out there?" I demanded, pointing at the spot Mason had indicated. "He says they were going out to that road. But they couldn't have walked there before the sun came up, and he claims they're there."

Dimitri's eyes narrowed thoughtfully. "Not that I know of." He took the map from me and brought it to the other guardians to check with them. While they talked, I glanced back at Mason.

"You better be right about this," I warned him.

He nodded.

"Have you . . . have you seen them? The Strigoi and their captives?"

He nodded.

"Is Eddie still alive?"

He nodded, and Dimitri walked over.

"Rose . . ." There was a strange sound to Dimitri's voice as he brought the map back, like he couldn't entirely believe what he was saying. "Stephen says there are caves right at the base of the mountain here."

I met Dimitri's eyes, no doubt looking just as astonished as he did. "Are they big enough—"

"Big enough for the Strigoi to hide out in until nighttime?" Dimitri nodded. "They are. And they're only five miles away."

TWENTY-SIX

I T WAS ALMOST IMPOSSIBLE to believe. The Strigoi were practically right next door to us, waiting for nightfall so that they could finish their escape. Apparently, in the chaos of the attack, some of the Strigoi had obscured their tracks while others had made it look as though they might have exited through any number of points on campus. Caught up in our own aftermath, no one had given it much thought. The wards had been restored. As far as we were concerned, the Strigoi were gone, and that was what mattered.

Now we had an odd situation before us. Under normal circumstances—not that a massive Strigoi attack was normal—we would have never pursued them. Those kidnapped by Strigoi were usually written off as dead, and, as my mother had pointed out, guardians rarely knew where to look for Strigoi. This time, however, we knew. The Strigoi were essentially trapped. It presented an interesting dilemma.

Well, it wasn't a dilemma to me. I honestly couldn't figure out why we weren't in those caves right now, flushing out the Strigoi and looking for survivors. Dimitri and I hurried back, anxious to act on our news, but we had to wait until all the guardians gathered.

"Do *not* interrupt them," Dimitri told me as we were about

to walk into the meeting that would decide our next course of action. We stood near the doorway, speaking in low voices. "I know how you feel. I know what you want to do. But ranting at them isn't going to help you get your way."

"Ranting?" I exclaimed, forgetting to speak softly.

"I see it," he said. "That fire's in you again—you want to tear somebody apart. It's what made you so deadly in the fight. But we're not fighting right now. The guardians have all the information. They'll make the right choice. You just have to be patient."

Part of what he said was true. In preparation for the meeting, we had relayed all our information and then done some more searching. Investigation had revealed that several years ago, one of the Moroi teachers had taught a geology class and mapped the caves out, providing us with everything we needed to know about them. The entrance was five miles from the Academy's back borders. The caves' longest chamber was about half a mile long, the far side letting out about twenty miles from the dirt road on the map. It had been believed that landslides had blocked both entrances. Now, we realized, clearing those out wouldn't be too difficult with Strigoi strength.

But I wasn't sure I trusted what Dimitri said about the guardians making the right choice. Minutes before the meeting began, I appealed to my mother.

"Please," I told her. "We have to do this."

She looked me over. "If there's a rescue, it's not going to

be a 'we' thing. You aren't going."

"Why? Because our numbers were so badass the first time that no guardians died?" She flinched. "You *know* I can help. You know what I did. I'm a week away from my birthday and only a few months away from graduation. You think something magical's going to happen before then? I've got a few more things to learn, yeah, but I don't think that's big enough to stop me from helping. You guys need as much help as you can get, and there are plenty of other novices who are ready too. Bring Christian, and we'll be unstoppable."

"No," she said quickly. "Not him. You should have never gotten a Moroi involved, let alone one as young as him."

"But you saw what he could do."

She didn't argue that. I saw the indecision on her face. She glanced at the time and sighed. "Let me check something."

I didn't know where she went, but she was fifteen minutes late for the meeting. By then, Alberta had already debriefed the guardians on what we'd learned. Mercifully, she skipped the details about how we'd gotten our data, so we didn't have to waste time explaining the ghost part. The caves' layout was examined in detail. People asked questions. Then decision time came.

I braced myself. Fighting Strigoi had always meant relying on a defense strategy. We attacked only when attacked. Previous arguments for an offensive had always failed. I expected the same now.

Only it didn't come.

One by one, the guardians stood up and expressed their commitment to going on the rescue mission. As they did, I saw that fire Dimitri had spoken of. Everyone was ready for a fight. They wanted it. The Strigoi had gone too far. In our world, there were only a handful of places that were safe: the Royal Court and our academies. Children were sent to places like St. Vladimir's with the certainty they would be protected. That certainty had been shattered, and we wouldn't stand for that, especially if we could still save lives. An eager, victorious feeling burned in my chest.

"Well, then," said Alberta, glancing around. I think she was as surprised as I was, though she too had been in favor of a rescue. "We'll plan the logistics and head out. We've still got about nine hours of daylight to go after them before they leave."

"Wait," said my mother, standing up. All eyes turned to her, but she didn't bat an eyelash under the scrutiny. She looked fierce and capable, and I was immensely proud of her. "I think there's one other thing we should consider. I think we should allow some of the senior novices to go."

This started a small outcry, but it only came from a minority. My mother gave an argument similar to what I had given her. She also maintained that novices would not be in the front lines but that we would serve more as backup should any Strigoi get through. The guardians had almost approved of this idea when she dropped another bomb on them.

"I think we should bring some Moroi with us."

Celeste shot up. She had a huge gash on the side of her face. It made the bruise I'd seen on her the other day seem like a mosquito bite. "What? Are you insane?"

My mother fixed her with a calm look. "No. We all know what Rose and Christian Ozera did. One of our biggest problems with Strigoi is getting past their strength and speed to go in for the kill. If we bring fire-using Moroi, we have a distraction that will give us an edge. We can cut them down."

A debate broke out. It took every ounce of self-control I had not to join in. I remembered Dimitri's words about not interrupting. Yet as I listened, I couldn't help my frustration. Every minute that passed was another minute we weren't going after Eddie and the others. It was another minute in which someone might die.

I turned to where Dimitri sat beside me. "They're being idiots," I hissed.

His eyes were on Alberta, as she debated a guardian who usually worked the elementary campus. "No," murmured Dimitri. "Watch. Change is happening before your eyes. People are going to remember this day as a turning point."

And he was right. Once again, the guardians slowly signed on with the idea. I think it was part of that same initiative that made them want to fight in the first place. We had to get back at the Strigoi. This was more than our fight—it was the Moroi's too. When my mother said she'd gotten a number of teachers to volunteer—they absolutely wouldn't allow students for this—the decision was made. The guardians were going after the Strigoi, and novices and Moroi would go with them.

I felt triumphant and exultant. Dimitri was right. This was the moment our world would change.

But not for four hours.

"More guardians are coming," Dimitri told me when I once again expressed my outrage.

"In four hours, the Strigoi could have decided to have a snack!"

"We need an overwhelming show of force," he said. "We need every edge we can get. Yes, the Strigoi could kill a couple more before we get there. I don't want that, believe me. But if we go in unprepared, we could lose more lives than that."

My blood boiled. I knew he was right, and there was nothing I could do about it. I hated that. I hated being helpless.

"Come on," he said, gesturing toward the exit. "Let's take a walk."

"Where?"

"It doesn't matter. We just need to get you calmed down, or you'll be in no shape to fight."

"Yeah? Are you afraid of my possibly insane dark side coming out?"

"No, I'm afraid of your normal Rose Hathaway side coming out, the one that isn't afraid to jump in without thinking when she believes something is right."

I gave him a dry look. "Is there a difference?"

"Yes. The second one scares me."

I resisted the urge to elbow him. For half a heartbeat, I wished I could close my eyes and forget about all the hurt and bloodshed around us. I wanted to lounge in bed with him, laughing and teasing, with neither of us worried about anything else except each other. That wasn't real, though. This was.

"Won't they need you here?" I asked.

"No. Most of what they're doing now is waiting for the others, and they have more than enough people right now to help plan the attack. Your mother's leading that."

I followed his gaze to where my mom stood, in the center of a group of guardians, pointing with sharp, forceful motions toward what looked like maps. I still never quite knew what to think about her, but watching her now, I couldn't help but admire her dedication. There was none of the dysfunctional annoyance I usually experienced around her.

"Okay," I said. "Let's go."

He took me on a loop around campus, and we surveyed some of the aftermath. Most of the damage wasn't to the campus itself, of course. It was to our people. Still, we could see some signs of the attack: damage to buildings, bloodstains in unexpected places, etc. Most noticeable of all was the mood. Even in full daylight, there was a darkness around us, a heavy sorrow that you could almost reach out and feel. I saw it on the faces of everyone we passed.

I half-expected Dimitri to take me through where some of the injured were. He steered clear of that, however, and I could guess why. Lissa was helping out there, using her powers in small doses to heal the wounded. Adrian was as well, though he couldn't do nearly as much as her. They'd finally decided that it was worth risking everyone knowing about spirit. The tragedy here was too great. Besides, so much about spirit had gotten out at the trial that it had probably only been a matter of time anyway.

Dimitri didn't want me near Lissa while she was using her magic, which I found interesting. He still didn't know if I really was "catching" her madness, but he apparently didn't want to take any chances.

"You told me you had a theory about why the wards broke," he said. We'd extended our circuit of campus, not far from where Jesse's society had met last night.

I'd nearly forgotten. Once I'd pieced it together, the reason had been perfectly obvious. No one had really asked many questions about it, not yet. The immediate concerns had been to get new wards up and tend to our own people. The investigation would occur later.

"Jesse's group was doing their initiation right here by the wards. You know how stakes can negate wards because the elements go against each other? I think it's the same thing. Their initiation rights used all the elements, and I think they negated the wards in the same way."

"Magic is used all the time on campus, though," pointed out Dimitri. "In all the elements. Why has this never happened before?"

"Because the magic isn't usually happening right on top of the wards. The wards are on the edges, so the two don't usually conflict. Also, I think it makes a difference in how the elements are being used. Magic is life, which is why it destroys Strigoi and why they can't cross it. The magic in stakes is used as a weapon. So was the magic in the torture session. When it's used in that sort of negative way, I think it cancels out good magic." I shivered, recalling that sickening feeling I'd felt when Lissa had used spirit to torment Jesse. It hadn't been natural.

Dimitri stared at a broken fence that marked one of the Academy's boundaries. "Incredible. I never would have thought that was possible, but it makes sense. The principle really is the same as for the stakes." He smiled at me. "You've thought about this a lot."

"I don't know. It just sort of fell together in my head." I glowered, thinking of Jesse's idiotic group. Bad enough they'd done what they did to Lissa. That was enough to make me want to go kick their asses (though not kill them anymore— I'd learned *some* restraint since last night). But this? Letting Strigoi into the school? How could something so stupid and petty on their part have led to this sort of disaster? It almost would have been better if they'd tried to make this happen, but no. It had come about through their glory-seeking game. "Idiots," I muttered.

The wind picked up. I shivered, and this time it was from the chilly temperature, not my own unease. Spring might be coming, but it certainly wasn't here yet.

"Let's get back inside," Dimitri said.

We turned around, and as we walked toward the heart of the secondary campus, I saw *it*. The cabin. Neither of us slowed down or obviously looked at it, but I knew he was just as acutely aware of it as I was. He proved it when he spoke a moment later.

"Rose, about what happened—"

I groaned. "I knew it. I *knew* this was going to happen."

He glanced over at me, startled. "That what was going to happen?"

"*This*. The part where you give me the huge lecture about how what we did was wrong and how we shouldn't have done it and how it's never going to happen again." Until the words left my mouth, I didn't realize how much I'd feared he would say that.

He still looked shocked. "Why would you think that?"

"Because that's how you are," I told him. I think I sounded a little hysterical. "You always want to do the right thing. And when you do the wrong thing, you then have to fix it and do the right thing. And I know you're going to say that what we did shouldn't have happened and that you wish—"

The rest of what I might have said was smothered as Dimitri wrapped his arm around my waist and pulled me to him in the shadow of a tree. Our lips met, and as we kissed, I forgot all about my worries and fears that he'd say what we'd done was a mistake. I even—as impossible as it seems—forgot about the death and destruction of the Strigoi. Just for a moment.

When we finally broke apart, he still kept me close to him. "I don't think what we did was wrong," he said softly. "I'm glad we did it. If we could go back in time, I'd do it again."

A swirling feeling burned within my chest. "Really? What made you change your mind?"

"Because you're hard to resist," he said, clearly amused at my surprise. "And . . . do you remember what Rhonda said?"

There was another shock, hearing her brought up. But then I recalled his face when he'd listened to her and what he'd said about his grandmother. I tried to remember Rhonda's exact words.

"Something about how you're going to lose something. . . ." I apparently didn't remember it so well.

"'You will lose what you value most, so treasure it while you can.'"

Naturally, he knew it word for word. I'd scoffed at the words at the time, but now I tried to decipher them. At first, I felt a surge of joy: *I* was what he valued most. Then I gave him a startled look. "Wait. You think I'm going to die? That's why you slept with me?"

"No, no, of course not. I did what I did because . . . believe me, it wasn't because of that. Regardless of the specifics—or if it's even true—she was right about how easily things can change. We try to do what's right, or rather, what others say is right. But sometimes, when that goes against who we are

. . . you have to choose. Even before the Strigoi attack, as I watched all the problems you were struggling with, I realized how much you meant to me. It changed everything. I was worried about you—so, so worried. You have no idea. And it became useless to try to act like I could ever put any Moroi life above yours. It's not going to happen, no matter how wrong others say it is. And so I decided that's something I have to deal with. Once I made that decision . . . there was nothing to hold us back." He hesitated, seeming to replay his words as he brushed my hair from my face. "Well, to hold *me* back. I'm speaking for myself. I don't mean to act like I know exactly why you did it."

"I did it because I love you," I said, like it was the most obvious thing in the world. And really, it was.

He laughed. "You can sum up in one sentence what it takes me a whole speech to get out."

"Because it's that simple. I love you, and I don't want to keep pretending like I don't."

"I don't either." His hand dropped from my face and found my hand. Fingers entwined, we began walking again. "I don't want any more lies."

"Then what'll happen now? With us, I mean. Once all of this is done . . . with the Strigoi . . ."

"Well, as much as I hate to reinforce your fears, you were right about one thing. We can't be together again—for the rest of the school year, that is. We're going to have to keep our distance."

I felt a little disappointed by this, but I knew with certainty he was right. We might finally have reached the point where we weren't going to deny our relationship anymore, but we could hardly flaunt it while I was still his student.

Our feet splashed through slush. A few scattered birds sang in the trees, undoubtedly surprised to see so much activity in daylight around here. Dimitri stared off into the sky ahead, face thoughtful. "After you graduate and are out with Lissa . . ." He didn't finish. It took me a moment, but I realized what he was about to say. My heart nearly stopped.

"You're going to ask to be reassigned, aren't you? You won't be her guardian."

"It's the only way we can be together."

"But we won't actually be together," I pointed out.

"Us staying with her gives us the same problem—me worrying more about you than her. She needs two guardians perfectly dedicated to *her*. If I can get assigned somewhere at Court, we'll be near each other all the time. And in a secure place like that, there's more flexibility with a guardian's schedule."

A whiny, selfish part of me wanted to immediately jump in with how much that sucked, but really, it didn't. There was no option we had that was ideal. Each one came with hard choices. I knew it was hard for him to give up Lissa. He cared about her and wanted to keep her safe with a passion that almost rivaled my own. But he cared about me more, and he had to make that sacrifice if he still wanted to honor his sense of duty.

"Well," I said, realizing something, "we might actually see more of each other if we're guarding different people. We can get time off together. If we were both with Lissa, we'd be swapping shifts and always be apart."

The trees were thinning up ahead, which was a shame, because I didn't want to let go of his hand. Still, a surge of hope and joy began to blossom in my chest. It felt wrong in the wake of such tragedy, but I couldn't help it.

After all this time, after all the heartache, Dimitri and I were going to make this work. There was always the possibility he could get assigned away from the Court, but even so, we'd still manage to get some time off together every once in a while. The time apart would be agony, but we would make it work. And it would be better than continuing to live a lie.

Yes, it was really going to happen. All of Deirdre's worries about me coping with conflicting pieces of my life would be for nothing. I was going to have it all. Lissa and Dimitri. The thought that I could be with both of them was going to make me strong. It would carry me through this Strigoi attack. I'd tuck it away in the back of my mind, like a good luck charm.

Dimitri and I didn't say anything else for a while. Like always, we didn't have to. I knew he was feeling the same happy buzz I was, despite that stoic exterior. We were almost out of the forest, back in sight of the others, when he spoke again.

"You'll be eighteen soon, but even so . . ." He sighed.

"When this comes out, a lot of people aren't going to be happy."

"Yeah, well, they can deal." Rumors and gossip I could handle.

"I also have a feeling your mother's going to have a very ugly conversation with me."

"You're about to face down Strigoi, and my mother's the one you're scared of?"

I could see a smile playing at his lips. "She's a force to be reckoned with. Where do you think you got it from?"

I laughed. "It's a wonder you bother with me then."

"You're worth it, believe me."

He kissed me again, using the last of the forest's shadows for cover. In a normal world, this would have been a happy, romantic walk the morning after sex. We wouldn't be preparing for battle and worrying about our loved ones. We'd be laughing and teasing each other while secretly planning our next romantic getaway.

We didn't live in a normal world, of course, but in this kiss, it was easy to imagine we did.

He and I reluctantly broke apart and left the woods, heading back toward the guardians' building. Dark times were ahead of us, but with his kiss still burning on my lips, I felt like I could do anything.

Even face down a pack of Strigoi.

TWENTY-SEVEN

NONE OF THE OTHERS appeared to have noticed our absence. More guardians, as promised, had shown up, and we now had almost fifty. It was a veritable army, and much as with the Strigoi, the numbers were unprecedented, aside from old European legends of great epic battles between our races. We had more guardians on campus, but some had to stay behind to protect the school. A lot of my classmates had been drafted for that duty, but about ten or so (including me) were accompanying the others to the cave.

An hour before departure, we met again to go over the plan. There was a large chamber near the far side of the cave, and it made the most sense for the Strigoi to be there so they could head out right away once night came. We were going to attack from both ends. Fifteen guardians would go in from each side, accompanied by three Moroi each. Ten guardians would remain at each entrance to hold back any escaping Strigoi. I was assigned to watch the entrance on the far side. Dimitri and my mother were part of the groups actually going inside. I wished desperately that I could have been with them, but I knew I was lucky to be along at all. And on a mission like this, every job was important.

Our little army set out, moving at a brisk pace to cover the five miles. We figured that it would take a little over an hour, and there would still be enough daylight for the fight and return trip. No Strigoi would be stationed outside on guard duty, so we could reach the caves undetected. Once our people were inside, however, it was almost a given that the Strigoi's superior hearing would immediately alert them to the attack.

There was little conversation as we approached. No one felt like chatting, and most talk was of a logistical nature. I walked with the novices, but every once in a while, I'd glance over and meet Dimitri's eyes. I felt like there was an invisible bond between us now, so thick and intense that it was a wonder everyone couldn't see it. His face was battle-serious, but I saw the smile in his eyes.

Our group split when we reached the closest entrance to the cave. Dimitri and my mother were going in here, and as I gave them one last glance, my feelings had little to do with my earlier romantic interlude. Everything I felt was worry, worry I'd never see them again. I had to remind myself that they were tough—two of the best guardians out there. If anyone would come out of this, it was them. I was the one who needed to be careful, and as we walked the half-mile around the mountain's base, I carefully placed my emotions in a small compartment in the back of my mind. They'd have to stay there until this was over. I was in battle mode now and couldn't let my feelings distract me.

When we were almost to our entrance, I caught a silvery flash out of the corner of my eye. I'd been keeping the assorted ghostly images that lived outside of the wards away, but this was one I wanted to see. Glancing over, I saw Mason. He stood there, saying nothing, wearing his perpetually sad expression. He still seemed unusually pale to me. As our group passed by, he held up one hand, as a farewell or benediction, I didn't know.

At the cave's entrance, our group split up. Alberta and Stan were leading the group in. They stood poised at the entrance, waiting for the exact time they'd agreed upon with the other group. Ms. Carmack, my magic teacher, was among the Moroi going in with them. She looked nervous but determined.

The moment came, and the adults disappeared. The rest of us stood there, lined up in a ring around the cave. Gray clouds hung in the sky. The sun had begun its descent, but we still had awhile.

"This is going to be easy," murmured Meredith, one of three other girls in the senior class. She spoke uncertainly, more to herself than to me, I think. "A slam dunk. They'll take out the Strigoi before any of them realize it. We won't have to do anything."

I hoped she was right. I was ready to fight, but if I didn't have to, it'd mean everything had gone as planned.

We waited. There was nothing else to do. Every minute felt like an eternity. Then we heard it: the sounds of fighting. Muffled cries and grunts. A few screams. All of us tensed, bodies so rigid we nearly snapped. Emil was our leader on this, and he stood closest to entrance, stake in hand and sweat forming on his brow as he peered into the darkness, ready for any sign of a Strigoi.

A few minutes into it, we heard the sound of footsteps running toward us. Our stakes were ready. Emil and another guardian drew closer to the entrance, ready to jump in and kill the fleeing Strigoi.

But it wasn't a Strigoi who came out. It was Abby Badica. She was scraped up and dirty, but otherwise, she was alive. Her face was frantic and streaked with tears. At first, she screamed when she saw all of us. Then she realized who we were and collapsed into the arms of the first person she could get to—Meredith.

Meredith looked surprised, but she gave Abby a hug of reassurance. "It's okay," Meredith said. "Everything's okay. You're in the sun."

Gently, Meredith unwrapped Abby and led her to a nearby tree. Abby sat at its base, burying her face in her hands. Meredith returned to her position. I wanted to comfort Abby. I think we all did, but it would have to wait.

A minute later, another Moroi came out. It was Mr. Ellsworth, the teacher I'd had in fifth grade. He too looked worn, and his neck showed puncture marks. The Strigoi had used him for feeding but hadn't killed him yet. Nonetheless, despite what horrors he must have faced, Mr. Ellsworth was calm, his eyes alert and watchful. He recognized the situation and immediately stepped out of our circle.

"What's going on in there?" asked Emil, his eyes on the

cave. Some of the guardians had earpieces, but I imagined in the midst of battle, it was hard to report back.

"It's a mess," said Mr. Ellsworth. "But we're getting away—in both directions. It's hard to tell who's fighting who, but the Strigoi are distracted. And someone . . ." He frowned. "I saw someone using fire on the Strigoi."

None of us answered. It was too complex to get into right now. He seemed to realize that and withdrew to sit near a still-sobbing Abby.

Two more Moroi and a dhampir I didn't know soon joined Abby and Mr. Ellsworth. Each time someone came out, I prayed that it would be Eddie. We had five victims so far, and I had to assume that others were escaping at the entrance closest to the school.

Several minutes passed, though, and no one else came out. My shirt was drenched, soaked through with sweat. I had to shift my hold on the stake every once in a while. My grip was so tight that my fingers were locking up. Suddenly, I saw Emil flinch. I realized he was getting a message through his earpiece. His face showed intense concentration, and then he murmured something back. Looking up at us, he pointed at three novices.

"You—take them back to the school." He gestured at the refugees, and then turned toward three of the adult guardians. "Go in. Most of the prisoners have gotten out, but our people are trapped. There's a stalemate." The guardians moved in without hesitation, and a few moments later, the novices and their charges took off.

That left four of us, two adults—Emil and Stephen—and two novices, me and Shane. The tension around us was so thick, we could barely breathe. No one else was coming out. No more reports were being made. Emil glanced up and looked alarmed. I followed his gaze. More time had passed than I realized. The sun was significantly lower. Emil suddenly flinched again as another message came through.

He looked at all of us, his face troubled. "We need more in there to cover the escape on the other end. It doesn't sound like we've lost many. They're just still having trouble with the retreat."

Many, he'd said. Not *any*. That meant we'd lost at least one person. I felt cold all over.

"Stephen, you go in," said Emil. He hesitated, and I could read his dilemma like a book. He wanted to go in too, but as the leader for this side, he was supposed to stay stationed here until the last possible moment. He was on the verge of disobeying those orders, I realized. He was considering going in with Stephen and leaving Shane and me out here. Yet, at the same time, he couldn't bring himself to leave two novices here alone, should something unexpected happen. Emil exhaled, and he looked us over. "Rose, go with him."

I didn't waste a moment. Following Stephen, I slipped into the cave, and immediately, that nauseous feeling rolled over me. It had been cold outside, but it was colder still as we moved deeper. It was also darker. Our eyes could handle a fair amount of it, but it soon became too much. He flipped on a small light attached to his jacket.

"I wish I could tell you what to do, but I don't know what we'll find," he told me. "Be ready for anything."

The darkness in front of us began to fade. The sounds grew louder. We picked up the pace, glancing in all directions. Suddenly, we found ourselves in the large chamber shown on the map. A fire burned in one corner—one the Strigoi had made, not anything magical—that was providing the light. Looking around, I immediately saw what had happened.

Part of the wall had fallen in, creating a pile of stones. No one had been crushed under it, but it had almost entirely blocked the opening to the other side of the cave. I didn't know if magic had caused it, or if the fighting had. Maybe it had been a coincidence. Whatever the reason, seven guardians—including Dimitri and Alberta—were trapped now by ten Strigoi. No Moroi fire users had been caught on this side, but the flashes of light coming through the opening in the cave-in showed me that they were still fighting on the other side. I saw bodies lying on the floor. Two were Strigoi, but I couldn't make out the others.

The problem was obvious. Getting through the opening would require someone practically crawling. It would put the person in a vulnerable position. This meant these Strigoi needed to be taken out before the guardians could make their escape. Stephen and I were going to help even the odds. We came up from behind the Strigoi, but three of them sensed us somehow and turned toward us. Two jumped Stephen, and the other came at me.

Instantly, I kicked into battle mode. All the rage and frustration poured out through me. The cave made for close fighting quarters, but I was still able to evade him. In fact, the close space was to my advantage because the Strigoi, with his larger size, had trouble ducking and dodging. I stayed out of his reach mostly, though he did grab hold of me long enough to slam me against the wall. I didn't even feel it. I just kept moving, going on the offensive. I eluded his next attack, got in some blows of my own, and, with my small size, managed to slip down and stake him before his next hit. I pulled out the blade in one smooth motion and went to help Stephen. He'd taken out one of his attackers, and between us, we finished the last one.

That left seven Strigoi now. No, six. The trapped guardians—who were having difficulty in their pinned position—had killed another. Stephen and I jerked the Strigoi closest to us out of the circle. He was a strong one—very old, very powerful—and even with the two of us, he was hard to take down. At last, we did. With the Strigoi numbers reduced, the other guardians were having an easier time getting to the rest. They started freeing themselves from their trapped position, and their numbers alone were now an aid.

When the Strigoi count was down to two, Alberta yelled at us to start escaping. Our alignment in the room had changed. We were now the ones surrounding the last two Strigoi. This left the path clear for three of the guardians to escape via the way I'd come in. Stephen, meanwhile, crawled through the hole to the other side. Dimitri staked one of the two Strigoi. One left. Stephen stuck his head back in and shouted something to Alberta that I couldn't quite make out. She yelled something back without looking at him. She, Dimitri, and two others were closing in on the last Strigoi.

"Rose," yelled Stephen, beckoning.

Follow orders. That's what we did. I left the fray, scrambling through the hole more easily than he had, thanks to my smaller size. Another guardian immediately followed after me. No one was on this side of cave-in. The fight had either ended or moved on. Bodies showed that things had been intense, however. I saw more Strigoi, as well as a familiar face: Yuri. I hastily looked away toward Stephen, who was helping another guardian through. Alberta came next.

"They're dead," she called. "It sounds like there are a few more blocking the retreat down here. Let's finish this before the sun comes up."

Dimitri came last of all through the gap. He and I exchanged brief, relieved glances, and then we were on the move. This was the long part of the tunnel, and we hurried down it, anxious to get our remaining people out. At first, we encountered nothing, and then flashes of light indicated a fight up ahead. Ms. Carmack and my mother were fighting three Strigoi. My group closed in, and in seconds, the Strigoi were down.

"That's it for this group," my mother gasped out. I was grateful to see her alive too. "But I think there are more here than we thought. I think they left some behind when they went to attack the school. The rest of our people—that survived—have already made it out."

"There are other branches in the cave," said Alberta. "Strigoi could be hiding in there."

My mother agreed. "They could be. Some know they're overwhelmed and are just going to wait us out and escape later. Others may come after us."

"What do we do?" asked Stephen. "Finish them off? Or retreat?"

We turned to Alberta. She made a quick decision. "We retreat. We got as many as we could, and the sun is dropping. We need to get back behind the wards."

We took off, so close to victory, fueled by the disappearing light. Dimitri was beside me as we moved. "Did Eddie get out?" I hadn't seen his body, but I hadn't been paying much attention either.

"Yes," said Dimitri, breathing ragged. God only knew how many Strigoi he'd fought today. "We had to practically force him out. He wanted to fight." That sounded like Eddie.

"I remember this curve," my mother said as we rounded a corner. "It's not much farther. We should see light soon." Thus far, we were only guided by the jacket lights.

I felt the nausea only a split second before they attacked. At a T intersection, seven Strigoi jumped us. They'd let the earlier party escape, but they'd been lying in wait for us, three on one side and four on the other. One guardian, Alan, never saw it coming. A Strigoi grabbed him and snapped Alan's neck so quickly that it looked effortless. It probably was. It was such a mirror to what had happened to Mason that I nearly came to a standstill. Instead, I doubled back, ready to get into the fray.

But we were in a narrow part of the tunnel, and not all of us could get through to the Strigoi. I was stuck in the back. Ms. Carmack was beside me, and she had enough visibility to light up a couple of the Strigoi, making it easier for those guardians in the fight to stake them.

Alberta caught a glimpse of me and a couple other guardians. "Start retreating!" she yelled.

None of us wanted to leave, but there wasn't much we could do. I saw one guardian fall, and my heart lurched. I hadn't known him, but it didn't matter. In seconds my mother was on the Strigoi attacker, driving her stake through his heart.

Then I lost sight of the fight as I rounded another corner with the three guardians with me. Farther down the corridor, I saw faint purplish light. The exit. Faces of other guardians peered in at us. We'd made it. But where were the others?

We ran to the exit, emerging into the air. My group clustered by the opening, anxious to see what had happened. The sun, I was dismayed to see, was nearly gone. The nausea hadn't left me, which meant Strigoi were still alive.

Moments later, my mother's party came tearing down

the hall. By the numbers, one more had gone down. But they were so close. Everyone around me tensed up. So close. So, so close.

But not close enough. Three Strigoi lay in wait in one of the alcoves. We'd passed them, but they'd let us go by. It all happened so fast; no one could have reacted in time. One of the Strigoi grabbed Celeste, his mouth and fangs going for her cheek. I heard a strangled scream and saw blood everywhere. One of the Strigoi went for Ms. Carmack, but my mother jerked her away and shoved her forward toward us.

The third Strigoi grabbed Dimitri. In all the time I'd known him, I'd never seen Dimitri falter. He was always faster, always stronger than everyone else. Not this time. This Strigoi had caught him by surprise, and that slight edge was all it had taken.

I stared. It was the blond Strigoi. The one who had spoken to me in the battle.

He grabbed Dimitri and pulled him to the ground. They grappled, strength against strength, and then I saw those fangs sink into Dimitri's neck. The red eyes flicked up and made contact with my own.

I heard another scream—this time, it was my own.

My mother started to double back toward the fallen, but then five more Strigoi appeared. It was chaos. I couldn't see Dimitri anymore; I couldn't see what had happened to him. Indecision flashed over my mother's features as she tried to decide to flee or fight, and then, regret all over her face, she kept running toward us and the exit. Meanwhile, I was trying to run *back* inside, but someone was stopping me. It was Stan.

"What are you doing, Rose? More are coming."

Didn't he understand? Dimitri was in there. I had to get Dimitri.

My mother and Alberta burst out, dragging Ms. Carmack. A group of Strigoi were after them, skidding to a halt just on the edge of the waning light. I was still fighting Stan. He didn't need the help, but my mother grasped a hold of me and tugged me away.

"Rose, we have to get out of here!"

"He's in there!" I screamed, straining as hard as I could. How could I have killed Strigoi and not been able to break free from these two? "Dimitri's in there! We have to go back for him! We can't leave him!"

I was rambling, hysterical, shouting at them all that we had to go rescue Dimitri. My mother shook me hard and leaned close so there were only a couple inches between us.

"He is dead, Rose! We can't go back in there. The sun will be down in fifteen minutes, and they are waiting for us. We're going to be in the dark before we can get back to the wards. We need every second we can get—it still may not be enough."

I could see the Strigoi gathered at the entrance, their red eyes gleaming with anticipation. They completely filled the opening, ten I believed. Maybe more. My mother was right. With their speed, even our fifteen-minute lead might not be enough. And yet, I still couldn't take a step. I couldn't stop staring at the cave, back where Dimitri was, back where half of my soul was. He couldn't be dead. If he was, then surely I would be dead too.

My mother slapped me, the pain snapping me out of my daze.

"Run!" she yelled at me. "*He is dead*! You are not going to join him!"

I saw the panic in her own face, panic over me—her daughter—getting killed. I remembered Dimitri saying he'd rather die than see me dead. And if I stood there stupidly, letting the Strigoi get me, I'd fail both of them.

"Run!" she cried again.

Tears streaming down my face, I ran.

TWENTY-EIGHT

THE NEXT TWELVE HOURS were the longest in my life.

Our group made it back to campus safely, though most of it was done at a run—which was hard with so many injured. The entire time I felt nauseous, presumably because Strigoi were near. If they were, they never caught up to us, and it's possible I was simply sick from everything that had happened in the caves.

Once back behind the wards, the other novices and I were forgotten. We were safe, and the adults now had a lot of other things to concern themselves with. All of the captives had been rescued—all the ones that were alive. As I'd feared, the Strigoi had decided to munch on one before we got there. That meant we had rescued twelve. Six guardians—including Dimitri—had been lost. Those weren't bad numbers considering how many Strigoi we'd faced, but when you took the difference, it really meant we'd only saved six lives. Had the loss of all those guardians' lives been worth it?

"You can't look at it that way," Eddie told me as we walked toward the clinic. Everyone, prisoners and raiders, had been ordered to get checked out. "You didn't just save those lives. You guys killed almost thirty Strigoi, plus the ones on campus.

Think about all the people they would have killed. You essentially saved all those people's lives too."

A rational part of me knew he was right. But what did rationality have to do with anything when Dimitri might be dead? It was petty and selfish, but in that moment, I wanted to trade all those lives for his. He wouldn't have wanted that, though. I knew him.

And through the tiniest, smallest chance, it was possible he wasn't dead. Even though the bite had looked pretty serious, that Strigoi could have incapacitated him and then fled. He could be lying in the caves right now, dying and in need of medical care. It drove me crazy, thinking of him like that and us unable to help. There was no way we could go back, however. Not until daytime. Another party would go then to bring back our dead so that we could bury them. Until then, I had to wait.

Dr. Olendzki gave me a quick check, decided I didn't have a concussion, and then sent me on my way to bandage my own scrapes. She had too many others to worry about right now who were in far worse condition.

I knew the smart thing was to go to my dorm or to Lissa. I could have used the rest, and through the bond, I felt her calling to me. She was worried. She was afraid. I knew she'd find out the news soon, though. She didn't need me, and I didn't want to see her. I didn't want to see anyone. So rather than go to my dorm, I went to the chapel. I needed to do something until the caves could be checked out. Praying was as good an option as any.

The chapel was usually empty in the middle of the day, but not this time. I shouldn't have been surprised. Considering the death and tragedy of the last twenty-four hours, it was only natural that people would seek comfort. Some sat alone, some sat in groups. They cried. They knelt. They prayed. Some simply stared off into space, clearly unable to believe what had happened. Father Andrew moved around the sanctuary, speaking to many of them.

I found an empty pew in the very back corner and sat there. Drawing my knees up to me, I wrapped my arms around them and rested my head. On the walls, icons of saints and angels watched over all of us.

Dimitri couldn't be dead. There was no way he could be. Surely, if he was, I would know. No one could take a life like that from the world. No one who had held me in bed like he had yesterday could really be gone. We had been too warm, too alive. Death couldn't follow something like that.

Lissa's *chotki* was around my wrist, and I ran my fingers over the cross and the beads. I tried desperately to put my thoughts into the forms of prayers, but I didn't know how. If God was real, I figured He was powerful enough to know what I wanted without me actually saying the right words.

Hours passed. People came and went. I got tired of sitting and eventually stretched myself across the length of the pew. From the gold-painted ceiling, more saints and angels stared down at me. So much divine help, I thought, but what good were they really doing?

I didn't even realize I'd fallen asleep until Lissa woke me up. She looked like an angel herself, the pale hair hanging long and loose around her face. Her eyes were as gentle and compassionate as those of the saints.

"Rose," she said. "We've been looking all over for you. Have you been here the entire time?"

I sat up, feeling tired and bleary-eyed. Considering I hadn't slept the night before and had then gone on a massive raid, my fatigue was understandable.

"Pretty much," I told her.

She shook her head. "That was hours ago. You should go eat something."

"I'm not hungry." *Hours ago.* I clutched her arm. "What time is it? Has the sun come up?"

"No. It's still about, oh, five hours away."

Five hours. How could I wait that long?

Lissa touched my face. I felt magic burn through our bond, and then the warm and cold tingling coursed through my own skin. Bruises and cuts disappeared.

"You shouldn't do that," I said.

A faint smile crossed her lips. "I've been doing it all day. I've been helping Dr. Olendzki."

"I heard that, but wow. It just feels so strange. We've always kept it hidden, you know?"

"It doesn't matter if everyone knows now," she said with a shrug. "After everything that's happened, I had to help. So

many people are hurt, and if it means my secret getting out
. . . well, it had to happen sooner or later. Adrian's been
helping too, though he can't do as much."

And then, it hit me. I straightened up.

"Oh my God, Liss. You can save him. You can help
Dimitri."

Deep sorrow filled her face and the bond. "Rose," she
said quietly. "They say Dimitri's dead."

"No," I said. "He can't be. You don't understand. . . . I
think he was just injured. Probably badly. But if you're there
when they bring him back, you can heal him." Then, the craziest thought of all came to me. "And if . . . if he did die . . ." The
words hurt coming out. "You could bring him back! Just like
with me. He'd be shadow-kissed too."

Her face grew even sadder. Sorrow—for me now—radi-
ated out from her. "I can't do that. Bringing people back from
the dead is a huge power drain . . . and besides, I don't think
I could do it on someone who has been dead, um, that long. I
think it has to be recent."

I could hear the crazy desperation in my own voice. "But
you have to try."

"I can't. . . ." She swallowed. "You heard what I said to the
queen. I meant it. I can't go around bringing every dead person back to life. That gets into the kind of abuse Victor wanted.
It's why we kept this secret."

"You'd let him die? You wouldn't do this? You wouldn't
do this for me?" I wasn't shouting, but my voice was definitely

too loud for a church. Most everyone was gone now, and with the level of grief around here, I doubted anyone thought too much of an outburst. "I would do *anything* for you. You know that. And you won't do this for me?" I was on the verge of sobbing.

Lissa studied me, a million thoughts swirling in her mind. She assessed my words, my face, my voice. And like that, she finally got it. She finally realized what I felt for Dimitri, that it was more than a teacher-student bond. I felt the knowledge light up in her mind. Countless connections suddenly came together for her: comments I'd made, ways that Dimitri and I acted around each other . . . it all made sense to her now, things she'd been too blind to notice. Questions immediately sprang up too, but she didn't ask any of them or even mention what she'd realized. Instead, she just took my hand in hers and pulled me close.

"I'm so sorry, Rose. I'm so, so sorry. I can't."

I let her drag me away after that, presumably to get food. But when I sat at the cafeteria table and stared at the tray in front of me, the thought of eating anything made me sicker than being around the Strigoi had. She gave up after that, realizing nothing was going to happen until I knew what had happened to Dimitri. We went up to her room, and I lay down on the bed. She sat near me, but I didn't want to talk, and I soon fell asleep again.

The next time I woke up, it was my mother beside me.

"Rose, we're going to check the caves. You can't go into

them, but you can come to the school's borders with us if you want."

It was the best I could get. If it meant I could find out what had happened to Dimitri a moment sooner than if I stayed here, I'd do it. Lissa came with me, and we trailed behind the assembled guardian party. I was still hurt by her refusal to heal Dimitri, but a part of me secretly thought she wouldn't be able to hold back once she saw him.

The guardians had assembled a large group to check the caves, just in case. We were pretty sure the Strigoi were gone, however. They'd lost their advantage and had to know that if we came back for the dead, it would be with renewed numbers. Any of them that had survived would be gone.

The guardians crossed over the wards, and the rest of us who had followed along waited by the border. Hardly anyone spoke. It would probably be three hours before they came back, counting travel time. Trying to ignore the dark, leaden feeling inside of me, I sat on the ground and rested my head against Lissa's shoulder, wishing the minutes would fly by. A Moroi fire user created a bonfire, and we all warmed ourselves by it.

The minutes didn't fly, but they did eventually pass. Someone shouted that the guardians were coming back. I leapt up and ran to look. What I saw drove me to a halt.

Stretchers. Stretchers carrying the bodies of those who had been killed. Dead guardians, their faces pale and eyes unseeing. One of the watching Moroi went and threw up in a bush. Lissa started crying. One by one, the dead filed past us. I stared, feeling cold and empty, wondering if I'd see their ghosts the next time I went outside the wards.

Finally, the whole group had gone by. Five bodies, but it had felt like five hundred. And there was one body I hadn't seen. One I'd been dreading. I ran up to my mother. She was helping carry a stretcher. She wouldn't look at me and undoubtedly knew what I'd come to ask.

"Where's Dimitri?" I demanded. "Is he . . ." It was too much to hope for, too much to ask. "Is he alive?" Oh God. What if my prayers had been answered? What if he was back there injured, waiting for them to send a doctor?

My mother didn't answer right away. I barely recognized her voice when she did.

"He wasn't there, Rose."

I stumbled over the uneven ground and had to hurry up to catch her again. "Wait, what's that mean? Maybe he's injured and left to get help. . . ."

She still wouldn't look at me. "Molly wasn't there either."

Molly was the Moroi who had been snacked on. She was my age, tall and beautiful. I'd seen her body in the cave, drained of blood. She had definitely been dead. There was no way she'd been injured and staggered out. Molly and Dimitri. Both their bodies gone.

"No," I gasped out. "You don't think . . ."

A tear leaked out of my mother's eye. I'd never seen anything like that from her. "I don't know what to think, Rose.

If he survived, it's possible . . . it's possible they took him for later."

The thought of Dimitri as a "snack" was too horrible for words—but it wasn't as horrible as the alternative. We both knew it.

"But they wouldn't have taken Molly for later. She'd been dead a while."

My mother nodded. "I'm sorry, Rose. We can't know for sure. It's likely they're both just dead, and the Strigoi dragged their bodies off."

She was lying. It was the first time in my entire life that my mother had ever told me a lie to protect me. She wasn't the comforting kind, wasn't the kind who would make up pretty stories in order to make someone feel better. She always told the harsh truth.

Not this time.

I stopped walking, and the group continued filing past me. Lissa caught up, worried and confused.

"What's happening?" she asked.

I didn't answer. Instead, I turned and ran backwards, back toward the wards. She ran after me, calling my name. No one else noticed us because honestly, who in the world was stupid enough to cross the wards after everything that had happened?

I was, although in daylight, I had nothing to fear. I ran past the place Jesse's group had attacked her, stepping across the invisible lines that marked the boundaries of the Academy's grounds. Lissa hesitated a moment and then joined me. She was breathless from running after me.

"Rose, what are you—"

"Mason!" I cried. "Mason, I need you."

It took him a little while to materialize. This time, he not only seemed ultra-pale, he also appeared to be flickering, like a light about to go out. He stood there, watching me, and although his expression was the same as always, I had the weirdest feeling that he knew what I was going to ask. Lissa, beside me, kept glancing back and forth between me and the spot I was speaking to.

"Mason, is Dimitri dead?"

Mason shook his head.

"Is he alive?"

Mason shook his head.

Neither alive nor dead. The world swam around me, sparkles of color dancing before my eyes. The lack of food had made me dizzy, and I was on the verge of fainting. I had to stay in control here. I had to ask the next question. Out of all the victims . . . out of all the victims they could have chosen, surely they wouldn't have picked him.

The next words stuck in my throat, and I sank to my knees as I spoke them.

"Is he . . . is Dimitri a Strigoi?"

Mason hesitated only a moment, like he was afraid to answer me, and then—he nodded.

My heart shattered. My world shattered.

You will lose what you value most. . . .

It hadn't been me that Rhonda was talking about. It hadn't even been Dimitri's life.

What you value most.

It had been his soul.

TWENTY-NINE

NEARLY A WEEK LATER, I showed up at Adrian's door.

We hadn't had classes since the attack, but our normal curfew hours were still in effect, and it was almost bedtime. Adrian's face registered complete and total shock when he saw me. It was the first time I'd ever sought him out, rather than vice versa.

"Little dhampir," he said, stepping aside. "Come in."

I did, and was nearly overwhelmed by the smell of alcohol as I passed him. The Academy's guest housing was nice, but he clearly hadn't done much to keep his suite clean. I had a feeling he'd probably been drinking nonstop since the attack. The TV was on, and a small table by the couch held a half-empty bottle of vodka. I picked it up and read the label. It was in Russian.

"Bad time?" I asked, setting it back down.

"Never a bad time for you," he told me gallantly. His face looked haggard. He was still as good-looking as ever, but there were dark circles under his eyes like he hadn't been sleeping well. He waved me toward an armchair and sat down on the couch. "Haven't seen much of you."

I leaned back. "I haven't wanted to be seen," I admitted.

I'd hardly spoken to anyone since the attack. I'd spent a lot of time by myself or with Lissa. I took comfort from being around her, but we hadn't said much. She understood that I needed to process things and had simply been there for me, not pushing me on things I didn't want to talk about—even though there were a dozen things she wanted to ask.

The Academy's dead had been honored in one group memorial service, although their families had made arrangements for each person's respective funeral. I'd gone to the larger service. The chapel had been packed, with standing room only. Father Andrew had read the names of the dead, listing Dimitri and Molly among them. No one was talking about what had really happened to them. There was too much other grief anyway. We were drowning in it. No one even knew how the Academy would pick up the pieces and start running again.

"You look worse than I do," I told Adrian. "I didn't think that was possible."

He brought the bottle to his lips and took a long drink. "Nah, you always look good. As for me . . . well, it's hard to explain. The auras are getting to me. There's so much sorrow around here. You can't even begin to understand. It radiates from everyone on a spiritual level. It's overwhelming. It makes your dark aura downright cheerful."

"Is that why you're drinking?"

"Yup. It's shut my aura-vision right off, thankfully, so I can't give you a report today." He offered me the bottle, and

I shook my head. He shrugged and took another drink. "So what can I do for you, Rose? I have a feeling you aren't here to check on me."

He was right, and I only felt a little bad about what I was here for. I'd done a lot of thinking this last week. Processing my grief for Mason had been hard. In fact, I hadn't even really quite resolved it when the ghost business had started. Now I had to mourn all over again. After all, more than Dimitri had been lost. Teachers had died, guardians and Moroi alike. None of my close friends had died, but people I knew from classes had. They'd been students at the Academy as long as I had, and it was weird to think I'd never see them again. That was a lot of loss to deal with, a lot of people to say goodbye to.

But . . . Dimitri. He was a different case. After all, how did you say goodbye to someone who wasn't exactly gone? That was the problem.

"I need money," I told Adrian, not bothering with pretense.

He arched an eyebrow. "Unexpected. From you, at least. I get that kind of request a lot from others. Pray tell, what would I be funding?"

I glanced away from him, focusing on the television. It was a commercial for some kind of deodorant.

"I'm leaving the Academy," I said finally.

"Also unexpected. You're only a few months out from graduation."

I met his eyes. "It doesn't matter. I have things to do

now."

"I never figured you'd be one of the dropout guardians. You going to join the blood whores?"

"No," I said. "Of course not."

"Don't act so offended. That's not an unreasonable assumption. If you're not going to be a guardian, what else are you going to do?"

"I told you. I have things I have to take care of."

He arched an eyebrow. "Things that are going to get you into trouble?"

I shrugged. He laughed.

"Stupid question, huh? Everything you do gets you in trouble." He propped his elbow up on the couch's arm and rested his chin in his hand. "Why'd you come to me for money?"

"Because you have it."

This also made him laugh. "And why do you think I'll give it to you?"

I didn't say anything. I just looked at him, forcing as much womanly charm as I could into my expression. His smile went away, and his green eyes narrowed in frustration. He jerked his gaze away.

"Damn it, Rose. Don't do that. Not now. You're playing on how I feel about you. That's not fair." He gulped more vodka.

He was right. I'd come to him because I thought I could use his crush to get what I wanted. It was low, but I had no choice. Getting up, I moved over and sat beside him. I held his hand.

"Please, Adrian," I said. "Please help me. You're the only one I can go to."

"That's not fair," he repeated, slurring his words a little. "You're using those come-hither eyes on me, but it's not me you want. It's never been me. It's always been Belikov, and God only knows what you'll do now that he's gone."

He was right about that too. "Will you help me?" I asked, still playing up the charisma. "You're the only one I could talk to . . . the only one who really understands me. . . ."

"Are you coming back?" he countered.

"Eventually."

Tipping his head back, he exhaled a heavy breath. His hair, which I'd always thought looked stylishly messy, simply looked messy today. "Maybe it's for the best if you leave. Maybe you'll get over him faster if you go away for a while. Wouldn't hurt to be away from Lissa's aura either. It might slow yours from darkening—stop this rage you always seem to be in. You need to be happier. And stop seeing ghosts."

My seduction faltered for a moment. "Lissa isn't why I'm seeing ghosts. Well, she is, but not in the way you think. I see the ghosts because I'm shadow-kissed. I'm tied to the world of the dead, and the more I kill, the stronger that connection becomes. It's why I see the dead and why I feel weird when Strigoi are near. I can sense them now. They're tied to that world too."

He frowned. "You're saying the auras mean nothing? That you aren't taking away the effects of spirit?"

"No. That's happening too. That's why this has all been so confusing. I thought there was just one thing going on, but there've been two. I see the ghosts because of being shadow-kissed. I'm getting . . . upset and angry . . . bad, even . . . because I'm taking away Lissa's dark side. That's why my aura's darkening, why I'm getting so enraged lately. Right now, it just sort of plays out as a really bad temper. . . ." I frowned, thinking of the night Dimitri had stopped me from going after Jesse. "But I don't know what it'll turn into next."

Adrian sighed. "Why is everything so complicated with you?"

"Will you help me? Please, Adrian?" I ran my fingers along his hand. "Please help me."

Low, low. This was so low of me, but it didn't matter. Only Dimitri did.

Finally, Adrian looked back at me. For the first time ever, he looked vulnerable. "When you come back, will you give me a fair shot?"

I hid my surprise. "What do you mean?"

"It's like I said. You've never wanted me, never even considered me. The flowers, the flirting . . . it rolled right off you. You were so gone for him, and nobody noticed. If you go do your thing, will you take me seriously? Will you give me a chance when you return?"

I stared. I definitely hadn't expected this. My initial instinct was to say no, that I could never love anybody again, that my heart had been shattered along with that piece of my soul that

Dimitri held. But Adrian was looking at me so earnestly, and there was none of his joking nature. He meant what he said, and I realized all the affection for me he'd always teased about hadn't been a joke either. Lissa had been right about his feelings.

"Will you?" he repeated.

God only knows what you'll do now that he's gone.

"Of course." Not an honest answer, but a necessary one.

Adrian looked away and drank more vodka. There wasn't much left. "When are you leaving?"

"Tomorrow."

Setting the bottle down, he stood up and walked off into the bedroom. He returned with a large stack of cash. I wondered if he kept it under his bed or something. He handed it to me wordlessly and then picked up the phone and made some calls. The sun was up, and the human world, which handled most Moroi money, was also up and awake.

I tried to watch TV while he talked, but I couldn't concentrate. I kept wanting to scratch the back of my neck. Because there was no way of knowing exactly how many Strigoi I and the others had killed, we'd all been given a different kind of tattoo instead of the usual set of *molnija* marks. I'd forgotten its name, but this tattoo looked like a little star. It meant that the bearer had been in a battle and killed many Strigoi.

When he finally finished his calls, Adrian handed me a piece of paper. It had the name and address of a bank in Missoula.

"Go there," he said. "I'm guessing you have to go to Missoula first anyway if you're actually going on to anywhere civilized. There's an account set up for you with . . . a lot of money in it. Talk to them, and they'll finish the paperwork with you."

I stood up and stuffed the bills in my jacket. "Thank you," I said.

Without hesitating, I reached out and hugged him. The scent of vodka was overpowering, but I felt I owed him. I was taking advantage of his feelings for me in order to further my own devices. He put his arms around me and held me for several seconds before letting go. I brushed my lips against his cheek as we broke apart, and I thought he might stop breathing.

"I won't forget this," I murmured in his ear.

"I don't suppose you'll tell me where you're going?" he asked.

"No," I said. "I'm sorry."

"Just keep your promise and come back."

"I didn't actually use the word *promise*," I pointed out.

He smiled and pressed a kiss to my forehead. "You're right. I'm going to miss you, little dhampir. Be careful. If you ever need anything, let me know. I'll be waiting for you."

I thanked him again and left, not bothering to tell him he might be waiting a long time. There was a very real possibility that I might not be coming back.

The next day, I got up early, long before most of campus was awake. I'd hardly slept. I slung a bag over my shoulder and walked over to the main office in the administrative building. The office wasn't open yet either, so I sat down on the floor in the hallway outside of it. Studying my hands as I waited, I noticed two tiny flecks of gold on my thumbnail. They were the only remnants of my manicure. About twenty minutes later, the secretary showed up with the keys and let me in.

"What can I do for you?" she asked, once she was seated at her desk.

I handed her a stack of papers I'd been holding. "I'm withdrawing."

Her eyes widened to impossible size. "But . . . what . . . you can't . . ."

I tapped the stack. "I can. It's all filled out."

Still gaping, she muttered something to me about waiting, and then scurried out of the room. A few minutes later, she returned with Headmistress Kirova. Kirova had apparently been briefed and was looking at me very disapprovingly down her beaklike nose.

"Miss Hathaway, what's the meaning of this?"

"I'm leaving," I said. "Quitting. Dropping out. Whatever."

"You can't do that," she said.

"Well, obviously I can, since you guys keep withdrawal paperwork in the library. It's all filled out the way it needs to be."

Her anger changed into something sadder and more anxious. "I know a lot has gone on lately—we're all having trouble adjusting—but that's no reason to make a hasty decision. If anything, we need you more than ever." She was almost pleading. Hard to believe she'd wanted to expel me six months ago.

"This wasn't hasty," I said. "I thought a lot about it."

"Let me at least get your mother so we can talk this out."

"She left for Europe three days ago. Not that it matters anyway." I pointed to the line on the top form that said *date of birth*. "I'm eighteen today. She can't do anything anymore. This is my choice. Now, will you stamp the form, or are you actually going to try to restrain me? Pretty sure I could take you in a fight, Kirova."

They stamped my packet, not happily. The secretary made a copy of the official paper that declared I was no longer a student at St. Vladimir's Academy. I'd need it to get out the main gate.

It was a long walk to the front of the school, and the western sky was red as the sun slipped over the horizon. The weather had warmed up, even at night. Spring had finally come. It made for good walking weather since I had a ways to go before I made it to the highway. From there, I'd hitchhike to Missoula. Hitchhiking wasn't safe, but the silver stake in my coat pocket made me feel pretty secure about anything I'd face. No one had taken it away from me after the raid, and it would work just as well against creepy humans as it did with

Strigoi.

I could just make out the gates when I sensed her. Lissa. I stopped walking and turned toward a cluster of bud-covered trees. She'd been standing in them, perfectly still, and had managed to hide her thoughts so well that I hadn't realized she was practically right next to me. Her hair and eyes glowed in the sunset, and she seemed too beautiful and too ethereal to be part of this dreary landscape.

"Hey," I said.

"Hey." She wrapped her arms around herself, cold even in her coat. Moroi didn't have the same resistance to temperature changes that dhampirs did. What I found warm and springlike was still chilly to her. "I knew it," she said. "Ever since that day they said his body was gone. Something told me you'd do this. I was just waiting."

"Can you read my mind now?" I asked ruefully.

"No, I can just read you. Finally. I can't believe how blind I was. I can't believe I never noticed. Victor's comment . . . he was right." She glanced off at the sunset, then turned her gaze back on me. A flash of anger, both in her feelings and her eyes, hit me. "Why didn't you tell me?" she cried. "Why didn't you tell me you loved Dimitri?"

I stared. I couldn't remember the last time Lissa had yelled at anyone. Maybe last fall, when all the Victor insanity had gone down. Loud outbursts were my thing, not hers. Even when torturing Jesse, her voice had been deadly quiet.

"I couldn't tell anyone," I said.

"I'm your best friend, Rose. We've been through every-thing together. Do you really think I would have told? I would have kept it secret."

I looked at the ground. "I know you would have. I just . . . I don't know. I couldn't talk about it. Not even to you. I can't explain it."

"How . . ." She groped for the question her mind had already formed. "How serious was it? Was it just you or—?"

"It was both of us," I told her. "He felt the same. But we knew we couldn't be together, not with our age . . . and, well, not when we were supposed to be protecting you."

Lissa frowned. "What do you mean?"

"Dimitri always said that if we were involved, we'd worry more about protecting each other than you. We couldn't do that."

Guilt coursed through her at the thought that she'd been responsible for keeping us apart.

"It's not your fault," I said quickly.

"Surely . . . there must have been a way. . . . It wouldn't have been a problem. . . ."

I shrugged, unwilling to think about or mention our last kiss in the forest, back when Dimitri and I had thought we'd figured out a solution to all of our problems.

"I don't know," I said. "We just tried to stay apart. Some-times it worked. Sometimes it didn't."

Her mind was a tumble of emotions. She felt sorry for me, but at the same time, she was mad. "You should have told me," she repeated. "I feel like you don't trust me."

"Of course I trust you."

"Is that why you're sneaking off?"

"That has nothing to do with trust," I admitted. "It's me . . . well, I didn't want to tell you. I couldn't bear to tell you I was leaving or explain why."

"I already know," she said. "I figured it out."

"How?" I asked. Lissa was full of surprises today.

"I was there. Last fall when we took that van into Missoula. The shopping trip? You and Dimitri were talking about Strigoi, about how becoming one makes you something twisted and evil . . . how it destroys the person you used to be and makes you do horrible things. And I heard . . ." She had trouble saying it. I had trouble hearing it, and my eyes grew wet. The memory was too harsh, thinking of sitting with him that day, back when we were first falling in love. Lissa swallowed and continued. "I heard you both say you'd rather die than become a monster like that."

Silence fell between us. The wind picked up and blew our hair around, dark and light.

"I have to do this, Liss. I have to do it for him."

"No," she said firmly. "You don't have to. You didn't promise him anything."

"Not in words, no. But you . . . you don't understand."

"I understand that you're trying to cope and that this is as good a way as any. You need to find another way to let him go."

I shook my head. "I have to do this."

"Even if it means leaving me?"

The way she said it, the way she looked at me . . . oh God. A flood of memories flitted through my mind. We'd been together since childhood. Inseparable. Bound. And yet . . . Dimitri and I had been connected too. Damn it. I'd never wanted to have to choose between them.

"I have to do this," I said yet again. "I'm sorry."

"You're supposed to be my guardian and go with me to college," she argued. "You're shadow-kissed. We're supposed to be together. If you leave me . . ."

The ugly coil of darkness was starting to raise its head in my chest. My voice was tight when I spoke. "If I leave you, they'll get you another guardian. Two of them. You're the last Dragomir. They'll keep you safe."

"But they won't be you, Rose," she said. Those luminous green eyes held mine, and the anger in me cooled. She was so beautiful, so sweet . . . and she seemed so reasonable. She was right. I owed it to her. I needed to—

"Stop it!" I yelled, turning away. She'd been using her magic. "Do *not* use compulsion on me. You're my friend. Friends don't use their powers on each other."

"Friends don't abandon each other," she snapped back. "If you were my friend, you wouldn't do it."

I spun back toward her, careful not to look too closely into her eyes, in case she tried compulsion on me again. The rage in me exploded.

"It's not about you, okay? This time, it's about me. Not

you. All my life, Lissa . . . all my life, it's been the same. *They come first.* I've lived my life for you. I've trained to be your shadow, but you know what? I want to come first. I need to take care of myself for once. I'm tired of looking out for everyone else and having to put aside what *I* want. Dimitri and I did that, and look what happened. He's gone. I will never hold him again. Now I owe it to him to do this. I'm sorry if it hurts you, but it's my choice!"

I'd shouted the words, not even pausing for a breath, and I hoped my voice hadn't carried to the guardians on duty at the gate. Lissa was staring at me, shocked and hurt. Tears ran down her cheeks, and part of me shriveled up at hurting the person I'd sworn to protect.

"You love him more than me," she said in a small voice, sounding very young.

"He needs me right now."

"I need you. He's gone, Rose."

"No," I said. "But he will be soon." I reached up my sleeve and took off the *chotki* she'd given me for Christmas. I held it out to her. She hesitated and then took it.

"What's this for?" she asked.

"I can't wear it. It's for a Dragomir guardian. I'll take it again when I . . ." I had almost said *if*, not *when*. I think she knew that. "When I get back."

Her hands closed around the beads. "Please, Rose. Please don't leave me."

"I'm sorry," I said. There were no other words to offer up.

"I'm sorry."

I left her there crying as I walked toward the gate. A piece of my soul had died when Dimitri had fallen. Turning my back on her now, I felt another piece die as well. Soon there wouldn't be anything left inside of me.

The guardians at the gate were as shocked as the secretary and Kirova had been, but there was nothing they could do. *Happy birthday to me*, I thought bitterly. Eighteen at last. It was nothing like I had expected.

They opened the gates and I stepped through, outside of the school's grounds and over the wards. The lines were invisible, but I felt strangely vulnerable and exposed, as if I'd leapt a great chasm. And yet, *at the same time*, I felt free and in control. I started walking down the narrow road. The sun was nearly gone; I'd have to rely on moonlight soon.

When I was out of earshot of the guardians, I stopped and spoke. "Mason."

I had to wait a long time. When he appeared, I could barely see him at all. He was almost completely transparent.

"It's time, isn't it? You're going . . . you're finally moving on to . . ."

Well, I had no clue where he was moving on to. I didn't know anymore what lay beyond, whether it was the realms Father Andrew believed in or some entirely different world that I'd visited. Nonetheless, Mason understood and nodded.

"It's been more than forty days," I mused. "So I guess you're overdue. I'm glad . . . I mean, I hope you find peace. Although I kind of hoped you'd be able to lead me to him."

Mason shook his head, and he didn't need to say a word for me to understand what he wanted to tell me. *You're on your own now, Rose.*

"It's okay. You deserve your rest. Besides, I think I know where to start looking." I'd thought about this constantly over the last week. If Dimitri was where I believed he was, I had a lot of work ahead of me. Mason's help would have been nice, but I didn't want to keep bothering him. It seemed like he had enough to deal with.

"Goodbye," I told him. "Thanks for your help. . . . I . . . I'll miss you."

His form grew fainter and fainter, and just before it went altogether, I saw the hint of a smile, that laughing and mischievous smile I'd loved so much. For the first time since his death, thinking about Mason no longer devastated me. I was sad and I really would miss him, but I knew he'd moved on to something good— something really good. I no longer felt guilty.

Turning away, I stared at the long road winding off ahead of me. I sighed. This trip might take awhile.

"Then start walking, Rose," I muttered to myself.

I set off, off to kill the man I loved.

As always, I can never express enough gratitude to the friends and family who hang with me through the ups and downs that go along with writing a book—let alone one as powerful as this. Many thanks to David and Christina for their speedy beta reading; to I.A. Gordon and Sherry Kirk for their help with Russian; to Synde Korman for her help with Romanian; to my agent Jim McCarthy who is wise and does all the hard stuff for me; to editors Jessica Rothenberg and Ben Schrank for all of their guidance; to the Team Seattle authors for their distraction and good cheer; and to Jay for being infinitely patient...and even making a good joke once in a while.

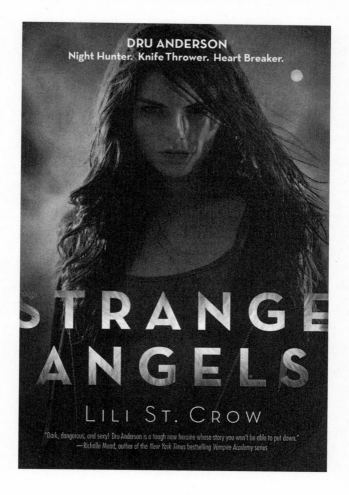

didn't tell Dad about Granmama's white owl. I know I should have.

There's that space between sleep and dreaming where things—not quite dreams, not fully fledged precognition, but weird little blends of both—sometimes get in. Your eyes open, slow and dreamy, when the sense of *someone looking* rises through the cotton-wool fog of being warm and tired.

That's when I saw it.

The owl ruffled itself up on my windowsill drenched in moonglow, each pale feather sharp and clear under icy light. I hadn't bothered to pull the cheap blinds down or hang up the curtains. Why bother, when we—Dad and me—only spend a few months in any town?

I blinked at the yellow-eyed bird. Instead of the comfort that means Gran is thinking about me—and don't ask how I know the dead think of the living; I've seen too much *not* to know—I felt a sharp annoyance, like a glass splinter under the surface of my brain.

The owl's beak was black, and its feathers had ghostly spots like cobwebs, shadows against snowy down. It stared into my sleepy eyes for what seemed like eternity, ruffling just a bit, puffing up the way Gran always used to when she thought anyone was messing with me.

Not again. Go away.

It usually only showed up when something interesting or really foul was about to happen. Dad had never seen it, or at least I didn't think so. But he could tell when I had, and it would make him reach for a weapon until I managed to open my mouth and say whether we were going to meet an old friend—or find ourselves in deep shit.

The night Gran died the owl had sat inside the window while she took her last few shallow, sipping breaths, but I don't think the nurses or the doctor saw it. They would have said something. By that point I knew enough to keep my mouth shut, at least. I just sat there and held Gran's hand until she drained away; then I sat in the hall while they did things to her empty body and wheeled it off. I curled up inside myself when the doctor or the social worker tried to talk to me, and just kept repeating that my dad would know, that he was on his way—even though I had no clue *where* he was, really. He'd been gone a good three months, off ridding the world of nasty things while I watched Gran slide downhill.

Of course, that morning Dad showed up, haggard and unshaven, his shoulder bandaged and his face bruised. He had all the ID, signed all the papers, and answered all the questions. Everything turned out okay, but sometimes I dream about that night, wondering if I'm going to get left behind again in some fluorescent-lit corridor smelling of Lysol and cold pain.

I don't like thinking about that. I settled further into the pillow, watching the owl's fluffing, each feather edged with cold moonlight.

My eyes drifted closed. Warm darkness swallowed me, and when the alarm clock went off it was morning, weak winter sunshine spilling through the window and making a square on the brown carpet. I'd thrashed out of the covers and was about to freeze my ass off. Dad hadn't turned the heater up.

It took a good twenty minutes in the shower before I felt anything *close* to awake. *Or* human. By the time I stamped down the stairs, I was already pissed off and getting worse. My favorite jeans weren't clean and I had a zit the size of Mount Pinatubo on my temple under a hank of dishwater brown hair. I opted for a gray T-shirt and a red hoodie, a pair of combat boots and no makeup.

Why bother, right? I wasn't going to be here long enough for anyone to care.

My bag smacked the floor. Last night's dishes still crouched in the sink. Dad was at the kitchen table, his shoulders hunched over the tray as he loaded clips, each bullet making a little clicking sound. "Hi, sweetheart."

I snorted, snagging the orange juice and opening the carton, taking a long cold draft. I wiped my mouth and belched musically.

"Ladylike." His bloodshot blue eyes didn't rise from the clip, and I knew what that meant.

"Going out tonight?" That's what I said. What I meant was, *without me?*

Click. Click. He set the full clip aside and started on the next. The bullets glinted, silver-coated. He must have been up all night with that, making them and loading them. "I won't be in for dinner. Order a pizza or something."

Which meant he was going somewhere more-dangerous, not just kinda-dangerous. And that he didn't need me to zero the target. So he must've gotten some kind of intel. He'd been gone every night this week, always reappearing in time for dinner smelling of cigarette smoke and danger. In other towns he'd mostly take me with him; people either didn't care about a teenage girl drinking a Coke in a bar, or we went places where Dad was reasonably sure he could stop any trouble with an ice-cold military stare or a drawled word.

But in this town he hadn't taken me anywhere. So if he'd gotten intel, it was on his own.

How? Probably the old-fashioned way. He likes that better, I guess. "I could come along."

"Dru." Just the one word, a warning in his tone. Mom's silver locket glittered at his throat, winking in the morning light.

"You might need me. I can carry the ammo." *And tell you when something invisible's in the corner, looking at you.* I heard the stubborn whine in my voice and belched again to cover it, a nice sonorous one that all but rattled the window looking out onto the scrubby backyard with its dilapidated swing set. There was a box of dishes sitting in front of the cabinets next to the stove; I suppressed the urge to kick at it. Mom's cookie jar—the one shaped like a fat grinning black-and-white cow—was next to the sink, the first thing unpacked in every new house. I always put it in the bathroom box with the toilet paper and shampoo; that's always the last in and first one out.

I've gotten kind of used to packing and unpacking, you could say. And trying to find toilet paper after a thirty-six-hour drive is no fun.

"Not this time, Dru." He looked up at me, though, the bristles of his cropped hair glittering blond under fluorescent light. "I'll be home late. Don't wait up."

I was about to protest, but his mouth had turned into a thin, hard line and the bottle sitting on the table warned me. Jim Beam. It had been almost full last night when I went to bed, and the dregs of amber liquid in it glowed warmer than his hair. Dad was pale blond, almost a towhead, even if his stubble was brown and gold.

I've got a washed-out version of Mom's curls and a better copy of Dad's blue eyes. The rest of me, I guess, is up for grabs. Except maybe Gran's nose, but she could have just been trying to make me feel better. I'm no prize. Most girls go through a gawky stage, but I'm beginning to think mine will be a lifelong thing.

It doesn't bother me too much. Better to be strong than pretty and useless. I'll take a plain girl with her head screwed on right over a cheerleader any day.

So I just leaned down and scooped up my messenger bag, the strap scraping against my fingerless wool gloves. They're scratchy but they're warm, and if you slip small stuff under the cuff, it's damn near invisible. "Okay."

"You should have some breakfast." *Click.* Another bullet slid into the clip. His eyes dropped back down to it, like it was the most important thing in the world.

Eat something? When he was about to go out and deal with bad news alone? Was he *kidding*?

My stomach turned over hard. "I'll miss the bus. Do you want some eggs?"

I don't know why I offered. He liked them sunny-side up, but neither Mom or me could ever get them done right. I've been breaking yolks all my life, even when he tried to teach me the right way to gently jiggle with a spatula to get them out of the pan. Mom would just laugh on Sunday mornings and tell him scrambled or over-hard was what he was going to get, and he'd come up behind her and put his arms around her waist and nuzzle her long, curling chestnut hair. I would always yell, *Ewwww! No kissing!*

And they would both laugh.

That was Before. A thousand years ago. When I was little.

Dad shook his head a little. "No thanks, kiddo. You have money?"

I spotted his billfold on the counter and scooped it up. "I'm taking twenty."

"Take another twenty, just in case." *Click. Click.* "How's school going?"

Just fine, Dad. Just freaking dandy. Two weeks in a new town is enough to make me all sorts of friends. "Okay."

I took two twenties out of his billfold, rubbing the plastic sleeve over Mom's picture with my thumb like I always did. There was a shiny space on the sleeve right over her wide, bright smile. Her chestnut hair was as wildly curly as mine, but pulled back into a loose ponytail, blonde-streaked ringlets falling into her heart-shaped face. She was beautiful. You could see why Dad fell for her in that picture. You could almost smell her perfume.

"Just okay?" *Click.*

"It's fine. It's stupid. Same old stuff." I toed the linoleum and set his billfold down. "I'm going."

Click. He didn't look up. "Okay. I love you." He was wearing his Marines sweatshirt and the pair of blue sweats he always worked out in, with the hole in the knee. I stared at the top of his head while he finished the clip, set it aside, and picked up a fresh one. I could almost feel the noise of each bullet being slid home in my own fingers.

My throat had turned to stone. "'Kay. Whatever. Bye." *Don't get killed.* I stamped out of the kitchen and down the hall, one of the stacked boxes barking me in the shin. I still hadn't unpacked the living room yet. Why bother? I'd just have to box it all up in another couple months.

I slammed the front door, too, and pulled my hood up, shoving my hair back. I hadn't bothered with much beyond dragging a comb through it. Mom's curls had been loose pretty ringlets, but mine were pure frizz. The Midwest podunk humidity made it worse; it was a wet blanket of cold that immediately turned my breath into a white cloud and nipped at my elbows and knees.

The rental was on a long, ruler-straight block of similar houses, all dozing under watery sunlight managing to fight its way through overcast. The air tasted like iron and I shivered. We'd been in Florida before this, always sticky, sweaty, sultry heat against the skin like oil. We'd cleared out four poltergeists in Pensacola and a haunting apparition of a woman even Dad could see in some dead-end town north of Miami, and there was a creepy woman with cottonmouths and copperheads in glass cages who sold Dad the silver he needed to take care of something else. I hadn't had to go to school there—we were so busy staying mobile, moving from one hotel to the next, so whatever Dad needed the silver for couldn't get a lock on us.

Now it was the Dakotas, and snow up to our knees. Great.

Our yard was the only one with weeds and tall grass. We had a picket fence, too, but the paint was flaking and peeling off and parts of it were missing, like a gap-toothed smile. Still, the porch was sturdy and the house was even sturdier. Dad didn't believe in renting crappy bungalows. He said it was a bad way to raise a kid.

I walked away with my head down and my hands stuffed in my pockets.

I never saw Dad alive again.

WILL DRU DISCOVER JUST HOW SPECIAL SHE REALLY IS?

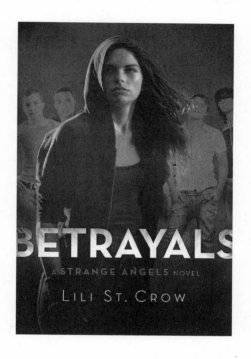

FIND OUT IN BETRAYALS COMING NOVEMBER 2009